THURSDAYS AT COCONUTS

BETH CARTER

SOUL MATE PUBLISHING
New York

THURSDAYS AT COCONUTS

BETH CARTER

Cover Design by Christy Caughie

This book is a work of fiction. The names, characters, places, and incidents are the products of the author's imagination or are used fictitiously. Any resemblance to actual events, business establishments, locales, or persons, living or dead, is entirely coincidental.

Published in the United States of America by

Soul Mate Publishing

P.O. Box 24

Macedon, New York, 14502

ISBN: 978-1-61935-580-4

eBook ISBN: 978-1-61935-534-7

www.SoulMatePublishing.com

To my husband, Bob.

Your ongoing love and support

helped make my dreams come true.

Thanks for your patience

while I chained myself to my desk

and forgot to cook dinner.

You are my Prince Charming.

I love you.

Acknowledgements

To my precious grandmother, Evelyn Jones, who only got to read the first three chapters. After reading them, she said, “Forever more.” I love and miss you, Grandma. ~ Sugar Plum

To my girlfriends who served as an early focus group and critiqued several chapters (over pizza and wine): Brenda Howard, Cindi Taylor, Karen Schaefer, Sarah Smith, Sharon Smith, and Marsha Maroney. These wonderful women gave me the oomph and encouragement to finish my manuscript.

To my beta readers: Amanda Brown, Stephanie Jarkins, Jan Marler Morrill, and Shirley McCann. Thank you for your invaluable input and friendship.

To my local writers’ groups: Ozarks Romance Writers, Sleuths’ Ink Mystery Writers, and Ozarks Writers League. Thank you for your support, invaluable lessons, and inspiration.

To my mom, Carol Holmes, and daughter, Amy Highfill Grabher, who are my biggest cheerleaders. I love you! My stepdaughters, Jessica Connolly and Allison Twist, have also been a great support and to my sister, Alison Holmes, who penned a novel, which inspired me to do the same.

To my writing mentors (beginning in middle school through college): Don Sharp, Laura Fleetwood, Jo Van Arkel, and Allan Young. I learned from the best!

To Marsha Maroney, M.S., CCC-SLP, Speech-Language Pathologist, who was amazing when I asked for information and exercises for the stroke victim. Her assistance was invaluable.

To my brother, Steve Holmes, who provided input concerning police lingo and procedures. I can't tell you how he knew. It's top secret.

To Erin Brown, freelance editor and former women's fiction editor for St. Martin's Press, who I hired to provide an overall manuscript evaluation. Erin gave me constructive criticism and said three things that I held on to for dear life: "You're a strong writer, excellent storyteller, and I hope your manuscript doesn't end up in a slush pile."

To Larry Smith, Editor of SMITH Magazine and founder of the Six-Word Memoir project. You helped me tiptoe into the wonderful world of publishing. "It all started with six words." Thank you.

To the rest of my wonderful family, friends, Facebook and Twitter pals, and my CHS buddies. I appreciate your ongoing support and enthusiasm.

I'd like to thank the cover designer, Christy Caughie. Last but not least, a huge thanks to Debby Gilbert, senior editor of Soul Mate Publishing, for believing in my novel and making my dreams come true!

Chapter 1

I can't go through with this. Suzy bit her bottom lip and clutched her phone, unable to dial. *Should I call and confront him?* She took a deep breath and paced. Her heels clacked on the hardwood floors. The cheery yellow walls annoyed her. Her throbbing ears competed with the loud swish of her chiffon wedding dress as she fumed.

Suzy rubbed her knotted shoulders as she peered out the dressing room window watching the unknowing guests filter into the chapel. They chatted and laughed, dressed in their wedding best. She held on to the curtain for strength as she watched friends and family parade inside to wait for the bride—to-be. To wait for *her*. Suzy angrily brushed away tears and adjusted her strapless, beaded wedding dress for the hundredth time. At that moment, she made up her mind. She didn't have a choice.

Determined, she dabbed her eyes with her grandmother's lace hanky—her something old—and did her best to reapply mascara. The guests were going to be in enough shock without looking at a raccoon-eyed bride. Suzy glanced at the clock. The ceremony was minutes away when her father appeared in the doorway.

"Ready, Suzy?" Gianni asked, smiling broadly.

Suzy managed a small smile for her handsome, half-Italian father. While she would have much preferred to inherit her father's olive skin and dark, curly hair, she had her mother's Irish red hair and easily sunburned porcelain skin.

"You look beautiful, sweetie. Absolutely stunning. You're the most gorgeous bride in the world."

Suzy blew out her breath and touched her chignon. She wanted to rip it out, throw on some jeans and run. Instead, she stared at the floor avoiding her father's eyes.

"Thanks, Dad." Suzy's voice wavered but she continued. "You look very debonair in that tux, more handsome than ever but—" A sob caught in her throat as she looked into her father's deep, brown eyes.

"Listen, Dad, there's going to be a change. I'm going to walk myself down the aisle—"

Her father's eyebrows shot up. "You don't want me to walk you down the aisle? What's wrong?"

Suzy held up one hand. "I'm really sorry. I know you were looking forward to escorting me but—" She wiped her nose with her hand. "Please, Dad. Just trust me."

Brows knitted together, Gianni stared at her and didn't say a word.

Suzy could see the bewilderment in his eyes.

He walked toward her and gently placed his hand on her shoulder. "I don't understand, but if this is what you want, I'll abide by your wishes. It's your day." He reached for her hand and held it just as he did when she was a young girl. "You'll always be my little girl and I'll always love you. Don't forget that when you walk down the aisle." His voice was soft and tears filled his eyes.

Suzy threw her arms around his neck and sobbed uncontrollably. "I love you, too, Daddy." With her hanky, she attempted to wipe her tears off her father's tux and gray silk tie.

Gianni's voice turned solemn as he pushed the hanky away. "Don't worry about the silly tux. I wish you would tell me what's wrong." He ran his fingers through his hair. "This is obviously more than just wedding day jitters." Gianni touched Suzy's cheek with the back of his hand and stared into her eyes. "I'm worried about you."

Suzy blinked away tears and blew her nose. She wadded the tissue into a ball and threw it into a gold wastebasket.

"Trust me. You'll know soon enough. I just can't go into it right now. Everyone is waiting. Just let me get through this my way, on my terms."

Gianni gazed toward the sky as if for an answer. He nodded gravely. "Okay. I can't imagine what this is about, but I'll go sit by your mother in the chapel, if you're sure."

Suzy nodded, unable to speak. Her father kissed her cheek and walked toward the door. Gianni turned and looked over his shoulder at her, worry and confusion clouding his eyes.

She forced herself to rally and blew him a kiss. "It'll be okay, Dad. *I'll* be okay. Just go sit by Mom," she said as cheerfully as she could as he vanished out of sight.

Suzy exhaled loudly. *God, I wish Alex were here. She would know exactly what to do. I can't believe her boss insisted she attend a mandatory board meeting on my wedding day. What could possibly be so urgent at the bank? I need my best friend.*

Suzy decided to do the next best thing. She called her niece who was assisting with the guest book, praying that Mia's cell phone was on. Suzy dialed the number and waited. Thankfully, on the third ring, her niece answered.

"Mia, please go to the beverage table just outside the chapel and bring me a bottle of champagne. Hurry."

"Okay. Aunt Suzy, are you sure you want to drink *before* you get married?"

"I'm positive. Hurry."

Mia returned with a chilled bottle of champagne. She handed it to Suzy and shifted from foot to foot.

"Rats. I forgot to bring a glass. Do you want me to find one?"

"No, hon. This is all I need. Thanks."

Suzy hugged Mia good-bye, peeled off the foil, and popped the cork, which hit the ceiling. She turned the bottle up to her mouth and chugged the bubbly as quickly as she could. She needed all the courage she could muster.

Chapter 2

As usual, Alex was running late. Balancing the steering wheel with her left knee, she applied pink lip-gloss and glanced in the rearview mirror. Satisfied with the new color, Alex peered into her purse. *Where are those gold hoops? And what could this urgent board meeting be about? How could it be more important than my best friend's wedding?*

It wasn't like the bank president to be unreasonable but Alex was irritated that she had to miss Suzy's wedding. She pulled out her phone to call her friend. It was dead. She had forgotten to charge it. *Crap. Now, I can't even call Suzy.* With a big sigh, Alex shoved the dead phone into her purse.

Alex glanced up. The light was still red so she continued to dig in the deep black hole of her purse for earrings. She fished wildly through her bag, cursing the fact that whatever she needed was always in a different pocket or crevice.

Suddenly, she felt a small movement followed by a thud. Her body lunged forward. *Oh, God.* She had a feeling she knew what had just happened but was afraid to look up. In denial, Alex fixated on the contents of her purse. Her pulse raced as she tried to will the thud away and pretend it never happened. Alex cursed under her breath and finally got the nerve to look out the windshield.

Damn it. I knew it. I've hit a car.

Alex squinted as she made out the type of car. The vehicle was white with large black letters on the back and sides. The lights on top were a dead giveaway. Sweat broke out on her top lip and her heart pounded.

I rolled right into a . . . police car. Oh, my God. Shit. Shit. Shit.

Alex pounded her steering wheel and threw her offensive purse onto the floorboard. Feeling paralyzed, she wondered whether she should get out of her car. A minute or two passed, seeming more like an hour. Eventually, the officer stepped outside his vehicle. Alex's heart thrashed against her chest as a tall, very cute uniformed officer sauntered toward her.

Lowering her window, Alex said, "Hi, Officer. I'm so sorry. I must have taken my eyes off the road for a second. I guess I rolled right into you. Is there a lot of damage? Are you okay? Oh, my God. I can't believe this. I've never done anything like this. Listen, I can pay for any damage. Should I get out?" The handsome officer waited for her to take a breath and looked as though he were suppressing a smile.

"License, please. And registration."

Alex released her seatbelt and reached for the hateful purse on the floor. The purse that had caused this mess.

"Here's my license." She handed it to the officer. "I need to open my glove box for the registration."

She eased her car manual out of the glove box, thumbed through an envelope, and found the paperwork immediately. Thank goodness for OCD at times like this. At least she was organized.

"Here's my car registration." She held the paper out the window.

The policeman nodded. "I also need proof of insurance."

"Oh, right." Alex opened her wallet and removed an insurance card. "Here, Officer."

He took the forms of identification and disappeared into his patrol car.

Meanwhile, Alex broke into a full-body sweat. She wiped the back of her neck with a tissue and checked her lipstick for good measure. She dabbed at her lips with shaky hands. She knew she'd be late for the mysterious bank meeting now. Suddenly, that was the least of her worries. Nervously fidgeting with the radio, Alex wondered if she should call into work. According to the clock on the dashboard, everyone would already be in the boardroom, plus the little fact that her phone was dead meant she couldn't contact anyone at the bank to tell them what had happened.

This is just perfect. First, I miss my best friend's wedding. Then, I rear-end a cop. Now, I'm going to be late to work—again.

Alex hated to walk into the conference room with fifty sets of eyes staring at her. She could just feel their minds at work. *Why don't you get up earlier, Alex? Why can't you get here on time, Alex?* Her tardiness infuriated her most of all.

Alex leaned against the headrest and took ten deep breaths. *What was taking the cop so long?* She wanted to see if there was any damage to the police car, and to her Mustang, for that matter, but she didn't dare get out. She didn't want to make another wrong move and further irritate the officer. Alex decided to search once more for her stupid gold hoops while she waited. She should throw them away. Damn earrings.

After what seemed like an eternity, she watched the officer stride back to her car. *He must have run a background check or something.* She noticed his straight back, broad shoulders and the confident way he carried himself. Her eyes wandered down to his . . . gun and she got all jittery again.

As the officer appeared at her window, his voice boomed, "Step out of the car, please."

Alex jumped. She was a bundle of nerves. He was going to handcuff her and take her away right then and there. She was going to go to jail because she'd hit a police car. Her mind raced. *Who can bail me out? Suzy is in the middle of her wedding and Mom and Dad are in Canada. Crap.*

Alex opened her car door and slowly stood up. Even though she wore three-inch heels, the officer, well over six feet tall, towered above her. Her black sleeveless turtleneck dress with a wide gold belt hugged her curves and she noticed the officer eyeing her appreciatively. Alex tucked her long blond hair behind her ears and took a deep breath. Then she put both hands behind her back.

The officer cleared his throat. "That won't be necessary."

Alex thought she heard him chuckle.

"I'm not going to handcuff you. I just thought you'd like to see the damage to the cars."

"Oh, right," she whispered. "Yes, I would."

Alex traipsed toward the patrol car and squatted down to inspect the damage. She turned her head from side-to-side, squinting. She examined both bumpers and couldn't detect one black smudge. No dents. Nothing. She smiled, stood, and looked at the officer expectantly.

"No harm done," he said. "But next time you need to be careful, Mrs.—?"

"It's Ms.," she corrected him. "Alexandra Mitchell. Most people call me Alex."

The officer extended his hand and smiled.

Alex noticed he had an adorable dimple.

"Nice to meet you, Ms. Mitchell. I'm Sgt. Tony Montgomery. Why don't you get back into your car and go to work? Did you say you work at a bank?"

She didn't recall mentioning it but nodded affirmatively. "Yes, I work at Community National Bank."

"I'm sure you need to get to work. Listen, Ms. Mitchell. Pay attention to what you're doing, okay?" His clear blue eyes pierced hers. "Keep both hands on the wheel and look straight ahead. I'm not sure what you were doing when you took your eyes off the road but you were lucky today."

Alex wasn't about to tell him she was putting makeup and earrings on. She met his direct gaze. "I'll look straight ahead from now on. I promise. Thank you." Her voice broke. "I was so afraid." Her eyes filled with tears and her legs felt wobbly. She reached for the door handle to steady herself.

"Don't worry, Ms. Mitchell." The officer seemed to soften. "Just be careful next time."

"I will." She climbed into her car and smiled at the officer with relief.

"Just one more thing." The cute officer bent down and leaned into her window.

Alex caught a whiff of his cologne and felt her cheeks flush.

He handed paperwork to her. "Here are your documents. I hope you don't mind but I made a note of your phone number."

Her eyebrows shot up. "Um, well, no, I don't mind." Alex shifted in her seat. She was actually thrilled but puzzled. "Wait. Only my address is on my license, isn't it?"

"That's all I need. I do pretty good police work." He flashed that adorable dimple and white teeth again.

Alex relaxed and decided to be bold. "I guess the least I could do is buy you some coffee. And maybe a doughnut." She laughed. "I know that's lame but I couldn't resist." She glanced at the clock. "For now, I've got to get to work. I'm late for an important meeting."

"I like doughnuts," he teased. "Do me a favor and don't speed. I'll take you up on that coffee sometime, Ms. Mitchell. Have a nice day." He patted the roof of her car with his left hand and walked back to his patrol car.

Alex swallowed as she stared at the detective's muscular backside and broad shoulders. She couldn't believe her bad luck had turned good. She had rear-ended a police car but there was no damage. Secondly, the cop was gorgeous and he wanted to get together with her. This was going to be a great day after all, except for missing the meeting and Suzy's wedding.

Alex resisted the temptation to speed to the bank. She didn't dare risk another cop encounter. When she arrived at Community National Bank, she punched in the code on the back door. The parking lot was full which meant board members were still there. *Maybe I can still make part of the meeting.* Alex rushed inside but her shoulders dropped as soon as she saw the open boardroom door. That meant the meeting was over.

Distraught, Alex scanned the lobby for her boss, Jim Hooban, the bank president. She spotted him by the teller windows talking to Mr. Tummons, the surly senior board member. *Great. Just great.* When Jim saw Alex, he gave her a stern look.

Of all days to be late. He's going to kill me. Maybe fire me.

Her stomach churned. She watched some board members mill around the lobby while others headed for the front door. Alex shifted from foot to foot, wishing she could become invisible. She didn't know what had taken place. After all, a mandatory Saturday meeting was atypical. Alex tried to blend in with the woodwork and made her way across the back of the lobby, quickly darting inside her corner office. She glanced at the glass walls and yearned to hide under her desk. Her lovely corner office offered little privacy and reminded her of a fish bowl. She hated it.

Alex didn't bother turning on the light and set her purse beneath her desk. She finally worked up the nerve to make eye contact with her boss. As head of marketing, she didn't want to appear out of the loop. When Jim noticed Alex, he motioned her over. She walked slowly across the lobby.

Jim didn't bother with his usual friendly greeting. "Did you forget this was a mandatory board meeting? Where were you?" His voice boomed all the way to the teller window.

Tears pricked Alex's eyes. Her boss had never yelled at her. "I'm sorry, Jim. I was involved in a minor accident." She noticed Mr. Tummons had cocked his head to listen. She dug deep and found her professional voice. "Whenever it's convenient for you, I'll fill you in on what happened."

The board member excused himself and Jim followed Alex into her office. He closed the door too loudly.

"I'm *very* disappointed in you. This was an extremely urgent meeting. You needed to be here." Jim cleared his throat. "I know your friend was getting married today. Does that have anything to do with your tardiness?"

Alex shook her head. "No. Absolutely not. Maybe I was distracted but—" She crossed and uncrossed her arms. "Please sit down. I'll tell you what happened."

She told Jim the entire story while he listened and nodded. She could see he relaxed slightly and almost hid a smile. His eyes crinkled as she finished.

Alex sighed and leaned forward on her elbows. "So, that's why I missed the meeting. I'm sorry. I know I've disappointed you. You can call the CCPD and check it out yourself."

"No need for that. You're as trustworthy as they come. You're lucky you didn't damage the police car. I wish you had been at the meeting but it's over."

Jim paced in front of Alex's desk as he updated her. "Our board was approached by Sunshine America Bank. Sunshine wants to buy Community National as well as other community banks."

Alex's eyebrows shot up. "Oh, no."

"That's right. CNB would have become part of their corporate entity located on the East Coast." Jim ran his hand through his brown hair. "A few of our bank locations would have closed and several employees would have lost their jobs. There would have been changes in upper management as well, most likely my position." He shoved one hand in his pocket and glanced toward the lobby, which was nearly empty.

He leaned across Alex's desk. "The urgency of the meeting was due to the fact that some of CNB's board members had been approached individually and were intoxicated by the stock price. I was afraid we wouldn't be able to get a majority vote. The conversation became heated, but luckily, the board voted to decline Sunshine's proposal. We're still locally owned." Jim sighed and smiled.

Alex leaned back in her chair. "Thank goodness they came to that realization. Now I see why this meeting was so urgent."

"I wasn't able to tell you beforehand due to the confidentiality agreement. I thought we might need your vote today but it all worked out. Now, let's concentrate on the good things at CNB."

Alex stared at her boss. "What do you have in mind?"

"I want you to create a branding campaign pointing out the positive reasons for banking locally."

"I'm on it." Alex smiled at her boss. "Thank you again for understanding."

Jim nodded, opened the door, and left her office.

Alex turned on her computer and glanced at the time. She smiled. Suzy would be married by now and she couldn't wait to hear all about her best friend's wedding.

Chapter 3

Hope dreaded going home. She knew most people couldn't wait to get home after work but they didn't have what she had waiting—hippie parents. Make that hippie parents who refused to get normal jobs and depended on her for food and especially beer. Hope had missed the Ozarks, but sometimes wondered if she had made the right decision by moving back to the Midwest.

Now, every day was the same—counseling kids at school, feeding her parents, fighting with her parents—and repeat. Just like the movie *Groundhog Day*.

She stopped by the store to buy bread, chips, and beer. God knows she'd never hear the end of it if she forgot the beer. Her parents, Larry and Montana, always had the munchies from pot and certainly couldn't afford their own groceries. How could they? Neither one had a job unless you counted Montana's colorful macramé plant holders that she sold at endless garage sales. Hope wasn't exactly on Wall Street with her meager high school counselor salary, but she managed.

Once Hope pulled onto her street, she spotted her parents' familiar, yellow Volkswagen Microbus with tie-dye peace signs and daisy decals adorning the sides. Just seeing that ridiculous vehicle made her shoulders droop.

She parked in front of her drab, tan duplex with shrubs that sorely needed trimming. The half brown, half green lawn was patchy at best. She noticed one of the brown shutters was crooked and the screen door had a hole in it that was somehow getting bigger by the day. A green garden hose now draped across the drive and the barbecue grill was beside the garage instead of on the back patio. *It's too much trouble to recoil the hose and return the grill to the backyard?*

Her parents' old VW bus, Betsy, actually had a bed in the back, seventies-style. They had it stocked with hard rock music on cassettes and even a few eight tracks. Hope did share their love of sixties and seventies music but their commonality seemed to end there.

Sure, it was great in high school when she had the *cool* parents who smoked weed and didn't mind if she got in at two in the morning. All of her friends loved the fact that Hope could drink beer, smoke pot, or paint her walls any color of the rainbow. She was allowed to wear short skirts, lots of makeup, have parties, and play rock music loudly. Very loudly.

Hope's friends had always put her parents on a pedestal. *If they only knew.* They told Hope how lucky she was and constantly complained about their boring, strict parents. But Hope had always envied her friends. She *wanted* a curfew. She didn't want her parents to let her smoke pot or drink beer. The parents of Hope's friends were all grown up. Unfortunately, hers still acted like teenagers.

The Strict Parents all had corporate careers or were retired, had large houses, nice cars, and traveled the world. Meanwhile, Hope's parents eked out a living with odd jobs. Montana sold macramé plant hangers at flea markets and had constant garage sales. Larry mowed lawns and painted houses—if and when he felt like it. Hope's house was never a priority to him. Most of the time, her parents were either stoned or asking for money.

Hope hadn't had the nerve to tell her best friends from high school, Suzy and Alex, that she had moved back to town. She was too embarrassed about her unchanged situation and her looks. They were both gorgeous and she had a curvy—okay fat—body and unruly hair. *Hell. Can't something be right in my life? If I at least had an accent, I might be considered cool.*

She sighed, ready to face her parents. Balancing her purse and schoolbag in one arm and groceries on her hip, Hope banged on the front door with her knee.

"Mom? Dad? Help me open the door."

Larry was sprawled on her tan couch as usual. His dirty blond hair adorned her green pillow. He had a beer in one hand and the television remote in the other. He glanced at her and held up both hands as if the remote and beer were glued to them.

He yelled, "Montana. Hope needs help with the door."

Actually, Montana wasn't her mother's real name. It was Claire. Claire is "much too stiff" she had said. Years ago, when Larry and Montana rode through Montana on borrowed Harleys, they fell in love with the area and the name. It had stuck ever since.

The screen door creaked open when Montana finally appeared.

"Have a good day?"

"Yes, Mom."

Hope darted toward her kitchen. Just once, she'd like to come home to an empty house and watch the television shows *she* wanted to see—or maybe not have the television on at all.

Hope's purse clattered to the floor and the contents spilled as she struggled with the groceries. Montana picked up the objects and shoved them inside Hope's purse.

"Thanks," Hope muttered as she eyed her mother's short denim shorts, black Harley tee and pink flip-flops. She had to admit her mother has a nice body—far nicer than hers. She could never figure out why she was short and stocky and her parents were tall and lean. Hope could feel the fat bulging over her own bra strap and stared down at her round belly. She envied her mother's smooth blond hair, which was usually worn in a youthful ponytail.

Montana started putting the groceries away. She knew where Hope stored her groceries as well as Hope did.

"You seem stressed. Let me cook dinner tonight."

"That'd be nice."

"BLT's, dip and chips comin' up," Montana said as she clanged the frying pan onto the stove. Hope retreated to her bedroom to finish her latest romance novel. *Just what I want to do. Read about some happy, sappy couple while I eat dinner with my parents at home. I don't know why they bother having a trailer. They're always here. Probably didn't pay their electric bill again.*

Hope picked up the phone to call Alex and tell her she was back in town. Before the first ring she lost her nerve and hung up.

"Dinner's ready," Montana yelled.

Hope threw her book on the floor and wondered how she could get her life back.

Chapter 4

The chapel overflowed with calla lilies, sweet-smelling purple lilacs and white candles. Trailing green ivy and lilacs were on the end of every pew, tied with lavender organza. The floor-to-ceiling windows offered breathtaking views of the wooded scenery outside. Two horses nibbled on the grass several feet away and squirrels ran up and down the trees. Guests chatted and stared ahead at the striking wedding party. The two bridesmaids and Suzy's sister, the maid of honor, wore strapless deep purple dresses and the groomsmen were dressed in black tuxes and silver ties. Dean, her husband-to-be, had a mile-wide smile as he eagerly eyed the back of the chapel.

When the organist began playing the wedding march, a hush fell over the crowd. The photographer snapped pictures as guests craned their necks to get a glimpse of the bride. Suzy appeared in the doorway and the smell of the fragrant lilacs filled her nose as she fought back tears.

Dressed in a strapless, beaded white gown, Suzy stood at the back of the chapel alone, feet planted as if they were concrete blocks. She glanced at the one-carat diamond solitaire on her left hand and took a deep breath. The organist was nearly through the entire wedding march and frowned in puzzlement as Suzy stood in place. She stopped playing for a moment, then dramatically repeated the song.

Suzy tried to smile at the adoring guests who glanced in her direction. *If they only knew.* Her stomach churned and her head pounded. *This is supposed to be the most perfect day of my life.*

Suzy willed her feet to move forward. In a daze, she somehow walked down the aisle, minus her father and minus her large bouquet. She glanced and nodded at the onlookers vying for her attention. Some were already taking photographs. The official photographer snapped photos a few feet ahead of her. She could see the curious look on his face since she wasn't smiling. When Suzy saw her parents, her heart plummeted and tears pricked her eyes. She didn't have the nerve to look at her son, Jon. She knew she'd lose it.

Willing herself to keep her tears at bay, Suzy trudged toward the front of the chapel. The long aisle seemed never ending. She couldn't make eye contact with Dean. Not yet. As Suzy climbed the final three stairs to the altar and stood beside Dean, she turned to the guests and motioned with her hands for everyone to sit down.

Looking surprised, Dean raised his eyebrows and mouthed, "Where's your dad?"

Suzy ignored him and held her quivering chin high. Fortified by the champagne she guzzled earlier and with a shaky voice, she said, "Thank you for coming here but there will *not* be a wedding today." She swallowed hard and said a quick, silent prayer for courage.

She could hear whispers as she found more words. "I know this is a shock. I want you to go ahead and enjoy the reception. Eat the food, drink, and dance to the band. I won't be here but you should enjoy the party. And thank you for your gifts but please pick them up as you leave."

She turned a hardened face toward her sister, Tara. Tara's face was pale, her blue eyes wide. Suzy clutched her grandmother's hanky, and spoke firmly and loudly so the guests in the last pews could hear.

"I especially want to thank my maid of honor, my sister, for sleeping with my husband-to-be last night and keeping me from making the biggest mistake of my life."

With that, Suzy yanked off her engagement ring and threw it at Dean. His face turned ashen and sweat beaded on his forehead. She hiked up her dress and practically sprinted down the aisle. There was a chorused gasp and then the chapel was eerily quiet.

When Suzy reached the back of the chapel, she glared once more at Dean who looked like a little boy who had shattered the Hope diamond. She glanced at her parents who held each other and sobbed. She looked toward her son and saw that his jaw was set. Dean's dad looked angry while his mother fanned herself with the wedding program. Before she ran out, Suzy heard Tara wailing. Gaping mouths, gasps, and shocked stares were all Suzy remembered as she continued running. *How did I, a wedding planner, end up with the mother of all weddings?*

Suzy removed her heels and ran barefoot to the guesthouse. Once inside, she ripped off her wedding dress and yanked open every drawer looking for scissors. She wanted to cut her dress to shreds, tiny shreds, and then mail the pieces to Dean and Tara.

Unable to find scissors, she started to cry again and flopped onto the large stool. She put her head in her hands and spread her dress on the floor like a crime scene victim.

Stripped down to her white garter belt and lacy strapless bra, Suzy yanked what seemed like a hundred hairpins out of her bun. Her red hair tumbled past her shoulders. The miniature white orchids carefully placed around her bun dropped to the floor. She wiped her nose with the back of her hand and heard footsteps outside.

Bang. Bang. Bang. Suzy bolted upright as the loud knocking continued. *God, what if that's Dean?* The last thing she wanted was to talk to anyone, especially him. She put her trembling hands over her ears as she heard the familiar voices of her parents.

"Suzy, open up. Please," her father pleaded, his voice cracking.

She couldn't bear to hear him cry. "Wait a second. Let me get dressed."

She changed into the white capris and black tank she had worn to the chapel and unlocked the door. Her parents burst into the room, wrapping their arms around her. Gianni spoke first.

"Honey, are you okay? Never mind. That's a dumb question. Sweetheart, how did you know about this . . . this horrible thing?" He added, "Are you sure? I can't believe Tara would do this to you."

"She did, Dad."

"I have a hard time believing that. How do you know?" demanded her mother, Ellie. She and her mom always had conflict for some reason. Suzy was a daddy's girl and Tara had clearly been her mother's favorite.

Suzy blew her nose and threw the tissue away, missing the basket. "I know because someone photographed Tara and Dean in bed. They were naked in some sleazy motel room and didn't even bother to close the curtains. The pictures show the room number, the bed, a bottle of wine, everything."

"What? When did you get this photo?" Gianni asked.

"This morning. Someone slid them under the guesthouse door as I was putting on my wedding gown. I didn't even notice the envelope at first."

"Who took the pictures?" Ellie demanded.

"How would I know? And who the hell cares?" Suzy snapped, her jaw set. "Pictures are worth a thousand words, as they say."

Her mother pressed. "Was there a return address?"

"No, there wasn't a return address, Mother. The large, glossy photos were in a big, brown envelope. It was blank on the outside. Since it wasn't mailed, there's no postmark. Someone just slid it under my door, as I said."

"How about a note?" Gianni asked as he rubbed his daughter's shoulders.

"There was a short note, Dad. It was on an index card."

"What did it say?"

"You need to know about this."

Gianni and Ellie looked at one other. Ellie fidgeted with her purse.

"Did you recognize the handwriting?" she asked.

"It was typewritten."

"I still can't believe Tara would do such a thing. She's your sister. She loves you. Could that picture have been doctored?" Ellie asked.

Suzy was beyond irritated that her mother didn't believe her. This was *her* wedding day, her disaster, yet all her life it had been poor Tara this and poor Tara that.

She glared at her mother. "I wondered that, too. I thought it could have been photoshopped, so I wanted to be sure." Suzy paced like a caged lion.

"That's why I walked down the aisle and made the announcement like I did. I wanted to see their reactions. I think Tara's loud sobbing and the look on Dean's face said it all, don't you? They gave me my answer."

She grabbed a tissue and angrily wiped the mascara from under her eyes. "Whoever took the photo wanted me to know about it and I'm glad. As much as it hurts now, I wouldn't want to be married to a man like that."

Her mother continued. "I just don't get it. I wonder who took it?"

"Oh, my God. Mom, who the hell cares who took the photo?" Suzy sat back down on the stool and stared at her dad willing him to silence her mother.

Gianni sighed. His shoulders slumped. "What are you going to do? We were all going to live nearby. We bought a house for you and Dean near us. That was going to be our surprise wedding gift." He sat on the stool beside her.

"I guess Tara has a new house," Suzy said, trying to laugh. "I certainly won't be living there. That was very generous of you but I need to be here with Jon anyway." She forced a smile.

Jon burst into the room. "Mom. What the hell is going on?

"Just like I said in the chapel. Your Aunt Tara and my almost-husband had a fling."

Jon punched the wall. "I'll kill the son of a bitch. I already had a few choice words with him. I never trusted that guy but I can't believe Aunt Tara would do this to you."

"Me neither," Suzy shook her head and gazed at the wall.

Her mother started to open her mouth but closed it, thankfully.

Ellie stared blankly out the window. "What are we going to do? You're sisters. We love you both. If this is true, Tara has done the unspeakable but I still can't believe this."

"Believe what you want, Mom. Their reactions confirmed it for me. I'm going home and I want to forget this ever happened. Like a bad dream or something. I want to forget that I ever knew Dean and I also want to forget that I have a sister right now."

Ellie gasped.

Suzy looked in the mirror at her tear-stained face. Her professionally applied makeup was a mess. "I'm going home to take a hot bath and then I'm going to bed."

Ellie opened her mouth as if to suggest something.

Suzy interjected, "I don't want company."

She gathered her shoes and purse, then scooped up her wedding dress. Suzy dramatically crammed it into a tiny wastebasket until a white, poofy ball billowed over the top of the gold trashcan.

Ellie sucked in her breath. "What are you doing? Are you throwing that beautiful dress away?"

Suzy couldn't believe her mother's denseness. "Yes, Mom," Suzy said through gritted teeth. "I'm throwing the damn dress away. Why would I keep it? For Halloween? I don't want any reminders of this day. None."

Ellie stared at the trashcan and looked at Gianni. He shook his head. Ellie apparently got the message because she didn't go near the dress.

Jon paced the room like a tiger in a cage. His fists were in balls. A dark vein popped out on his forehead. Suzy touched her son's arm. "I repeat. He isn't worth it."

Jon stared at his mother in wonder.

"Some day, some year, I'll get past this. Maybe I'll even forgive Tara. But that will be a long time coming, if ever. For now, I don't want to speak to her. I hope you'll respect that. I need time to heal, if that's possible. If she marries Dean, fine. Just don't expect me to attend the wedding. Suzy managed a small smile. In fact, they can move into the house you bought for us. I hope I never set eyes on that bastard again. Now, I'm going home. I'm exhausted."

Gianni had always been an intuitive father. He walked toward Ellie, put his hands on her shoulders, and steered her toward the door. He could gauge his daughter even at times when her mother was still in a fog. Ellie opened her mouth but Gianni knitted his brows and she got the message.

Gianni took his daughter's hand. "What can we do for you, honey? Do you want me to get your car? Drive it around the back?"

"I'll go with Grandpa to get the car," Jon said.

"Yes and please hurry." The last thing Suzy wanted was to make conversation with curious wedding guests. "I don't want to talk to anyone, especially Dean or Tara. They've humiliated me enough for a lifetime." Suzy picked up her phone and threw it against the wall. It somersaulted off, hit a loveseat and bounced onto a green rug. "Damn phone. I can't even break a phone properly."

"You have every right to be angry. Maybe you should take a long, hot soak in the tub," offered Ellie. "Call Alex. She always cheers you up."

"She's at some important bank meeting. Besides, I want to be alone."

"Are you sure that's a good idea?" asked Ellie nervously.

"I really want to be alone. I'm mentally and physically fatigued. I'm not going to call Alex tonight. I don't want to talk about this for one more second."

Gianni and Jon were already out the door when Suzy handed Ellie her yellow going-away dress. "You can have this or return it. I don't want any memories of today."

Suzy pulled her red hair into a high ponytail and waited for her dad and son to bring the car around the back. Ellie, thankfully silent, stared out the window and brushed away tears. When she spotted Gianni, she rushed Suzy out the back door. They climbed into Suzy's parents' car and drove to Suzy's silver SUV, which Jon had mercifully moved to the back of the lot.

Gianni leaned back and took his daughter's hand. He kissed the top of her hand. "I love you, Suzy Q." His words caught in his throat. Ellie rubbed his back. She looked at Suzy, tears in her eyes. "I'm sorry this happened. I love you, too."

Suzy hunkered low in the back seat. She didn't want to be spotted.

"I'll be okay. I love you both." She launched herself out of her parents' car, ran to her SUV, with her large green purse banging against her back. She glanced back at Gianni and Ellie. She noticed Gianni laid his head against the steering wheel.

"Damn, Tara and Dean. Damn them." Suzy pounded her steering wheel with her left fist, put her car into gear and left skid marks as she sped away. Jon's eyes bulged as he reached for the seatbelt.

Chapter 5

Once they pulled into the driveway, Jon and Suzy both rocketed out of the car like human cannon balls.

"I'm not going to Europe. I can't leave you like this."

"Yes, you are, Jon. This trip is a graduation gift from your dad. I'd feel doubly worse if you stayed here. I'd be guilt ridden on top of the betrayal by my fiancé. That's not a good combination."

Jon glanced toward his gigantic duffel bag on the floor. "I wouldn't feel right leaving you."

Suzy picked up the heavy bag and heaved it toward her son. "I love you. I appreciate your wanting to stay here with me but I'd be miserable about not only the almost-wedding but about ruining your trip."

Jon looked hesitant but glanced at his watch.

"I know you're on a tight schedule. Go. Take the car and leave it at the airport. Alex can drive me there tomorrow to collect the car. I have another set of keys.

Jon smiled for the first time since the incident. "If you're sure."

"I'm positive."

"You're the best mother in the world."

Suzy wrapped her arms around her son's neck. "And you're the best son. Now, give me a kiss and have a safe flight. Don't forget to call your mother when you arrive."

Jon gave Suzy a bear hug embrace. "Call me if you need me to come back. You know I will. I love you." He sauntered toward the front door and heaved the heavy bag over his shoulder. He peered back. "I'm sorry this happened. Dean's a douchebag."

Suzy laughed at his description. "Cheers to that. I love you, too. Now, goodbye." She waited until she could no longer hear the car engine and went to bed.

Suzy tossed and turned and punched her tear-stained pillow. She stared at the ceiling. She should have been on her honeymoon enjoying tropical Jamaica. She fixated on the plane tickets on the nightstand. She could still fly there alone but no longer had the desire for a fun, sunny vacation. The clock showed four in the morning. Suzy trudged to the bathroom and took a sleeping pill. She couldn't sleep and kept picturing Dean and Tara in bed. It made her sick to her stomach. She tried to block out the hurtful images and finally, thankfully fell asleep.

When she woke at nine, she bolted out of bed and drank a pot of coffee. Pacing the kitchen floor and fuming, she wanted to call Dean and give him a piece of her mind—and Tara, too, for that matter. But they didn't deserve it. She wasn't going to give them the satisfaction. She wanted to erase both of them from her thoughts and let them suffer from their public embarrassment. Who knows? Maybe they were glad they were caught and were happily in each other's arms. Maybe one of them arranged to have the photo taken. Suzy slammed her coffee cup into the sink where it shattered. Picking up the pieces, she cut her finger and started crying from exhaustion and anger.

Suzy needed help. She needed Alex. She called her best friend and asked her to meet at Coconuts in an hour. Suzy could tell by Alex's voice that she was perplexed. Alex would have expected Suzy to be on her honeymoon and must have deduced from Suzy's somber voice that something was terribly wrong. Thankfully, Alex didn't press her.

Suzy drummed her fingers on the table and glanced around the familiar restaurant. The best friends had a weekly ritual—Thursdays at Coconuts. In the land-locked Midwest, this beach-like bar and restaurant, complete with fake palm trees and coconut drink holders, at least felt like a vacation getaway. Coconuts was their oasis. Each week, they served as each other's therapists and comforted, counseled or provided one another with a necessary kick in the butt. The friends jokingly coined their weekly get-together *friendapy.*

Suzy glanced at her watch. *Does Alex always have to be late?* She was about to order a second glass of cabernet when Alex barreled inside.

"So sorry. I was behind a moron who was out for a leisurely Sunday drive. The car in the other lane had me boxed in so I couldn't pass Grandpa." Alex leaned over and squeezed her best friend. "I got here as fast as I could." She stared into Suzy's eyes. "What's going on? Why aren't you on your honeymoon?" Alex's forehead crinkled with worry. She glanced at Suzy's almost-empty wine glass.

"Drinking a little early, aren't you?"

Suzy's eyes filled with tears and a loud sob escaped. Alex put her hand on Suzy's arm as she watched Suzy take a big gulp and polish off her wine.

Alex's eyes widened. "Honey, what happened?" She stroked Suzy's red hair.

Suzy blew her nose and wiped her eyes. Alex placed one hand over Suzy's and with her other, motioned to the server for a drink. It was still early but whatever had happened, it was obvious she'd need to imbibe, too.

Gus appeared at the table. "Chardonnay as usual?" Alex nodded and added, "And another cabernet." Gus disappeared.

When the server was out of earshot, Suzy told Alex her wedding nightmare in vivid detail. To punctuate the disaster, she pulled out the photos of Tara and Dean. Wide-eyed, Alex glanced at the pictures, then shoved them forcefully into the envelope. She sat still, obviously in shock, as Gus delivered her wine.

After she took a large gulp, her icy eyes met Suzy's.

"What an asshole. What a prick. I never liked that bastard. And your sister. What a bitch."

Suzy rolled her teary eyes. "They're all that and more. I can't believe my own sister would do this to me. And the man who I thought I was going to spend the rest of my life with . . ." she sobbed. "How could I have been so wrong? So stupid? I'm never dating again." Her voice got louder with each statement. Suzy laid her head on the table and wept.

Alex rubbed Suzy's back and fought back her own tears but she was more angry than sad.

She leaned down against the table and spoke into Suzy's ear. "I can't believe I wasn't there to help you through this. God, I'm so sorry. You were all alone. That makes me sick. What can I do?"

Suzy's mouth curved into a half smile. "Hire a hit man."

"Done."

They both giggled. "We need to gorge on some unhealthy appetizers." Alex again motioned for Gus and ordered coconut shrimp, crab cakes, fries, and more wine.

She shook her head. "I can't believe this. I'm in complete shock. I can only imagine how difficult it was for you to stand in front of every—" her voice caught in her throat. "You're so brave. I'm really proud of you." Alex leaned back. "What did your parents say?"

Suzy blew her nose again. Loudly. "My parents are in shock too. They talked to me afterward as I was looking for scissors to shred my dress."

Alex laughed. "I don't blame you. Go on."

"Actually, I feel sorry for my parents. They're in a tough spot because they love my sister and me. Mom still can't believe Tara would do such a thing. Me neither. It's unthinkable."

She stared into her empty wine glass. "Needless to say, I won't be attending any family get-togethers any time soon—

probably not in this decade." Her voice rose angrily. "I could care less if I ever set eyes on Dean or Tara again."

Alex patted her arm. "I'm glad you're getting angry. You need to go through all the stages of mourning. What are they? Shock, denial, anger, acceptance . . . something like that. Sweetie, this *will* get better. You will heal and move on. You deserve someone better. It's too bad Ken—"

"I know, I know. Biggest mistake of my life. I should have married Ken when I had the chance in college. Now, he's married. All the good ones are gone. Isn't that what they always say?"

Gus brought over a huge tray of steaming food. "You girls must be hungry." He laughed and set down the food.

"You don't know the half of it," Suzy said.

Alex got up to use the rest room. When she returned, Suzy was scooting her food around the plate.

"I want to call Tara and give her a piece of my mind," Alex said.

"Don't bother," Suzy said. "It's over."

Alex watched Suzy play with her food. "You've got to eat. Listen, Dean had us all fooled with his boyish good looks and goofy smile. There are good guys out there, I promise. In fact, there's a cute new loan officer at work. I'll ask if he's dating anyone."

Straightening her green ruffled shirt, Suzy wiped away tears. "No, don't try to fix me up. I made it through my first divorce. I'll make it through this betrayal. I'm definitely not ready to date, if ever." She popped a coconut shrimp in her mouth.

"Besides, I have my hands full with upcoming weddings. Ironic, huh? My second wedding never took place, I'm divorced and a wedding planner. Let's just hope my brides don't find out what a failure I've been with my own marital bliss."

Alex chewed her crab cake and watched her best friend. "You'll meet the right guy one of these days. A really good one. You've had rotten luck, for sure, but as far as your career, you're definitely in the right business. You're a great wedding planner. Any bride would be lucky to have you plan her wedding. I think the best thing for you to do is stay busy, lean on me, and drink vats of wine."

"Whatever you say, Great Sage." Suzy finally smiled.

Alex waved Gus over and requested coffee. She wracked her brain trying to decide how to help her best friend when Suzy broke the silence.

"I don't want to talk about my disaster right now. It's too depressing. Help me get my mind off that bastard and tell me who this mystery man is already."

Alex's eyebrows shot up. "How did you know?"

"I know you inside and out. I'm your best friend, remember? I can tell when you've met a guy. Spill."

Chapter 6

A huge smile came over Alex as Gus placed two steaming zebra print mugs in front of them. Alex held her warm coffee trying to decide where to begin.

"I did meet someone. You're *never* going to believe this. He's a cop and I rear-ended him on the way to my meeting yesterday."

Suzy choked on her coffee. "What did you just say?"

"You heard me." Alex relayed the entire story.

Suzy slapped her hand to her forehead. "My God. You're lucky you weren't thrown into jail or something. Alex, you've got to stop running late all the time. What's his name?"

"Sgt. Tony Montgomery."

"This is too funny." Suzy laughed hard. "I needed this. Only *you* could crash into a cop and have him ask for your phone number. If I didn't love you, I'd hate you."

"Ha ha," Alex said. "I know. I was lucky. Guess no more makeup while driving. Wait until you meet him. Tall, dark, and handsome. Cliché but true. He's gorgeous with a chiseled jaw, an adorable dimple, and ocean blue eyes—sort of a younger, taller George Clooney."

"Okay, I do hate you." Suzy leaned back in her chair. "I'm not surprised you're interested in a cop."

"Why?"

"Even in high school you loved guys in uniform. You dated the football quarterback and the basketball star."

"Not at the same time." Alex shrugged her shoulders. "So I was slightly superficial."

Suzy studied Alex as she sipped her coffee. "Have you talked to him since the 'accident?'"

"Um, yes."

"And?"

"There's not much to tell." He called to see if I had whiplash or anything so we agreed to have coffee this morning at The Coffee Drip." Alex looked away. "He's, um, married."

Suzy's mouth flew open. "What? I don't know if I want to hear this after yesterday."

"I know. I know. I'm sorry." Alex rested her chin on her hand. "The thing is, Tony *is* married but she sounds like a horrible woman. They've been married for eight years. He said before they were married they hadn't dated long and he was thinking of ending the relationship because they didn't have much in common. Apparently, the night he was going to break it off, she told him she was pregnant so, being the gallant guy he is, he married her."

Alex stirred her coffee. "Tony said his wife had affairs early on, and he even caught her in bed with a guy. It's such a waste. She doesn't appreciate him. He seems kind from what I can tell. He deserves better. And it doesn't hurt that he's drop-dead gorgeous."

Suzy stared intently at her friend and spoke more sternly than she intended. "The fact that his wife has had affairs doesn't excuse that little detail that he's married. Why would he stay with her? I can't imagine anyone putting up with that."

"Me neither. I asked him that very question. Tony said he stays for his son, Joey. It's obvious he loves that little guy. You should have seen his face light up when he talked about him. Over coffee today, we had barely started talking when he pulled pictures out of his wallet to show me what Joey looks like. He's a proud papa."

Suzy said, "You know how I feel about my son. There's nothing like that unconditional love. How old is Joey?"

Alex brightened. "Eight. Tony said they go everywhere together. Any time he's off work, he said he's with Joey, his buddy. He told me Joey is his world." She sighed. "Isn't that sweet? I know I shouldn't talk to him anymore but he's such a nice guy and his wife treats him terribly. Tell me what to do."

Suzy leaned across the table and looked Alex in the eye. "You know what to do. Walk away. *You'll* be the one to get hurt."

Alex was silent.

"You know I'm right. And if you don't walk away, be careful, my friend. We shouldn't both have our personal lives in ruins. Only one disaster at a time, please."

Suzy looked through her purse and pulled out some shiny red-tinted lip-gloss. She traced her lips perfectly without the use of a mirror, then stared at Alex. "I'm curious. What did you two talk about besides the fact that he's married to a cheating wife and you rear-ended him?"

"It was kind of hard to talk. He kept getting calls from the station and from his snitches—"

"Snitches? What's that? You just met a cop and you're already using police lingo."

"That's what the cops call 'informants.' Tony said snitches often give information in order to get a lesser charge and to get in the cops' good graces. He also talked about how jaded he's becoming. I'm sure his home life doesn't help matters." Alex sipped her coffee.

"I could see the sadness in his eyes but I'm not sure if that's from his bad marriage or from dealing with unsavory characters on a daily basis. I feel sorry for him."

"This whole married cop thing makes me nervous. I'm surprised he was so open with you."

"I was too. He said he doesn't get a lot of down time so maybe he wanted to fill me in quickly."

"Are you going to see him again?"

I'm not sure. I know I shouldn't. He gave me his business

card and cell number and said to call anytime, 24/7." Alex pulled his card out and slid it across the table.

Sgt. Tony Montgomery
Crystal City Police Department

Suzy stared at the card and handed it back. "I've never dated a cop and I'm not sure I would. Do what you want, Alex. You're an adult. I'll love you and support you no matter what but I don't want you to get hurt." Suzy set her mug down. "Listen, I'm exhausted. I couldn't sleep last night and I'm suddenly very tired."

Alex noticed the bags under Suzy's eyes. "It's no wonder you couldn't sleep after the day you had."

Suzy picked up her purse and reached for the bill. Alex grabbed it.

"Let me get this. It's the least I can do."

Suzy agreed for once and headed for the door. Halfway across the room, she turned and walked back to the table.

"Thanks for cheering me up, or at least giving me something new to think about. I need your friendship now more than you'll ever know. I love you." She leaned down and hugged Alex.

"I love you too, hon. It'll get better. And I'll check into that hit man."

Alex watched Suzy leave and asked Gus for decaf coffee. She was lost in her thoughts about Suzy when she felt a body standing too close over her right shoulder.

"Hi. I thought I might find you here," Sgt. Montgomery said.

Alex jumped. "Ooh, you gave me a start. How did you know I was here?"

"You mentioned you meet a friend here once a week. Mind if I sit down?"

"Um, no."

Sgt. Montgomery was obviously off duty since he was holding a beer.

Wracking her brain, Alex didn't recall mentioning Coconuts to the officer but couldn't remember much of what was said after the shock of rear-ending him and finding out he was married earlier. Plus, this was Sunday, not Thursday, their usual girls' night out.

Alex glanced at her watch. "I was about to leave but guess I could stay a little longer. Not much longer, though. I have one of our infamous eight o'clock meetings at the bank tomorrow."

"What are you drinking? Let me buy you a drink."

"Decaf coffee now. I was drinking a chardonnay."

Sgt. Montgomery ordered white wine and a second Budweiser for himself. Alex didn't want another drink but didn't object either.

Chapter 7

"It was great getting to know you a little better this morning. I'm sorry we kept getting interrupted. That's my life." He took a swig of beer. "I hope I didn't bore you with cop stories."

"Actually, it was fascinating, Sgt., er, Tony."

"I'm glad you remembered. Call me Tony."

Gus brought over the wine and beer and looked at Alex sideways. She knew he wasn't used to seeing her at Coconuts with guys but she didn't offer an introduction.

Suddenly the cop's jaw tightened and his light blue eyes turned to ice. "Remember when I told you earlier that I'm becoming jaded? That's partially due to the scumbags I encounter and partly due to the truth I've discovered after years on the force. Do you want to know the truth?"

"The truth. What are you talking about? You're so mysterious. Are you going to tell me the famous 'secret' that everyone talks about?" Alex giggled.

He didn't crack a smile. "The truth is simple. I know what drives people to commit crimes. After fifteen years as a cop, I've learned that all crimes are caused by one of four things. Want to know what they are?"

Alex leaned forward. "You've got my attention. What's the truth?"

"Money, sex, power, or drugs." He ticked each one off with his fingers. "It's that simple. Think about all the crimes you've heard about. They can all be traced to one or a combination of those four." He took another swig of beer.

Alex was quiet while she considered corporate crimes, hate crimes, child abuse, domestic violence, robberies, and drug deals. She shivered.

"I guess you're right. Money. Sex. Power. Drugs. I've never thought about it like that. But it makes sense. I don't know how you deal with police work every day. I really don't."

He held her gaze.

"It's in my blood. My dad and grandfather were cops. It's all I've ever known. Most of the time I enjoy it. Someone has to deal with society's low-life. Might as well be me."

"Let's stop talking about crimes. You have quite a family legacy. Tell me about them."

"Grandpa was a beat cop. He walked around the square for years. Would have bored me to tears but he enjoyed it. He got to know all the shop owners, restaurant regulars and the homeless people. He knew everyone's name and never forgot a face." Tony's eyes crinkled.

"He was a great cop and so proud of his uniform. He told me he dreamed of being a cop his whole life. It's all he ever wanted to do."

Alex sipped her wine. "Is he retired now?"

Tony sat up even straighter and swallowed. He looked away but Alex thought she detected tears in his eyes as his jaw clenched. She sat still, waiting. After a long silence, he spoke.

"Grandpa was killed in the line of duty."

"Oh, no." She touched his arm. "I'm very sorry."

Tony was clearly shaken but tried to hide his emotions while veins popped out on his forehead.

"Some two-bit robber held up a convenience store just off the square. Grandpa and his partner took the call and when they entered the store, the scumbag shot at both officers. Grandpa took a fatal bullet but his partner lived."

Tony stared into his beer. "Grandpa died for a measly $200."

"I don't know what to say. That's horrible." Alex studied Tony who was doing a good job of gathering himself.

"It's okay. He lived a good life. He did what he wanted to do and knew the risks."

Alex shuddered. "What about your dad?"

"He's a lieutenant in the force. Big man on campus and a real teddy bear. He prefers deskwork now that he's older. He doesn't want to run down back alleys chasing someone. I don't blame him. He works a lot of cold cases. Has a few that really haunt him. He plans to take early retirement, has bought some land, and wants to be a cattle farmer."

Tony ran his fingers through his hair. "I don't blame him. I think he'll enjoy farm life."

"Are you close?"

"Yes, but I'm so busy with Joey that I only see Dad at work and holiday dinners. Joey loves to fish with his Grandpa, though." Tony downed his beer.

"Enough about me and this cop stuff. How are you? You look fabulous, by the way." Tony looked at her from head to toe, slowly taking in her long blond hair, big green eyes, and tall, athletic body.

Alex felt her cheeks flush and worried that her red splotches would make an appearance. They always did when she was embarrassed. She tugged at the collar of her red sweater and wished she had on a turtleneck.

"Tell me about your bank job."

Alex stammered. "Uh, I don't know. Same old boring bank stuff. Oh, we were nearly gobbled up by a large mega bank but thankfully the board voted against it. That's about it, no bank robbers or anything. Actually, I shouldn't laugh about that." Alex knocked on the wall, slightly superstitious.

"I'm sure you have plenty of security cameras. All banks do."

"Yes, we all have buttons in our offices to turn on the

cameras. We also have a security officer who keeps track of our private addresses, cars, children, you know, just in case."

"Of a hostage situation."

"Yeah, right. You'd already know that." Alex felt a chill run down her spine. "Let's change the subject."

"Tell me about your friend. I saw her leave your table a few minutes ago."

"She's my best friend in the world. Her name is Suzanne Jacobs and she's a wedding planner, even though she has had very unlucky weddings herself."

"What do you mean?"

"Long, horrible story for another time." Alex rolled her eyes.

"How long have you known her?"

"Since before high school. In fact we were both in the Kiltie Drum & Bugle Corps. She was the majorette and I was drum captain." Alex smiled as she remembered all the cold, wintry parades and football games where they marched with bare legs under their short, red plaid kilts, often kicking mud onto their white spats and shoes. She remembered being especially touched during parades when older men would salute them or place their hands over their hearts as they marched by. Alex told Tony about some of their high school escapades and the Kiltie midnight kidnappings before she finished her wine.

"Bet you girls had a blast. Wish I'd known you then."

Again, Alex felt her cheeks burn.

"Anything else you want to share? I'm enjoying getting to know you."

Alex tingled with delight. *This gorgeous cop wants to get to know me.*

"That's about it. I wish I could meet up with the former bagpipe captain, Hope Truman. She used to march right in front of me. Suzy, Hope and I were very close in high school. Hope moved away several years ago and we lost touch, unfortunately."

Tony grinned. "You'll never believe this but I know where Hope Truman works. She must have moved back."

"You know Hope? How? I know you're a cop but I didn't think you had a spontaneous rolodex spinning in your head."

"If I were that impressive, the chief would promote me to lieutenant in a heartbeat." Tony cleared his throat, preparing for the big announcement.

"Hope is a counselor at Hilltop High School on the north side of town. I had to break up a disturbance during a football game there last year. She apparently counsels at-risk kids. Some of her students were involved in the altercation. We met in her office the following day to fill out a school report."

Alex shook her head. "I can't believe she moved back and didn't contact me. I can't wait to call her. Thanks." Alex glanced at her silver cuff watch. "I've got to go. Early day tomorrow."

Tony paid the bar tab, pulled out Alex's chair and they walked to her car. "I hope I see you soon." He leaned down and kissed her lightly on the cheek. Alex caught a faint whiff of his musky cologne.

"I've never been so happy to be rear-ended before," he said, eyes twinkling.

Tingly and wobbly, Alex got into her Mustang, telling herself not to get involved with a married man. It's wrong. It will go nowhere. *I'll be the one to get hurt. Suzy's right. And he's a cop. Another good reason. His job is too dangerous.*

As she crawled into bed that night and pulled a comforter over her, Alex's mind swirled. *I can't get involved with a married cop, or a married anything, for that matter.*

Chapter 8

Suzy felt like she had been punched in the gut. Staring out the window, she wondered if she'd ever get over what Dean and Tara did to her. She sipped her coffee but would have preferred alcohol. But it was just eight in the morning.

She didn't want to be alone and rattle around in her house all day. Normally, she liked nothing better than to fill the house with fresh air by opening her white French doors onto the patio. She'd sit outside with a book, coffee or wine wearing a big, floppy hat since she sunburned easily. Her patio was small but cozy. Three large ferns hung on the lattice ceiling and white metal patio furniture sported plush, navy cushions.

Her house paid homage to Laura Ashley. Suzy would have been happy in the era of long dresses, hats, and white gloves. She tried to keep her formality bent at bay since her eighteen-year-old son was casual. He would complain that he didn't feel comfortable in a "proper" house. If he had his way, her house would have a contemporary décor with black leather furniture, gleaming, chrome mirrors and not a knick-knack in sight. Sometimes her son was an enigma to Suzy. Jon made good grades, graduated in the top ten percent of his class and received several college scholarships. That's why his dad gave him such an extravagant graduation trip to Europe. Occasionally Jon would share a bit about school or his long-time girlfriend Vanessa but he didn't give Suzy the details she craved.

Her son was much like his dad, Bill—reserved with a medium build and brown curly hair. Suzy laughed when she thought about Bill and their mismatched marriage. His house would be a far cry from hers. She hadn't seen it since their divorce years ago but would bet money that it had a lodge-like feel, complete with beer holders in the chair arms and deer heads adorning the walls.

Suzy watched a redbird perch in a tree. For some reason, this made her think of her high school love, Ken, maybe because their school colors were red and black. She absent-mindedly twirled her red hair between her fingers, wondering where he lived and who he married. The bird flew away as her thoughts wandered to college. She and Ken had been inseparable until they each received scholarships to separate colleges. They tried a long-distance relationship but their young age and hormones got the best of them. They reluctantly agreed to date other people and Suzy got pregnant. Her boyfriend at the time, Bill, proposed immediately and they had a rushed, courthouse wedding. She knew Bill wasn't her soul mate but they tried to make it work because of their son, Jon. She cursed herself often for ending her relationship with Ken but would never regret her first marriage due to the outcome--her wonderful son.

Suzy turned from the window and walked toward her couch. She loved her blue and white floral sofa, oversized china hutch filled with her grandmother's antique dishes, and especially the piano in the corner. Jon often asked her why they had a piano since neither of them played. "We will someday" was always her response.

Suddenly, the naked image of Dean and Tara crept into her mind and Suzy frowned in disgust. *Why am I thinking about all the men in my life today?*

Trying to busy herself, she glanced at her appointment book. Misty's wedding was fast approaching. Naturally, she had the bride from hell to deal with. She wasn't in the mood for Misty today. She wasn't in the mood for anything.

Suzy finished a pot of coffee and forced herself to shower. It had been a couple of days. Her hair was dirty and she knew she'd feel better if she showered and put makeup on. Afterward, she almost felt human and invited Alex to lunch. She decided to wear a cheerful yellow floral sundress and headed to Coconuts. And waited.

Alex came bursting through the restaurant door like she was sliding into home plate.

"Hi. Sorry I'm late."

Suzy held up her hand, tired of the excuses. She was not in the mood. Suzy had already ordered a salad, and Alex noticed she had barely touched her food.

"You need to eat. You look like you've already lost weight." Alex's brow furrowed with concern. Suzy was a mother and usually the one who took care of her.

"Have I ever found the wonder diet." Suzy pushed salad around her plate.

Alex motioned for the server and ordered iced tea and a house salad. "I have some good news."

"What?"

"When you left Coconuts, the cop showed up and—"

"Wait a minute. What do you mean he showed up? Is he stalking you?"

Alex laughed. "Of course not. He said I had mentioned that we always go to Coconuts and—"

Suzy interrupted again. "We go to Coconuts on *Thursdays*. That was a Sunday. We made an exception because of my wedding disaster, remember?"

"You're missing the point. Let me tell you the good news. Tony, er, Sgt. Montgomery knows where Hope works. Isn't that great?"

"Really? That *is* great. Where does she work?"

"Hilltop High School. She's a counselor." Alex took a big bite of salad. "Anyway, as soon as I get back to work tomorrow, I'm going to call her. Are you up for getting together this Thursday if she's free?"

"Absolutely. I need to stay busy and I'd love to see Hope. I have a wedding this weekend so I've got to snap out of it."

"No rest for the weary. Are you sure you're ready for a wedding?"

"It's my job so I don't have a choice. My bride, Misty, is counting on me. Besides, most of the work is done." Suzy jumped as her phone vibrated in her lap. "That's Misty. She's a spoiled brat and needs her hand held frequently. At least it'll get my mind off my own problems."

Alex nodded and wiped her mouth. "I'm going shopping. T.J. Maxx is calling."

She placed her hand over Suzy's. "Will you be okay? I'm worried about you."

"I'm a big girl." Suzy's phone vibrated again. She ignored it. "Maybe I'll call my son and see where he's backpacking today. That's one nice thing his dad did for him. A trip to Europe. Not too shabby. I'm sure he's having the time of his life."

"Good idea. Call Jon and remember, you're a gorgeous, intelligent, savvy redhead. Any man would be lucky to have you. You're going to be fine—better than fine."

Suzy took a long sip of tea. "I hope you're right."

She finally picked up her non-stop vibrating phone and glanced at the screen. "It's Misty again. I've got to run. I must have an angry bride by now. Wish me luck." She rushed out the door with her cell phone to her ear.

Chapter 9

Her bride *was* furious. Suzy held her phone far away from her head as her bride bellowed. "Where have you been and why aren't you taking my calls? I need you here. *Now*."

"Misty, calm down. What's the problem?" Suzy was glad to have the distraction even if it was from a bratty bride.

"The problem is *I'm* getting married in two days and my wedding planner isn't taking my calls," shouted Misty.

Yes, ma'am; at your service, ma'am; right away, ma'am, thought Suzy.

"Where are you, Misty? I'll come and join you."

"I'm at the florist. The pink orchids are on *back* order. Can you believe it? They're suggesting purple or white orchids instead. I don't *want* purple or white orchids; I want pink," she wailed.

"I'm on my way. Why don't you go to Starbucks and get a latte to calm down. On second thought, maybe caffeine isn't such a great idea. Why don't you get some soothing chamomile tea? I'll be there in ten minutes." Suzy hung up, turned on the radio, and asked for patience.

As she pulled into Artistic Blooms, she took a deep yoga breath. *Just let me get through this wedding. I'm sure the next wedding will be a piece of* . . . then she spotted Misty. Her dark hair was pulled severely away from her face. Suzy made a mental note that she should try that style as a mini-facelift option. Misty wore all black as if in mourning. Her thin, pasty arms were crossed and her dark eyebrows furrowed. Suzy could see Misty's black sandaled foot tapping on the sidewalk. She climbed out of her car.

"Hi, Misty—"

"It's about *time* you got here. I've been here for *hours*. I have a lot to do, you know. You're supposed to be available to me." Misty huffed and put her hands on her hips.

"Right." Suzy cleared her throat. "I'm here now. Calm down, everything will be fine. Let's find the florist and talk about this pink orchid dilemma, shall we?"

Misty glared at Suzy but Suzy ignored Misty's attitude and nudged her inside Artistic Blooms. She rang the bell on the counter and soon heard the owner's footsteps coming from the back of the shop.

"Hellllllooooo," Marc said as he waltzed in. "How's my favorite wedding planner?" He air kissed Suzy on each cheek.

"Cut the kissy-faced greetings. I want to know where my pink orchids are," Misty snapped.

"Well, now. Aren't we testy?" Marc looked at Suzy and rolled his eyes. "As I tried to tell you earlier, the pink orchids have been back ordered, temporarily, because the delivery truck driver had a terrible accident on the highway." Marc clucked his tongue. "The poor man veered to miss a deer and overturned his semi-truck. I understand he's in the hos—"

"I don't care about your little truck-driver story. I want pink orchids for my wedding. It's in two days, people. My favorite color is pink. I want PINK." Misty's eyes bulged.

Marc and Suzy exchanged knowing glances.

"Can I interest you in white orchids? They're very chic, you know," Marc said as he picked lint off his navy silk shirt. He was wearing slim designer jeans with a studded silver belt. He anxiously touched the small silver hoop in his ear as he waited for Misty's answer.

"Are you deaf?" Misty yelled. "I want *pink*. Is that so difficult? Why can't anyone understand that? My colors are pink and black. That's what I want. Period." Misty stomped her foot like a child.

"Under the circumstances, I think pink roses would look beautiful. Marc, will you pull some from the cooler and show Misty," Suzy suggested.

"But I wanted *orchids*. I paid for orchids. Roses are so traditional," Misty wailed.

"Roses are classic and pink roses would look perfect in your bouquet. You'll see," Marc shouted as he bent over the cooler. He gathered six long-stemmed pink roses and perfectly tied black ribbon around the stems, candy-cane style. "See, pink and black, your colors. There." Marc proudly shoved his creation under Misty's nose.

"Well, I do like the black ribbon and that is a pretty shade of pink. I don't know. I really wanted ..." She shifted from foot to foot. "I guess they'll—"

"Good. Let's go with the pink roses. Excellent decision." Before Misty could change her mind, Suzy added, "Now, let's get on with the rest of your list." Suzy winked at Marc.

Marc asked Misty to sign a Change of Order form. He had dealt with difficult brides before; he knew the drill. "You've made the right decision, Misty. You're going to have a beautiful wedding. I'll have it all set up before you arrive. No worries."

Suzy gathered her purse and planner as she steered Misty toward the door. "Bye, Marc. You're the best. See you tomorrow." They walked out the door, bells jangling behind them.

In the parking lot, Misty was calmer but still pouted. "Come on, Misty. You're about to get married. It should be the happiest day of your life. Cheer up."

"I'm a bundle of nerves," Misty admitted. "We still have a lot to do. I hope you're not going to disappear on me again."

"I'm all yours for the next two days."

"Good. Now, I'm afraid we won't have enough food."

"We've already gone over this. You told me you had a small food budget, and we decided against a sit-down meal for 300, remember? We have heavy hors d'oeuvres, champagne, wine, a wedding cake and the groom's cake. I am not one of those wedding planners who tries to get newlyweds into a financial bind. I'd love to see you have an incredible day, a great honeymoon, and still have a little money left over to start building your lives together."

"You sound like my mom," Misty groaned. "My friend had a full sit-down dinner plus *gifts* for all the guests. And she had 300 at *her* wedding, too."

"First of all, I am a mom. Secondly, don't try to keep up with the Joneses."

"Who are the Joneses?"

Suzy stifled a giggle. "That's a saying. It means don't try to have the type of wedding your friend had. Be yourself. What's important is to have your wedding with your own unique touches. That's what your guests will remember and that's what should be important to you and Todd, your soon-to-be-hubby."

"Okay, enough preaching. Remind me what kind of finger food we're going to have."

Suzy checked her planner. "Mini crab cakes, baby quiche, chilled shrimp and cocktail sauce, a veggie tray with hummus, a fruit tray with strawberry yogurt, deviled eggs, and a variety of smoked cheeses and meats. Each will be on large, tiered silver platters. It'll be a beautiful presentation, I promise. Plus, we'll have red and white wine on every table and champagne will be served prior to the toasts."

"Well, I guess that's okay. I mean it's better than peanut butter and jelly sandwiches."

Suzy laughed. "A lot better. Your guests won't go hungry. Besides, your wedding is at three in the afternoon. It's not exactly the dinner hour. That's why we chose that time of day, remember?" Suzy patted Misty's arm. "Stop worrying. Everything will be perfect."

"I guess you have it under control." Misty stared at

her shoes. "One other thing. I don't know what to give my bridesmaids. Will you buy their gifts? I don't have time."

Suzy frowned. "That's not exactly the job of a wedding planner. They should be personal gifts from you."

Misty pouted. "But you weren't available when I needed you and I kept waiting and waiting. Now I'm out of time," she whined. "And we have the rehearsal dinner tonight."

"Oh, all right," Suzy gave in. "I'll go to Things Remembered at the mall and have some nice gifts engraved. Do you want to give all five of them the same gift?"

"Yes, just spend about thirty dollars each. I'm running low on cash."

"Done. Consider the gifts bought. I think engraved picture frames would be nice. Then, you can promise to place a wedding photo inside later. I'll even wrap them for you with pink paper and black bows."

Misty's mouth formed into what looked like a sincere smile. "Thank you. The gifts sound perfect. I'm sorry if I was a brat earlier. I didn't realize how much there was to do. Weddings are *hard*. That pink orchid thing put me over the edge."

Suzy smiled and patted Misty's arm. "Don't worry. This is common among brides. I've gotten used to it. Weddings are nail biters until the very end. That's why I'm here to help. Just promise me one thing."

"What?"

"That you'll cheer up and enjoy your wedding."

"I promise." Misty smiled.

Suzy hugged her nervous bride and left for the mall.

Chapter 10

Alex glanced at the clock on her dashboard and pressed harder on the gas pedal.

Why do we have so many damn morning meetings? Is a freakin' afternoon meeting too much to ask?

Scolding herself for putting on lipstick at yet another stoplight, Alex spotted a cop behind her. No way. Her heart pounded as she slowly sat her purse in the passenger seat. With sweaty palms, she adjusted and glanced in the rearview mirror. Surely that isn't, the bright sunlight blocked her view.

She gulped. Finally, the police car pulled beside her. Alex looked over, spotted a female officer, and breathed a sigh of relief. She drove slowly to work.

Pulling up to Community National Bank, Alex drove into the nearest stall. She strolled through the lobby and spotted Stu, the bank security officer. He was her height with toned arms and legs from competing in marathons. Stu had a great smile, dark tan, and warm personality to match. She was glad his office was next to hers.

Every office was surrounded by glass which Alex hated since she didn't have any sense of privacy. She was the only female officer on the lower level and stuck out like a sore thumb attracting long-winded sales guys like a moth to a flame.

As she rounded the corner, Alex nearly bumped into Stu who wore a continual, sweet smile.

"Hey, nice tie. Only real men wear pink." She winked at him. "Gotta run upstairs to my meeting. By the way, I met a nice cop the other day."

Stu followed Alex and stood beside her desk.

"Really? How did you meet him?"

"Sorry, no time to chat. Marketing meeting's in one minute. I'll tell you later."

She glanced at Stu. "Why are you frowning?"

"Be careful. You're a beautiful, single woman with a high-profile position at this bank. You need to watch who your friends are."

Alex blushed, then cocked her head.

"Sheesh. Relax. He's a cop, for Pete's sake. What are you worried about?" She glanced at her watch. "God, now I'm late. Crap."

She grabbed a legal pad and bounded the stairs two at a time.

"Sorry, boss, I was talking to Stu about an, uh, security matter and lost track of time."

"Anything I need to know about?" asked Jim, the bank president.

"No, no, nothing at all."

She switched into professional mode and laid her marketing material on the conference table, hoping to change the subject. Alex distributed an agenda, as she did every Monday morning. The marketing committee consisted of the president, three executive vice presidents, and herself. All men. All morning people.

She glanced around the table as she handed out packets for each of them.

"I have three media proposals for your review. First, I suggest we sponsor the children's hospital fundraiser to help purchase neo-natal equipment. Secondly, I recommend we buy five high-profile billboards at the city's busiest intersections. I've highlighted the billboard locations on the attached map. I'll grab some coffee while you study the map."

When she returned to the table with a Styrofoam cup of coffee, Alex continued.

"Finally, I recommend we renew our television contract with Ozarks5. They've agreed to honor the same rates as last year which is unheard of but we're a big client and I negotiated that price."

She smiled and downed her much-needed coffee.

As the executives reviewed the marketing material, her thoughts trailed to Tony. *Focus.* She refilled her cup as they read the material.

"Last year, we greatly increased our name recognition through the use of billboards and commercials. Ozarks5 has the highest ratings in town and worked well for us. I'd like to continue branding Community National Bank (CNB) with some fresh, new commercials featuring our home-town lenders, and of course, featuring you, Jim."

The bank president smiled. Alex knew he loved the camera.

After a few questions, the marketing committee voted unanimously to renew the television contract and reserve the billboard space. Alex made notes and picked up the hospital sponsorship.

"This is more of a feel-good, community relations effort but we need to be good corporate citizens and what better way than to partner with the local hospital's fundraiser for premature babies. It will be great exposure for the bank and we'd love to pick up some of their five thousand employees' accounts, wouldn't we?"

Jim grinned. "Yes, we would. You're always thinking, Alex. You've done a tremendous job in getting CNB into the Twenty-first Century with television, billboards and the Internet. We trust your sound judgment."

Feeling her cheeks flush, which she hated but couldn't control, Alex looked at her boss.

"Thanks. That means a lot."

Alex was the first marketing director the bank had ever hired and she worked hard to make them proud of their employment decision. She knew she was good at her job and she loved it, except for those hateful morning meetings.

Alex gathered the marketing material and headed toward her office. She called her sales rep at Ozarks5 to give him the good news. They agreed to schedule a shoot in three weeks after she had a chance to write the thirty-second television spots and work with the lenders on their respective scripts.

She hung up and promptly called the billboard company to reserve the premium locations and promised to work on the copy and artwork within two weeks. She then emailed the director of the obstetrics department at the hospital regarding CNB's sponsorship.

Satisfied, she relaxed and her mind wandered to Tony. That man had quite an impact on her. She scolded herself for daydreaming, ever the workaholic, and stared at the screen trying to summon copy for television scripts. Her mind was blank. She rummaged in the desk drawer for a stopwatch to time the thirty-second spots that would eventually come to her.

She watched customers line up at the teller windows to get cash and deposit checks. Judy was busy opening new accounts for several customers, hopefully, after that big Certificate of Deposit promotion she ran recently. Marla and Rexanna were busily typing up loan documents for several of the bank's commercial customers.

Alex stared at the computer screen. Finally, some ideas about not merging came to her and she drafted possible scripts for two hours' straight, stopping only to rub her tired wrists. She was proofreading the scripts when she heard a knock on her door.

Chapter 11

She looked up as a huge arrangement of pink roses blocked the door. Alex couldn't see the deliveryman's head because the bouquet was so enormous.

"For me?"

"Are you Alexandra Mitchell?"

"Yes."

"Then these are for you. Where do you want them?"

Alex looked around her already crowded desk and her credenza along the side wall. She moved a pile from her desk and made room for the roses on the corner.

The delivery guy set them down and placed a form in front of her to sign.

"Who are they from?"

"Someone who likes you, I guess."

Alex signed the form and the man left. She looked through the pink blooms but couldn't find a card. She chased after the delivery man and caught him in the parking lot.

Breathless, she said, "Sir, there's no card attached. Did it fall out in your truck?"

"No, ma'am. The florist told me the caller wants to remain anonymous. He specifically stated that. Have a nice day." He climbed into his truck and drove off.

He, Alex thought. *Could they be from Sgt. Montgomery? He wouldn't send me flowers. He's married, and besides, we just met.*

When she got to her office, Stu walked in smiling like a Jack-O-Lantern. "Well, well. Looks like someone has an admirer, unless it's your birthday."

"No, it's not my birthday. I'm not sure who they're from. There's no card and the delivery man said the guy wants to remain anonymous."

"They're from the cop," Stu said.

"How can you be so sure?"

"I'm a guy. I know guys. Just leave it at that. He's got good taste, though, in flowers and in women. See ya. I'm going home."

"Bye, Stu. And thanks. I think." She winked.

Alex secretly hoped they were from Sgt. Montgomery, even though she knew he shouldn't be sending her flowers. The only other person who might have sent them could be the new dorky, cowboy boot-wearing loan officer who always managed to belly up to the break room coffee pot every time she went for a refill. He invariably had a runny nose, wiped it on the back of his hand, and then grabbed the coffee pot handle. Alex groaned, hoping the roses weren't from him.

After the flower delivery, she couldn't concentrate on bank work and opened the phone book, scanning it for Hilltop High School's phone number. She dialed and an elderly woman answered.

"Hello. Do you have a counselor by the name of Hope Truman?"

"Yes, hold please."

Alex could barely wait to talk to her long-lost friend.

You've reached the voicemail of Hope Truman. I can't come to my phone right now. Please leave a message and I'll get back to you soon. Have a great day.

"Hi, Hope. This is Alex. Alexandra Mitchell. Gosh, I can't believe you're back and living right under my nose. I can't wait to get together with you. Suzy Jacobs is excited, too. We'd love to meet with you and wondered if you're free on—" The machine cut her off.

Alex hit redial and finished her message. "Damn. Sorry. I always talk too long on machines. I'm doing it again. Hope, it's me. Alex. Call me at Community National Bank at 555-5555. Suzy and I want to get together with you. Bye."

Now that she had made contact, albeit via voicemail, Alex straightened three piles on her desk and dusted her computer screen and keyboard. She glanced at the roses as the trilling phone interrupted her cleaning.

"Alexandra Mitchell, Marketing."

"Alex!" Hope screamed. "God, it was so good to hear your voice. I've had a lousy day—a lousy two years, really. Hearing your voice made my day. Yes, yes, yes, let's go to lunch! How about tomorrow?"

They agreed to meet at Rosa's Mexican Restaurant and Alex said she'd call Suzy.

"Do you and Suzy Q look as gorgeous as ever? You two always have made me look bad but I love you anyway. I've gained twenty pounds and my dark hair is as unruly as Einstein's. I still have a sparkling personality, though. I'm just waiting for Jimmy Fallon to call." Hope laughed.

"I've missed you, Hope. Let's meet at eleven thirty and beat the lunch crowd. See you tomorrow at Rosa's. Order a margarita for me if you beat me there. It'll be five o'clock somewhere. Bye."

Chapter 12

The next day, Alex drove to Rosa's Mexican Restaurant still not knowing who had sent the flowers. She had received a quick call from Tony but he didn't mention the roses so she wasn't about to ask. He did ask if she had reached Hope. Alex frowned thinking about the beefy, snotty-nosed loan officer. *They're probably from him.*

She pulled into the parking lot and couldn't wait to see Suzy and Hope. Her snakeskin stilettos clicked on the floor as she spotted Suzy sitting in a booth munching on chips and salsa.

"Hi, girl. How's it going? You look great." Suzy appeared to be making a miraculous comeback.

"Thanks. Bank attire. Alex struck her best red carpet pose and ran her hand along her sleek ivory skirt and silky brown blouse. I call it 'The Boardroom Look.'"

"I'd call that The Sexy Boardroom Look." Suzy smiled. "God, I'm so glad it's Friday. Let's have a margarita and start our weekend."

"Yeah, I think I can manage one margarita. How are you? I'm still worried about you."

"Don't be. I'm getting better each day. My sister probably did me a favor. Of course, it'll be a cold day before I ever tell her that."

Alex studied Suzy's blue eyes to see if she was telling the truth. "You're so strong, Suzy. I'm—"

Suzy cut her off. "I'm fine. Really." Suzy stared at her menu and peered over the top. "Stop worrying. I'm staying busy planning weddings. I have a doozy of a bride right now.

At least she keeps my mind occupied." Suzy dipped a chip in salsa. "Now, let's celebrate getting reacquainted with Hope. Speaking of, where is she?"

Alex stared at her friend and hoped Suzy felt half as good as she was letting on. She wasn't going to press her.

Suzy read her mind. "Stop it. Today is about Hope. I can't wait to see her." She straightened her black skirt and green cardigan. "This will be the fun point of my weekend. After today, I have a thorny wedding. At the very least, a prickly bride." She stared at her cell phone, which kept vibrating in her lap. "It's the bride from hell again. She can just wait a couple of hours. I'm not going to answer this right now."

Alex laughed and picked up a chip. "Good for you. Let's relax and have a good time." Alex stared at the front door.

Minutes later, in walked a short, slightly chubby brunette. It was undeniably Hope with her cute dimples, unruly hair, and chocolate brown doe eyes. She was wearing brown pants, a turquoise tee, and flat brown sandals, sensible school attire.

Hope looked around the restaurant and spotted Suzy and Alex. She rushed toward their table. Smiling from ear to ear, she said, "Hi, you two. Sorry I'm late. I was counseling a student. Now, let me take a good look at you."

Alex and Suzy stood to give her a group hug.

"Okay, I officially hate you. Why didn't either of you gain a pound after high school? You both look even better, if that's possible. I give up. Pass the chips."

For over an hour, Alex and Suzy attempted to bring Hope up to date. Alex talked about her marketing projects at the bank and about rear-ending the cop.

Suzy said she was divorced with an eighteen-year-old son and pulled out a picture of Jon. Then she regaled Hope with her most recent bridezilla stories.

Alex noticed Suzy didn't mention her near-miss wedding.

Hope explained her students at school were on both ends of the continuum—either on the honor roll or at risk. "Since it's summer, most of the students are gone, but the staff and some faculty are working. We have a few summer classes and intramurals, that sort of thing, so students are in and out of my office."

The server reappeared with a new basket of chips.

After nearly two hours and two margaritas later, Alex announced she had to get back to the bank. "I've got a lot of work to do. If I don't leave now, I'll be at the bank after the drive-thru tellers leave and that always gives me the creeps."

"Alex, you'd better chew some gum," Suzy offered. "I think your conservative boss might frown if he smelled alcohol on your breath."

Pulling out her credit card to pay the bill, Alex said, "Don't worry. Seeing Hope was a celebration. I don't do this regularly. Besides, I can guarantee you the bank will look like a ghost town about now. Most of the guys will already be on the golf course."

Alex flashed a smile at Hope. "It was so great catching up with you. Please join us each week for cocktails. We always meet on Thursdays at Coconuts right after work."

"Can you make it?" Suzy asked.

"Is the Caribbean Sea blue? I'm not losing touch with you two again."

Chapter 13

After lunch, Hope stared into her bathroom mirror.

Mirror, mirror on the wall, who's the ugliest one of all? Let me answer that. Me.

She thought about how good Alex and Suzy looked and knew she overate because she was depressed about her parents. *Isn't it just swell that I'm in my thirties and still supporting my parents?*

She hadn't told anyone at Hilltop High School about her home situation. How could she? She didn't want her fellow teachers to know about her hippie parents. They wouldn't respect her as a counselor if she couldn't get her own life together. Seeing Alex and Suzy again gave her encouragement that she could eventually open up to them for advice. As she glared at her frizzy hair, Hope heard the screen door creak open.

"Yoo-hoo, Hope," yelled Montana as she tapped on the screen door while simultaneously walking inside.

"Are you home?" Montana walked in wearing her usual cut-off denim shorts and black tee adorned with a colorful peace sign.

"Got a beer, Hope? I've been mowin' all day and really worked up a thirst." Larry flopped on the couch, kicked off his grassy sneakers and flung his long, dirty blond hair over the couch cushion.

"Sure, Dad."

"How about a beer for the old lady, too?"

Hope hated how he referred to her mom as his "old lady" but knew it was useless to discuss it yet again.

"I'll get you and Mom both a beer. I went to the grocery store yesterday and restocked."

"Why don't you call us Larry and Montana?" asked her father. "We've told you that since you were a kid, Hope. You can call us by our first names. We're all equals." Focused on the television, Larry flipped through the channels.

Hope bristled. "Because you're my mom and dad, that's why. I *like* calling you 'Mom' and 'Dad.' Can't we have some small sense of normalcy in our relationship?" Hope asked more strongly than usual.

Larry and Montana exchanged curious glances. "Sure, whatever you want."

Changing the subject, Hope's mother asked, "How was school today?" Before Hope could answer, Montana produced something bright orange from her scraggly denim purse. "Look, I made another macramé plant hanger for your office. I just finished it today. Do you like it?" She proudly twirled the orange planter in the air.

Hope eyed the planter. Just what she needed—another macramé plant holder. How many did she have now? Twenty? Someday her mother would burst into the Twenty-First Century.

Always polite, Hope said, "Thanks, Mom. It's beautiful. I love the color. It'll brighten my drab gray office. Have a seat and I'll get the beer."

"Mind if I smoke a joint?" Larry pulled one from his front pocket. "It's been a rough day—"

"Yes, I mind. The neighbors might smell it and I'll be the one who gets into trouble since I own this house. Please respect that," she huffed. "I can't risk getting arrested. I'd lose my job. Geeze."

"What has gotten into you?" Montana asked. "You seem tense." She walked over to rub her shoulders but Hope turned away.

I just wish you were normal parents, she wanted to say. Hope walked into the kitchen and opened the refrigerator.

Montana followed and stared at her daughter.

Hope preempted her questioning. "I'm fine. Just a tough day at school." She pulled cold beer from the refrigerator. "Here."

Larry shouted from the living room, "Mind if we stay a couple hours and watch TV? Ours is on the blink."

And, naturally, you don't have the money to have it repaired.

Hope handed Larry a beer and watched it foam over the sides as he popped the top. He licked it off.

"Sure. Watch TV. I've got laundry to do anyway. Do you want me to order a pizza? I don't feel like cooking."

"Pizza sure would hit the spot but we're a little short on cash," Larry said.

"What's new?" Hope muttered as she walked into the kitchen.

"What, honey?"

"Nothing. I'm looking up the phone number for Pizza Cravings."

Chapter 14

Alex pressed the gas pedal, late for work, when she saw red lights swirling in her rearview mirror. *Not again. My insurance rates will triple this time. Crap.*

Banging her fist against the steering wheel, she cursed herself and slowly pulled over to the curb, waiting for the cop to appear. She hoped he'd tell her how fast she was going, give her a ticket and get it over with. When the cop appeared at her window, she looked up and saw a smiling Sgt. Montgomery.

"Morning, Alex. Going a little fast, don't you think? Don't worry, I'm not going to give you a ticket. That is, if you'll agree to have lunch with me today."

"God. You scared me to death. My heart's racing. Did you know it was me?"

"Yeah, I figured you took this path to work and I was on my way to get a doughnut anyway." He chuckled.

"Very funny. Can I go now? I've got another eight o'clock meeting."

"Yes, if you'll agree to that lunch."

"Okay, where?"

"How about that new salad bar place. I'm watching my waistline."

"Cranberry's Salad Toss?"

He nodded.

"See you at noon. Gotta run." Alex sped off, looked in the rearview mirror, and watched Sgt. Montgomery shake his head. She smiled.

At noon, she settled into a booth at Cranberry's and waited. She took off her red blazer and straightened her white lace blouse as he walked up.

As Tony slid across the seat, Alex said, "Thanks for not giving me a ticket. I know I drive too fast."

He smiled. "My friends won't let you off so easily—lunch in lieu of a ticket. Just be careful, okay? You look amazing, by the way."

Alex blushed. "Thanks. You don't look half bad yourself." She admired him in his police uniform which fit nice and tight in all the right places.

"Why are you sometimes in uniform and occasionally in regular clothes?"

"Different assignments. I'm a detective, so at times, I'm in civilian clothes. But today, I volunteered to go to some schools to talk about the DARE program. I love the kids. When we do that, it's better to be in uniform."

Alex nodded. She liked this guy better all the time. "Let's order and then chat. I'm starving and I've got a billboard deadline today."

"Sounds important. I'd like to know more about your job." Tony scanned the menu.

When the server appeared, he ordered a BLT and Alex ordered a spinach salad with cranberries, feta cheese and pine nuts. He changed his order to match hers.

"Why don't you tell me about your job first? What made you decide to become a police officer?"

"That's easy. It's in my blood. I'm a third generation cop, remember? Collectively, my dad and grandfather served this city for seventy years. How could I not continue that legacy?"

Alex chewed her salad thoughtfully. "That's impressive and noble. I thought maybe your grandfather's death while on the force might have scared you off.

Tony's jaw clenched. "It made me want to be a cop even more."

Alex nodded. "I can understand that. How long have you been an officer?"

Tony hesitated. "Well, let's see, I started right after high school and attended evening college to get my criminology degree, so it's been fifteen years. Long enough to become jaded."

"There's that term again. I get it that you're jaded. You've mentioned that several times. Have you ever had to shoot anyone?"

"I've had to show my weapon many times but I've never shot a person, if that's what you mean. I've shot into the air, I've shot deer and birds, but that's about it."

"Oh, I love deer. How could you shoot those beautiful animals?"

"Are you a tree hugger, too? Hunting season actually does them a favor. Deer are overpopulated in this area and would starve to death if hunters didn't kill them. They'd die a slow, painful death by starvation."

"Much worse than a speeding bullet right to the heart." She shuddered. "Let's talk about something else."

Tony laughed. "I don't think you'd make it as a hunter or a police officer. Tell me about your job. How long have you worked at the bank and how did you land such a great job?"

Alex took two more bites of salad and washed it down with peach tea. She told Tony how she met the bank president at a basketball game. She had dated the basketball coach and just happened to sit by a bank board member at a game. The more they talked the more he insisted on introducing her to the bank president since they apparently needed help with marketing.

Alex wiped her mouth. "So, I took my resume to the next game, and *voilà,* that's how I was hired."

"At a basketball game?"

"Well, that's how I got my foot in the door. I actually had three different interviews. It was quite a long process, but in the end, I won them over. The rest is history, as they say." She wrinkled her nose. "I hate all the early meetings though."

Tony sipped his Diet Coke. "That's an interesting story, Alex. What do you do as marketing director?"

"Some days I do a bit of everything and wear a lot of hats. I'm in charge of our television and radio commercials, branding campaigns, community relations projects, bank promotions, print ads, trade shows, billboards, web copy, you name it."

Tony raised his hand. "Whew. You're wearing me out. You have a big job, don't you?" He stared into Alex's green eyes.

"Yeah, but I can handle it. I thrive on stress. I'm very Type A, a total perfectionist." She glanced at her watch as they waited for the bill. "Speaking of which, I've got to run or I'll never meet my deadline."

"Go ahead. I'll get the bill."

Alex fished in her purse for some cash.

"Hey, I said I'll get it. Lunch was my idea. Marketing directors may make more than cops but I can handle a couple of salads."

"Ha. Don't bet that I make more than you. Banks pay notoriously low. We may be surrounded by cash but they don't dole it out to the employees. Thanks, Tony. I'll catch the next one. I've got to run."

Tony stood up and gave Alex a kiss on the cheek. She caught a glimpse of herself in a mirror on the wall and noticed her face matched her red blazer. *Why does this married cop have this effect on me?* Alex was uncomfortable with her feelings toward him. She knew she needed to end it and fast as she stared at his tall, hard body walking back toward the table. It took all of her reserve to keep from running back to him.

Chapter 15

Suzy enjoyed a steaming cup of coffee in her home office. Dressed in a T-shirt Jon had sent her from Italy sporting the Italian flag, she took in her office trying to get motivated for her next wedding. An antique desk with petite rosebuds painted down the legs took center stage. Two pink and black—Suzy's logo colors—striped chairs were in front of the desk for bride consultations. Marc supplied her with fresh flowers weekly—his thanks for her bridal referrals. A handsome credenza showcased enlarged photos of the many weddings she had planned. Suzy kept the pictures displayed for two reasons—to show prospective brides the variety of weddings she had planned, and as a reminder that wedded bliss does exist.

She laughed out loud as she looked at the animal lover bride who wanted her dog to be her maid of honor. That was the only wedding where dog treats were on Suzy's to-do list. She lovingly picked up the frame featuring a bride who was driven to the altar in her great-grandfather's old Model T. Several of her weddings featured horse and carriage rides and traditional church weddings. Suzy touched the frame featuring a beautiful sunset overlooking a Crystal Lake wedding and glanced at a photo of lush rose petals paving a bride's path as she strolled through the Japanese Gardens.

She loved the variety of the weddings she planned. Every one was vastly different. Even the bridezillas gave her something new to focus on. Getting completely immersed in the details kept her mind off her divorce and near-miss wedding, not to mention her lack of male companionship.

In spite of her own failures, she smiled and gave herself an invisible pat on the back. *I've done a smashing job with these weddings, if I do say so myself.*

The irony of being a wedding planner never failed to amuse her. Her thoughts occasionally drifted to Tara and Dean and it still hurt like hell. In fact, Suzy hadn't spoken to her sister since that shocking day and didn't care if she ever saw her again. Her parents had called several times but said they had no choice but to accept Dean and Tara. Suzy loved her parents but their relationship had become strained. Her relationship with Tara and Dean was nil.

Good riddance. Suzy was happy when her ringing phone jarred her thoughts.

"Hello, Weddings by Suzanne. Suzy Jacobs speaking."

"Hi, Suzy. My name's Maria and I need help planning my wedding."

Suzy detected a faint Spanish accent and thought the bride sounded nervous.

"Certainly. When is the big day?"

"Well, that's the thing. We just found out I'm six weeks' pregnant and I really want to have this wedding before I start showing. Can you pull it off in two months? The doctor said I probably won't start showing until my fourth or fifth month, but I don't want to push it."

Suzy cradled the phone between her ear and shoulder and thumbed through her planner. "Let's see. I do have a weekend available at the end of next month but it depends on how elaborate you want your wedding to be. The invitations will have to be chosen and sent off immediately in order to get them back in time. Will you be able to move quickly on making decisions? That's the only way we can pull this off."

"Yes. Absolutely. I've cleared my schedule and am at your disposal." Maria breathed a sigh of relief. "You were recommended to me by Misty. She was very happy with her wedding and said I could trust you. Thank you so much for taking this on at the last minute."

Misty. The girl who wanted pink—and only pink—orchids. She ended up being a happy customer. Will wonders never cease?

Suzy and Maria agreed to meet within the hour. Suzy hung up and hopped in the shower. She decided to wear a pink floral skirt in honor of Misty for referring her. As she combed her hair, she pushed her own unhappy thoughts out of her mind and tried to think happy, creative thoughts about Maria's upcoming nuptials.

They decided to meet at The Coffee Drip. Suzy ordered a mocha coffee as a flustered, Hispanic woman with large breasts spilling out of her blouse came rushing in. She held a thick file and, in her rush, dropped it. Pictures and papers scattered like snowflakes.

Suzy bent down to help her. "Are you Maria by chance?"

"Yes."

Suzy extended her hand and introduced herself. "Let me help you sort these out." She steered Maria toward a table.

Flustered and slightly sweaty, Maria said, "I brought some pictures to show you from the festival where I met my fiancé." Maria fanned herself with a napkin.

Suzy smiled. "Relax. This will be fun. And your pictures will help expedite the process. Would you like some coffee?"

"No, I'm cutting back on caffeine. I'll order some decaffeinated green tea."

After Maria got her tea, she slid into the booth and Suzy took in Maria's pretty face. She had plump cheeks and large calves but her thick mane of black hair, large dark eyes, and pearly white smile were enviable. Suzy began pouring over the pictures.

"These are beautiful, Maria. Is this the annual hot air balloon festival in Albuquerque, New Mexico?"

"Yes," Maria gushed. "It was my first time to go. The balloons were beautiful, absolutely breathtaking. That's where I met Scott. He goes there every year and showed me all around." She flashed a wide smile. "Afterward, we started dating. Is there any way we can incorporate the hot air balloon festival into our wedding? I'd like to surprise Scott. He's been so supportive about the unexpected pregnancy. I want to give him a special day."

Suzy liked Maria right away and knew she would be an easy bride, a refreshing change. Her mind raced with ideas as she asked Maria about their wedding budget. It was above average and she guessed since they were both in their thirties, they had each managed to put aside a comfortable nest egg. Still, Suzy wanted them to stick to a budget—especially with a baby on the horizon.

After thumbing through the pictures, she said, "I have a few ideas. First of all, just like all the brightly colored balloons, I'd suggest each bridesmaid's dress be a different, jewel-toned color. You could go with floor length, tea length or a cute above-the-knee balloon hemline."

Maria clapped her hands together. "I love that idea. We could use red, blue, green, and yellow—all the bright colors that you see not only on the balloons but also in New Mexico."

"Good. I'm glad you like it."

"What about the groomsmen? What should they should wear?"

Suzy sipped her coffee and pondered the idea. "I'd put them in black tuxes with a brightly colored tie to coordinate with whichever bridesmaid they'll be escorting."

Maria looked thoroughly relieved. "Perfect! You're so quick with ideas! I'm glad Misty recommended you. This gives me a good start."

Suzy excused herself and walked up to the counter to refill her coffee. She looked back at Maria who looked much more relaxed than she did when she walked in with papers flying everywhere. Suzy took great joy in making other people's weddings a special memory.

When she returned to the booth, Suzy said, "Your first priority is invitations. They need to be ordered right away. I recommend Calligraphy & More. I know the owner, Tina, and if you tell her your situation, she'll put a rush on them. Discuss your hot air balloon theme, and she'll take it from there. She's very good. You could even have two colorful hot air balloons on the invitation with your names printed on them, unless you think that's corny."

"No, I love that idea." Maria scribbled down the store and owner's name in her turquoise journal and made two intertwining balloons with the names *Scott* and *Maria*.

Suzy patted the journal. "This gives me another idea. New Mexico is well known for its beautiful turquoise and silver jewelry. What would you think about wearing turquoise and diamond jewelry with your white wedding dress and maybe even a beautiful silk turquoise sash to tie it all together? Your fiancé's tie could also be turquoise."

"I think that's a fabulous idea. I think *you're* fabulous." Maria teared up. "I can't believe you've given me so many ideas already. This is such a relief—"

"Hey, I love the creative process. It's fun. And it's my job. No worries and no tears, okay? Now, before you can get invitations printed you'll need a date, time, and location."

Maria hurriedly wrote down Suzy's instructions. Suzy noticed her scribbling madly and pulled out a form. "Here, hon. I have this all typed out. Just fill in the blanks and give it to Tina. She'll take it from there. Have you and your fiancé thought about a wedding venue?"

"We'd like an outdoor setting with flowers. Do you know any place like that?"

"How about the Botanical Gardens just east of town? The flowers are gorgeous and they have a large pavilion for the DJ or band, food, cake and dancing. You can rent tables and chairs and there are restrooms off the pavilion. What do you think?"

"I forgot all about that place. It would be perfect. My friend had a wedding there and the setting is beautiful. I'll check with Scott but I'm sure he'll be fine with it."

"Why don't you do that? In the meantime, I'll give the Botanical Gardens a call and put a tentative hold on a couple of dates." Suzy looked at her calendar and made some notes. "Talk this over with Scott and call me later today so I can lock in a date and you can order the invitations. Then, let's meet in a few days to talk about the menu and music. I have another idea but I want to check on it first before I tell you. It will be grand if it works out." Suzy smiled mysteriously.

"Thank you, thank you, thank you! You'll never know what a lifesaver you've been." Maria giggled. "I can't wait to hear about your grand idea! Thanks again for meeting me on such short notice." Maria hugged Suzy, gathered her papers and left.

Chapter 16

A few days after having lunch with Tony, Alex had a particularly hard day at work. She rubbed her shoulders and wrists. She had spent the entire day creating marketing brochures and displays for an upcoming trade show. Thank God the work day was over. She turned her computer off and decided to reward herself with some new shoes.

She pulled her Mustang convertible, top down, into the parking lot of Shoe Surplus. Walking inside, she noticed they had a Buy-One-Get-One-Free sale. She smiled to herself. That would fit her budget. Alex was a serious bargain shopper. Her favorite store was T.J. Maxx. Suzy had always kidded her that she should name her first child either T.J. or Maxx.

Looking at the shelves of shoes, Alex walked down the sandal aisle and stopped by the dress shoes when she was nearly knocked over by a toddler with blonde curls bobbing. The little girl was wearing a white frilly dress and lacy socks. A stocky, masculine-looking woman ran breathlessly behind her.

"Grab her, grab her," yelled the woman. "I'm her mother and I'm afraid she'll dart outside into the parking lot."

As the toddler got closer, the mother looked at Alex with pleading eyes. "Please grab her."

Alex was already squatting on the floor trying to find her shoe size so she simply stuck out her left arm and the youngster ran right into her. Alex smiled so the little girl wouldn't be frightened. "It's okay, honey. Your mom is right behind you."

Alex looked up into what she thought would be a grateful mother's face only to hear her blood-curdling screams,

"Help! Help! She's trying to kidnap my child! Somebody help me!"

Dazed, Alex slowly started to comprehend what was happening. She felt as if her feet were in quick sand. Her heart pounded as she slowly pulled away from the little girl and stood up. But not before a hulky Gold's Gym-type security guard appeared at her side. The guard reached for Alex's arm as the mother continued screaming "help" at the top of her lungs.

Alex jerked her arm away. "You've got this all wrong, sir. This woman asked, no, practically *begged* me to stop her child. The little girl was running amok in the store and I simply did what the mother asked me to do. She scanned the store to see if anyone had witnessed the event but didn't see a soul. "This is a huge misunderstanding."

"She's a liar," hissed the mother. "She was trying to kidnap my baby. My poor baby." She forced tears and held her startled toddler to her large, heaving bosom.

Alex's eyebrows shot up. "This is a bunch of crap. I'm leaving."

"No, I'm afraid you aren't, ma'am," the muscular guard said. "I've already called the CCPD and they're on their way. They'll want to question you. You aren't going anywhere, lady."

Alex was floored. She wanted to run. "What? You must be kidding me. I came in here to buy some fucking shoes. This lunatic woman started yelling at me to 'grab her child' and I stupidly did as she asked. Now, you're telling me I have to talk to a police officer about this?" She put both hands on her hips. "Have all of you gone mad?"

The little girl started to cry. Loudly.

Alex looked past the security guard to see other shoe patrons had finally gathered and were gawking at her. They whispered and pointed at Alex who was becoming more humiliated by the second.

Pointing an accusing finger at Alex, the girl's mother said, "She was trying to kidnap my child, my baby. Arrest her."

"Oh my God," was all Alex could manage. All she could think about was the fact that she would be fired from the bank if she were arrested. She could lose her job over this stupid woman. Banks obviously do not employ people with arrest records. Her stomach was doing back flips. She felt as if she were going to vomit. Alex seriously thought about making a run for the front door when Sgt. Montgomery walked in. Alex relaxed slightly. Thank goodness for small favors. She took a deep breath.

When the mother saw the officer, she yelled, "She tried to kidnap my child. She *touched* my child." The woman pointed a stubby finger toward Alex.

"Ma'am, I'll get your statement in a minute," Sgt. Montgomery said forcefully. He looked at the security guard. "We need to separate these two. Do you have a separate room where I can take Miss . . . ?" He looked at Alex to fill in the blank.

"Mitchell. Alexandra Mitchell." It donned on Alex that he didn't want anyone to know they were acquainted.

He looked Alex directly in the eye and said, "I'm Sgt. Tony Montgomery."

Alex nodded meekly.

Turning toward the security guard, Tony said, "I'd like to take Miss Mitchell's statement in another room. Then, I'll speak with the mother." He added, "Do you have security video that I can observe?"

Alex looked at the guard hopefully.

The guard shook his head. "We only have cameras *outside*." He grunted and led Alex and Sgt. Montgomery to a small closet of an office and closed the door.

When the guard left, Alex let out big, gulping sobs. "Thank God you're here. I was scared to death." Alex wiped her nose with the back of her hand. "I don't know what I would have done if another officer had shown up. Tony, this woman is crazy, absolutely nuts." Alex could barely catch her breath between sobs. Tony handed her a tissue.

"Tell me what happened," he said as he placed his large hand over hers.

Alex blew her nose. "She asked me to grab her child. Those were her exact words. The kid was running away from her and I instinctively and stupidly did as she asked. I had no idea she was trying to set me up."

"You're right. It's probably a setup and most likely one of her many scams. She probably noticed your nice clothes and jewelry and hoped to take advantage of you. Maybe talk you into keeping everything quiet by giving her some cash. She sounds like a pretty good con. This probably isn't the first time she has pulled a stunt like this. I'll get to the bottom of it when I check her record. Try to relax. I know you aren't a kidnapper or child molester." He placed his hand on her shoulder and squeezed it.

Alex took a deep breath.

"Sit still and try to calm down while I take her statement. I'll check and see if she has a record. I'll be back soon."

Tony came back twenty minutes later after he ran a background check. She had prior arrests in Arkansas and Oklahoma where she had pulled similar kidnapping scams. He placed the woman under arrest and called a social worker to place the child in state custody. Tony told Alex she was free to leave and lucky that the woman didn't try anything more dangerous.

The hulky, obviously disappointed, security guard slumped away to his small office where Tony had the woman handcuffed.

Wringing his hands and sweating profusely, a nerdy twenty-something Shoe Surplus manager apologized profusely to Alex. He told her to pick out two pairs of shoes on the house. She asked for a rain check since she was no longer in the mood to shop. Still shaking, she walked to her car with wobbly legs.

Tony met up with Alex in the parking lot. “I’m off duty now. I called the station to have another officer take her to jail. Want to grab something to eat?”

“Only if it includes alcohol. I need a stiff drink.”

“I bet you do.”

Chapter 17

After Maria left, Suzy refilled her coffee, bought a fruit and tuna plate and settled back into the booth. She opened her purse and fished out mail she had plucked from her mailbox on the way out. Among the junk mail and magazines, was a postcard from her son. Suzy excitedly pulled it to the top of the heap.

Hi, Mom! Greetings from Italy. Having a great time. The food is fantastic. Pizza and wine every day! Rome is amazing. I saw Michelangelo's Sistine Chapel. Doubly amazing. On my way to France soon. Hope you're okay. I worry about you. Miss you.

Ciao and much love,
Jon

Suzy held the postcard to her chest and smelled it, hoping for a faint scent of Jon. She reread the postcard three times. She missed her son but was glad her ex had given him the adventure of a lifetime. Even if Bill was a horrible, distant husband who loved golf more than her, she had to admit he was a great dad. Suzy and Bill were married for ten years. They shared custody, and even though they were not good as a couple, they jointly attended Jon's activities throughout his school years, helped him with college visits, and occasionally spent holidays together as a family.

Bill was a real guy's guy. He wouldn't be caught dead wearing pink, even though Suzy once tried to convince him that real men wore pink. He also couldn't understand her career choice and how she could be content planning weddings for other people. When Suzy established Weddings by Suzanne, Bill told her he'd rather have someone drive a nail through his head than plan weddings for a living.

Suzy surmised that as long as Bill had golf and team sports, he was happy. He would be perfectly satisfied living the rest of his life in a sports bar, drinking beer, and yelling at the television with his buddies. Sports, plus a little hunting added to the mix. Bill loved to deer and elk hunt. Every fall he planned an extensive—and expensive—outing to Chama, New Mexico, to hunt elk with a few other die-hard hunters.

Taking a bite of a juicy strawberry, Suzy wondered what they ever had in common other than being madly in love in school. When Suzy became pregnant, she had just started college. Her parents were not pleased that she had gotten pregnant so young and shortly after she and her high school boyfriend, Ken, had broken up. After Suzy and Bill's quick, modest courthouse wedding, she dreamed of planning memorable weddings for others.

When Jon was born, Suzy had to fight Bill over their son's name. Bill wanted to name their son Hunter for obvious reasons but Suzy won the argument. After Bill finally agreed to name their son Jon, he told her he hated the spelling, saying it was an odd way to spell his name. Bill wanted the more traditional spelling. Suzy argued that "Jon" seemed more modern. She won the battle.

Jon graduated with honors from high school, and after his European vacation, he planned to go to college and major in English. He loved to write, dabbled with short stories and poems, and had some success with getting a couple of short stories published in anthologies. His goal was to write a novel. An important novel. What about, Suzy wasn't sure.

Jon dated the same girl, Vanessa, throughout high school. Suzy adored Vanessa and secretly hoped they would marry. She wanted to plan a blowout wedding for them. She had even jotted down a few ideas unbeknownst to Jon. Vanessa was a pretty, petite girl who thought the world revolved around Jon. Suzy noticed he could be a little distant toward Vanessa but attributed that to Jon's mirroring his dad's behavior.

Suzy put the postcard in her purse and decided to call her son. She looked at her watch to calculate the time difference. It was eleven in the morning in the Midwest, which meant it was around five o'clock in Europe, depending on where he was. She dialed Jon's number and couldn't wait to hear his voice.

"*Bonjour*, Mom." He obviously recognized his mother's cell number.

"Hi, honey. It's so good to hear your sweet voice! Are you still in Italy? Are you eating enough? When are you coming home?"

Jon laughed. "One question at a time, Mom. I've been in Italy the past two weeks and loved it. I think I ate pizza every day for lunch. I've probably gained weight. Now, I'm in Paris, thus the *bonjour*."

"I get it."

"How are you anyway? Have you heard from Dean or Tara?"

"No. Thank goodness. I don't want to talk about it. I'm fine. I promise."

Suzy could hear Jon blow out his breath. After an awkward silence he said, "You need to stop working so hard and go on a vacation, Mom. You'd enjoy Europe."

"Someday I'll make it across the big pond. How's the food in France?"

"It's tiny compared to our portions in the Midwest. No wonder we're so fat and Europeans are skinny." He laughed. "Of course, the wine is amazing. Europeans know how to live. They drink wine for lunch and dinner every day."

Suzy chuckled and nodded her head in agreement even though he couldn't see her.

"I wish I could eat at a little sidewalk café with you right now. I miss you. Have a nice glass of French wine for me, okay? Do you need any money?"

"No, Mom, I'm set. I've been frugal and have really made my savings last. You'd be proud. I even wash my socks and underwear out at night and dry them with a blow dryer."

"Well, I'm not sure I'd go to that much trouble." Suzy laughed.

Jon continued, undaunted. "I've found several cafés with reasonable prices. A couple of them that normally throw extra food out are giving me food at the end of the evening."

Suzy frowned into the phone. "Are you eating garbage, Jon? Let me wire you some money."

He cackled. "I'm not dumpster diving. Certain restaurants know I'm backpacking. I guess they're taking pity on me. The food is in a nice container. It's not covered in coffee grounds or anything."

Suzy chuckled. "Thank goodness. Tell me more. We haven't talked in so long."

"I haven't done all the touristy stuff. I'd rather talk to the locals. Actually, several have invited me to stay in their homes. They feed me and let me sleep for free. Of course, I've helped out with odd chores here and there to help pay for my room and bo—"

"You're staying with complete strangers? I don't think I want to hear this," Suzy said in complete dismay. "Jon, you don't know these people. They could rob you, steal your identity, or worse. What are you thinking?"

"Geeze, Mom. I'm a big boy now. All grown up. You worry too much. I'm a good judge of character. Give me some credit. No one is going to hurt me. You're overreacting."

"Well, you must be lonely there by yourself. I can just picture you walking and eating alone every day. Solitude has its limits."

"I'm having a blast. And I'm not lonely. Actually, I've kind of met someone."

Suzy cradled the phone between her ear and shoulder and drained the coffee.

"You've met someone? What about Vanessa? You've dated for three years. She'll be devastated. She thinks you hung the moon, Jon." Suzy sighed. "Surely this is just some little European romance."

Jon paused before he answered. "I think it's more than a little European romance but I'm going to give it a few more weeks before I tell you any details. Don't worry about Vanessa. I think, actually, I know she had the idea I wasn't happy during our senior year. Hopefully, she's dating now, too. I'm not the best person for her. I think she realized that before I left."

Suzy stared into her phone more confused than ever. She didn't want to hang up but was suddenly at a loss for words.

"Whatever you say. I just want you to be happy. This is really coming out of left field, though. What's this girl's name? Is she American, Italian, or French?"

"I'll explain everything when I return to the states, okay? Just trust me. I've got to run. Love you, Mom. Bye." Jon quickly hung up.

Suzy was beyond confused but at least satisfied that her son was safe, healthy and happy. That was what was most important she told herself. She picked up her purse, laid a tip on the table and left. Half of her wanted to call Vanessa but she knew she shouldn't meddle—or should she?

Chapter 18

After the shoe store incident, Tony followed closely behind an upset Alex as she drove to Rosa's Mexican Restaurant. They immediately ordered two giant margaritas and gorged on chips, salsa, guacamole, chicken enchiladas, and rice. As usual, Alex examined her silverware for cleanliness and her glass for lipstick smudges. Tony noticed this habit of hers at lunch the other day but didn't say anything.

Alex swallowed hard and looked into Tony's eyes. "You really helped me out today. You were my hero." She still had the sniffles from crying. "I hope you know that."

"No sweat, Alex, it's all in a day's work."

"Not exactly *my* typical day. I'm still shaking." She held out her hand to prove it. Tony reached for it and gently kissed the top of Alex's hand like a dashing Englishman. Alex blushed, took a big gulp of her margarita as her mind raced.

She was afraid to broach the subject of his home life but was having a hard time containing her feelings for him, so she jumped right in, as usual.

"So, how's it going at home?" she asked awkwardly. "Are you still happily or not-so-happily married?"

"Actually, I have some news. I've talked to an attorney. I'm separated. It sounds cliché but life is short. I think that's finally starting to sink into my thick head."

Alex could hardly contain her excitement and wanted to throw her arms around Tony's neck. Then she immediately felt guilty that she was happy a marriage might end.

"Separation is a big step, Tony. I mean, um, what does your wife think?"

"She knows neither one of us is happy. We've stayed together for Joey for years. I think the separation might help," he added with an expression Alex couldn't quite read.

"Where are you staying, if I might ask?"

"On the couch."

Alex's mouth flew open. "What? You're still sleeping in the same house and you call that 'separated?'"

"It's a big step for me. I want to be near Joey, go to his activities, things like that. I don't want to be a weekend dad."

She sighed as tears filled her eyes. She turned her head so Tony wouldn't notice.

"I think I understand." She was more disappointed than she would have expected. "So, a separation means you might stay together and you might not. Is that it?"

"We'll see how it goes. I know this must be hard on you. I'm sorry and I don't expect you to wait around if you don't want to. I don't want to be one of those cliché guys with a woman on each arm. You deserve more than that." He reached for her hand but she kept it firmly in her lap.

"I hope you understand this isn't about my wife. It's about Joey. I've got to put him first, plain and simple." He stared down at the table. "She could care less if I was with you because she's certainly doing what she wants but you deserve more. Much more."

Alex felt like she had been punched in the stomach for the second time that day. *A separation but he's sleeping on the couch?* That's all she remembered out of the entire conversation. *I don't want to get any more attached. I can see the writing on the wall.*

"Listen, this has been a rough day and I've got to go home. Thanks again for everything at the shoe store. You truly were my hero today." Alex's voice shook as she dug her car keys out of her purse and walked toward the door.

Tony put money on the table and walked Alex to her car.

As they stood by her Mustang, he leaned forward. "Mind if I hug you?"

He was standing close and smelled so good, too good. Clean. Yummy. She desperately wanted to kiss him but knew there might not be any going back.

"It's getting late. I have an early meeting tomor—"

Tony lightly pinned her to the car. When she opened her mouth to finish her sentence, he leaned down and kissed her. A long, deep, sweet, and salty kiss. She felt his tongue explore her mouth and tingled from head to toe—and especially in between. After the passionate kiss, Alex looked into his compelling blue eyes.

"You're killing me, you know. You're a married man. I can't do this. I've got to go." Alex forced herself to pull away from him.

Tony took half a step back and placed his fingers under her chin, tilting her head until she met his gaze. "Actually, I'm a separated man but I understand. I'll talk to you soon." He kissed Alex on the forehead and opened her car door.

She drove home in a daze with Tony's scent on her clothes. What a shitty and wonderful night all balled into one. *What am I going to do about my extreme crush on this guy? Am I falling in love with a married—separated man?*

Chapter 19

After school, Hope walked to her car. She had a newfound bounce in her step since she had reconnected with Alex and Suzy. Meeting them at Coconuts would be a refreshing change from going home to her hippie parents. Humming a tune, she stopped abruptly when she heard the song, "Takin' Care of Business," blaring in the parking lot. She jerked her head around and spotted a yellow bus sporting several daisy and peace sign decals. Hope groaned as she walked toward Larry and Montana.

"Hey, Hope. Groovy song, huh? Want me to turn it up?"

"No, Dad. I can hear it just fine. As a matter of fact, the entire neighborhood can hear it." Hope listened to the words: "*Working hard at nothing all day.*" That should be my parents' theme song, she thought.

"Rock on," Montana said as her head bopped to the music. Hope stared at her mom's tanned legs and bare feet sprawled across the dash. She seemingly didn't have a care in the world.

Hope scanned the parking lot to see if any students or teachers were around. "What are you doing here?" she hissed.

"We seem to have a little problemo with 'ol Betsy here. We're, uh, outta gas." Larry smiled expectantly at Hope.

Montana shrugged and added, "We're short on bread, honey."

"Get in, Hope. Want a beer?" Larry asked.

Hope's eyes bulged. Through gritted teeth, she said, "Are you trying to get me fired? Do you know how often we preach to our students about not drinking and driving? What's wrong with you two?"

Larry and Montana exchanged glances but said nothing.

Hope held her nose in the air and sniffed. "What's that I smell?" She looked horrified. "Are you smoking pot on the school parking lot? On *my* school parking lot?"

"Relax, Hope. Seems to me you could use a joint yourself," Larry said easily.

Hope ran her fingers through her frizzy hair and pulled out her wallet.

"Here's a twenty. Go get some gas. Don't use this for beer." She thrust the bill toward Montana. Larry was tapping to the beat of the song, using the steering wheel as a drum.

"Don't ever come here like this again. And don't ever smoke pot anywhere near my house or school."

Larry stopped tapping.

"What has gotten into you? You're so tense lately," Montana said.

Hope's eyes filled with tears. As usual, guilt gripped her. It was hell being an only child.

"Please. Just take the money and get some gas. You can go to my house if you want. I have some leftover hamburger in the fridge. Grill it if you want. The charcoal and lighter fluid are by the steps.

Larry smiled. "A burger sure would hit the spot. First things first. Do you have a gas can on you?"

"You mean you're completely out of gas? I thought you were just low. Why didn't you buy some earlier?"

Larry shrugged and held up two fingers.

"Two reasons. We're flat-busted broke and the gas gauge don't work."

Hope huffed and got in her car. She drove up to her parents' hippie mobile.

"Get in. I'll drive you to the nearest station."

Hope now regretted telling her parents they could come over and cook burgers but it was too late.

I wonder what Alex and Suzy are doing? Probably the usual—having a perfect day.

The next day Alex awakened in a state of confusion. She rubbed her eyes and sat up in bed. *Was that shoe store incident a dream?* She knew it wasn't and jumped out of bed. She poured water into the coffee pot and laid out clothes for work. She wanted to tell Jim before any witnesses could give him any sordid information. Her job was important to her and she wanted to be the first to tell her boss exactly what had happened.

She quickly showered, poured the coffee into a CNB thermos, and threw on a navy blouse and a gray pin-striped suit. She placed silver earrings and a necklace into her purse, knowing she could manage her makeup and jewelry at stoplights. Old habits were hard to break.

Arriving at Community National Bank early, for once, Alex walked toward her office through the dark, isolated lobby. *It's eerie here when no one is around.* As she approached her door, she saw a man sitting in a chair in her office. Alex nearly jumped out of her skin. She tiptoed toward her office and could see a man in a suit drinking out of a CNB coffee mug. She relaxed. Thank God. She couldn't take any more surprises. It was her boss.

I guess he's already heard the news. One of our customers was probably shopping at Shoe Surplus. Jim's probably going to fire me for sullying the bank's reputation.

Alex walked up and put her hand on his shoulder. "Morning."

"You're early, Alex. I was just sitting here enjoying the peace and quiet before we launched into our meeting."

"Uh, are we meeting in my office?"

"I know you're working on a new branding campaign. Before you get too far into it, I wanted to give you a heads up. The board wants to change CNB's name. There are too many community banks around and way too many with the word 'community' in them." Jim grinned and sipped his coffee as Alex placed her heavy purse on the floor.

"Go on."

"We want to differentiate ourselves from other community banks. Become more of a state-wide entity. We'll still maintain our local flavor but plan to build several more banks in smaller towns surrounding Crystal City. I'd like your recommendations for a new name for CNB. Something with state-wide appeal."

Alex looked at her boss with wide-eyed relief and realized she was still standing. She pulled out her chair and sat down.

"No problem. I'll have a list of prospective names to you by noon."

"I can always count on you." Jim stood and reached for the door handle.

"Would you mind sitting back down? I was involved in an incident last night and need to tell you about it," Alex said solemnly. Tears threatened her eyes.

Jim looked concerned and took a seat.

Alex relayed the entire shoe store incident as Jim listened with one eyebrow cocked. She told him everything—except the part about kissing the cop. She did tell Jim she knew the cop.

Jim took a small pad out of his shirt pocket and made notes. He asked her to repeat the sergeant's name, and smiled at her in a fatherly manner.

"Alex, don't worry about anything. I know what type of upstanding person you are. You're a huge asset to this bank. If word gets out about this, we will stand behind you one hundred percent. From what the officer told you, that woman has a record. You were the victim. I'm sure it shook you up but try and put it behind you—and maybe consider a different shoe store." He chuckled.

Alex breathed a sigh of relief and hugged her boss. "Thanks, Jim. I thought you'd understand but have to admit I was a little worried. I know how hard you've worked to build CNB's stellar reputation and don't want to be the one to leave a scar on the bank's good name."

Jim smiled. "Nothing more needs to be said. Speaking of the bank's good name, don't forget about a new one." He winked and left.

Loan assistants, new account reps and loan officers had already filed in and were seated at their desks. Alex headed straight to the coffee machine as tellers counted money and placed it in their drawers. Several employees talked animatedly about the previous night's ballgame. All looked normal in CNB-land.

After she filled her mug, Alex squeezed anti-bacterial gel onto her palm. She knew the employee coffee machine was a haven to who-knows-what-kind of bacteria. Satisfied that her hands were clean, she flopped into her chair and turned on the computer. Staring at the blank screen, she thought, *names.* T*hink of names.* Alex typed: *Sgt. Tony Montgomery.* No, not that name, she scolded herself. Focus.

Think of bank names for my good boss. That's the least I can do. She typed "New Name for Community National Bank" at the top. Then it came to her. The perfect name. Why hadn't another bank thought of this? There was no need for a long list. This was it. It couldn't be more ideal for a Missouri bank. She typed her recommendation in large bold letters and practically ran across the lobby to her boss's executive suite.

Chapter 20

Alex actually made it to Coconuts first and decided to order something other than wine. She felt almost celebratory and chose a key lime pie martini. She couldn't wait to tell Hope and Suzy about her scary shoe store incident and about Tony contacting an attorney. Finally.

As she looked around the room, she took note of some of the regulars. There was the guy in the cheap suit two tables over who wore so much cologne she could smell it five feet away. A heavyset, unlit cigar-chomping guy was seated at the end of the bar watching the sports channel. A homely man with a bad comb-over was perched in the far corner of the room in his favorite chair. A loud, bleached blonde barfly was on her usual barstool wearing a mini skirt, hoping to pick up a guy—any guy, apparently.

Coconuts almost made her feel as though she were on the beach. Along one wall was a mural depicting a beach scene with waves, a surfer, bikini-clad women and beach umbrellas dotting the sand. Large ferns were atop a half wall between the restaurant and the bar, most likely to diffuse the smoke. Alex especially liked the zebra print chairs and fake palm trees. Whenever she ordered something other than wine, which wasn't often, it always came in a hollowed out small, fake coconut cup.

Alex again noticed the gorgeous young woman with the designer clothes, stylish hair and perfect toothpaste-commercial white teeth. She was always with different guys who obviously weren't in her league. *I wonder what her story is?* Her curiosity was about to get the best of her when Suzy arrived.

"Hi. I get two points. I was early for once."

"You do get points. That's a first," Suzy teased.

"So, spill. How was the bride from hell? Did the wedding go off as planned?"

Suzy rolled her eyes. "When I left here last week, Misty was throwing a hissy fit over not having pink orchids. There was an accident involving the truck driver carrying the flowers but she couldn't care less about him."

"What did you do?"

Suzy held up her hand to get the server's attention. "We *finally* talked her into pink roses instead."

"What a spoiled brat. So the actual wedding turned out okay?"

"Yes, after that fiasco, it was truly a beautiful wedding. All the bridesmaids wore long, pink silky dresses, the groomsmen had matching pink ties, and the reception area was completely covered with pink candles and trails of pink rose petals."

Alex nibbled on the graham crackers covering the rim of her martini glass. "Sounds like the ceremony went off without a hitch."

"Except for her drunk uncle who knocked over the DJ's equipment. But she can't blame that on me. Now, I have a new bride, Maria, who is going to be a doll to work with. I'm planning a quick wedding since she's pregnant. It'll be a southwestern theme. Enough about all that. What's going on with you?" Suzy looked around. "I wonder where Hope is."

Gus appeared with zebra print drink menus.

Suzy looked at Alex's green key lime martini.

"That looks good. I'll have one of those. And are you working out again, Gus?"

He flexed his muscles, smiled and took their menus. Another key lime martini coming up."

Alex stared at the front door. "I'm surprised she's late. She was so excited to reconnect."

Alex glanced around the room and cleared her throat. "You won't *believe* what happened to me."

"What?"

Hope rushed up, looking frazzled. "Sorry I'm late. Long story."

Alex relayed the entire shoe store incident emphasizing the mother's claim of attempted kidnapping. Suzy and Hope sat agog, mouths open.

"Holy hell. What a scam," Hope said.

"Thank goodness that cop knew you. I guess it was fate that you rear-ended him. What if they had taken you to jail before they checked her record?" Suzy shook her head.

"Well, if I had gone to jail, even under suspicion, I would have lost my job."

Gus appeared with their drinks.

Hope stared at him. "One more, please."

Suzy held up her drink. "Here's to Sgt. Tony—"

"Montgomery," Alex supplied.

"Here's to Sgt. Montgomery," Hope repeated.

They clinked their glasses and Suzy furrowed her brows, shaking her head. "You never know when to help someone these days. It's scary. You tried to do a good deed and that horrible woman set you up. That makes me mad."

"I know. Believe me I'll be careful if and when I try to be a Good Samaritan again. There's more." Alex felt her cheeks burn.

"More? What? Spill," Hope said.

"After the scary episode, Tony was off duty and suggested dinner, so I went. Afterward, he kissed me. I mean the best kiss ever." She blew out her breath. "I didn't want it to stop but—"

"Alex, he's married," Suzy scolded.

"They're separated."

"Oh, good. Where's he living?" Hope asked.

"Well, that's the thing. He's still living at home to be close to his son. But he's sleeping on the couch."

"Right," Suzy said.

"Right," Hope echoed as she and Suzy exchanged looks.

Alex gulped her martini and waved her hand. "I know. I know. It's not a good sign. I can't help my feelings for him. And he really helped me out the other day. I'm trying to hold back. I really am."

"Just be careful. It's never a good idea to get involved with a married man, especially a married cop," Suzy warned.

"Yes, Mom. Enough about me. What about you, Hope? Anything new?"

Hope rolled her eyes and drained her drink.

"What's wrong?" Suzy asked.

"Same old thing. My hippie parents," Hope said.

"What about your parents?" Alex asked.

"Yeah, you had the coolest parents in the world," Suzy said.

"We all *wanted* your parents," Alex added.

Hope groaned. "In school, everyone thought they wanted to trade for my parents, but trust me, you wouldn't now."

"Are you kidding? They were so cool. You didn't have a curfew, they let you drink beer in school and wear the shortest skirts," Alex said.

Suzy agreed. "Alex and I had strict parents. We couldn't date until we were sixteen and couldn't go to parties unless there was a chaperone. We would have given our right arm for your freedom."

"And where are your parents today?" Hope asked indignantly. "I bet they're successful. I bet they never ask you to pay their bills. I bet they don't hang out at your house because it has air-conditioning. I bet they don't eat all of your food." She motioned to get Gus's attention.

"Your parents probably don't have hair down to their shoulders, seventies style, and they probably own something besides jeans, tie dye and Harley T-shirts." Hope crossed her arms defiantly. "Do your parents go to sleep stoned or drunk? *Now*, whose parents would you like to have?"

Suzy and Alex looked stunned.

Alex saw the despair and sorrow in Hope's eyes. "They're still doing drugs? You're paying their bills?" Don't they work?"

Embarrassed, Hope leaned across the table so no one would overhear. She explained that her parents had few and far between odd jobs like lawn mowing, painting or snow shoveling but never could quite make ends meet.

"They certainly wouldn't stand for one of the 'establishment' jobs where they had to work in an office from nine to five. They've never had a salary, let alone benefits. Once, they even talked about joining the fair and becoming carneys. Actually, I think they'd fit right in." Hope managed a laugh.

Suzy touched Hope's arm. "Sweetie, we had no idea. You shouldn't pay their bills. You're enabling them."

"Don't you think I know that? I'm a counselor," Hope said crossly.

"The problem is, I can tell other people what they should be doing. I can see that very clearly but when it comes to my own parents, it's tough, you know? How do I tell them to get their act together? How can I say I'm not going to pay their electric bill or let them eat my food?" Hope's voice wobbled as she wiped a tear off her cheek.

Gus brought another round of key lime martinis and Hope quickly downed hers.

Alex rubbed Hope's shoulder. "It's like you've reversed roles, isn't it, hon? Actually, I guess they've always acted like kids. I agree with Suzy. They should be standing on their own two feet. We're here when you need us. Anytime you need to talk, okay?"

"Yeah, well, that's enough for tonight," Hope said. "It's draining. And depressing. I had to give them gas money tonight. That's why I was late. They were parked in the school parking lot, music blaring, drinking beer, and smoking pot. Can you believe it?"

Hope threw up her hands. "Counselors in high school don't make much money, but they think I'm rich because they've never had an annual salary in their lives. I'm sure they're at my house right now watching television and grilling hamburgers. They're always behind on their electric bill and can't afford cable, so they come to my house. They're probably cleaning out my fridge right now." Hope sniffled. "I can't have a life until my parents get one of their own." Tears slid down her cheeks.

Alex handed Hope a tissue and waved Gus over. "We need a round of coffee. We have some business to take care of."

Over their steaming mugs, Suzy suggested possible jobs for Larry and Montana. "Why don't they try temp work? They can do some type of work outside like landscaping or working for a billboard company."

"What about working in a factory or a hospital? Hell, I'd work at McDonald's if I couldn't pay my bills. I'm not too good for that," Alex added.

"Same here. It sounds like they need some tough love," Suzy said.

"You've got to stand up to them." Alex eyed her friend.

They spent several minutes trying to think of gigs for Hope's parents. Hope thanked them for their moral support. She was determined to help her parents get on the right path—get on any path. "Let's change the subject."

Chapter 21

Hope drove home thinking about her beautiful, polished friends, Alex and Suzy. She wished she could find a genie in a bottle, make a wish and become either one of them for a month or even just one glorious day.

She wasn't jealous but was beginning to loathe her own life. It seemed as though every day was doom and gloom. There was never anything to look forward to. Every time she took one step forward, she took at least five steps back.

Adding to her miserable mood, rain pounded on her windshield. She turned the wipers on high as thunder boomed and lightning cracked. She slowed her pace as the streets became slick. The last thing she needed was a wreck.

Her mind wandered. *I'm a good person. I love my job, my friends, and my students. Why do I have the loser parents? Why do I have ugly, frizzy hair to match my short, squatty body, not to mention a crappy wardrobe*? Hope groaned aloud and turned her wipers up higher.

It's probably not even raining on Alex and Suzy right now.

Feeling deflated and having difficulty seeing, Hope wiped her hand over her foggy windshield. She turned on her high beams and could barely see one car length ahead. If only it were January, she would make a resolution to get control of her life. Maybe she would anyway. She hated living like this. She was a fun person. She just had to find herself again.

Lost in her thoughts, Hope drove on autopilot. Somehow she made it home in the torrential downpour. Pulling up to her duplex, she saw her mailbox smashed to smithereens on the ground. *What the hell?* She pulled up her driveway, peering through the back-and-forth wipers and heavy rain. Squinting, Hope groaned as she noticed her garage door was also smashed in.

Shit. She yelled to herself. Who could have done this? Hope parked her car on the driveway, afraid the crushed garage door would get stuck if she tried using the electric opener. Naturally, her umbrella was at school. Holding her purse over her head, Hope got out in the pouring rain and ran toward the front door. *I wonder if the jerk left a note. Yeah, right, like some good citizen is going to tell me they careened into my mailbox and garage.*

She reached the cover of her front door overhang and rummaged in her purse for her house key. Before she could get the key in the lock, her cell phone rang. She turned it on as water dripped on her head.

A hazy sounding Montana stammered, "Hope, Hope, are you there? Hope. It's Montana . . . I mean it's Mom. I have some . . . bad news to tell you. Somehow, we, we— hit your mailbox and garage. It was an ac—accident." Her mother paused, apparently waiting for a response. "Are you there?"

After a stunned silence, Hope unclenched her jaw and stared at her phone. She wanted to heave it through the front window.

"Yes, Mom, I'm here. Are you drunk? Is that how you *accidentally* hit my mailbox and garage?"

"No, I'm . . . not drunk," she slurred. "We invited a couple of friends over and had those burgers of yours. I guess we, maybe we, partied a little too much." She coughed and added, "But I'm not druunnk."

"Whatever. This is so typical."

"Are you mad? I'm sorry."

"I'm standing in the pouring rain. I've got to get inside. Are you and Dad okay?"

"Yeessss," Montana said drunkenly.

"It sounds like you're just dandy. I don't know how you managed this. But then I don't know how you manage most things." Hope worked her key in the door and continued her lecture. "It's going to cost me a lot of money to fix my garage door. I think my deductible is a thousand dollars. Do you realize that? I work at a high school, remember?" Her voice cracked and a sob escaped. "I don't have a thousand dollars just lying around."

"I'm sorry. I wish we could help but, you know, we don't have—"

Hope cut her off. "I know the drill. You don't have any money. I'll take care of it. Goodnight, Mother."

Hope was so angry she wanted to smash something. But her parents had already taken care of that. *Why won't they grow up? Why do they have to be my parents?* Hope didn't bother to turn on the lights. She sat at her kitchen table and cried in the dark. Water dripped off her hair and clothes making a puddle on the cheap vinyl floor. She was ashamed of her parents and equally ashamed of herself for enabling them. Suzy and Alex were right. She had to stop. They needed tough love.

After a twenty-minute crying jag, Hope jammed her wet clothes in the washing machine and put on warm pajamas and socks. She was chilled to the bone. She towel dried her hair, which hung in dark curls around her face. She dazedly sat on the side of her bed. She was so furious she didn't think she could sleep. She needed a plan. A Parental Plan. As her mind swirled with possibilities, she was out.

Chapter 22

On the way home from Coconuts, it began pouring. Alex turned on her wipers. Her windshield fogged while her mind raced. When she pulled up to her house, something looked different. She didn't remember leaving a light on in the kitchen. She was always good about turning off lights to conserve energy. Thunder boomed and lightning cracked. Alex jumped and decided she just had the jitters from the storm.

As she pulled into her garage, she noticed the door leading to her kitchen was open. She never left it ajar. She hated bugs and knew there were all kinds of bugs in the garage that would creep into her house. Uneasy, Alex sat in her car trying to remember if she had left the house quickly.

Her breathing quickened as her heart pounded against her chest. She wiped her sweaty brow, wondering if she should back up and drive away. She couldn't stand the fact that someone might be in her house. She pulled out her cell phone and called Tony but he didn't answer. She didn't want to use the emergency pager number he gave her until she knew it was a true emergency.

She slowly unbuckled her seatbelt and walked gingerly toward the open door. She walked on tiptoes so her heels wouldn't clack on the concrete floor. Alex stood on the step leading from the garage to the kitchen and cocked her head to listen. She hoped whoever might be inside couldn't hear her pounding heart.

Frozen on the step, she listened. After about fifteen minutes of silence except for her own heavy breathing, she walked inside. She quietly sat her purse in the corner but kept her cell phone and car keys in her hand. She scanned the room and decided she would jump out the back door onto the deck if someone appeared.

Swallowing, she tried working saliva into her dry mouth. Alex bent down and took off her shoes, then started walking from room to room. Her breathing seemed extra loud even to her. No one was in the kitchen, dining area or living room. The foyer was dark and quiet. She walked toward her bedrooms with apprehension and was horrified that someone might be lurking in a closet or under a bed.

Alex carefully opened a hall closet door filled with towels and sheets. It creaked. She cursed under her breath and picked up a flashlight so she could bop someone over the head if necessary. The guest room was empty and so was her office. She didn't know if she could work up the nerve to walk through her own bedroom. She gripped the flashlight and checked her walk-in closet. It was empty. She looked in the bathroom and the shower. Empty. Finally, she got up the courage to look under her bed. Thankfully, no one was there. Alex let out a loud breath, not realizing she had been holding it.

She walked more confidently toward the living room and double-checked the front and back doors. Both were locked. Standing in the dark wondering what to do, she jumped and dropped the flashlight when her cell phone rang.

"What's up?" Tony asked casually.

"Thank goodness it's you. I just about had a heart attack tonight."

"Why? What's wrong?"

"Well, I was at Coconuts with the girls—"

"Right," he said. "You go there every Thursday. Out kind of late for a work night aren't you?"

"Hope had some family issues. We talked longer than usual. That's not the point. When I got home, things didn't look right. My kitchen light was on and the door between my garage and kitchen was open. I never leave it open and I'm sure I didn't leave that light on. I feel like someone has been in here."

"Are your front and back doors locked?" Tony asked.

"Yes, I just checked them."

"And your windows. Are any broken?"

"No. Everything looks fine." Alex rubbed the back of her neck, starting to feel foolish.

"Then, you must have left the light on and the door open. Otherwise, how would anyone have gotten in?

"I don't know," Alex mumbled, feeling silly.

"Do you want me to come over?"

"Would you? That would calm my nerves."

"On my way." He hung up.

Alex looked at the clock. One in the morning. She knew she would have a hard time getting up for work but also knew she couldn't sleep in this state. And there was that little fact that she wouldn't mind seeing Tony again.

She made decaf coffee and changed out of her work clothes into jeans and a Cardinals baseball shirt. Then she brushed her teeth—just in case.

Within minutes, she heard a soft knock on the door. She looked through the peephole. It was Tony. She unbolted the deadbolt and opened the door.

"Hi. Thanks for coming over on such short—"

Tony gently pressed Alex against the wall and kissed her long and hard. "There. Now, you're okay," he said soothingly. "I'm here to protect you. Protect and serve. That's what I do," he chuckled. "I've missed you, Alex."

Still shaking from a possible intruder, Alex discovered she was reeling even more from the longing kiss. She wanted Tony in her heart but knew in her mind that she couldn't have him. Not yet anyway. But maybe kissing was okay. *She didn't have to act like a nun, did she?*

Tony steered Alex toward the couch and continued to kiss her lips, trailing down her neck. “I don’t know how much longer I can wait. I’ve got to have you,” he said huskily. He ran his hand across her breast.

Alex quivered. Her insides ached for him. She kissed him hard, then, using all her willpower, did her best to gently push him away. She hated to turn him down. She wanted him as much as he wanted her.

“We can’t Tony. You’re still married. I want you. God, I want you. But this isn’t right. Why in the hell are you staying with that woman if she can’t stay out of the sack with other guys?”

“You know why. Joey. We’ve talked about this.”

“I don’t know how you stand it. I couldn’t go on like that.”

“I’ll put up with a lot for my kid. Joey means everything to me. He’s my buddy. I love that little guy.” Tears filled Tony’s eyes.

Alex softened. She kissed the tears off his cheek and looked into his baby blue eyes. She was falling for this guy no matter how hard she tried to place a protective shield over her heart.

“Your son will love you no matter what. You don’t have to live in the same house to be a great dad. In fact, there must be a lot of tension at home. Don’t you think Joey picks up on that? It’s not healthy.”

“We hide it pretty well, I think. But she’s not a good wife and not the same woman I married. Actually, I don’t know if we were ever madly in love. When we dated and were about to break up, she told me she was pregnant.” He stared at his wedding band. “I was raised to do the right thing.”

Alex studied his gold wedding band. She wished she could give this woman a piece of her mind. If only she had the chance, she would show Tony how a real woman would behave. A good woman.

"We can't sit here kissing. As much as I want to, I don't trust myself." She pulled herself out of Tony's grip. It was the last thing she wanted to do. She'd much rather jump into bed with Tony and have him ravage her, then hold her all night and make love again the following morning. She knew she couldn't. It wasn't right. She had to fight her feelings.

Tony groaned and removed his arm from her waist. "If you say so. You're making me take a lot of cold showers lately. I don't know if you're aware of that."

She was happy she at least had that effect on him. Maybe that would help him decide if he wanted to continue living with the wife-from-hell or have a chance at a happy life.

"Before I leave, let me double check all your rooms and closets. I'm starving. Want to get something to eat?" I'm craving yogurt."

"But I just made coffee," Alex protested.

"We'll take it with us."

After checking Alex's doors and windows, they got into her car and drove to The Yogurt Shoppe. They ordered at the drive-thru window because, after all, they couldn't be seen together during the wee hours of the morning. As Alex drove, Tony fed her small bites of peach yogurt. He ran the spoon over her lips sensuously and then put the spoon into his own mouth. He fed her like this over and over—very, very slowly. She thought she was going to have an orgasm eating yogurt. A yogurt orgasm. This sexy cop completely undid her.

As they turned down Yorkshire Road, several police cars, lights flashing, blocked the road. A long line of traffic was stopped in front of them.

"Shit. I forgot about this. Turn here." He sunk down in his seat. "Get off this road."

"What's going on?"

"A DWI checkpoint. I can't believe I forgot they were

doing this. Several of my buddies are out there. They would have recognized me." He wiped his brow.

Chalk this up to reason one thousand and fifty why I shouldn't date a married man. She drove home feeling completely alone, even though Tony sat beside her. They rode in silence, both realizing they were almost "had."

Tony walked inside and placed both hands around her face. "I guess this is goodnight."

He leaned forward for another longing kiss but Alex turned her head so his mouth landed on her cheek.

"We need to slow this down, Sgt. Montgomery. You've got a big decision to make. I'm crazy about you. I think you've already figured that out. I know you care about me too. But I don't want to sneak around, eat at drive-thrus, and worry about being seen on a street in the town where I live."

Tony scanned her face. "I understand. I don't like it either. I get where you're coming from and I agree." He kissed her lightly and lingered a little too long. "I'll be in touch soon." He caressed her cheek with the back of his hand. "I wish I had the answer."

As Alex watched him trudge away, tears sprang to her eyes. She locked the deadbolt and climbed into bed still wearing her clothes. *He does have the answer.* She punched her pillow. *He just won't act on it.*

She tossed and turned and jumped out of bed. Alex turned the computer on in her bedroom and typed: MATCH.COM.

Chapter 23

Suzy woke up early and checked her notes for Maria's wedding. They decided to meet at The Pancake House to finalize details. Suzy grabbed her camel briefcase where she kept individual files for each bride. She thumbed through it to make sure she had the file for Maria and Scott. Satisfied, she turned the radio on and hummed to Blake Shelton's "Honey Bee."

She laughed to herself. *I must find a wedding where I can use that song.*

She scanned her closet and chose a yellow sundress. Suzy pulled her sleek red hair into a high ponytail and applied mascara. She finished her look with coral lip-gloss and sunscreen. Suzy's dermatologist insisted she wear 50 SPF sunscreen under her makeup. She hated it because it made her face feel greasy, but after years of his warnings, she had finally given in. Suzy often tried to mask her part-Irish heritage and porcelain skin with fake-tanning products.

As Suzy entered the hallway, her phone rang. She ran to pick it up. "Hello."

"Hi, Suzy. This is Maria. Do you mind if Scott joins us for our breakfast meeting?"

"Of course not. I'll meet you in twenty minutes. Will that work?"

"Yes. See you soon."

Suzy was excited to meet Scott. She hoped he was deserving of this sweet, pregnant girl. She had really taken a liking to Maria.

Pulling up to The Pancake House, Suzy picked up her briefcase and the white sweater she always kept in her car. She cursed to herself about restaurants always being cold.

Suzy asked the hostess for a table for three and sat down. She laid out her paperwork and ordered coffee while she waited. In a few minutes in walked pretty, dark-haired Maria and a very handsome, very tall Scott. He had short brown hair and the build of a Navy Seal. He seemed quite the gentleman as he greeted Suzy while simultaneously pulling out Maria's chair.

Suzy liked him already. She shook his hand. "You must be Scott." She winked approval to Maria. After introductions, they chatted as Scott retold how they met in Albuquerque. He explained that they were both gawking at the same hot air balloon when they bumped into each other.

"We fell to the ground and I pulled Maria up. We talked for an hour and went to dinner." He smiled at his fiancée. "We haven't been apart since. It was love at first sight."

"What a sweet story. You two are going to have a great marriage and be wonderful parents. I can tell." She noticed they didn't seem the least upset about their order of events. Scott and Maria rarely took their eyes off one another and ordered the same breakfast—oatmeal with rye toast on the side and a small orange juice. Suzy also ordered a sensible breakfast of fruit and wheat toast.

"Let's get down to business, shall we? Maria, did you find dresses for the bridesmaids?"

"Yes." Maria excitedly pulled out pictures of balloon-hemmed dresses in vivid red, royal blue, green and bright yellow. She spread out pictures of matching silk ties and said she had already rented black tuxes.

"The dresses are beautiful. Great job. Have you had any luck with your own dress?"

"I've narrowed it down to two and am going to let Scott help me choose."

"I guess you're not superstitious." Suzy stirred her coffee.

"What do you mean?"

"Most brides won't let their grooms see them in their gown before the wedding."

Maria laughed. "I'm not worried about silly things like that." Scott leaned over and kissed Maria on the cheek.

"Let's talk about the menu. What's your favorite food? I recommend we stay with the southwestern theme for our meal."

Scott and Maria looked at one another and simultaneously said, "Spinach enchiladas!"

Suzy laughed and made a note. "Sounds like you're definitely in sync on that menu item. What else?"

"The usual Mexican fare—guacamole, salsa, chicken fajitas and soft tacos," Maria suggested.

"Sounds fabulous. We can place sombreros among the platters of food and I'll use brightly colored linen napkins to match the bridesmaids' dresses. If you want place settings at the head table, we can write guests' names on big red peppers rather than using traditional place cards." Suzy took a bite out of a juicy strawberry.

Maria clapped her hands. "Didn't I tell you Suzy was the best wedding planner in the whole world?" She looked at Scott adoringly. "This is going to be the perfect wedding to the perfect guy."

Scott gave her an *aw shucks* look. "No, it's going to be the perfect wedding to the perfect girl." He placed his large hand over Maria's.

Suzy didn't know if she could take much more sappiness but was happy for the lovebirds. She had planned weddings for brides and grooms in the past who had fought up to the last minute. This was a refreshing change.

Waiting until the server refilled her coffee, Suzy continued. "Sounds like we have the food covered. And I know a great caterer. Did you have anyone in mind?"

"No. We don't know any caterers. Use whomever you want," Maria said.

"Done. I also recommend keeping the drinks simple to help keep the cost down. Let's stay with the southwestern theme. How about margaritas and sangria as your signature drinks? Of course, you'll probably want champagne for the toasts."

"Sounds great," Scott said.

Maria leaned forward. "Suzy, what's your grand idea? You told me you were going to check on something incredible. Well, what is it? We can't wait any longer."

Suzy smiled, pulled out a special folder and laid it on the table.

Chapter 24

Suzy and Hope arrived at the same time at Coconuts. Suzy was dressed in a flirty black and white skirt and a black top. Hope wore khaki Capri pants, a boxy brown top and sensible, flat sandals. Alex stole the show in a sexy red suit, black patent heels, and a large gold statement necklace.

"Alex, you look gorgeous. Big day at the bank today?" Suzy asked.

"As a matter of fact, yes. It was a very big day. I pitched my suggested name change to our board of directors." She grinned a mile wide. "And they loved it! The board unanimously approved the name change. And—" She paused for suspense.

"What?" Suzy and Hope asked in unison.

"They promoted me to vice president." Alex beamed.

Both women jumped up and hugged Alex. "This calls for a celebration," Suzy said.

Hope waved Gus to the table while Alex talked non-stop. "I'm thrilled they liked the new bank name and I'm beyond excited about my promotion. As far as the name change, now comes the hard part, all the branding."

Gus brought over chips and salsa.

"Compliments of the house, ladies, and your drinks are on me." Gus grinned. "I overheard something about a promotion."

Alex flashed a grateful, pearly smile. "You're the best."

Hope bit into a chip. "What exactly does branding mean?"

"Customers and the general public must easily identify

our new name and logo. It should be immediately identifiable with our new bank name."

"I still don't get branding," Hope admitted.

"When you see a big red bull's eye, what store do you think of?"

"Target."

"Exactly. They've done a brilliant job with branding using the bull's eye, the color red, and certain music during their commercials. Of course, Target is a corporate giant and it's just little old me coming up with a branding strategy. Essentially everything with the bank's old name must be changed."

"Like what?" Hope asked.

"Exterior signage, business cards, letterhead, billboards, TV spots, and Internet banking." She ticked the items off using her fingers. "I'm going to be swamped for months but I'm happy they liked my suggested name." Alex reached for a chip.

"Thinking about all that makes my head hurt. I'd rather plan weddings, but congrats, sweetie." Suzy raised a pretend glass since Gus had yet to bring her wine. "Here's to Alex."

"So, what's the new name anyway?" Hope asked.

"It was so obvious after I thought about it. They wanted a name with state-wide appeal, so I came up with, drum roll, please."

Alex drummed her two index fingers on the table.

"CNB will now be called Show-Me Bank, or SMB for short. What do you think?"

"Of course. Our state motto." Suzy's wine arrived. "It's perfect."

"Bravo," Hope echoed.

Gus passed around zebra-print menus. Alex ordered one of every appetizer to celebrate.

"There goes my diet," Hope said. "Just kidding. I'm never going to diet. I like food too much. Besides, guys hate bony women." She laughed.

The spring rolls, avocado dip, crab cakes, potato skins, and stuffed mushrooms arrived.

Alex held her wine glass up to the light checking for smudges. She then subtly inspected her silverware and placed it in her lap, never on the dirty table where people put their disgusting bathroom-floor, feces-laden purses.

Hope and Suzy had seen her routine many times. They cackled so hard they nearly fell off their chairs.

"What's so funny?" Alex asked.

"How can we put this delicately? Dear, sweet Alex. We love and adore you but you entertain us with your OCD," Hope said.

"What are you talking about?"

"I've looked through your cabinets. The glasses are in rows but they don't touch, horror of horrors. Your spice drawer is in alphabetical order. When we went grocery shopping, you straightened the bananas and the broccoli."

Alex's mouth flew open. "I did not—" She caught herself straightening the salt and pepper shakers on the table. "Oh. You might be right."

Hope almost choked on a spring roll she was laughing so hard. "Honey, I know I'm right. In your pantry, there's a shelf for fruit, another for veggies, and one for soups." She looked at Suzy. "Don't even think about putting fruit on the veggie shelf. I made that mistake once."

Suzy bit her lip to keep from laughing. She patted Alex on the arm. "Don't be mad at us but you know your canned goods are lined up like soldiers, like items together, with the fresh stock rotated, just like at the grocery store. Oh, well. I could use some of your organizational skills."

Alex gave both Hope and Suzy a playful punch. "Hey, enough. I'm not that bad, am I? Everyone has little quirks. Sheesh." She popped a crab cake into her mouth and shook her finger at her friends.

Alex smiled as she tied her discarded straw holder into a knot.

"That's another thing you do," Hope said.

Alex rolled the empty straw holder into a ball and threw it at her. "Ha ha."

"And don't ask her to walk barefoot, especially on dry wooden floors," Suzy added.

"What is this? Pick on Alex Day? Shut up." Alex crossed her arms, pretending to be upset.

"I think it's cute. You're cute. We can't let that vice presidential promotion go to your head," Suzy said.

"Come on. I just have a *touch* of OCD. I don't get up in the middle of the night to straighten the fringe on the rugs. Enough about me." She drained her drink. "What's going on with you, Hope?"

Hope looked at her friends with sad doe eyes. Obviously stalling, she took a bite of a spring roll and reached for a second one before answering.

"My parents drove into my mailbox and garage. Smashed them both to smithereens."

"What? How?" Suzy asked.

"Same old thing. They were drunk, stoned, or both. I've been talking to the insurance people about my deductible. I don't really want to talk about it."

Alex and Suzy looked at one other.

"I'm sorry. I wish they'd grow up," Suzy said.

"That pisses me off. They put such an unnecessary strain on you," Alex said. "Surely there's something good going on in your life." She leaned across the table and took her friend's hand.

Hope's face halfway lit up. "My students are my salvation. I have two groups of kids—either the at-risk kids, most of whom have parents like me, so I relate to them best. I love my honor students, too. They challenge me. I'm proud of all my kids."

Suzy grinned. "See what a difference you're making in these kids' lives? You should feel great about that."

"I do. It keeps me sane."

"What exactly do you do at school?" Alex asked.

"Every day is different but I mainly help the academic, high-achieving kids with their college applications and essays or I hold hands and counsel the students who have horrible home lives. They're all good kids and often come back to see me after they graduate." Hope pushed a frizzy curl out of her eyes.

"That says a lot about you," Suzy said.

"I love my job but there are some negatives about working at a school."

"What?" Suzy and Alex echoed in chorus.

Hope slid a dreaded pink slip across the table.

Suzy's eyebrows shot up. "Were you fired?"

Hope laughed. "Thankfully, no. This little pink slip, ladies, is what the principal hands out to students, faculty, and staff when there's a lice alert."

"Ewww," Alex said as she scratched her head.

"I know. Gross." Hope laughed. "But you get used to it."

"I don't think so. Are the kids freaking out?" Suzy asked.

"The girls are. They went to Walgreens on their lunch hour to buy RID and used it in the school bathroom. They were lined up at the sinks helping each other. Every single one was late to class. But the guys think it's hilarious. They're acting like monkeys and picking pretend nits off each other and eating them."

"Sounds just like the guys I went to school with." Suzy laughed.

Hope noticed both Suzy and Alex were scratching their heads and subtly scooting slightly away from her—especially Alex.

"Hey, relax. I don't have lice. I used the RID, too. Look at my scalp!" She leaned over so the women could examine it.

"Can we talk about something else?" Alex clawed at her head one last time and glanced at her watch. "It's nearly midnight. I'll never wake up in time for work tomorrow." She stood and brushed crumbs off her red suit.

"I didn't realize it was so late. I've got to run too. Maria and Scott's wedding is coming right up."

"Good luck with that," Alex said.

"Congrats again, Alex," Hope added.

They paid the bill, hugged, and drove their separate ways.

As Hope pulled up to her house, she saw a large note attached to the front door. She parked outside the garage since the door was crumpled. What a day. First, a lice alert. Now what?

Chapter 25

She walked up to the door and read the note. It was written in her mother's loopy handwriting with her childish manner of dotting every "i" with a heart.

Hi, Hope!!!

We borrowed a friend's RV and are driving to Washington, D.C. to protest this damn war. Exciting, huh? We'll see you in a week or so. Watch the news. Maybe we'll be on TV!!!

Love and Peace,

Montana and Larry (AKA, Mom and Dad)

P.S. Thanks for the beer and snacks. Hope you don't mind. We needed some grub for the road.

Hope wasn't surprised. Nothing about her parents surprised her any more. She stared at the large peace sign her mother had drawn at the bottom of the page and started talking to no one in particular.

"Sure, no problem. Help yourself to my food. Drive halfway across the country. I'll just keep working with the insurance guy to fix my damn garage door and mailbox. Don't worry. You two have a merry road trip."

Hope sulked into her kitchen and opened the cabinets. She gasped. The shelves were nearly bare. Her parents had taken cereal, chips, peanut butter, crackers, squeeze cheese, raisins, granola bars, bottled water, beer, soda, and anything else that wasn't nailed down. Tears welled in her eyes. She shook her head and walked away. Her meager counselor's salary barely paid her bills but her parents couldn't seem to grasp that.

Walking toward her bedroom, Hope fumed. She wondered when her parents came up with the idea to hop into an RV and drive to Washington, D.C. Yet, what was holding them back? Certainly not a job. She wondered whose RV they had borrowed. *God only knows how they're going to pay for the gasoline.*

Hope could just picture Montana wearing short cut-offs and Larry with his signature tie-dye shirt. They'd go to every truck stop for meals. Larry would most likely pull out his guitar and literally sing for his supper. The windows would be down with rock music blaring. Their long, stringy blonde hair would be blowing in the wind. Recently, Larry had sported a long braid down his back like Willie Nelson. Each night, they'd probably sit around some campsite, make friends with other hippies, belt out songs, drink beer or smoke joints. Even though they drove her crazy, she hoped they would be safe.

Hope looked in her bedroom mirror and checked her scalp again. She wondered why she didn't inherit her parents' straight, blond hair. Pulling her frizzy, brown hair down the middle to check her part, she decided another dose of RID might make her hair fall out. She rummaged in her drawer, found some comfortable PJ's and fell fast asleep.

When she awoke the next morning, she searched for something to eat. At least they left half a box of Cheerios and coffee. She made coffee, ate dry cereal, and turned the television on. CNN was reporting breaking news near the White House. Behind the reporter, throngs of protesters chanted and held signs declaring "Peace not War." Hope sipped her coffee and watched. Police officers with batons tried to hold the protesters at bay. The crowd was inflamed. *Just perfect.* The angry mob yelled at the cops arms outstretched, forming a human barricade. Hope squinted to see if she could see her parents in the crowd. It was impossible; there were too many people.

The demonstration made her uneasy. She sipped her coffee and tried to shake off her worry. She hated the war but admired the military men and women for putting themselves on the line. She admired their patriotism, sacrifice, and focus. Some of her students had visited recruiters' offices. Many were attracted to the college benefits and sign-on bonuses. Others were simply patriotic. Hope was proud of her students who had joined the military but worried about them often. Lost in her thoughts, she glanced at the large clock in her kitchen. She had to shower and leave.

When she reached Hilltop High, a teacher in the hallway said, "Did you see those protesters this morning? It really got out of hand. The police had some on the ground in handcuffs." The teacher shook her head disapprovingly. "Others were thrown in a paddy wagon and hauled off."

Hope shuddered, thinking the worst. When she walked into her office, her favorite unruly student was sitting in a chair across from her desk.

"Britney, why aren't you in class?"

"I need to talk to you." The freckled redhead's voice cracked.

"What's wrong?"

"It's my parents. I hate them. I ran away last night."

Hope could see fear and hurt in Britney's eyes. "Where did you stay? Do your parents know where you are?"

"I was with a friend." Britney wiped her runny nose with her sleeve. "They don't know where I am and they don't care."

Hope could relate but didn't say so. "I'm sure they're very concerned about you. What's your phone number?" She reached for the telephone.

"Please don't call them," Britney pleaded. "They're getting a divorce. My mom already has a boyfriend. She's much more interested in him than me. I can't go home. I won't go home. Can I stay at your house for a while? Please?"

Hope hated to turn her down. "Britney, I'm sorry but our school policy doesn't allow that. It could look inappropriate."

"I won't eat much. And I won't tell anyone."

Hope felt her own eyes fill with tears. She loved her students but knew she couldn't take the risk. "Listen, Britney. Come back to my office after school and I'll take you out for pizza. Would you like that?"

She bobbed her head.

Hope continued, "Afterward, I'll have to take you home. I'm sure your parents are worried sick. For now, you need to get to class."

Still sniffling, Britney picked up her ratty backpack, and left.

Later that day, Hope worried about Larry and Montana and wondered if they were still protesting. She sat at the computer with an honor student, Billy, and helped him search for college scholarships. As she pointed to her favorite financial aid site, her phone rang.

"Hope Tru—"

"It's Montana. I mean Mom. We're in trouble."

"Where are you?"

"I don't know how to tell you this but we're in jail."

"Mom. What the—?" She caught herself since Billy was in her office. "What happened?"

"Please don't be mad. This is my only phone call so listen, okay? We need bail money. Can you go to the bank and wire some money?"

Hope couldn't believe her ears. "How much?"

"Five hundred." Montana paused. "Each."

"I don't have one thousand dollars, Mom. I'm still trying to fix the garage door, remember?"

"Are you going to leave us in jail? You're our only chance. You've got to find the money somewhere. They're telling me I have to hang up. Here's the name of the jail. Please help us." Montana hung up.

Hope stared into the phone, hung it up forcefully, and jotted down the information. Because of Billy, she composed herself but wanted to throw something. Anything.

"Billy, I have a situation. We'll have to finish this search tomorrow."

"Okay, Mrs. Truman. Same time tomorrow?"

Hope felt her face tighten and nodded. Billy must have sensed something awry and gathered his school folder quickly.

Hope didn't know who to ask. She didn't have the money. She decided to call Alex at the bank.

After Hope explained the situation, Alex agreed to loan her the money. Alex explained she wasn't exactly swimming in money but did have a few thousand in savings and was happy to help her friend.

"Come over around four thirty before the lobby closes and I'll help you wire the money. We'll keep this between us. I know you have your hands full with them. It's almost like having children, isn't it?"

Hope could barely speak. She was so relieved, albeit embarrassed, and finally got past the lump in her throat to express her gratitude. After she hung up, she slammed her fist on the desk. *Why won't they grow up?* Then, she remembered Britney.

Chapter 26

Hope gripped the steering wheel of her gray Honda, embarrassed she had to impose on Alex to bail out her parents. She was sick and tired of their antics and was ready to give them a piece of her mind. As soon as they returned from D.C., she would put her foot down. No more shenanigans.

After leaving the bank, she tried to console Britney over pizza and knew all too well what her young student was going through with a deadbeat parent. Later when she took Britney home, Hope spent fifteen minutes on the porch being chewed out by Britney's mother who told her to butt out of their lives.

The next day after school Hope groaned when she saw her parents' rickety yellow VW bus in her driveway, leaking oil all over the concrete. *They must have driven nonstop after I sprang them from jail.* She screeched to a loud stop and walked toward her house.

The door was open and the stereo blared "Never Been to Spain" by the Three Dog Night. The volume nearly blew out her ear drums. Completely stoned or drunk, her parents slept right through it. Larry was sprawled on the couch and Montana snored in the recliner.

I'm surprised they're not in my bed.

Shirtless, Larry had on grungy, ripped jeans, his long hair braided. The television remote was in his hand, yet he was sound asleep. Montana had passed out with her latest lime green macramé creation in her lap.

Hope opened the refrigerator to see that it was nearly bare. Again. No way. She had just restocked after they cleaned her out before D.C. Bags of opened chips scattered the counter, half-eaten microwave popcorn was in a large mixing bowl and a bag of chocolate chip cookies lay open on the table, already attracting ants. The trashcan overflowed with beer cans and bottled water.

She shook her head at the mess and suspected her parents had the munchies from smoking pot. Hope fumed and gritted her teeth. This was it. She wasn't going to enable them one more day. Alex and Suzy were right. Larry and Montana needed tough love. No more sponging and living off their daughter. Hope stomped into the living room and turned off the blaring stereo.

"Get up. GET UP," she screamed. "Now."

Her parents awakened out of their stupor. Montana stretched while Larry blinked and yawned.

Hope glared at them. "I've had it. Listen to me. You need to get a life and get out of mine."

"Hey, Hope," Larry said, dismissing her as if he hadn't heard a word she said. It was though he had completely forgotten being sprung from jail.

Hope ran her fingers through her frizzy hair. "Listen up. Both of you. I'm sick of you coming over to *my* house, eating *my* food, watching *my* television, and drinking *my* beer. I can't keep supporting you like this. I'm tired of taking care of you. I've had it." She started sobbing. "Do you hear me? I'm. Sick. Of. This. No more."

Larry opened his mouth as if to say something and mercifully closed it.

"Why can't you two be normal?" She crossed her arms defiantly and sniffed the air. "I smell marijuana. Are you trying to get me arrested? Do you want me to lose my job? What is wrong with you two?"

Hope's voice got louder. "GROW UP. I'm done." She grabbed the remote out of Larry's hand and threw it across the room. It smashed a lamp.

Montana and Larry sat mute, probably still trying to focus.

Finally letting loose years of pent-up anger and frustration, Hope exploded. "Just look at your hair, Dad. It's twice as long as mine. Do you see other men with hair past their shoulders? This isn't the seventies anymore. And Mom, you look ridiculous. You dress like a cheap teenage whore. I don't know how I ended up with parents like you," Hope said through loud gulping sobs.

Larry edged himself from the couch and slowly started to stand.

"Sit down. I'm not finished," Hope yelled.

"Do you even *remember* that I bailed you out of jail? I didn't have one thousand dollars. I had to get a loan from my friend. I also just paid for the garage door that one of you smashed. Do you remember *any* of that or are you too stoned to remember? You're both a total embarrassment." Hope sat on the floor, put her head in her hands, and wept.

Larry seemed oblivious or indifferent. It was hard to tell. Montana stared at Hope, still slightly dazed.

"Hope, we'll leave but we don't have any bread. Can you help us out?" Larry asked.

Montana looked at Hope eagerly.

"Bread as in wheat or rye?"

"Cash. Dough. You know what I mean," Larry said.

"No one calls it 'bread' anymore. When are you going to join us in this decade," she said hotly.

"Okay, money. We need some money. We didn't pay our rent before we went to D.C. and now our hard ass manager wants two months' rent. We don't have it. Otherwise, he said he'll evict us. If that happens, we'll have to move in with you."

"If that's okay with you," Montana added with a timid smile.

It was as if her outburst didn't register. As if they didn't hear a single word she had said. All her parents wanted was another handout. Hope was furious. She felt like her shirt was going to rip open like the Incredible Hulk. She put her hands on her hips with her feet planted defiantly.

"No, it is *not* okay. Get a job. *Any* job. I'm not a money tree. I've already spent money on you that I didn't have. The well is dry. Get it? Can you get that through your thick, stoned heads?"

Larry looked dumbfounded. "What are we going to do?"

"That's your problem." Hope screamed through clenched teeth. "Now, take your beer and get out. I want you both out of here. Don't come back until you have a job and can support yourselves." Tears streamed down her checks. She was surprised by her resolve. And proud of herself. She had finally stood up to her parents.

Larry and Montana didn't say a word. They finally seemed to get the message. They gathered their shoes, extinguished what was left of their joints, and walked toward the front door.

The screen door creaked open. Larry walked out and looked over his shoulder. "I'm sorry."

"Don't worry. We won't come back unless you invite us." Montana's voice had a new edge.

Her father's apologetic comment made Hope cry harder. What had she done? She had now isolated herself from her own parents. She had told her own parents to get a life and leave her alone. She had kicked them out of her house. She was their only child. Hope ran to the door to hug them. She wanted to tell them she still loved them before they got into their pathetic old jalopy and sped away. But it was too late. She could hear the song, "Papa Was a Rollin' Stone," blaring as they rounded the corner. What an appropriate song, she thought. "*Wherever he laid his hat was his home...*"

Hope paced. She couldn't call her parents because they couldn't afford a landline phone. She had stopped paying their cell phone bill, so they were phoneless. She tried to tell herself she did the right thing. She had to let them go. Tough love. That's what Suzy and Alex had suggested. So why did she feel so terrible? Hope fell to the floor and bawled. She felt guilty. Terribly guilty. Wiping her tears on her shirt sleeve, she told herself over and over that she did the right thing. After second-guessing her decision to throw her parents out, Hope cried herself to sleep on the cold, hard kitchen floor.

Chapter 27

Suzy was almost sad Maria and Scott's wedding was nearly over. They had been the ideal couple to work with. She glanced around the outside reception. Guests lingered by the food and bar. The DJ played the song, "Celebrate." Maria's bridesmaids sipped margaritas, laughing. Their brightly colored dresses were perfect. Standing beside one another, they looked like a box of colorful crayons. The groomsmen looked smart in their black tuxes and gem-colored ties while carefully—and some not-so-carefully—munching on tacos and spinach enchiladas. Suzy grimaced at the thought of a taco stain on one of those gorgeous ties.

The southwestern theme was a hit. Platters of spicy food were surrounded by large Mexican sombreros. Clay candles adorned each table. For favors, guests received a miniature cactus in a small pottery planter tied with ribbons in jewel colors to match the bridesmaids' dresses. The piñatas were popular with the kids and guests praised the mouth-watering menu.

The grand plan looked as though it would go off without a hitch. Suzy looked up and mouthed a thank you for the perfect blue skies and slight wind. She took the microphone, calling the guests and wedding party to the nearby field. Everyone gathered in the field as Maria and Scott climbed into a brightly colored hot air balloon. The guests waved, whistled, and cheered as Maria and Scott slowly took flight. Maria leaned gingerly over the side, smiling from ear to ear. As the balloon ascended, her long lacy veil blew in the wind. Scott gave a thumbs up to the cheering crowd and gave his bride a lingering kiss. Everyone cheered as the balloon rose above the treetops.

Suzy arranged for Maria and Scott to have a romantic forty-five minute balloon ride prior to landing in an open field. A limousine was on standby to take them to the airport. She had ordered fruit, cheese, champagne, and two engraved flutes to be placed in their hotel suite, as a personal gift, upon their arrival in New Mexico.

At ease, Suzy allowed herself to bask in the glow of the lovely wedding and reception. It had been a perfect day for a delightful couple. She smiled dreamily. *Maybe this is my destiny. Maybe I'm here to fulfill other couple's dreams. This is a great life and I'm a darn good wedding planner.* She grinned to herself and watched the adoring crowd continue to wave and cheer.

When Maria and Scott had drifted out of sight, Suzy watched the catering staff clear the plates and wheel off the remaining wedding cake. The DJ wound up his cables and guests headed toward their cars. Her ringing cell phone jarred her idyllic thoughts.

"Is this Suzanne Jacobs, the wedding planner?" the caller asked in a brisk, southern drawl.

"Yes, this is Suzy Jacobs with Weddings By Suzanne."

In a terse voice the woman said, "My name is Mrs. Biltmore. I need to meet with you right away to discuss my daughter's wedding."

Suzy retracted her planner from her purse—an old habit she preferred over her Smartphone. She thumbed through the pages with her phone cradled between her shoulder and ear.

"I'm actually at one of my weddings right now. What day would you like to meet?"

"Don't you understand 'right away?' I mean *now*," Mrs. Biltmore demanded.

Suzy stiffened. *What a way to end a tranquil, gorgeous day.* As firmly as she could, she repeated, "As I said, I'm *at* a wedding I planned at the moment." She paused and took a deep breath, not one to turn down business. "I can be free in an hour. Would you like to meet at Coconuts?"

"Isn't that a bar?" Mrs. Biltmore asked with mock horror in her voice.

"It's actually a restaurant too."

"No, absolutely not. I don't step foot in tawdry bars."

"It's very nice and definitely not taw—"

Mrs. Biltmore cut her off. "I'd prefer to meet at *my* country club, the Biltmore Country Club. Surely you've heard of it. I can have a car pick you up. Where are you?"

Suzy smirked into the phone. "That won't be necessary. I know where the club is. I'll drive there myself."

"The Biltmore Country Club is not a 'club.' We've worked hard to build a reputable name and I'll have you call it by its proper name, thank you."

Suzy stifled a snicker. *What a bitchy broad.* But she found her professional voice.

"Certainly, Mrs. Biltmore. I'll meet you at the Biltmore Country Club. It's on Biltmore Road, correct?" she said in her sweetest, most accommodating voice.

"That's right. I'll see you in one hour sharp."

She apparently didn't catch the amusement in Suzy's voice.

Suzy turned her phone off and looked toward the skies. *I hope you're enjoying yourselves, Maria and Scott. Thanks for the sweet memories. I'm afraid this next wedding is going to be a doozy.*

She walked past the outdoor bar on the way to her car. The bartender had already carried off the liquor or she might have had a quick drink to bolster herself for what was sure to be an intriguing appointment. Satisfied that the cleanup was nearly finished, she said her goodbyes and drove away.

As Suzy pulled up to the country club, she spotted a short, frail-looking woman in a stylish, plum suit carrying an expensive ivory Chanel purse. The woman's arms were crossed and Suzy could see she was impatiently tapping a snakeskin shoe on the sidewalk. Suzy took a deep breath to ready herself, gathered a legal pad, and walked toward the massive wooden entrance. In the center of each door, was an enormous engraved "B." *Could this get any more pretentious?*

Somehow, the tiny woman held the heavy-looking door open with ease.

"Are you Suzanne Jacobs?"

"Yes, call me Suzy. You must be Mrs. Biltmore." Suzy extended her hand as she stepped inside the gold embellished foyer. *Donald Trump would be proud.*

Mrs. Biltmore kept her hands to her side. "I don't shake hands. Germs. Let's go inside and have a bite to eat. I'm starving. Then we'll discuss the wedding."

After they walked up a few wooden and brass stairs to the ornate landing filled with oriental rugs and gigantic floral arrangements, Mrs. Biltmore took a moment and looked at Suzy from head to toe. She could obviously see that Suzy was wearing an ivory ruffled sundress, bold turquoise jewelry and nude wedge sandals, a must for outdoor weddings so her heels wouldn't sink into the ground.

"Didn't you say you just came from one of your weddings?" Before Suzy could answer, Mrs. Biltmore added, "Don't you think you're dressed rather casually?"

Suzy blushed. "It was an outdoor wedding. I think I'm dressed perfectly."

Mrs. Biltmore waved her hand dismissively. "Oh, well. You'll be properly dressed for my daughter's wedding if I have to buy your dress myself. Come along." She waved impatiently. "Let's go inside the dining room. They're holding a table for us."

Suzy followed Mrs. Biltmore, wondering what the hell she was getting herself into.

Chapter 28

After viewing some of the laughable possibilities online, Alex decided to suspend any idea of Internet dating. Who had the time to weed through the losers, cheaters and con artists? Instead, she threw herself into her work. She spent the day creating artwork for the new Show-Me Bank billboards. Her thoughts wandered to Tony, as usual. Even though he was separated, she was glad she didn't have to search the Internet for a date. She knew she wasn't exactly *dating* Tony but loved having him around in, even in small doses and even if she shouldn't.

When she got up to stretch and get a drink, Alex was thrilled and surprised to see a patrol car sitting in front of her house. Tony usually drove an unmarked car. Her heart pounded even though their last discussion had been about trying to keep each other at arm's length. She had to admit she loved his surprise visits.

Alex glanced in the mirror, fluffed her long, blonde hair and sprayed a light mist of perfume. She walked outside and tapped on his car window. Tony lowered it and smiled. She could hear him talking to a dispatcher.

While listening, he cocked his head and his eyebrows furrowed. "I'll be right there." He turned to Alex. "That was Walgreens again. It's always either Walgreens or Target."

"What are you talking about? A robbery?"

"No." He laughed. "It's Mrs. Magilicutty. She's an old woman who shoplifts. I've worked out an agreement where the stores call me instead of questioning her. The stores know I'll pay for the items she takes if they don't press charges."

"Why would you do that?"

"She's elderly, a widow with no children. For some reason, she gets a kick out of shoplifting. She's been doing this for over a year. Must be a kleptomaniac." He shook his head and chuckled.

"What does she steal?"

"Silly things like lipstick, makeup, candy—even travel-sized toothpaste. I know seniors are on fixed budgets but I've seen Mrs. Magilicutty's house. It's nice. And she has a new car. She's either losing it or she enjoys the thrill, I'm not sure which."

"Why have you taken a special interest in her?"

"I was at Walgreens once in civilian clothing when I saw her put some nail polish in her pocket. The security guard came bounding over and was really rough with her. It pissed me off. She could have had a heart attack over some stupid nail polish."

His voice softened. "And she reminds me of my grandmother. Don't get me wrong. My grandmother didn't steal things but both ladies have white hair, large glasses and are stooped."

Laughing, he added, "She draws arched eyebrows so perfectly McDonald's would be jealous. And, just like my grandmother, she has a purse big enough to carry a raccoon." He laughed. "She can put a lot of merchandise in that big bag."

Alex laughed so hard her stomach hurt.

"That's why I took her under my wing. She's a quirky old lady who reminds me of my grandma. That's all." He grinned at Alex.

Alex's heart melted every time she saw him and even more so now knowing how Tony sticks his neck out for little old ladies.

Tony rubbed his forehead. "I can't bear to think of Mrs. Magilicutty with a record. Or worse, in jail with no one to bail her out. It's easier to just pay for the items she steals."

Alex was falling hard for this guy and fast—especially after hearing this softer side. She was used to hearing how jaded he was. She liked this part of his personality much better. She hoped if she ever got old and senile a nice police officer would look after her.

"So, that's the story. I'm heading to Walgreens now to pay for whatever she took. Want to come along?"

Alex's eyes widened. "You mean it's okay? To ride in the patrol car, I mean."

"No. It's completely against the rules but I can probably make an exception in your case. I mean we're just going to Walgreens and I'm officially off duty. I came straight to your house after my shift." He reached through the window and touched her hand. "I had to see you."

Alex's pulse quickened. "I'd love to go. This is exciting. No one will ever know. I'd like to see what it feels like to be a cop for a little while."

"Just let me go to the bathroom first," he said. They walked inside.

Alex quickly changed into jeans and a white T-shirt. When Tony reappeared, he tightened his gun and holster around his waist. His gun made Alex nervous. "Do you have to take that?"

He nodded. "Absolutely. Wouldn't be without it." He talked into his shoulder radio, telling headquarters he was going to Walgreens to take care of a small matter, even though he was off duty.

"Don't get into any mischief." The police dispatcher laughed.

"Ten four, good buddy," Tony joked back.

"Let's roll."

They climbed in and buckled up as Alex looked over her left shoulder at the bars between the front and back seat. She shuddered as she wondered how many criminals had been hauled to jail in this car. And how many germs were in the car. She placed her hands on her lap, trying to avoid touching anything.

After settling the score at Walgreens for a fake-tanning product Mrs. Maligicutty had stolen—*and why in the world would an eighty-something woman want a tan*?—they turned onto Oak Street and headed north.

"Want to go for a little ride?" Tony asked.

"Sure but this part of town is depressing."

"Why? Because it's run-down?"

Because all of the homeless shelters are here."

"At least they have shelters. If half of the SOB's would either get a job or get off drugs and alcohol, they'd be fine. Some of them have chosen this life over their own family. Many are scam artists. They're filth as far as I'm concerned." Tony clenched his jaw.

Alex thought he was too harsh but didn't say anything. She had to admit if she dealt with criminals all day she'd probably be hardened, too. When they got to Commercial Street, Tony headed west.

He leaned forward, mouth open. "I can't believe it. There's that little prick. I've been trying to catch that bastard for three months. He's a wily piece of shit."

"Uh. Aren't you off duty?"

"I'm not losing this bastard again. I've been searching for this scum far too long. Hold on."

Alex sat frozen as Tony slammed the gas pedal to the floor. She glanced at the speedometer. He was going nearly 80 miles per hour in a 30 mile per hour speed zone. She pressed the buckle on her seat belt to make sure it was securely latched.

"Sit tight." Tony flipped switches and in seconds had lights swirling and sirens blaring.

The rusted-out blue Camaro they chased really hugged the curves. Alex felt like she was in the Indy 500 and was afraid to utter a word. She didn't want to break Tony's concentration. Her heart raced as she swallowed hard, wondering how this was going to end.

Chapter 29

Tony was visibly agitated as the Camaro dangerously wove in and out of traffic. His nostrils flared and he squinted, even though the sun was setting and not in his eyes.

"You fucking son of a bitch," he shouted. "You're not getting away from me again." Tony increased his speed to 100 miles per hour.

Alex had a lump in her throat the size of a peach pit. She suddenly wished they were back in her cozy living room watching a movie.

"I've got to call for back up. This dirt bag isn't going to stop. Listen, Alex, if anyone asks, you're a reporter."

"A reporter?"

"Yes, you're doing some kind of story. Think of something. Fast. I have to concentrate. You shouldn't be in the patrol car with me unless you're a criminal or my partner. Listen, this guy is dangerous. He's one of the biggest meth dealers in town and I've been trying to catch the bastard for months. There's no telling how many lives he has destroyed with meth. I'd love nothing better than to run his skinny pockmarked ass up a flag pole."

Alex had never seen Tony in action before. Not in a high speed chase anyway. In addition to being scared out of her mind, she was getting an adrenaline rush and becoming strangely turned on. She stared at his chiseled face and would like nothing better than for him to pull over and take her. But she knew that wasn't about to happen. Not now.

Tony yelled into the microphone. "This is Sgt. Tony

Montgomery. I'm in pursuit of license number CTU 298, a blue, rusted-out Camaro, probably an '87.

"Copy that," said the gravelly voiced dispatcher. "What's your location?"

"Heading south on Courtney Avenue, just south of Commercial. Suspect is a known meth dealer. Send back up NOW. Whoever is patrolling the area needs to put down some spike strips on my command. I want to blow out this fucker's tires. Copy?"

"Sgt. Young is in your area. He's on West Alpine, heading in your direction."

"Copy."

Tony gripped the wheel and stared ahead with laser focus.

"Those spike strips sound like a good idea. I'm doing a story on the day in the life of a policeman."

"What?" yelled Tony as he concentrated on his driving while wiping sweat off his brow.

"If anyone asks, I'm a reporter doing a story on a day in the life of a policeman—or policewoman," she said.

"Got it. Sounds good." Tony bore down again on the gas pedal. The Camaro was now heading east on the Expressway toward Alpine.

Alex was afraid to look but glanced at the speedometer. It read 120 miles per hour. She realized she was holding her breath and was glad there weren't many cars on the road. She said a quick prayer that they wouldn't crash.

As Tony glanced to his left, Alex followed his line of vision and spotted another patrol car. The Camaro took a quick right.

"I'm going to catch that prick if it's the last thing I do. Sorry, Alex. Don't be scared. This bastard got away from me once. That's not going to happen again."

"I'm okay," Alex said shakily, wondering if her heart would burst out of her chest.

The scanner crackled. “Sgt. Montgomery. This is Sgt. Young. Are you ready for the spike strips? I’m about six blocks away.”

“Not yet. Stay with me. I want to make sure he doesn’t make a quick turn. Call for back up to block off the side streets.”

“Will do. Uh, when you drove past, it looked like you had a passenger in the car.”

Tony glanced at Alex and raised his eyebrows. “I do. A reporter.”

There was a long, loud silence before Sgt. Young responded with a sigh. “They always pick the best times, don’t they? The chief is going to love this one. Can’t worry about that now. Let’s get this jerk. I’ll head him off on Central Avenue.”

“Good. We’ll trap him. It’s a dead-end street. I want to haul him in. I’ve been trying to catch this pathetic piece of work for months. He’s been lying low. I was about to come to the conclusion that he was living in a cave in Afghanistan.”

Sgt. Young laughed. Alex got paler by the minute and Tony was visibly excited as he closed in on the Camaro.

Alex watched Sgt. Young turn his car sharply several yards ahead of the Camaro, blocking his path. Tony zeroed in behind him with one hand on the wheel and the other on his gun. Alex couldn’t breathe. They watched and waited for the Camaro to stop since both patrol cars had him trapped.

Instead, the driver floored it and drove right into Sgt. Young’s car. There was a huge fireball followed by black smoke. Tony slammed the brakes and skidded as his car turned sideways. He barely had the car in park and yelled “Stay here” as he ran toward Sgt. Young.

Alex sat frozen on the seat listening to scanner static and watching the growing blaze and black plume. As the blaze grew larger, she grabbed the hand-held microphone and pressed a button.

"Hello. Help. Send a fire truck. There's been an accident involving Sgt. Montgomery and Sgt. Young." She desperately fought back tears and looked out the window frantically searching for Tony. The smoke was so thick she could barely see five feet ahead.

The police radio came to life. A dispatcher barked, "Where is Sgt. Montgomery and what is your location?"

"Uh, we're on Central, just off the Expressway and Alpine."

"Who is this?" the dispatcher croaked.

"Um," Alex paused, afraid to lie but remembering what Tony had told her. "I'm a reporter. I was doing a story while riding with Sgt. Montgomery."

The dispatcher was all business. "Can you see Sgt. Montgomery or Sgt. Young?"

"No, I can't see anything. The smoke is very thick. Let me get out of this car and check."

"Stay where you are," the dispatcher barked. "Do not, I repeat, do not leave the patrol car under any circumstances. I'm sending back up, a fire truck, and an ambulance right now."

"Good. Thank God. Please hurry," begged Alex.

She sat there for what seemed like an eternity but was probably less than five minutes. She couldn't take it any more. She had to find Tony. Alex unhooked her seat belt, and knowing the meth dealer was out there somewhere, she opened her door as quietly as possible, trying to avoid a sound. She looked around through the smoky night but couldn't see Tony. She walked closer to the blaze. She was afraid to go too close, fearing the car could blow up at any minute.

Alex's eyes prickled with tears as she stared at the giant yellow and red fireball and the billowing dark smoke. Embers crackled and popped. Alex held her hand over her mouth and nose to block the strong smoke odor. She looked toward the street, willing the sound of helpful sirens. Trembling and cold, she crossed her arms in front of her. She had never felt so alone and scared in her life.

Chapter 30

As Suzy and Mrs. Biltmore entered the dining room, the servers stood ramrod straight when they spotted their employer. Suzy detected fear in their eyes and noticed how they managed to smile without actually looking Mrs. Biltmore in the eye.

"Hello, Mrs. Biltmore. Good evening, Mrs. Biltmore. How do you do, Mrs. Biltmore. Good to see you, Mrs. Biltmore," were some of the greetings Suzy heard from the deer-in-headlights staff.

She already felt sorry for them and could only imagine how they were treated. It was pretty obvious they were afraid of Mrs. B. That was going to be Suzy's new name for her. Privately, of course.

"Sit down. Sit down," said Mrs. Biltmore impatiently. "Menus, we need menus. And water." She barked at the servers as they scampered away like scared rabbits.

Immediately they were handed glasses with water and lemon slices. Menus were thrust in their hands and linen napkins placed in their laps.

"When is everyone here going to remember? I prefer *orange* slices in my water, not lemon." She pushed the water away as though it were a dirty sock.

"I apologize, Mrs. Biltmore. I'll get you some fresh water." The nervous server looked at Suzy. "Would you like orange slices as well, madam?"

"My water is just fine."

Mrs. B sighed. "Employees. You can't get good help

these days. We have such a high turnover here. I can't understand it."

Suzy squelched a snicker. She understood the problem immediately.

"Let's get down to it. My daughter, Emma, is getting married. This is her first marriage and I want it to be perfect. Do you hear me? Per-fect." She pursed her lips as she looked at Suzy.

"Got it. Actually, I strive for all of my weddings to be perfect. What type of wedding do you have in mind?"

"A good, old-fashioned southern wedding. We're from the south, you know. The Biltmores are from Atlanta, Georgia. We've brought our southern charm here to Missouri by offering the marvelous Biltmore Country Club to you people," she drawled.

Suzy almost choked on her water. Southern charm? You must be kidding.

"Go on," she urged, trying not to smirk.

"You tell me. *You're* the wedding planner. I want a lovely southern wedding. The best. Now where is my water with those orange slices?"

The server magically appeared and placed the water before her, timidly awaiting her approval. "A-are you ready to order, Mrs. Biltmore?" he stammered.

"I'm on a diet, as you should well know. My daughter is getting married and I've got to fit into my Versace dress." She cleared her throat. "Therefore, I'll have the Biltmore house salad, Biltmore dressing, on the side, and some low-fat crackers. And fruit. Whatever is fresh—and everything had better be fresh, right—" She leaned forward to read the server's name tag. "Ryan?"

"Yes, ma'am." He looked at Suzy. "What can I get for you?"

"I'll have the same. I'm easy to please." Suzy smiled at a grateful-looking Ryan.

Suzy wondered where the bride was. Shouldn't she be here with her mother? She couldn't resist asking the obvious. "Is Emma going to join us?"

Mrs. Biltmore's face clouded as she took a small sip of water. She waved over the server. "I'll have a glass of Cabernet too. Suzy, would you care to join me? I don't like to drink alone."

Suzy happily nodded. She could use a drink.

The server disappeared behind a mahogany bar showcasing a large hand-chiseled "B" on the front. Mrs. Biltmore waited until he returned while Suzy's question hung in the air.

Mrs. Biltmore smelled and swirled her red wine before taking a long, slow sip. "Well, you see, my daughter is not—how shall I put this? She's not in total agreement about this wedding. That is why she isn't here. In fact, she doesn't even know I'm meeting with you."

Suzy's brows knitted with concern. She took a sip of wine before further questioning.

"What do you mean? Why isn't she in agreement about the wedding?"

Mrs. Biltmore's heavily made up, wrinkled face looked strained. Her thin red lips were in a straight line.

"I really didn't want to get into all of this. I thought we could go ahead and plan the wedding, and in the meanwhile, my Emma will come to her senses. She always does."

Suzy leaned forward, giving Mrs. B her full attention. "This is very unusual. I'll need to know more before I agree to this wedding. Please continue."

Mrs. Biltmore looked from side to side, obviously to see if anyone was within earshot. They weren't. The servers, while on point, gave her a wide berth. And no one was seated within ten feet of their table. Suzy could see why.

Mrs. Biltmore held her chin high. "You see, Emma doesn't know what's best for her. *I* know what's best for her.

She thinks she's in love with this ridiculous man who doesn't have a good job, let alone a good pedigree. In fact," she leaned forward and whispered, "I don't think he's fully Caucasian. He may be part Hispanic or black or Italian or something. He's dark-skinned." She held her nose high and sniffed.

Suzy sat in horrified silence, afraid to make any statement whatsoever to this racist, domineering woman while on her turf. She couldn't believe what she was hearing—and from the bride's mother no less.

Mrs. Biltmore continued, "Don't get me wrong. I'm not a racist."

Suzy cocked her head but didn't utter a word.

"I'm not. I have friends of other races. A couple, anyway. This man is just not up to snuff and my Emma cannot marry him. I just won't have it."

She downed her wine. "Besides, I have the perfect man for Emma. His name is Lincoln. He comes from a good southern family. He's well bred, intelligent, and wealthy. I grew up with his mother. You see, Emma and Lincoln dated briefly in high school and he's still madly in love with her, plus I want Lincoln to be my son-in-law. End of story." She studied her liver-spotted hands briefly before making eye contact with Suzy.

Suzy squirmed in her chair. She could tell Mrs. B thought she was doing the right thing but couldn't believe this woman was so out of touch with her staff and especially with her own daughter. Suzy crossed and re-crossed her legs, stalling. An arranged marriage in the Twenty-first Century. She knew it happened in other countries but not in America. Surely not. She could barely believe her ears.

"How old is Emma, may I ask?"

"She's thirty-five. That's another reason why she needs to make the right choice *now*. I can't wait much longer to have grandchildren. It's important that we carry on the Biltmore name in the proper way with the proper blood line." She dabbed her painted lips and refolded her napkin.

"If my Emma marries this—this low life and comes to her senses later, she'll lose precious baby-making years. We can't have that. It has to be done correctly the first time around. That's why I'm taking charge."

Suzy's mouth flew open. "But to a man she doesn't love? Does this Lincoln fellow even know you're doing this?"

"Of course he knows," Mrs. Biltmore snapped. "And it's not your place to judge. You just need to worry about the wedding details. You're a wedding planner, aren't you? We're wasting time. Let's get down to the wedding plans. Take out a pad and make notes."

Suzy's stomach gnawed at her and it wasn't from hunger. She didn't want to be a part of anything so shady and wrong. She wondered if Mrs. Biltmore even knew the background of the other man—the man Emma loved. Somehow, she doubted it. She sighed, pulled out a legal pad and a pink Weddings by Suzanne pen. Then, she immediately stuffed them back in her briefcase.

"I'm sorry, Mrs. Biltmore, but I can't be your wedding planner—or Emma's wedding planner." Suzy reached for her purse and scooted her chair back.

Mrs. Biltmore leaned forward and hissed. "You will do this. I'll pay you handsomely. You came highly recommended to me by our florist at Artistic Blooms—that gay guy. What's his name? Marc, I think. He's a *wonderful* floral designer. Very creative. Just. You know."

Suzy bit her lip to keep from laughing imagining any interaction between Mrs. Biltmore and Marc.

"He recommended you and I certainly don't have time to interview other wedding planners, nor the desire. I trust his judgment. Emma will come around. Just pretend you don't know anything about this and go about planning the wedding. It'll all work out. It always does. I always get my way." She smirked.

Suzy had little doubt about that.

Suzy sat up straight and gulped her wine. "Here are my terms. I'll try this for one month. If it doesn't work out, I'll recommend another wedding planner. And I'd like to meet Emma."

Mrs. Biltmore folded her arms. "Excuse me. *I* set the terms here. I'm the client, *you*'re my employee."

Suzy visibly winced and picked up her briefcase ready to storm off.

Mrs. Biltmore softened slightly. "I didn't mean to come across so harshly. I've had a rough time lately—a bad year. You will meet Emma in good time. Don't worry. And I'll pay you generously." To prove it, she pulled out her checkbook and wrote out a large sum. As Mrs. B pushed the check across the table, Suzy's eyes widened when she saw all the zeroes.

"Consider this a sign-on bonus." Mrs. Biltmore patted the check. "Now, that should allow you to provide me with your utmost attention. I don't want you working on any other weddings while you work on mine, I mean, on Emma's. And if the wedding goes off without a hitch, there'll be a substantial bonus for you." She smiled as though she were putting together a corporate merger.

Suzy couldn't take her eyes off the huge check Mrs. Biltmore effortlessly wrote out for fifty thousand dollars. She had never received a sign-on bonus and her retainer was normally a fraction of that. The check seemed to grow larger in her hands. She looked up with a jolt as the server appeared. She turned the check upside down.

He sat their salads down and refilled their water. "More wine?"

"Yes, and go find another apron," Mrs. Biltmore barked. "Yours has a disgusting stain on it. I'm losing my appetite and I'm sure our members are too."

The server practically galloped away.

Another server brought their food and Mrs. Biltmore stuck her fork tines daintily into the dressing and then into her salad. Meanwhile, Suzy glopped the dressing on top of her Biltmore salad, which was admittedly delicious. The salad consisted of large beets, salad greens, caramelized walnuts, bleu cheese, and of course, the infamous Biltmore salad dressing, which was apparently top secret according to Mrs. B.

Both women ate in silence for a few minutes. Suzy realized she hadn't eaten much food at Scott and Maria's wedding because she had been too busy with last-minute details.

The server emerged with fresh glasses of wine, donning a new apron. Mrs. Biltmore nodded her approval. She looked at Suzy. "Well, don't just sit there. Get out your pad. We have planning to do."

Suzy quickly weighed her options. She didn't have another wedding in the works and could really use the commission off an extravagant wedding. She had wanted to do some landscaping and expand her deck for years. But she wondered if it would be worth it to work for such a—well, a bitch. She knew this was wrong on so many levels. But she was a single mom who had a son starting college, plus her own expenses.

Her mind drifted to Emma. Maybe she could meet with her and turn the situation around. She knew Mrs. B would be next to impossible to work for. Suzy wished she had Alex's fortitude. She knew Alex would delight in telling Mrs. B off. Alex would point out dirty smudges on the glasses, tear up the check, and tell her where to shove it. But Suzy wasn't like Alex. She was a people pleaser and a bit of a dreamer. Somehow, she wanted to find a way to help Emma have the wedding of her dreams. Sighing, she reached down and again pulled out her legal pad with her customary pink and black pen poised in the air.

"That's better." Mrs. Biltmore almost smiled. "Now, as I said, I want a southern wedding. Lots of southern charm and hospitality, just like me."

Chapter 31

"Tony! Tony! Can you hear me?" Alex called into the smoke-filled night. She remembered her mace that she always kept in her purse. Naturally, it was in the patrol car. She decided to retrieve it, walked through the wall of smoke and waved her hands in an attempt to clear the air.

Just as she felt the door handle, a hand clamped over her mouth. Someone began dragging her away. She tried to scream but it was futile. She could tell by the forcefulness that it wasn't Tony. Alex stiffened knowing she must have walked right into the hands of the meth dealer. Tears pricked her eyes from the smoke—and from sheer fear. Her mind raced. She wondered if the druggie would kill her or hold her hostage.

Still clamped over her mouth, his hand smelled of cigarettes. She could see his grimy black thumbnail just below her right eye. He dragged her toward a large shrub and her heart thrashed against her chest. *Oh, God. What if he rapes me? Help me.* Alex broke into a cold sweat and prayed for Tony to find her.

She twisted her body, trying to wriggle free. She had to fight back. She wasn't going to make this easy for the jerk. As she squirmed, she felt a hard barrel against her back. *Oh, shit. A gun.*

"Stop struggling, bitch," he hissed. "If you don't do as I say, I won't have any problem blowing your brains out. Got it?" He jammed the gun barrel harder into her lower back.

As nightmare scenarios raced through her head, long-overdue sirens finally filled the smoky night. Alex squinted to determine how close the rescuers were and craned her neck to watch and listen. Through the smoke she could see two fire trucks, four police cars, and an ambulance swarm the scene. Then, she heard a twig snap. She froze. Maybe the drug dealer had an accomplice. She'd never get away from two of them.

"Let her go," yelled Tony "or I'll shoot." The criminal jumped and loosened his grip. Alex stumbled forward. Tony's face was black with smoke and his gun was pointed at the criminal's dirty brown hair. Alex noticed Tony had hurt his leg because he limped.

The meth dealer took a long look at Alex, up and down from head to toe. She shuddered. His gnarly teeth were rotten and his face was dotted with red splotches. He looked much older than his voice. He ogled Alex. She felt bile rise in her throat.

He continued holding a gun on her and challenged Tony. "I want a deal. I'll let her go if you let me walk."

"You're surrounded, stupid ass. Look around. You don't stand a chance. Let her go." Tony pulled the hammer back on his Glock. "My finger's on the trigger and I've got an itchy finger, scumbag."

The meth dealer shoved Alex into a large shrub and ran. She watched as he rounded the corner and ran toward the back of the house, which was apparently empty or else the owners were hiding on the floor. Her wobbly legs barely supported her as she attempted to stand. She hoped the new cops on the scene weren't trigger-happy and wouldn't think she was a criminal too.

Several officers rushed in, all with guns drawn. Alex's heart thrashed in her chest.

"Guns down," Tony commanded. "She's a reporter. He ran back there." He pointed with his gun and took off in the direction of the dealer. Two cops ensued in the foot chase while another ran toward the smoldering blaze.

"Get back in the patrol car," an officer demanded. "We don't want any reporters getting hurt."

She paused, worried about Tony.

"NOW," he yelled.

Alex shakily obeyed. One officer ran toward the smashed patrol car as Alex jumped into the patrol car and locked the doors. She cracked the window so she could hear. Firefighters had already pulled out long hoses and doused the flames. EMT's and paramedics carried stretchers. The entire area was filled with men and women in uniform scrambling like uniformed ants on an anthill.

Too bad I'm not a reporter. This would be a great story. Suddenly she remembered Sgt. Young, the cop who had assisted Tony in the pursuit to begin with. It was his patrol car going up in flames. Alex moved across to the driver's seat to get a better view. She was jarred out of her thoughts by the curt voice of the dispatcher.

"Sgt. Montgomery. Sgt. Montgomery, do you copy?" Alex guessed she was already in big trouble for being involved but decided to give some sort of update. She picked up the hand-held microphone.

"Sgt. Montgomery is in pursuit of a meth dealer."

"Who is this?" barked a different dispatcher.

"Alex, um, Macy," she lied.

"Who are you?"

"I'm a reporter." She lied again.

He paused. "Tell me what you see, Ms. Macy."

Alex cleared her throat. "Well, Sgt. Montgomery is chasing a meth dealer on foot, two or three other cops are following them, everyone has their guns drawn, firemen are putting out the fire from two crashed cars—one a patrol car and the other belonging to the meth dealer. Oh, and an ambulance is on the scene." She thought that was a pretty good description for being so shook up and afraid.

"And Sgt. Young. Do you see him?"

"No, no, I don't." She felt sad as she peered out the windshield. "An officer is near his car, though, looking around." She craned her neck. "Maybe he'll find him. I hope he's okay."

"Thank you for the update, Ms. Macy. Who are you with?"

"Sorry?"

"You said you're a reporter. Who are you with?"

I'm going to go to jail if I keep lying. This is the police. They'll check my story. She didn't think she had any other choice except to keep up the charade. Alex ran her fingers through her hair, biding for time. "I'm with a small-town paper doing a story on big city cops. It's a newspaper in Avilla. You've probably never heard of it."

"The Avilla Advertiser? My grandmother lives in Avilla."

What are the chances? I'm doomed.

Alex thought on her feet. "Actually, it's an independent paper just starting out. The Avilla Independent. In fact, this story will be in our debut issue."

Alex couldn't believe how easily the falsehoods flew out of her mouth. *Now I'll have to create a newspaper layout and hire a printer to somehow make this look legitimate. Shit.*

Chapter 32

Ka-boom! Alex jumped when she heard the explosion as Sgt. Young's patrol car exploded into a huge fireball. She hit the floor and covered her head with her hands. Pieces of metal and debris flew through the smoky air hitting the hood and trunk. A large chunk of debris landed on the hood and bounced, cracking the windshield.

Alex huddled in the floor and cried. *What if Tony was near the car? What if Sgt. Young was still in the car? What if he was..."* She didn't want to think about it. She rolled the window down a few inches so she could hear. Smoke filled the patrol car and burned her eyes. She heard footsteps, running, shouting and then a boisterous cheer.

"I found him," shouted an officer near the blaze that was now a small campfire, thanks to the firemen who quickly attacked the flames.

"Sgt. Young is alive!" an officer yelled.

Alex climbed up and squinted. Fanning the smoke in the car, she watched the scene through the partially open window. The air was beginning to clear and she heard an officer say Sgt. Young had been thrown several feet into some thick bushes.

"Get a stretcher over here. I think he has two broken legs," yelled an officer.

Relieved, Alex blinked back tears as she watched the paramedics place a stiff board under the young officer, strap him in, and lift Sgt. Young onto the stretcher. Simultaneously, they placed an oxygen mask over his face.

The officer who first found Sgt. Young turned toward Tony's patrol car. He raised his eyebrows as he spotted Alex peeking out the window. He bounded toward the vehicle.

"Who the hell are you?"

Alex knew she should stop being untruthful but the story came out of her mouth so easily, plus she didn't know what else to say. She definitely couldn't say she was falling in love with a married Tony.

"I'm a reporter for a small-town newspaper." She stared directly at the officer. "I was riding along with Sgt. Montgomery to report on the day in the life of a police officer."

"You picked a helluva day, lady." The officer leaned into the window and stared coldly into her eyes. He looked familiar but Alex couldn't place him. Maybe he was a bank customer.

"Roll up that window and lock the doors," he barked. "This is police business. We still have an assailant on the loose and don't need a reporter taken hostage. Hurry up."

Alex obeyed and rolled up the window. The doors were already locked. She had almost forgotten the meth dealer was still outside with the explosion and excitement of finding Sgt. Young. She leaned back in her seat as the police radio came to life again.

"Unit two? Unit two. What's the status?" a female dispatcher asked.

"This is Alex, uh, Macy. I can give you an update. They just found Sgt. Young. He's alive." She smiled with relief, even though she had never met the man.

"What's his condition?"

"He's with the paramedics. I heard one officer say he might have a broken leg or two."

"And Sgt. Montgomery?"

Alex frowned. "I wish I knew. I'm so worried about To— Sgt. Montgomery." Crap. She almost blew her cover. She rephrased her sentence. "Sgt. Montgomery is still pursuing the meth dealer as far as I know."

"Alleged meth dealer," corrected the dispatcher.

"Right. Anyway, I don't see them. Oh, wait—" Alex's eyes got as large as coasters as she watched Tony drag the handcuffed meth dealer toward the car. He jiggled the handle and banged on the window. "Open up, Alex."

She unlocked the doors.

"Get in," Tony growled as he shoved the guy in the back seat. The dealer tried to spit on Tony but he dodged the spray. Alex watched, horrified.

"Turn around, Alex, and buckle up. We're going to have a little party back at the station." He glared at the meth dealer and got behind the wheel. "Not a word out of you, asshole."

The officer who had earlier looked familiar to Alex walked up to Tony's side of the car.

"Hey, bro," said the officer. "Who's the girl?"

Tony grunted. "None of your concern."

"She's a looker. You always get the lookers, don't you, bud?"

"Shut up." He closed his window in the officer's face and Alex noticed Tony's jaw was set. She could tell the other officer got a kick out of needling Tony.

"Who's that?"

"Don't worry about him. He can be a real pain in the ass. Listen, I hope you got a good story for your paper. I know you got more than you bargained for." He motioned with his head toward the criminal.

Alex understood. "Right. Yes, this will be a great story. I'm just glad you and the other officer are okay." The stench of body odor from the back seat moved to the front like a heavy curtain. Alex wrinkled her nose.

Tony gripped the wheel and sped away. "We're going straight to the station with this scumbag. You wait in the lobby and try to slip out a side door during the chaos. The chief won't want any reporters around." Tony ran his fingers through his hair.

"I'm going to catch hell for this. Let's just hope the chief is in a good mood." Tony shot a look at the suspect. "Not a word out of you. Not one word, prick."

Alex stared at Tony's clenched jaw and sweat beads on his forehead. His shirt was torn and his face was black from the smoke. His muscular arms and hands had cuts and scratches. She watched the muscles tighten in his cheek and thought she had better be quiet as well. She could tell his nerves were frayed and wasn't exactly in top form herself. He rubbed his leg.

What a night. What was going to be a joy ride in a police car to help out a little old lady turned into a high-speed chase. Her stomach churned thinking about everything that could have gone wrong. Alex wasn't certain she could live like this. She knew she could never be a cop and wondered if she could date one.

Within minutes, they pulled up to the station. Television crews were everywhere. Someone had already alerted them. Alex found it ironic that *real* reporters with cameras and microphones lined the steps of the police station. She had to admit it; this was a great story. As they parked, cameras from every television station were pointed toward the patrol car, obviously waiting to get the first glimpse of the drug dealer.

"Great. I'm in huge trouble now." Tony groaned. "Alex, when you get out, they'll be shouting questions. Don't answer. Don't say a word. Just be quiet and walk a few feet behind us. Let me get out of the car first and get our friendly drug dealer off the streets for good."

"Got it."

Tony walked around the car. Cameras and microphones were immediately thrust in his face.

"Officer, is this the drug dealer police have been trying to catch for months?"

"Officer, would you like to make a statement?"

"Officer, who is that woman in the car?"

Tony ignored the reporters. "No comment. Stand back. Give us room. I don't want anyone to get hurt." As the reporters stayed in place, Tony commanded, "Step back *now*."

The reporters moved back a few feet giving him space to pull the guy out of the back seat. Still handcuffed with his arms behind his back, Tony grabbed the dealer's filthy elbow and dragged him up the steps.

Alex kept her distance several feet behind wishing she could disappear as the cameras rolled. She walked into the lobby afraid of being questioned by other police. Luckily, all eyes were on Tony and the suspect. They dragged the criminal away and surrounded Tony, patting him on the back. Some gave him high fives and others asked about Sgt. Young's condition. Reporters swarmed Tony like bees. Alex was able to slip out a side door and practically galloped across the street to a convenience store. She called a cab and gratefully headed home.

Her nerves were shot. When she got home, she poured a large glass of chardonnay and lit a soothing lavender candle. She took the wine into the bathroom and showered. She wanted to wash every body part the druggie had touched. Twice. Exhausted, she flopped on the couch and turned on the evening news.

BREAKING NEWS read the bold, red crawl across the screen.

Alex held her breath as she watched the video. The camera zeroed in on the patrol car, on Tony, and finally on the meth dealer. The next shot was of Tony taking the handcuffed suspect up the steps. There was no close-up of Alex, but when she saw her backside walking up the stairs, she winced. A brief mention of the "unknown" female in the patrol car was reported, but thankfully, the reporter focused on the meth dealer and how police had been trying to catch him for months according to her sources. She showed the mug shot of the dealer and video of his house where meth had allegedly been cooked. The reporter discussed the household ingredients used to make meth and how addictive the substance is.

"Crap," Alex said aloud to no one. *What if someone recognizes me from behind? I hope Tony doesn't get into trouble. I hope I don't get into trouble.*

The ringing phone jarred her.

"I only have a minute," Tony said. "Listen, I'm in deep shit here with the police chief. Deep, deep shit. I can't tell if he's at all happy that we got this scum off the streets because he's so angry that you were in the car. Apparently, the reporters have video of you. I hope no one can ID you. Keep quiet about this. The chief is reprimanding me for having a reporter in the car, for not getting your assignment authorized beforehand, and for that little fact of putting your life in danger. He's afraid you'll sue the CCPD." Tony blew out his breath.

"Because of this, I have to work a boring desk job and check prisoners in for a month, maybe more. The chief said I cannot be in contact with you, 'that lady reporter.'"

"How will they know if we talk?"

Tony exhaled again. "They're cops. They'll know. They have tracking devices. Listen, I'm lucky that's all they're doing. They could have demoted me. I can't talk any longer. I've got to interrogate this guy. I won't be reachable, even by phone. They'll know if you call me, so don't. That's all I can say. I shouldn't be telling you this much."

"But—"Alex said desperately.

"I'll call you in a month or so when my punishment is over. Gotta go." He hung up.

Alex stared at the phone in her hands, willing it to give her answers. *How am I going to handle this by myself? What if the police chief calls me? What if someone at the bank recognized me?* On top of her personal concerns, she was now worried about Tony, especially since she couldn't call him or see him. She wanted to discuss this with Suzy or Hope but Tony made it clear to keep quiet. She wasn't sure she could. Thank goodness it was the weekend. Maybe all the car chase talk would die down by Monday. Sick with worry, Alex refilled her wine and wondered how she would handle this mess.

Chapter 33

At the Biltmore Country Club, Suzy almost choked on her salad thinking about Mrs. B's so-called "southern charm." She hid her displeasure behind her burgundy napkin emblazoned with a golden "B."

When she could see she was getting her way with Suzy, Mrs. B became noticeably excited as she talked about her plans for her daughter's wedding.

"I want you to figure out how to incorporate horses. We're big horse people, you know. Actually, I've thought about having the groomsmen ride in on horses—some of the winners from the Kentucky Derby, of course. We own several horses and Lincoln absolutely loves the horse races." She dabbed her mouth. "What do you think?"

Suzy wondered whether Emma liked horses. "That's a unique idea. Let me think it over." She wrote "horses" on her legal pad.

Waving her hands in the air, Mrs. B continued. "And I want the bridesmaids to wear large hats—just like they do at the Kentucky Derby and in all the lovely cities of the South. Can you manage finding beautiful hats?

Suzy nodded and made another note. "That won't be a problem. I love hats too. I'll find some beautiful ones."

Mrs. Biltmore actually smiled showing slightly coffee-stained teeth. With all her money, Suzy wondered why she didn't have them whitened.

Suzy took another bite of salad. "Have you thought about a location? Where will the wedding be held?"

Mrs. B gave her a stern look. "Where in heavens do you think? The Biltmore Country Club, naturally." There is a grand wooden spiral staircase that Emma can walk down or she can enter through our fabulous foyer into the Grand Dining Room and out onto the limestone patio area.

"So will the wedding be outside or just the drinks beforehand?"

"Everything will be outside. We'll set up white chairs on the grounds and I want slip covers on each chair with fragrant, perfect lilies and magnolias tucked inside big chiffon bows on the back of each one."

"You've given this a lot of thought."

Mrs. B nodded. "Don't interrupt." She pointed toward Suzy's legal pad. "Keep writing. Don't miss any details. I'm a detail person." She waved her hand with a flourish. "The chairs should be arranged theatre style with an aisle down the middle. And," Mrs. B leaned forward. "This is very important, I do not want any bird crap on the chairs. Do you understand? They must be inspected closely *right* before the guests are seated. We cannot have our refined friends sitting in bird doo."

Suzy bit her lip to keep from giggling. She could only imagine Mrs. B's designer-wearing wealthy friends sitting in bird poop. Picturing the scene, she suppressed a chuckle with her napkin as the server appeared with a dessert tray. Suzy's mouth watered as she eyed the tempting chocolate cheesecake, pecan pie, carrot cake, and tiramisu.

"Remember my diet?" Mrs. Biltmore said. "Don't tempt me with dessert. I don't want to *hear* about dessert. I don't want to *see* a dessert. Why can't you people remember anything?" She waved the offensive tray away. The server started to turn on his heel but Mrs. Biltmore called him back.

"I do want coffee. Decaf. Black. How about you?"

"The same," Suzy answered meekly, feeling sorry for

the server. She bet the servers drew straws to determine who had to serve Mrs. B; this poor schmuck drew the short one.

The waiter appeared with a shiny silver coffee pot and set down two porcelain cups etched with a gold rim. Naturally.

"This cup has a crack in it. My God, do I have to go in the kitchen and run this place myself?"

The server picked up the cup, examined it and squinted, apparently trying to find the crack. He shrugged and left to find another cup.

Suzy finished her second glass of wine and felt her cheeks getting warm.

The server returned with a new cup for Mrs. Biltmore.

"Is this decaf?"

He nodded.

"It had better be. If I'm still awake at two in the morning, I'll have your head."

The server shifted his feet and scurried away.

They both sipped coffee while Suzy pondered the wedding. She wanted to leave and think about the entire situation but she didn't dare until she was dismissed. She was definitely not going to cash that large check for a while—just in case Mrs. Biltmore got out of hand—well, more out of hand.

"How about music? Have you thought about what kind of music Emma would like?"

"We want a harpist and violinists. Maybe trumpets. Classical music, of course. Everything will be charming and chic. Lincoln likes the blues, so maybe a saxophonist, too."

"Do you think anyone will want to dance afterward? Perhaps you'll want a DJ or a band?" suggested Suzy, half fearful of the answer.

"Oh, I suppose the younger crowd would enjoy that. I'll have to trust your judgment, I suppose, but I don't want any of that dreadful rap music. And no hard rock."

Suzy made a note. "I get the picture. This will be a

beautiful wedding but I'd really like to meet Emma. Would it be possible to arrange a meeting with her?"

"I told you I'm handling this," Mrs. Biltmore said. "We don't need to bother Emma just yet. I'll let you know when."

Suzy nodded, knowing she couldn't push her luck. "What is the date for the wedding?"

"I don't have a date. I need to talk to Lincoln first. I'll get back to you." She tapped her fingers together. "That's enough for today. We covered more ground than I expected. I must go meet and greet our members now. Would you mind seeing yourself out?"

Suzy knew she was being dismissed and was more than happy to leave the stuffy room and unpleasant company. "Just let me know the date when you can."

As an answer, she received a curt wave of dismissal and Mrs. B's back. Suzy gathered her pad and purse and headed to her car. She was weary from shifting gears from a sweet, beautiful wedding to this betrayal of a wedding. Her nagging conscience told her not to work on the Biltmore wedding. But the money was hard to resist.

Chapter 34

Driving home from the country club, she tried to conjure up happy thoughts, wanting to end the day on a good note. As she pulled up to her stone house, Suzy immediately relaxed. She loved her older home with its manicured rose bushes and red door. She had toyed with painting it pink to match her logo but thought that would be overkill. Besides, the neighbors probably wouldn't like it.

Suzy walked inside enjoying her cozy surroundings, her nest. The hardwood floors gleamed and the gorgeous sunset shone through the patio doors. A stone fireplace was in the corner of her small hearth room, just off the kitchen. Suzy loved that room. It was her favorite getaway where she often curled up with a good book, lit candles or listened to music. Suzy's pale pink office was on the other end of her house. She purposely kept it that way to ensure a haven away from her business. This was a perfect example of a day when she needed the separation most.

When she created Weddings by Suzanne, Suzy knew she would occasionally have some difficult brides and mothers. Wedding planning makes for frayed nerves but she hadn't counted on someone as hateful, conniving, and domineering as Mrs. B—not to mention racist. That woman made her former bride Misty look like a puppy dog.

Suzy fished the fifty thousand dollar check out of her purse and stared at it agog. She laid it on the counter under an antique bride and groom figurine. She wasn't ready to think about the check and the baggage it carried—or the hoops she'd have to jump through to earn it. At the same time, she was unable to keep her eyes off it.

The power that little piece of paper held. *Mrs. B must be worth millions. This is probably a drop in the bucket. Pocket change.* Suzy shook her head in wonder. To her, it was nearly a year's annual salary. *I hope this thorny wedding is worth it.* She put on her practical Mom hat and told herself she had a business to run and a son starting college. Suzy took a deep breath and decided to make the best of the situation, hoping to intervene on Emma's behalf. Somehow, some way, she hoped to plan a wedding for Emma and the man she truly loved.

After making some chamomile tea, Suzy walked into the hearth room and settled into her favorite yellow and blue floral chair. She thought about Maria and Scott who were honeymooning by now. Their glowing faces in that hot air balloon made it all worthwhile as she sipped her hot tea, trying to calm her frayed nerves. She glanced at the neglected mail on her counter. Suzy walked over and thumbed through the pile. Mostly bills, junk mail, and magazines. As she returned the mail to her counter, a postcard fell out. It was from Jon. Just what she needed.

Dear Mom,

I have exciting news for you. I know I should wait until I return from France but I'm bursting at the seams. Remember I told you I've met someone? Well, we're both returning to America. It's getting serious, Mom. Very serious. I know what you're thinking. Don't worry about Vanessa. She's okay with this. I've talked to her. Can't wait to see you. We'll be there in two weeks!

Love,
Jon

Could this day hold any more surprises? Suzy trusted her son's judgment and couldn't wait to set eyes on him and this new girlfriend of his. Today of all days, she could have used a hug from Jon. Suzy refilled her tea. Exhausted, she walked into her bedroom, placing the postcard on her nightstand so she'd see it first thing in the morning.

Before turning out the light, Suzy glanced at a framed photo of Jon and Vanessa at their high school prom. He looked so handsome in his tux and Vanessa was wearing a knee-length yellow sequined dress. She decided to hide the photo in her drawer since his new girlfriend from Europe probably wouldn't be pleased to see it. Bleary-eyed, Suzy turned out the light and nearly fell asleep before her head hit the pillow.

Ring. Ring. The grating phone made Suzy jump. She squinted at her alarm clock. It was two in the morning. She wondered if Jon had gotten the time zones mixed up.

"Hello," she answered groggily.

A wide-awake Mrs. Biltmore said, "I think that little twerp gave me caffeinated coffee at lunch—probably on purpose. I can't sleep, can you?"

"Yes. I was sound asleep, Mrs. Biltmore. Can this wait until tomorrow?"

"It *is* tomorrow. I have a couple of ideas. Do you have your pad handy?"

Suzy rubbed her eyes and sat up. She grabbed a post-it and pen by the lamp.

"I'll give you five minutes."

They discussed a few more details—rather, Mrs. B *told* Suzy about a few more details and hung up. Suzy tossed and turned, punching her pillow a few times before she fell back asleep.

At six o'clock her shrill phone awakened her. Suzy groaned and fumbled with the receiver. "Yes," she said sharply.

"Good morning, Suzy. Are you up? It's a beautiful day."

Doesn't this woman sleep?

Suzy sighed, "No, I'm not up. You woke me up at two this morning, remember? Can we talk later, Mrs. Biltmore? Please?"

"This won't take long. What do you think about trumpeters on horses standing on either side of the aisle? Wouldn't that look smart? They could play the wedding song or wedding march, whatever you call it. What do you think?"

"Wonderful. Can I sleep now?"

"I think you're just saying that to get me off the line. I want your true opinion. I've paid substantially for your expertise."

Suzy sat up in bed and brushed the hair out of her eyes. "I think trumpeters on horses would be nice. It would be quite distinctive, actually—almost like royalty."

"Ah. Like royalty." Mrs. B's voice perked up. "I'm glad you like the idea. I'll contact the horse owners. I know which horses I want. My favorite is a gray horse called 'Majesty.' I'll call you later today if I think of anything else." Click.

Suzy wanted to ask her to refrain from calling too late or too early but assumed that would be a useless waste of breath. This woman was accustomed to getting her way. That was obvious.

She pulled her blue comforter under her chin and tried willing herself back to sleep. Her mind drifted to Jon. Suzy flopped on her stomach and she buried her head under the pillow. It was useless. She couldn't sleep. She walked to the kitchen and made coffee. While she waited for the coffee to brew, she glanced at the calendar. No appointments today. Thank goodness. She needed a day off to catch up on bills, laundry and housework. She wanted everything to be perfect for when Jon and his new girlfriend arrived.

Chapter 35

Completely drained from the police chase the night before, Alex thrashed in bed and awakened much earlier than usual. She was still scared out of her mind and worried about Tony. She hoped it was all a bad dream but knew it wasn't. She hated not being able to talk to him. Alex decided to stay close to home. Maybe she'd even do laundry and exercise.

The television was on in the background. When she the news came on, Alex sat on the couch, glued to the screen. She flipped through four local channels hoping against hope that no one had gotten a close-up of her. Luckily, it was nearly the same video on every channel and the excitement of the story seemed to be fading.

Remembering she had forgotten to get her mail the day before, Alex walked outside. When she opened the lid, she screamed. A frog inside her mailbox jumped on her chest. Startled, she fell to the ground. The frog hopped away. Alex gathered herself off the ground, as a speeding white van nearly ran over her.

"Jerk." She yelled at the van pumping her fist in the air. "Watch where you're going." She brushed herself off and reached inside the mailbox. She dreaded touching the nasty, slimy frog mail and couldn't wait to throw the envelopes way and douse herself with antibacterial gel.

She studied the mailbox to see how the frog could have gotten in. There was only a small hole in the back, less than an inch in diameter. The lid had been tightly shut. She figured it must have been a neighbor kid playing a prank.

She walked back inside, set paper towels underneath the mail on the counter and reached for the antibacterial.

She threw the envelopes in the trash and organized her bills in one pile and magazines in another. A note from the middle of the stack fell out. In bold, block letters, it read:

I'M WATCHING YOU.

The message was typed on white card stock similar to cards that would be used in a debate match. She wondered if Tony had left the note to let her know he was around even though he was unable to talk to her. But why would he leave such a creepy, unsigned message? Alex shuddered and made coffee. She was beginning to feel out of control and was actually looking forward to her Monday morning bank meeting. She needed some sense of normalcy.

She turned the index card upside down and watched her favorite romantic movie, The Notebook. Alex cried at the end, as always, and napped in an effort to calm her frayed nerves.

Later that afternoon, the sun was ablaze and birds were singing. She could smell her fresh flowers through the open window and started to relax. She donned flip flops, cut-off denim shorts and a red tee and walked outside to water her flowers. The geraniums, hibiscus, impatiens and hostas were in full bloom and a rainbow array of colors. She loved gardening and looked forward to a restful evening of sitting in a lawn chair and reading, after she cleaned the deck. But she couldn't relax if things were dirty or unorganized. Alex hosed off the patio furniture and deck and couldn't believe how many cobwebs always sprang up seemingly overnight. Satisfied that everything was clean, she went inside to check the news online while the lawn furniture dried. Her phone rang as she typed "police chase and meth dealer" into the search bar.

"Hello."

Silence.

"Hello," she repeated, both agitated and scared as she heard the caller's heavy breathing.

"Who is this? Tony, is that you? Are you okay?"

More silence and heavy breathing.

"This isn't funny." Alex slammed the phone down.

Chapter 36

Alex closed her iPad and laid on the couch.

What's going on? First the frog, the van, the scary note and now this stupid call. Her nerves were raw but she convinced herself it was all a coincidence. She hadn't had breakfast so she ate breakfast for lunch. It seemed easier than a sandwich. She topped her Cheerios with strawberries and toasted some cinnamon bread. She pulled a bottle of Smart Water from the refrigerator, figuring some extra electrolytes couldn't hurt.

After eating, Alex spent the rest of the day on edge. She couldn't concentrate on a book or get into a movie, jumping at every sound. She needed company and invited Suzy over for dinner. When Suzy arrived, she opened the refrigerator.

"What are we going to eat?"

Alex laughed. "Guess I haven't shopped in a week or two. Let's go to the store."

Both exhausted from their respective weekends, they drove in unusual silence. Suzy grabbed a cart and spotted Alex on another aisle.

"You're straightening the produce again."

Alex picked up an orange and pretended to throw it at Suzy.

Suzy smiled. "I know you can't help it and the produce is much neater now. Maybe they'll hire you to arrange the store."

"Ha ha."

When they arrived at Alex's house, she started the grill and Suzy headed inside to pour wine for both of them. When she returned, Alex hugged Suzy.

"Thanks for coming over on such short notice. I know you're probably tired from your wedding this weekend."

"Friends are more important than rest."

They toasted that sentiment and enjoyed veggie burgers, chips, salsa, and watermelon. After they finished eating, Alex said, "You'll never believe my weekend."

"Mine was pretty eventful as well. You go first."

Alex told Suzy about the terrifying car chase, the explosion and the meth dealer. She knew Tony told her to keep it quiet but she had to tell *someon*e.

Suzy's eyes bulged as she leaned forward. Her mouth flew open while Alex relayed the scary car chase and the fact that the meth dealer had grabbed her. When Alex finished, Suzy gasped.

"What the hell was he thinking going off like that with you in the car? I can't believe this. Oh, honey."

Suzy grabbed her friend's hand. "You could've been killed. And now the cop is unreachable for weeks? What if someone is out there who knew this drug dealer? Someone who knows you were in the car? Maybe this person is trying to get to Tony through you."

Suzy watched her friend's face turn ashen and was immediately sorry she had put this idea in her head.

As Suzy spoke, Alex's knees nearly collapsed under her. She hadn't even thought about that possibility. Maybe that was who was scaring her this weekend.

But she put on a brave front. "Stop worrying. I'll be fine. The criminal doesn't know my name and my face wasn't on TV. He thinks I'm a reporter. Besides, his revenge would be against Tony." Alex shuddered. "I'm okay. Just shook up. Tell me something else. Quickly. I don't want to talk about this any more."

Suzy took a bite of her burger and amused Alex with Maria and Scott's fun, southwestern-themed wedding and hot air balloon ride. Then, she told Alex about Mrs. Biltmore.

Alex forced herself to eat while Suzy talked. Before Suzy

could finish regaling her with stories about Mrs. Biltmore, Alex spewed her drink and doubled over with laughter. "Thanks for the laugh. I needed that." She bit into a chip. "Are you sure you can handle her? You may need my help. First of all, I have a new name for her: Mrs. Bitchmore."

Suzy covered her mouth with her hand and giggled. "That's perfect. I hope I don't slip and actually call her that."

Alex added, "I feel sorry for her daughter. I hope you can talk some sense into this despicable old bag and I hope she's paying you well. She'd have to pay me a fortune to put up with her bullshit."

Suzy was unusually quiet and ate a bite of watermelon before answering. "The pay is very good. Plus, I feel sorry for Emma. My plan is to somehow get in touch with her and get this worked out. Emma should marry the man she's in love with. This whole thing is ridiculous."

"At least she's paying you well. That helps, I suppose. Want to watch a movie or spend the night?"

"I wish I could. I'm exhausted from the wedding and all the calls from Mrs. Bitchmore." Suzy laughed then yawned.

"I've got to get a good night's sleep. I'm sure I'll be hearing from the southern belle from hell again soon."

"Ha. That's another good name for her."

"You need to get a good night's rest after your harrowing weekend."

"You're probably right."

"Let me help you clean up."

"No, I've got it. I need something to do. I've got to stay busy."

"If you're sure. Thanks for the burger. It was tasty. I'm glad you invited me over. We both needed this." Suzy hugged Alex. "Lock your doors."

Alex was still on edge. She washed the dishes and triple checked the locks. Unable to sleep, she turned the television on and hoped she wouldn't receive any more scary calls.

Chapter 37

Two days later, Hope was delighted that Suzy had invited her girlfriends over for dinner. As she drove to Suzy's house, she continued to fret because she hadn't heard from her parents in a week. Of course, she had told them to stay away, but she was beginning to worry.

What if they don't have food? What if their landlord kicked them out? Her shoulders were tight and she had a tension headache from worry. Rubbing the knot on her left shoulder while driving with her right hand, she told herself to refrain from dropping by their trailer. Otherwise, they'd never change. Everything would go back to how it was. She had to stop enabling them. Her friends were right. *On the other hand, maybe it wouldn't hurt to drop by their house in a few days.*

When she pulled up, Hope was surprised to see that Alex had arrived first. She parked her gray Toyota and walked up to the door. They sat in Suzy's cozy hearth room where a fire crackled in the fireplace, even though it was warm outside.

"I love your house. It's so homey."

Suzy blushed. "Thanks."

"Want a drink? Tea, lemonade or wine?"

"Lemonade sounds great.

Alex was seated on the floor, Indian style, with her usual glass of chardonnay. She rose to greet Hope.

"Stay seated. Let's have relaxing girl time. What has been going on with you two?" Hope asked.

Alex and Suzy looked at one another, then had a laughing fit that went on for minutes.

"What's so funny?"

"Nothing funny, believe me," Alex said.

"You'd never guess. Maybe you'd like something stronger than lemonade," Suzy suggested.

"I'll go first." Suzy told Hope about Maria and Scott's wedding, then about the pretentious, obnoxious Mrs. Biltmore.

Alex chimed in. "I call her Mrs. Bitchmore."

"I can see why. What a witch. I can't believe a mother would do such a thing to her own daughter. Are you actually going to work for this obnoxious woman, Suzy?" Hope asked.

After fielding several questions, Suzy explained she had decided to give Mrs. B one month in an attempt to find a way to talk to Emma.

"But I have something else to tell you." Suzy frowned.

Alex and Hope looked at one another.

"There's more?" Alex sipped her chardonnay.

"You know Jon has been backpacking in Europe?"

Alex and Hope nodded affirmatively.

"Apparently he's met someone and is bringing her back to the states. He sent a post card and said it's getting serious. I can't believe it. I always thought he'd marry Vanessa. I'm kind of in shock."

"What is the girl's name? What does she do?" Hope asked.

"Do you know anything about her?" Alex asked.

"No, nothing. I assume she's European since Jon met her while abroad but he's being very mysterious. Maybe he met a celebrity. Who knows?"

Alex listened intently with her hand on her chin. "Some people do manage whirlwind romances, you know. I'm falling for the cop hard. And Suzy you've never gotten over Ken."

Suzy stared at her nails and bit her lip. "True. And I don't think I'll ever get over him. I can't believe I let him get away. But back to Jon. I guess I'll have to wait.

"When is he coming home?" Hope asked.

"They're due to arrive in two weeks. I'm sorry. I've taken up the entire evening talking about Mrs. Biltmore and Jon's new girlfriend. Alex, tell Hope your big news."

Hope's eyebrows shot up. "Wow. We let a few days go by and you both have big news. Now what?"

Alex reached for a chip and dipped it in the guacamole Suzy had set out. Then, she popped two cheese cubes in her mouth.

"Quit stalling and tell her," Suzy said.

Alex wiped her mouth and considered what Tony had said about talking about this. She had to tell her other closest ally. She knew both Suzy and Alex would keep it confidential.

In a hushed tone, Alex leaned forward. "Okay, but this is top secret. I mean it. Don't tell one person what I'm about to tell you. Deal?"

Hope nodded.

"What is it, mystery woman?" Hope asked. "Your secret is safe with me."

Since she had heard the story, Suzy sat quietly eating cheese and fruit.

Alex began by telling Hope how Tony took her to Walgreens in a patrol car to pay for stolen items for Mrs. Magilicutty.

"Huh? I'm already confused. Who's Mrs. Magilicutty?"

"An old woman who reminds Tony of his grandmother, apparently. She steals things and he pays for them."

"A klepto grandma. Interesting," Hope said.

"Anyway, it was going to be a short fifteen-minute drive but . . ." Alex looked heavenward and blew out her breath.

"Tony spotted a meth dealer he had been trying to catch and took after him like a greyhound at the races."

Hope's eyebrows formed one line. "And you were in the car?

Alex nodded while Suzy refilled their drinks.

Alex took a sip and continued. "Yes. Believe me, if I could have gotten out, I would have. Tony was in a white heat to catch this guy. We sped all over town going over 100 miles an hour—"

Hope sucked in her breath. "How did it end? Obviously, you're okay."

"Another officer was called to help, the meth guy was trapped at a dead-end street, there was a crash and the other cop's car blew up!" Alex held out her hands. "Look, I still get shaky talking about it."

Hope reached for her hand. "How are Tony and the other cop?"

"They're okay."

Hope stared at Alex with scared eyes. "Did you see the meth dealer?"

Alex's felt the blood drain from her face. "Yes. Like an idiot, I got out of the patrol car to try and find Tony and within minutes, the bad guy saw me and stuck a gun in my back." Alex's eyes filled with tears.

Hope sucked in her breath. "I can't believe this. Now, I'm shaking."

"Now, Tony's in trouble because I was in the car. The chief has him on desk duty and said he couldn't talk to the 'lady reporter.' That's me."

Hope rubbed her arms. "I've got goose bumps."

"It was a nightmare. In fact, I'm having nightmares now. Thankfully, everyone at the station was so distracted I was able to slip out the side door. So, remember, mum's the word."

Hope threw her arms around Alex's neck. "You were in a real police chase. What if you have to testify or something?"

Alex groaned. "That hadn't even occurred to me."

Suzy chimed in, "You hadn't told me the charming story about the klepto grandma. I can see why you're falling for this cop."

"Yeah, I think he's a good guy."

"A good, married guy," Suzy added.

Alex shrugged, stood and stretched. "I don't want to talk about this any more. It makes me jumpy. I'm going to develop a nervous tic or something. We've done all the talking. Hope, what's going on with you?"

Hope decided not to tell her friends about her recent altercation with her parents. She was slightly ashamed she threw them out of her house, even though she knew Suzy and Alex would approve of her tough love.

"Same 'ol, same 'ol. Parents who won't work and use me for money or food. Nothing different in my world." Hope sighed. "I love them. I just wish they were normal. I'm annoyed they're stuck in the seventies and won't work. I feel hopeless and I hate my stupid name. It makes everything worse."

"You're too hard on yourself. I know your parents are a handful." Suzy reached over and patted Hope's arm.

Lost in her thoughts, Hope continued eating. Between bites, she said, "Do you know my mother still wears a mood ring? A *mood* ring. Do they even sell those things anymore?"

"Does Montana have a pet rock too?" Alex asked. Everyone doubled over laughing. "Honestly, they *should* have a pet rock since they can't afford a real pet." Hope raised both arms in the air, "Why me?"

"You certainly didn't inherit their hippie gene," Suzy said.

"I'm sorry they're such a worry. I wish we could help you," Alex said.

"Being able to talk about it helps a lot. Enough about my parents. I'm getting depressed."

Hope looked at her watch. "It's getting late."

"Let's talk about something random and light-hearted." Alex looked at her friends.

Hope sat up straight. "What?"

"Ever think about the person you had sex with for the first time?"

Hope wrinkled her nose. "Why does it always turn to men? I don't have time for men."

"Are you a virgin?" Alex asked.

Hope felt her cheeks burn. "No. I've had sex."

"How many times?"

"You're nosy."

"Well?" Alex prodded.

"Three."

"Who was the first?"

"You wouldn't know him."

"From school?"

"I'm pleading the Fifth."

"So, was it Tommy or Jeff?"

"Shut up." Hope put her hands on her hips pretending to be mad.

"My first was Alan but you probably figured that. We dated for two years but I was a good girl in school. Of course, a month after I graduated—" Alex giggled.

Suzy grinned. "I lost my virginity to my childhood sweetheart, Ken, before we both moved away to college." Suzy stared into space. "I think about him so much. He's married now, I think. He was the last time I checked anyway. I always wondered what would have happened if—" Suzy stopped.

"I didn't know you still thought about Ken," Hope said.

"I remember him. Cute, sexy and smart. Finish your sentence. You always wondered what?" asked Alex.

"If we hadn't married other people, I wonder if we would have gotten married. We broke up when we went to different colleges. After I got pregnant with Jon, well, the rest is history. Ken always knew me better than anyone. I'll never find another guy like him." Suzy stared out the window wistfully.

"Maybe you should try and find him. Go to Classmates. com," Hope suggested.

"No. I checked Facebook a few times and saw that he was married. There were all these happy pictures of Ken, his cute wife, their dog, and their beautiful house. Vacations, anniversaries, you name it. I was depressed for two months. I'm not putting myself through that again. No more cyber stalking. I'll just chalk up losing Ken to my biggest mistake. That, and maybe agreeing to work with Mrs. Bitchmore," Suzy added.

Chapter 38

The next morning Alex sped to the bank, steering with her left knee as she put silver hoops on. She had a memory like a sieve when it came to her earlier rear-ending incident. She punched the code in the back door and walked through the lobby where Jim and Stu were visiting near the teller windows.

An employee's radio was on the counter playing soft music. Alex walked toward them to say hello when the radio announcer's urgent, booming voice caught her attention. She heard the words "breaking news" and stopped. She craned her head to listen, afraid it was about the car chase.

"One male and female in their late fifties were killed at two o'clock this morning when the vehicle they were in was hit by a Burlington Northern train in north Crystal City. According to the police report, the Volkswagen Micro Bus was crushed and pushed fifty yards into neighboring trees. The vehicle, an older 60's model, was covered with peace sign decals. The investigation is early and ongoing. Names of the victims are being withheld pending notification of relatives. Now back to our regular programming."

Alex broke out in a cold sweat. "Oh, my God. I may know who that is." She ran to her office and dialed Suzy's number. "Have you heard the news?"

"No. What?"

"Turn on the television. Hurry," Alex said. "There was a terrible train accident and the vehicle's description sounds like it could be Hope's parents. Hurry."

"Okay, wait." Suzy fumbled with the remote and saw "breaking news" at the bottom of the television screen. A reporter stood in front of train tracks giving a report.

"Well?"

"Shh. Let me listen."

After a few minutes Suzy came back on the line, asking rapid-fire questions.

"What should we do? Have you called Hope?

"I don't know what to do, and no, I haven't called her. If it's Larry and Montana, and I suspect it is, we can't let Hope be alone when she hears this. I'm leaving the bank now. I'll pick you up. Let's head over to Hilltop High School."

"I'll be ready."

Alex changed her voice mail—something her boss was a stickler about—telling callers she would be out of the office most of the day. She grabbed her purse and asked one of the loan assistants to cancel her appointments.

When she arrived at Suzy's house, Alex talked non-stop. "I have a bad feeling about this. I'm afraid it's them. How many people have an old hippie jalopy like that?" She gripped the steering wheel until her knuckles turned white. "I'm terrified for Hope."

Suzy bit her nails. "I'm afraid it's them, too.' She turned on the radio. "Let's see if there's an update."

Alex pulled into the Hilltop parking lot and saw two patrol cars near the front door. She looked at Suzy with dismay. "Unless there's a drug bust or some gang banger students, I'm afraid those cop cars are bad news."

Suzy nodded.

Alex's legs felt like jelly. They got out of the car, as if in slow motion. Neither spoke as they slammed the doors and walked toward Hope's office. Staring ahead, Alex spotted two uniformed officers through Hope's glass door. Hope was crying and nodding as a female officer crouched down to speak to her. Hope was seated in a chair blowing her nose with tissue after tissue.

Alex and Suzy watched the interaction and looked at one another hopelessly. Both burst into tears. Alex spoke first.

"It's obviously true. We've got to help her through this."

Suzy watched Hope through the door with tear-filled eyes. "I guess we should stand back and give the officers plenty of room." After what seemed forever, they stepped closer where Hope could see them through the glass.

When Hope spotted Alex and Suzy, she rushed toward her friends. Tears streamed down her red, splotchy face as she wrapped her arms tightly around Suzy and Alex's necks.

"I killed them. Oh, my God. I killed them." She let out a horrific moan, like a wounded animal caught in a trap. Hope fell to her knees and hugged herself, nearly in the fetal position.

Alex knelt down and put both hands on Hope's shoulders. She looked directly into her eyes.

"You're in shock, honey. You didn't kill them. A train hit their van. It's horrendous but you didn't have anything to do with it."

Suzy sat on the floor, flanking Hope on the other side. She stroked her hair.

"Sweetie, it was an accident. There are no words. This is a terrible, terrible tragedy. But we're here for you and will help you through this."

Hope sobbed uncontrollably, unable to catch her breath. Alex fished a tissue out of her purse and steered Hope toward a chair. Suzy stood. "I'll find some coffee."

The police officers came out of the office. One held a clipboard and told Hope she could complete the forms later. The female officer smiled at Alex, most likely relieved someone was there to console Hope.

"I did this." Hope turned toward Alex. "It's all my fault. I killed my parents."

The cops looked puzzled by her declaration but didn't press her.

Before Alex could respond, Suzy returned with three cups of coffee. "Here, honey, drink it black."

Alex put her arm around Hope's shoulders. "Why do you keep saying you killed them? They were hit by a train."

Hope inhaled and told Alex and Suzy about her huge fight with her parents.

Through gulping moans she said, "Two weeks ago, I kicked them out. Something in me snapped when I saw them sprawled out on my couch, eating my food and drinking my beer right after they returned from their protest where I—no Alex—bailed them out of jail. I threw a fit. A bitch fit. I screamed and yelled and told them they were horrible people and to get out of my life."

Suzy wiped Hope's runny nose and held her like a small child.

Alex handed her another tissue. "You didn't do anything wrong. You were doing what we—"

Hope interrupted. "I said I didn't know how they could be my parents. That I wanted them out of my house. This is the first time in my life I've lost complete control. Now look what happened." Practically hiccupping because she was crying so hard, Hope continued. "They must have been stoned out of their minds, worried about their next meal and not concentrating while they were driving. Now they're dead. See? It's my fault." Hope put her head on her knees and wept.

Suzy wiped her own tears and rubbed Hope's back.

"Please stop saying that. It's not your fault. You had nothing to do with this tragic accident. We all say things we don't mean. You weren't the cause of the accident. You have to believe that."

"But the last thing they'll remember is how I yelled at them. I'm a horrible daughter. I don't think I can live with myself now. I don't see how I can go on. I'm not sure I want to go on."

Suzy put both hands firmly on Hope's shoulders. "You do want to go on and you must go on. You have girlfriends and students who love you. We *need* you. Time is a wonderful thing. I know it's way too soon to think about healing but you've got to stop these destructive thoughts."

Suzy looked into Hope's bleary eyes and kissed her splotchy cheek. "They were probably so stoned the night you fought they didn't even remember what you said by the time they drove out of your driveway."

Alex bobbed her head in agreement and made a face as she sipped the bitter coffee.

"I hope you're right about that," Hope said.

Suzy shifted into total mom mode. "Larry and Montana knew how much you loved them. How much you did for them. You were the strong person in the family, the responsible one. You were the parent to your own parents. They weren't going to love you any less because of one argument. Maybe you opened their eyes before this accident."

Hope listened between sniffles.

"Suzy's right." Alex shifted in her seat and held Hope's hand. "Listen to her. She's a mom. She knows how parents and children interact."

Hope's sobs echoed off the wall. A few curious students glanced over but gave her a wide berth.

"Now, I don't have any parents. I hope I wake up and this is a terrible nightmare."

Alex handed Hope a coffee. "Here, sip this putrid coffee. I don't know how you drink this stuff but maybe it'll make you feel better."

Hope managed a small laugh. "Guess I'm used to it."

A tall, well-dressed, matronly woman walked up and introduced herself as Dr. Holmes, the Hilltop High School principal. First, she directed her attention to Hope, gathering her in a large, long hug.

"Take off as much time as you need. Don't worry about coming back to school any time soon. We'll take care of your students. We'll take care of everything."

The principal smoothed Hope's hair and kept her arm around her shoulders. "Call us anytime, dear. Everyone here loves you. I'll be in touch soon."

Hope nodded while managing a meek "thank you."

Dr. Holmes looked over her shoulder as she walked away.

"Will one of you drive her home?"

Suzy and Alex both nodded and the principal disappeared into her office. Alex followed her inside. "Excuse me? Did the officers tell you how this happened?"

"Yes, a witness saw the entire accident unfold. He was apparently stopped on the other side of the railroad tracks and reported the vehicle was parked in the middle of the tracks. He told police he heard "Proud Mary" blaring from the radio and could smell marijuana from several yards away. He added the woman danced outside the bus while the man was at the wheel."

The witness said he got out of his car, waved and yelled as loud as he could for the couple to leave the vehicle. He said the crossing lights were blinking indicating an oncoming train but the Trumans apparently didn't notice." The principal shook her head. "Such a tragedy."

She continued, "The officers surmised Hope's parents didn't hear the train's whistle either because of the very loud music or because of being stoned or both. It's a dreadful situation. I'm worried about Hope. Please take good care of her."

"How horrible. May I ask—" Alex looked at her feet not knowing how to continue. "Did they find the bodies?"

"That wasn't mentioned. I doubt they'd be in one piece but I really don't want to know those details, do you?"

"Guess not. Thank you for telling me, Dr. Holmes. We'll do all we can to help Hope with this crisis." Alex left the principal's office and saw Suzy gathering Hope's purse and sweater. Alex caught up with them as they trudged toward Alex's car.

They drove in silence except for Hope's ongoing wails. When they arrived at her house, the friends got on either side of Hope, practically carrying her inside. In the living room, Hope spotted a small swatch of her mother's lime green macramé plant holder peeking out from the side of the chair. She carefully pulled it out, hugged the planter to her chest and nearly choked on her sobs.

"Mom was making this plant holder when I yelled at them."

"I'm glad you have this. Why don't you take it to bed with you if it gives you comfort. I'm going to fix you some hot tea," Alex said.

Suzy led Hope to her bedroom and turned the comforter down. "Why don't you put on some PJ's or sweats and get into bed? We'll bring you some tea in a minute."

Hope stared blankly at Suzy as though she didn't comprehend what she was saying. She sat on her bed hugging the plant holder and rocking back and forth.

"Let me help you." Suzy pulled off Hope's shoes and began undressing her. She rummaged in Hope's drawers for some comfortable clothes. She put white crew socks on Hope's feet and helped her into gray sweats and a Hilltop tee.

Suzy hugged her again and assured Hope she'd be right back. She traipsed into the kitchen to find Alex.

Alex opened cabinet doors searching for mugs when Suzy entered the room. "What are we going to do? Hope is the counselor. I don't know how to handle these situations."

"I'm no counselor either but I am a mom. All we can do is shower her with love and let her grieve. We're going to have to rally around her for the next few weeks—help with food, household chores, and possibly the funeral arrangements. I think that's the best we can do."

Suzy helped Alex fill the mugs with tea. "We need to keep her preoccupied so she doesn't get severely despondent or depressed."

While Alex looked through the cabinets for food, Suzy found a prescription bottle for sinus medication near the sink. She noted the doctor's name and looked up her phone number. After Suzy brought the doctor up to speed about the accident, she asked, "Will you prescribe a sedative and some anti-anxiety medication? I think she'll need it."

Suzy listened, frowned, and said "I understand." She hung up and stared at Alex. "Stupid HIPPA laws. The doctor won't prescribe anything without seeing Hope first."

"Are you kidding me? After her parents were killed?" Alex crossed her arms. "Wait a minute. I have both of those medications. I take anti-anxiety medication for my occasional OCD issues."

Suzy smiled. "I'm glad to hear that, hon. Do you take them daily?"

"No."

"Maybe you should."

"This isn't about me. I also have some Ambien or you could pick up Tylenol PM or something similar to help Hope sleep."

Suzy grabbed her purse. I'm going to Walgreens to get the sleep aid. Maybe you can bring the anti-anxiety meds tomorrow. We could probably all use one.

Alex nodded. "I will. She needs drugs. This is too hard on her own. I'll make sure she isn't allergic to any medications, though. That's all we need right now."

Suzy found her purse and walked toward the door. "Mind if I use your car?"

"Of course not." She fished in her bag and handed the keys to Suzy. After Suzy left, Alex took soothing green tea into the bedroom. Hope was cuddling the macramé plant holder, sobbing and rocking in bed.

"I'm so sorry, hon. I feel helpless. Please tell me what I can do for you. I'll do anything."

"Just stay with me for a while. I don't want to be alone."

"No problem." Alex handed Hope the tea and sat on the bed.

She turned on the television for white noise and they watched Dr. Phil in silence. Luckily, today's show wasn't about feuding children and parents. It was about anorexia nervosa. They stared at the skeletal former model in silent shock.

"I certainly don't have to worry about that." Hope managed a small laugh. "My thighs get bigger if I so much as look at carbs."

"Stop it. You're a beautiful woman."

"I hate my looks. You and Suzy are gorgeous. It doesn't matter. I could care less right now. I just want my parents back." Hope buried her face in her pillow.

Alex wished Suzy would hurry. "Listen to me. You *are* beautiful—inside and out." She patted Hope's leg. "We'll help you get past this. You will get better. I promise."

"That's a hefty promise."

"Yes it is. But it's true." Alex pulled a sheet over Hope.

"Knock. Knock." Suzy entered the bedroom with pizza and a pharmacy sack.

"I've been smelling this pizza for fifteen minutes. I'm about to eat the cardboard box. Do you want to eat at the kitchen table or in here?"

"Thanks for the thought but I can't eat. How can I eat pizza when my parents just died?"

"You've got to eat to keep up your strength. Just try one piece." Suzy pulled a desk chair beside the bed and plunked the pizza on top of Hope's comforter. Alex ran into the bathroom and reappeared with a towel. She placed it underneath the box. "It's greasy."

Suzy looked at Hope and shrugged. "Gotta love our Alex."

Hope watched as Suzy and Alex hungrily ate the pepperoni pizza and drank Diet Coke. Hope realized she was starving and the smell wore her down. She held out a grateful hand and Suzy placed a slice of pizza on it.

When they finished, Suzy pulled out a sleep aid. "Alex and I agree you'll need some help getting to sleep. Here's a sleeping pill."

"I don't like pills. My parents always popped—" Hope started to cry.

"It's just for a week or two. They're not addictive."

Alex added, "I'd sure take them if I were you. Hell, I could use one myself. I've had trouble sleeping."

Suzy poured a pill into Hope's hand and handed her a Diet Coke. "Here."

Hope reluctantly took the pill and within minutes she could barely hold her eyes open. She laid back on the pillow. Alex pulled a sheet over her, and Suzy placed the phone near her bed.

"We're going to leave while you sleep. Call us any time, day or night."

Alex closed the curtains and picked up the empty pizza box. "We'll be back in the morning to check on you."

They turned out the kitchen lights and locked the front door behind them. Alex blew out her breath.

"This is a tough one. I hope we can get her through the next few days."

"We will," Suzy said.

Chapter 39

Over the next five days, Alex and Suzy took turns checking on Hope. One of them stopped by every morning and evening to bring food and make sure she took her meds. Suzy took a huge container of broccoli cheese soup, Mexican cornbread, and a large fruit salad. Alex bought a Honeybaked ham and made baked beans and a green salad. They bought a giant Sub sandwich, chips, and French onion dip. Hope had enough leftovers for two weeks.

A few nights after work, Suzy and Alex met with the funeral home director to help plan the arrangements at Hope's request. She wasn't mentally able to pull a funeral together.

The day before the funeral Alex checked on Hope. When she entered her bedroom, Hope was in bed, still wearing the same gray sweats she had worn for three days. The macramé planter was on the nightstand. Alex nudged her. Hope rolled over and rubbed her eyes.

Alex pointed to her sweats. "Aren't you sick of wearing these? Have you had a shower all week?"

Hope rolled over and mumbled something that sounded like "I don't know" into her pillow. She pulled the comforter under her chin. Staring at the wall, she said, "I don't want to change clothes. I don't want to shower. I'm never leaving my bedroom. I feel safe here."

Alex tugged at the comforter. "You've got to get out of bed. The funeral is tomorrow. Suzy and I have it all arranged. It'll be a beautiful service." She gently pulled on Hope's arm.

"Come on, sweetie. Sit up. You'll feel better."

Begrudgingly, Hope pushed herself up and stared into Alex's eyes.

"I don't want to go tomorrow. It's all my—"

"Stop saying that. It's not your fault. I know this is very, very hard but you've got to stop blaming yourself." Alex sat on the bed and put both her hands around Hope's still-blotchy face. "It's not your fault. It was an accident."

Hope leaned against Alex's shoulder and cried. Alex held her close, rubbing her back. When Hope's breathing slowed, Alex patted her leg and walked to her closet.

"Let me help you find something to wear tomorrow."

Alex chose a long black skirt, a white blouse with pearl buttons and black ballerina flats. She laid the clothes neatly on a chair beside the bed and looked squarely at Hope.

"Now, you're going to get some fresh air."

Hope opened her mouth to complain but Alex was determined. She sat Hope's tennis shoes in front of her.

"Just a short walk around the block. You'll feel better, I promise."

Alex pointed Hope toward the front door and they stepped out into the warm sunshine. The skies were a soft pale blue and cottony clouds swirled overhead. Hope put one hand above her eyes, squinting as the bright sun shone on her pale face. Alex hoped the sun would give Hope some much-needed color. She grabbed an extra pair of sunglasses out of her car and thrust them on Hope's face.

"Let's go."

They walked five blocks and saw children riding bikes and playing basketball. Two people were mowing, a redbird flew overhead, and a rabbit hopped across the street. A yellow Lab ran up as if to say hello. Hope bent down to pet him for a long time. When they rounded the corner toward the house, Suzy pulled up and jumped out of her car.

With a smile that nearly wrapped around her head, Suzy ran with outstretched arms, practically tackling friends.

"I'm so glad to see you outside. This is a big step."

Hope smiled like a shy, young girl. "I admit the fresh air feels good." She looked around. "But I want to go inside now before my neighbors interrogate me."

Alex agreed they'd accomplished enough for one day and protectively steered Hope inside.

"I'm tired of these leftovers," Suzy said. Alex overheard her on her cell ordering Chinese. While they waited for the delivery, Alex coaxed Hope into the shower. "Go shower. I'm the boss today."

Hope gawked at her.

"Pretty please. You'll feel better. When you get out, the food should be here."

Hope obeyed as fast as a turtle crossing an eight-lane highway. She trudged to her room, opened drawers and finally found clean jeans, a yellow shirt, and clean underwear. She disappeared into the bathroom. Twenty minutes later, she reappeared bundled in a thick, white towel with a smaller towel around her hair. Her eyes welled with tears.

"I have the best friends in the world. I can never thank you enough for all you've done. I couldn't have survived this without you. I love you both more than you know."

Alex and Suzy simultaneously wiped tears from their own eyes, then held Hope in a long, tight bear hug.

"That's what friends are for. We're here for each other in good times and bad."

Ding dong. Suzy went to the door and paid the delivery guy. She handed the bags to Alex as she searched her purse for money.

"Let me pay," said Alex and Hope in unison. Suzy dismissed them with her hand. "I've got it. I'm loaded," she joked.

Alex shrugged and looked at Hope. "I'll get the plates and drinks. Peach tea, everyone?"

They nodded and settled at the kitchen table instead of Hope's bedroom for once. Alex was happy the baby steps were beginning and could barely contain her excitement. It was obvious that Hope was slowly but surely beginning to heal. Alex set the plates and silverware out as Suzy dished up cashew chicken, sweet and sour chicken, rice, vegetables and egg rolls.

Hope rubbed her belly, eyeing the food. "I didn't realize I was hungry."

Alex and Suzy exchanged satisfied glances. They ate in silence for several minutes then Suzy took a deep breath and spoke.

"Alex and I have planned a Celebration of Life in honor of Larry and Montana. We hope that's okay with you." She looked toward Hope who nodded.

"We know they loved seventies music so there will be some great songs playing before, during and after the service." Suzy hesitated. "It won't be a traditional service, per se, but I think," she looked at Alex "*we* think it suits and honors them."

Suzy waited for Hope to respond. She had made a great deal of progress today and hoped this didn't set her back. Suzy glanced nervously at Alex.

Hope swallowed her chicken and smiled.

"I think a Celebration of Life is exactly what Mom and Dad would have wanted. They loved life—and especially music—it sounds perfect. Thank you both for planning the service. I just couldn't—" Her voice caught.

"I know tomorrow is going to be hard but somehow with you two and my students, I think I just might get through it."

Chapter 40

After cleaning the kitchen and getting Hope settled with a sedative and a funny movie, Alex and Suzy walked outside.

"I need a T.J. Maxx fix," Alex said.

"Have fun, oh great shopper." Suzy checked her cell and saw a text from Jon. Her face brightened.

"Jon's going to be here in three days. I can't wait to see him and meet his new friend. I think I'll go to the grocery store and stock up."

"Can't wait to meet the mystery woman. See you tomorrow. Big day." Alex climbed into her Mustang and left.

Suzy mentally compiled a grocery list as she drove. She spent an hour at the store buying all of Jon's favorites. As she rounded the corner near her home, she saw a strange car in her driveway.

I wonder if Jon got a different car. They must have arrived early. Good thing I bought some food. Suzy squinted but with the bright glare on the windows, she couldn't make out the passengers.

She parked her car and walked toward the Camry, struggling with the grocery bags. The car door opened and out stepped her long-lost sister, Tara.

Suzy's mouth flew open. She struggled to keep from dropping her bags. "What are you doing here? And where is Asshole of the Year?"

Tara walked tentatively toward her sister.

"I know you're mad at me. Very mad. I've left Dean. Please hear me out. I made a huge mistake. Can I come in?" She reached for a grocery bag.

Suzy's face hardened. "I don't need help. I can manage just fine, thank you. We don't have anything to talk about. You tried to ruin my life. You embarrassed me on *my* wedding day. You and Dean ruined it. What could you possibly say now? I'm not interested in hearing your story." Suzy stormed past her sister toward the house.

Tara cried out. "You're my sister. I want to make amends. This whole thing tore our family apart. Mom and Dad are miserable. They're caught in the middle. Please. Let me come in. I want to tell you the whole story. Then I'll leave."

Suzy sighed, then held the door open. Tara followed timidly behind, head bowed. Suzy plunked groceries on the counter and ignored her sister while she put away the cold items. She banged the canned goods on the shelves and slammed cabinet doors.

"You think you can pull a stunt like that, show up out of the blue, and I'm just going to forgive you, is that it?" Suzy glared at Tara. "It's always been poor, poor Tara. Well, little sister, I don't know if I can get past this one." Suzy brushed her hair out of her eyes and thrust the milk inside the refrigerator so hard she nearly knocked the other items over like bowling pins.

Tara braced herself against the kitchen counter, shoulders slumped. "I understand if you can't forgive me. I wanted you to know I realized what a jerk Dean was. We broke up two months ago. I put the house up for sale and the proceeds will go back to Mom and Dad."

Suzy softened slightly. "I'm glad to hear that. They should be reimbursed."

Tara stared at the floor. "I'm trying to move on. I've taken a new job and am relocating to Florida. Now that I'll be miles away, you've got to repair your relationship with Mom and Dad. They miss you terribly. They never took my side. Dad didn't anyway. He's heartbroken not seeing you." Tara looked hopefully into Suzy's eyes.

Suzy walked toward the window holding back the anger that filled her chest.

"I miss them, too. None of this would have happened if you hadn't—Wait a minute. I don't need *you* to tell *me* how to handle my parents. I just wanted time. It seemed like they sided with you and the adulterer. Of course I'll repair my relationship with them. I love them. I miss them."

Tears welled in Suzy's eyes and spilled down her cheeks. "I have a girlfriend who just lost her parents in a horrible accident." She plopped down in her favorite floral chair and sobbed. "Damn it. Life is too short for grudges."

She searched Tara's face. "I do want to know who took the picture of you two having sex and how it got to me."

Tara shifted from foot to foot. "You aren't going to like this but I'll tell you the truth. I had been dating the best man, Brent, for three weeks and joined up with the guys after the bachelor party. We shot some pool. We did shots. Several shots. Brent got mad, said I was flirting with Dean, and stormed off. I guess I was flirting with him. You always got the cuter guys. Anyway—"

She looked away, unable to face her sister.

"I was very drunk and very stupid. That's the bottom line. Apparently, Brent followed us. Dean and I went to a hotel and obviously didn't bother closing the curtains. We were both wasted. Brent must have taken the photos. No one else was at the bar that late."

Suzy watched her sister's cheeks redden.

"I'm deeply ashamed. I knew if I couldn't forgive myself that you certainly couldn't forgive me, so I broke up with Dean. Besides, it was wrong from the start. He probably would have cheated on me too and my sister is far more important than a cheater. That's why I'm moving away. I need a fresh start."

Suzy paced. She wanted to forgive Tara but not easily. Tara had put Suzy through hell on her wedding day. She couldn't let her off the hook just like that. She looked her sister straight in the eye.

"You're going to have to give me time to digest this. It won't happen overnight but I will forgive you, Tara. It's the forgetting that's hard. You're my sister and always will be. But I need time." She crossed her arms, hurt, and still defensive.

"I understand. I couldn't ask for more. I'm leaving for the airport in an hour and will start my job in a few days." Tara reached into her pocket. "Here's my card. I'll be working at a beach resort. Maybe I can send some beach wedding clients your way."

Tara pushed her business card across the counter toward Suzy. "Call me anytime. I'd be honored to have you back in my life. I love you. And I'm sorry." Tears ran down her cheeks.

Suzy softened. She couldn't stand it when anyone cried. She walked toward Tara and gave her a brief hug. "I forgive you but I meant what I said. I need time to heal. Good luck in Florida. I'm glad," she paused. "I'm glad you came by."

Tara stared thankfully into her sister's eyes.

"This is such a relief. Such a weight lifted. Thank you for listening. I was afraid you wouldn't speak to me." She took a deep breath. "Hopefully, we can repair our relationship and you'll visit me in Florida. When you're ready. I'll do anything to make this up to you." She glanced at her watch. "For now, I've got to catch my plane."

They hugged an awkward good-bye and Tara hopped into her rental car and left. Suzy stared out the window until Tara was out of sight. Tears pricked her eyes. She rubbed her arms even though she wasn't cold.

What a day. And tomorrow will be just as draining. She strode into her bedroom to change and noticed the answering machine light blinking. She pushed the button, hoping it was Jon with a travel update.

A pleasant-sounding southern voice said, "Suzanne Jacobs? I'm assuming this is Weddings by Suzanne. If it is, I would like to meet with you soon. My name is Emma Biltmore. I'm leaving town for a few days. I'll call you again when I return. Good-bye."

Suzy wondered how Emma had put two and two together.

This will be interesting. Maybe Mrs. B decided to involve Emma and gave her my number. Somehow, I doubt it.

Suzy's mind raced as she thought about meeting Emma. Her shoulders tensed, fearful of how Mrs. Biltmore would react. She had been very clear that there should not be any contact between them.

Suzy put her pajamas on and tried reading to unwind. She got involved in her novel and lost track of time. Her head barely hit the pillow when the phone jarred her. She glanced at the clock. It was midnight. *Surely, it isn't?* Picking up on the third ring, Suzy said "hel—"

"I had another thought. You're awake, aren't you? I can't seem to sleep much these days. This is Mrs. Biltmore, by the way."

"Yes, I know." Suzy yawned, trying to keep the disdain out of her voice. "What is it, Mrs. Biltmore? Do you realize its midnight?"

Mrs. Biltmore ignored the question and plodded on. "We need to meet with the chef at the Biltmore Country Club. He's fabulous. The best. Of course, I don't tell *him* that. It would go straight to his head and he'd ask for more money. I snagged him from a five-star hotel while traveling in Hawaii. Nevertheless—"

Suzy cut her off. "Can this wait? I have to go to a funeral in the morning."

"Just meet me at the Biltmore Country Club tomorrow at three. The lunch rush will have ended and surely your funeral will be over by then."

Suzy sighed, knowing Mrs. B wouldn't take no for answer.

"Fine. I'll be there. Good night." Suzy hung up, pulled the covers over her head, and willed herself to sleep.

At six o'clock she was awakened by her familiar Biltmore alarm.

"I called to remind you of our meeting this afternoon. I've lined up Chef York. He's going to prepare a taste-testing for Emma's wedding. See you at three." Suzy didn't get one word in before Mrs. B hung up.

She tried to sleep another hour but gave up after punching her pillow a dozen times. Yawning, she padded toward the kitchen to make some much-needed coffee. While eating raisin toast, pineapple yogurt, and a banana, Suzy reminded herself to focus on the funeral—and Hope. She'd handle Mrs. B. later. Oh, add Jon to the mix. All the personalities swirled through her head. Suzy wished she could sneak one of Hope's anti-anxiety pills. After eating breakfast, she took a long, hot shower, and changed into a black sheath and pumps in preparation for the Celebration of Life.

Chapter 41

Alex flopped in bed, dreading the funeral, and wondering how they'd get Hope through the day. She awoke early and left a message at the bank reminding her boss she wouldn't be in. She knew Hope would need her friends all day. Alex took a quick, steamy shower and smoothed her long blond hair with a flat iron. She wore a new black suit and applied makeup, all the while wondering if Hope was awake. She looked heavenward. *Please help us all get through today.*

Alex padded into the kitchen and poured Cheerios into a bowl. She added sweetener and a sliced banana. She made pumpkin coffee and popped an English muffin into the toaster. While she waited for it to finish toasting, an envelope on the floor near her front door caught her eye.

Alex picked the envelope up with dread. She turned it over. The envelope was sealed and blank on the front. She placed it on the counter while she buttered the muffin, poured milk on her cereal, and filled a coffee mug. When she couldn't stall any longer, she sat at the table and opened it. Inside, was a handwritten note.

Dear Alex,

While being away from you, I've had a lot of time to think and will just come out and say it. I'm falling hard for you and wanted you to know. You're right. I shouldn't stay in a bad marriage because of Joey. He'll always be my son no matter what. I realize that now. I miss you and can't wait to see you. It shouldn't be much longer. Can't wait!

Tony

P.S. Don't tell anyone about this.

The note both excited and confused Alex. *What does this mean? Is he going to get a divorce? Are we going to be together? Now with an even more nervous stomach,* she glanced at the clock, tucking the note in her purse. She fastened a silver heart locket around her neck, checked the lock on the door twice, and left for Suzy's house.

Chapter 42

Alex collected Suzy and drove to Hope's house.

"Do you think she'll be dressed?" Suzy shrugged but gave an optimistic smile.

Alex pulled up to Hope's house, took a deep breath, and walked toward the front door. Suzy got into the rear seat so Hope could sit up front.

Before Alex reached the door, Hope stepped outside. She was dressed in the clothes Alex had laid out the day before. Hope gave her friends a pensive smile and climbed into the front seat.

"Hi, Hope." Alex patted her arm.

Hope was extremely quiet. The silence was so thick it felt like another person in the car. They rode to the funeral home, arriving an hour early. Alex and Suzy wanted Hope to see the outpouring of love and support from her fellow teachers and students.

The two caskets were closed—and empty since the bodies were never found. Montana's purse was located at the scene, as was one of Larry's tennis shoes. But that was all. It was as if they had vanished. Alex shuddered to think about what had happened to their bodies at impact and certainly never discussed it with Hope. The less details the better.

Larry and Montana's pictures were on top of their respective brown caskets. A large collage filled with photos spanning several decades was displayed on a nearby easel. At least thirty floral bouquets, most likely from Hilltop High School students, faculty, and staff filled the dark, paneled room.

Hope shuffled toward the caskets, placing her hand on top of each, one by one. She stared at the photos for several minutes, finally kissing Larry and Montana's pictures. She wiped away tears, rejoined her friends and squeezed their hands. Alex held her breath, fearing Hope would have a meltdown.

As guests filtered in, several songs played in the background. Alex had gone through Hope's music selection and chose several. "Come Sail Away" by Styx was followed by "Papa Was A Rollin' Stone" by the Temptations. As people were seated, "Fooled Around and Fell in Love" by Elvin Bishop filled the air.

Alex feared the music would bring back vivid, painful memories but knew Hope shared her parents' love of music. She and Suzy worried it would sound more like a concert than a funeral but came to the conclusion that the service should be appropriate for Larry, Montana, and Hope—not everyone else.

Hope's shoulders heaved when she spotted some of her favorite students slide into a pew. Several teachers, neighbors, and friends of Larry and Montana dressed in their best black leather, some with fringe and riding boots, greeted Hope. Well-wishers hugged her and expressed their sympathy. Hope was quiet but attempted to smile through her tears as she hugged everyone.

Suzy whispered to Alex. "She's doing amazingly well. She must have taken a handful of those prescriptions."

Suzy arranged for her favorite wedding pastor to preside over the service. Before Rev. Browning took the podium, the song "Lean on Me" by Bill Withers played. When the song ended, the minister approached the front and motioned with his hands for everyone to stand. He said the Lord's Prayer and everyone spoke in unison, repeating the words.

Rev. Browning read Larry and Montana's obituaries from the newspaper, emphasizing the tragic accident and how their lives were taken too soon. He discussed the fact that the service was a Celebration of Life and how Larry and Montana had enjoyed life to the fullest. Holding his hands in the air, Rev. Browning expressed how they were now akin to free birds in heaven with no worldly worries. When the pastor finished, "Amazing Grace" by Elvis boomed through the speakers.

Alex dabbed her eyes and blew her nose. She heard sniffling throughout the funeral home and focused on Hope who appeared to be holding herself together well. *So far, so good.*

When the song ended, Hilltop's principal strode to the front. Dr. Holmes smiled at Hope and said several kind words about Hope's impressive relationship with her students and how she must have had wonderful parents to turn out so well. Hope nodded with gratitude. Alex could only imagine what Hope was thinking.

When Dr. Holmes finished, the minister said a final, uplifting prayer, then everyone filed toward the caskets to pay their respects. Many stared at the pictorial collage while "Crystal Blue Persuasion" played. Alex and Suzy stood beside Hope as they waited to depart for the cemetery.

After most had filed through, Hope walked toward the back of the funeral home where she noticed a man standing alone. He seemed transfixed by her.

The man was well dressed in a dark gray suit. He had dark, curly hair surrounding a bald spot. He was stocky, rather short, and had kind brown eyes which studied Hope. As she got closer, he smiled, motioning her over. Hope hesitated then walked toward the stranger.

He extended his hand. "I'm sorry about your loss. My name is Paul and—" He stammered. "I know you're in mourning right now, but when you're ready, I'd like for you to call me. It's important."

"Who are you? A bill collector?"

"No, no. Nothing like that. I'm sorry to intrude on a day like today, but I saw the obituary for Larry and Claire and knew I'd find you here."

"Her friends call her 'Montana.' You must not be a friend."

"I can explain everything. I've wanted to talk to you for a very long time." He stuffed his hand in his pocket and produced a business card.

"Call me. When you're ready. Please. It's very—" He paused, clearing his throat. "The sooner we talk the better." He held the business card toward Hope. "My office and cell numbers are on it. Call me any time, day or night."

Hope took the information. *I don't have time for a mystery man, especially today.* She looked into his chocolate brown eyes, wondering what he was up to. She thought she detected a tear and apprehensively shook his hand.

"I'll be in touch," she said, even though she wasn't sure she'd ever contact him. He thanked her and walked out the door.

Hope looked for her friends. She knew it was time to drive to the cemetery. She dreaded this part the most. She spotted Alex and Suzy on the steps outside.

"Who was that man?" Alex asked.

"I'm not sure. He said he needs to talk to me. That it's extremely important." Hope shrugged. "I can't imagine what it's about. He looks vaguely familiar but I can't place him. I don't think he's a bill collector or anything. He seems like a gentle, kind man but these days, who knows? He could be some kind of con artist."

"You can't be too careful." Suzy touched her arm. "It's time to leave." They climbed into Alex's car and followed the hearse to the cemetery.

The graveside service was short, especially since it started to rain. After the minister said a few words, Hope sauntered toward the opening in the ground. She threw two bunches of daisies onto each casket. She whispered toward the ground, then looked to the heavens. "Please forgive me. Goodbye, Mom and Dad. I love you."

Alex and Suzy exchanged tearful glances as they dabbed their eyes. Hope returned to the front row and sat between them. They held her hand until other friends and teachers walked up to pay their respects. After everyone left, Alex and Suzy put their arms through Hope's and guided her to the car.

Hope wiped her eyes and nose. "You're both wonderful. I don't know how I'll ever repay you for your kindnesses." She leaned her head back against the seat and blew out her breath.

Suzy leaned forward and stroked her hair. "You don't repay friends for being friends."

Chapter 43

After leaving Hope's house, Suzy entered the Biltmore Country Club at exactly three o'clock. She knew better than to be five minutes late. Mrs. B was standing in the foyer barking orders. A young, well-dressed woman stood, round shouldered, as though waiting to be whipped.

"I told you to update that mailing list a month ago," Mrs. B bellowed. "Dr. Klondike is no longer married to Mary. They're divorced and he's very angry he received yet another newsletter from us with her name on it. He doesn't want to see her name ever again."

She put her hand on her hip and leaned closer to the woman. "I don't want to lose him to another country club. This had better not happen again. Do you hear me?"

The scared-looking young woman bobbed her head and ducked into an office. Undoubtedly, she went straight to her computer to update the mailing list before Attila the Hun had her beheaded.

After her tirade, Mrs. B acknowledged Suzy with a curt nod.

"I hope you're hungry. I've ordered our top menu items for a tasting." She charged toward the dining room.

"Let's find Chef York."

As they stood inside the grand dining room, Suzy spotted a chubby chef wearing a starched white uniform and large chef's hat. From a few feet away, she could see the poor man's face was glistening with sweat.

Mrs. Biltmore approached him and made a face.

"Are you sweating? My God, did your perspiration drop into my food? Go clean yourself up and come back."

The chef scurried off while Suzy wondered if he would return or walk right out the front door. *Why would he or any of the employees put up with this obnoxious, rude woman? Then again, why was she putting up with her?* She decided Mrs. B must pay them all very well to endure this treatment.

The chef returned with a dry face and slightly damp hair. He extended his hand and introduced himself.

Before Suzy could speak, Mrs. B interrupted.

"She's Emma's wedding planner." The chef didn't feign his surprise.

"I've told Suzy all about you. I hope you live up to your reputation. Dazzle us. Now, tell us what you've prepared?"

Chef York walked toward the mounded platters and beamed.

With a flourish, he pointed to the beautifully presented food. "Our first menu features leg of lamb with plum sauce, herb risotto, green beans almandine, salad greens with champagne vinaigrette, and poppy seed rolls."

He then walked toward the middle section of the table. "If you prefer seafood, I've prepared pistachio encrusted salmon, roasted asparagus with balsamic vinegar, garlic mashed potatoes, a tomato and artichoke salad, and lemon muffins."

"Finally, we have peppercorn beef medallions, twice-baked potatoes, salad greens with dried cherries, mandarin oranges, and a blood orange vinaigrette accompanied by Hawaiian rolls."

Chef York smiled. "Of course, before the wedding, we'll have served appetizers, wine and champagne for toasts. The wedding cake and groom's cake will be dessert."

Suzy shook her head. "You made all of this for us?"

The chef blushed.

"These are superb choices. Divine. I don't think we can go wrong with either menu. I can't wait to sample it." Suzy noticed the chef relax. Of course, he was still awaiting approval from the Queen.

Mrs. Biltmore looked around impatiently. "Where are the servers with our drinks? And plates? We need plates."

Iced tea and plates arrived almost magically and Suzy and Mrs. Biltmore began eating. Suzy knew she was expected to try everything. Mrs. B's suspicious eyes studied her every move. Suzy wiped her mouth and observed Mrs. Biltmore appeared to be enjoying the food, although she would probably never admit it.

"Well," Mrs. Biltmore said. "What do you think?"

"Amazing. The food is delicious. Every morsel." She eyed the heaping platters again.

"What's your favorite?"

"I'd recommend the pistachio-encrusted salmon and peppercorn beef medallions. The vegetables and salads he prepared are perfect to accompany the entrees. I'd let Chef choose two or three of each. Guests always appreciate it when they have a choice."

Mrs. B nearly smiled.

"That's exactly what I was thinking. The food is good, isn't it? Maybe I shouldn't be so hard on Chef. He does an excellent job but I don't want it to go to his head."

Suzy wondered when she would feel comfortable enough to give Mrs. B some advice about people skills.

Chef York wandered out of the kitchen, looking in their direction. "Any decisions, ladies?"

Suzy went first. "Utterly delicious, Chef. We loved everything. For the wedding, we've decided on the seafood and steak for the entrees. You choose which vegetables, salads and bread to accompany them. You're the expert."

Chef York beamed. He stood taller, puffing out his chest like Superman. Suzy peered at the buttons on his apron wondering if they would burst. She felt a giggle but suppressed it.

Mrs. Biltmore shot Suzy a look. "Well done, Chef. I

want the best meal that has ever touched anyone's lips here in Missouri. I believe you've come up with an outstanding menu.

This wedding will be in all the society pages in Atlanta as well. I'll see to that." She narrowed her eyes with laser focus on Chef York. "*You* see to it that the food is perfect."

Suzy noticed a glint of perspiration reappear on his forehead.

"Yes, ma'am. I will. Thank you." He disappeared into the kitchen before she could change her mind.

Sipping her tea, Suzy wondered if she should mention Emma had called but decided against it.

"Mrs. Biltmore, I've had a very long morning. My friend buried her parents today. I'm going to check on her now."

Mrs. B looked startled. "Oh, my. That's too bad. Well, I hope she's—" She stopped herself as if she realized she was about to say something kind.

"Good-bye then." Mrs. B scooted her chair back and marched away.

Suzy watched her frail back wondering why she couldn't be nice for once. Suzy left in a hurry to drive directly to Hope's house.

Chapter 44

Since Suzy was dealing with Mrs. Bitchmore, Alex entertained Hope's school friends who dropped by following the service. Thankfully, plenty of staff and faculty had brought casseroles and side dishes. There was enough food for a football team.

When the guests finally left, Alex cleaned up the kitchen and tucked a weary Hope into bed. Alex called Suzy and told her not to worry about coming by. Exhausted, she drove home counting the minutes until her head hit the pillow. She pulled into the garage, put her purse on the kitchen floor, and kicked off her shoes. The phone was ringing off the hook.

Damn. I just want some peace and quiet. Ring. Ring. Ring. She stared daggers at the trilling phone.

"Hello," she said impatiently.

Silence.

"Who's there?" Alex pressed the phone against her ear trying to detect background noise.

She could hear breathing. "Speak or I'm hanging up." Alex waited a few seconds. Nothing. She slammed the phone down violently and ran her fingers through her hair.

Could that have been Tony? Maybe he couldn't talk and just wanted to hear my voice.

Alex checked to make sure the doors were locked and headed to her bedroom. Unsettled, she left the hall light on. She changed into her pajamas and tried to sleep. She was awakened at two in the morning by a loud pounding on her back door. It sounded like someone was using a large log to break down the door. She sat bolt upright in bed.

Oh, my God. Someone is trying to get in.

She crouched beneath her bedroom window and peeked underneath the curtain. She squinted in the dark trying to see if anyone was in her backyard. The pounding continued and her breaths were like rapid fire. She wiped sweat from her brow and reached for the landline phone on the night stand, cursing herself for leaving her cell phone and purse near the kitchen.

On the first try, she dropped the receiver. She then steadied her hand and dialed 9-1-1.

"What is your emergency?"

"Someone is trying to break into my house."

"Is your address 2121 South Marigold?"

"Yes."

"I'll dispatch officers to your area. In the meantime, get in your closet and take your cell phone with you. I'll stay on the line."

"I can't. My cell phone's in the kitchen near the racket. This landline in my bedroom is the only phone I can use." Alex swallowed. "Hurry. I'm scared. I feel like I'm going to have a heart attack."

"Try to relax, Miss—"

"Mitchell. It's a little hard to relax when—" Alex broke off with a sob. She squatted in the floor, afraid the person outside would see her shadow if she stood.

"The officers will be there soon. Just stay on the line."

Alex's heart pounded as she pressed the phone to her ear. She could still hear banging outside. "It's been over fifteen minutes. What's taking so long? What if they break in first?"

The receiver was slippery in Alex's sweaty hand. Her entire body was a pool of sweat. She could feel her heart pounding in her head.

"Just hold on. Are you okay?

"Apart from having a heart attack and maybe being assaulted, yeah, I'm peachy."

"You're doing great. The officers are close now." The dispatcher paused. Alex's eyes burned. "The officers have arrived."

"Doubtful," Alex said, "I didn't hear any sirens."

"They're coming in quietly. Do you still hear banging on the door?"

Alex listened. "No. It stopped."

"The officers are going to ring your doorbell now. One officer is in your backyard and one will be at your front door. I'll sign off since they're at your house."

"Okay. Thanks." *Ding dong.* She tied her robe tightly, trudged through the hallway and stared through the peep hole. Not seeing anyone, Alex froze. The doorbell rang again. She jumped and opened the door to a uniformed female officer.

"Ma'am, we've searched the backyard and sides of your house but don't see anyone. Do you mind if I come in and ask you a few questions?"

Alex motioned her inside just as a male officer joined her on the front step. He followed her in and looked at Alex.

"We didn't see anyone in your backyard. In fact, it's damp outside and there are no footprints on your deck." The two officers exchanged glances.

The male continued. "There would be footprints on your deck if someone had been at your back door. Are you sure you heard someone?"

"Am I sure?" Alex screeched. "Are you kidding me? I almost stroked out listening to them pound on my door. It sounded like someone was about to break it down! There *must* be footprints out there."

The female officer made a note on her pad while the male said, "We'll take another look, ma'am. Sit tight. We'll be back in a few minutes."

Alex walked to the kitchen sink, still afraid someone lurked in the back yard. She wanted hot chamomile tea to calm her nerves and filled the teapot in the dark. Fumbling in the cabinet, she plucked out a tea bag and turned on the stove. She sat on the kitchen floor waiting for the kettle to whistle.

The officers returned and assured her they had scoured every inch of her yard. No one was in the area. Alex thanked them but was still uneasy. She sipped half her tea and tried unsuccessfully to go back to sleep.

Was that a nightmare? Did I really hear pounding? Maybe I'm losing it.

Chapter 45

Suzy jumped out of bed. Jon and his girlfriend were due to arrive the following morning. She couldn't wait to see her son. Something gnawed at her but she couldn't quite put her finger on it.

She made a pot of coffee and turned on CNN. As she poured her first cup, her phone rang. Suzy hoped it would be Jon with a travel update. Instead, a pleasant-sounding young woman was on the line.

"Hello. Is this Suzanne Jacobs? This is Emma Biltmore."

"This is Suzy. I'm glad you called. I've wanted to talk to you for some time."

"Good. I'd like to get together. I found your pink Weddings by Suzanne pen on the table at the Biltmore. I put two and two together, checked with the servers and they confirmed that you've been meeting with my mother. Is that correct?"

Suzy hesitated and frowned into the phone, feeling guilty. "Yes, we've met a few times." Suzy could hear Emma take a deep breath.

"Might I inquire as to why a wedding planner—I assume you're a wedding planner—would be meeting with my mother? Last time I checked she wasn't getting married."

Suzy felt her cheeks get hot and a nervous laugh escaped her mouth. She looked around her darkened living room for an answer. She knew Mrs. Biltmore was going to be upset if she told Emma the truth but she didn't have any choice. Suzy couldn't lie to this pleasant woman.

She glanced at the fifty thousand dollar check that she had placed in a basket on the counter. She guessed she might as well rip that check up and throw it away. Suzy cleared her throat and told Emma the entire story.

When she was done, Emma said, "My mother. Only she would do such a thing. Just who does she think I'm going to marry? I know she doesn't approve of Bernie." She paused. "Let me guess. It's Lincoln. Am I right?"

Suzy felt like a child at time out.

"Yes, she mentioned someone named Lincoln."

"You know I should be furious with both of you."

Suzy sat in silence. She didn't want to provoke Emma but at the same time didn't blame her for being angry.

"I am extremely upset but I can tell you why I'm not in a rage. My mother has changed drastically over the past year. Ever since Dad died, she's been so lonely. She used to have many friends. She was the life of the party and involved in everything—charity work, golf, bridge, gardening, you name it. She never met a stranger and remembered everyone's name—from the maintenance man to the CEO. She absolutely loved life and loved people." Emma sighed. "Now, she's turned into a miserable old woman and takes it out on everyone. I'm sure you've been on the short end of the stick. She treats our employees like unwanted coyotes. It's embarrassing."

Suzy couldn't believe her ears. *Mrs. Biltmore used to be nice? She used to treat people kindly? The life of the party? A fun person who had many friends and loved life?* This did not describe the woman she knew. Not even remotely.

Emma chuckled. "Your silence says a lot. I know it sounds impossible to someone who just met her but it's true. My father and mother did everything together. They were soul mates in every sense of the word. When Dad had a sudden heart attack, Mom's world shattered. She couldn't take the pressure of being a widow or being in charge of the Biltmore Foundation. Her life as she knew it was over. She's putting up a tough front, but inside she's like a scared, abandoned puppy."

Suzy's opinion of Mrs. B did an immediate about-face. Now she pitied her.

"What do you want me to do? She's already given me a large sum of money. I haven't cashed the check because I was uneasy about the entire situation. Should I just return the check and be done with it?"

"No, keep the check. Mom needs a project. Maybe this will help her get over her depression. If she can focus on something other than her sadness, maybe it'll help."

"But I can't— It's too much."

"It'll be worth all the therapy in the world that she refuses to get. Just let her stay involved in this so-called wedding. Let her take the reins."

Suzy stared into the phone. "I'm confused. Are you going to go through with this and marry Lincoln?"

"Of course not. I don't love Lincoln. In fact, I can't stand the squirmy little guy. He's a snooty, narcissistic weasel. I'm in love with Bernie. We were going to elope but I knew mother would be heartbroken about that, so maybe I'll let her plan my wedding after all."

Emma chuckled. "But I'll be marrying Bernie, not Lincoln."

"How are we going to pull this off?" Suzy yanked drawers open looking for a legal pad and pen.

"Instead of Lincoln's name on the invitation, insert Bernie's name. Just keep me informed about the details and I'll nix what I don't agree with. I'll handle Mom. Don't worry about her. It will all work out. Trust me," Emma said.

Suzy chewed on her lip. "I don't like this. I haven't felt good about this since day one. It feels like fraud. I can't take money from your mother and plan a wedding that's a hoax."

"But it won't be a hoax. Her only daughter will get married—just to someone other than the ideal husband in her eyes. Mom will get to plan my wedding like she's always wanted. It will keep her busy, and hopefully, she'll come out of her depression and enjoy life again. It's a win-win."

Suzy somehow doubted that. It was hard to fathom Mrs. B being a nice person. She knew she'd be the one to get caught in the middle of this mess. She stared into the phone.

"I'm afraid your mother will see right through me. I'm sort of afraid of her," Suzy admitted. "Plus I've worked hard to build my reputation as a wedding planner. I don't want this to soil it. She appears to wield a lot of power. I'm worried about this."

Emma persisted. "I understand where you're coming from. Please trust me. Think about the fact that you'll be helping her focus on something other than losing Dad. It'll work out. I'll make sure of it. I've got to go. Just continue to take her calls and meet with her. Please call me with updates, okay?"

Suzy thought long and hard for a few seconds. She wasn't sure she was doing the right thing but Emma made a strong case and seemed like a reasonable person.

"Okay. You win. I'll continue to meet with your mother under one condition."

"Name it."

"If everything goes south and she starts to blame me—or worse yet, sue me—I want your word in writing that you're aware of this supposed wedding, and in fact, encouraged it."

"Fair enough. In fact, I'll type up a statement and email it for your approval later today. I see your email address on your pen. Don't worry. You won't be held accountable if Mom gets upset. You have my word. Now goodbye."

Suzy wondered if she should get Alex's input. She decided to keep it to herself. Alex had enough worries with the cop. Her mind swirled with this new revelation about Mrs. B.

She dialed Alex's number. "Do you think we should check on Hope today? I'm worried about her and need a break. I can be there in fifteen minutes."

"Sure. I'm at Starbucks getting a skinny vanilla latte. Want me to bring you one?"

"Yes. A *grande*, please. Grab one for Hope, too."

"Will do. See you soon."

Chapter 46

The two friends pulled up at the same time in Hope's driveway. They each carried the coffee as they knocked on the door. No one answered. It was unlocked and Alex nudged it open.

"Hope, are you here?" She stared around the empty living room.

"I'm in bed."

Suzy and Alex walked in and found Hope still in bed, puffy-eyed with her hair askew.

Alex held up a container. "I bought chocolate chip cookies. Chocolate is good for the soul, you know. And we have coffee."

"Thanks but I'm not hungry right now. I don't feel like doing anything." Hope sat in bed, looking puffy from too much sleep.

Alex straightened the throw on the bed and tidied the books on the shelf.

"God, Alex. Can you stop cleaning and straightening for one minute?" Suzy shook her head.

"Hope needs us, not a clean room."

"Someone is tense. Sorry. I didn't know what else to do. Want this skinny vanilla coffee, Hope?"

"How about a bottle of vodka. Got any of that?"

The women chuckled.

"I can add a shot of Bailey's," Alex suggested.

"Make it two shots, please. And bring it in here. I don't have the energy to get up."

"Uh, better not add alcohol with your meds, hon," Suzy said.

Alex left the room with Suzy on her heels.

Suzy's forehead crinkled. "What are we going to do? I thought she'd be better by now. Dr. Holmes is being very patient but I don't want Hope to lose her job. It's been a couple of weeks now. We need to find a way to get her back to school and in a routine."

Alex rummaged through cabinets looking for Bailey's Irish Cream for her own coffee. Her face brightened.

"I have an idea. Let's go to Hilltop and ask the students to write letters—"

Suzy's mouth fell open.

"That's brilliant. Hope needs to realize someone other than us needs her. She needs a reason to go on. It's perfect." Suzy hugged Alex. "Great idea, my friend."

Alex took the lid off her coffee and Suzy's. "I think we could use a shot."

"Here's to that."

They went back to Hope's bedroom and told jokes to try and cheer her up. Hope said she wanted to take a nap so Alex and Suzy left. Outside, they winked at one another as they climbed into their respective cars to hatch their plan.

The women drove to Hilltop and found the teachers' lounge. Teachers were getting ready to leave for the day but sat back down when they heard it was about Hope. After Alex explained her idea, the faculty happily agreed. They said they'd send letters of their own as well and asked the women to stop by in two days to pick up the notes.

In the parking lot, Alex beamed.

"This calls for another T.J. Maxx stop. Want to go?"

"No. Have fun, my little shopper. I need to get ready for Jon's visit. I just received a text. They're arriving tomorrow."

Chapter 47

Suzy took a quick shower and made the bed. The fridge was stocked and she made fresh coffee. She had placed fresh flowers in the kitchen and bedrooms and set out clean towels in the guestroom. Her phone buzzed. She glanced at the screen.

HI MOM.

WE'RE 15 MINUTES AWAY. SEE YOU SOON!

LOVE, JON

She grabbed a mixing bowl to make blueberry pancakes, Jon's favorite. She poured three glasses of orange juice, using the special company stemmed glasses. As the bacon sizzled in the pan, Suzy heard honking and turned off the stovetop.

She wiped her hands on her apron and checked her face in the hall mirror. She didn't want to greet Jon's new girlfriend with flour on her cheeks.

Suzy swung the front door wide and nearly cried when she saw John's familiar navy Volkswagen. She squinted as the sun glared off the windshield.

Jon stepped out of the car, smiling a mile wide, and looking thinner than she remembered. He spread his arms as Suzy rushed toward him. While they embraced, the passenger door creaked opened. Suzy turned to greet Jon's new girlfriend and her jaw dropped.

Out stepped a very tall, handsome man. Jon must have given him a ride from the airport. She peered into the back seat expecting a cute Italian girl to poke her head out but no one else was in the car. Suzy stared blankly at her son.

Jon nodded toward the tall, smiling man.

"Mom, meet Fernando."

Suzy felt unsteady. Fernando kissed her on each cheek as she stabilized her wobbly legs by leaning against the car.

"Um. Nice to meet you, Fernando."

Jon bounced toward his mother and slipped his arm through hers.

"Let's go inside. I'm starving.

Suzy took her hand off the warm car and tried to rally. She was perplexed to say the least by this jolt hand delivered by her son.

"I've, uh, made pancakes." Her voice faltered as she studied Fernando. "Do you like blueberry pancakes?"

"Relax, Mom. He won't bite. We're ravenous and we both love everything. Let's see what we can help you with in the kitchen."

Jon slung his well-worn backpack over one shoulder and Fernando grabbed his large black duffel bag out of the trunk. Both men followed Suzy inside.

Suzy suddenly wished she could spike her coffee. She walked straight to the coffee pot and poured a cup of black coffee. Normally, she took cream and sweetener. This was a black kind of day.

Suzy could barely make eye contact with Fernando. Instead, she focused on her son.

"Why don't you and your *friend* have a seat? It's almost ready."

Suzy gestured toward the chairs. Jon shrugged, glancing at Fernando who simply sat down. Jon followed suit.

"Mrs.— Suzy, I'd like to help," Fernando offered. "What can I do?"

Suzy wanted to tell him he could leave and go back to Europe but her manners wouldn't allow that.

"You're Jon's guest. Just have a seat. Jon, why don't you get your friend some coffee?"

"We don't drink coffee anymore. We're detoxing."

Suzy nodded. Her mind raced. “Then, will you get the butter and syrup out? I have sugar-free syrup if you prefer that.”

Fernando perked up. “That would be perfect. I’m on a diet.” He patted his 24-Hour Fitness stomach.

Suzy managed a laugh. “Yeah, you look pretty disgusting.”

That seemed to break the somber mood and they got through breakfast. Fernando offered to clean up so Suzy took the opportunity to go into the living room with Jon for a little chat.

They sat on the sofa while Jon patted her on the arm.

“I’m sure this is a bit of a shock.”

“A bit? That might be the understatement of the century.”

Suzy stared at Jon for several seconds.

“I don’t understand. I don’t get it, Jon. You’ve always dated girls. You dated Vanessa all through high school. I always thought you two would get—” She sighed and leaned back on the couch.

“What happened in Europe?”

“I realize how hard this must be for you.” Jon rested his chin on his hand. “I’ve known I was gay since I was thirteen. Maybe even before. I never told you or Dad because I knew it would go over like a lead balloon, so I hid it by dating Vanessa. I tried to force myself to like girls but it didn’t work.”

He walked toward the window. “Vanessa knows, by the way. We talked about it in high school. I think she thought she could change me.” He laughed as tears filled his eyes.

Jon turned to observe his mom. “Sorry if I’ve disappointed you.”

Suzy was still perplexed but walked toward Jon and rubbed his arm. “You could never disappoint me.” She looked directly in his eyes and held his chin with her hand.

“I love you and I always will. I want you to be happy. Are you happy?”

Jon nodded. "I'm very happy. He's amazing. This is the first time in my life I've been in love."

Suzy wasn't quite sure how to respond.

"You're going to have to give me some time, that's all. I'll come around. I don't have a problem with gays. I just—I just don't know how I missed this. I'm your mother. How is it that I—"

She shook her head. "I love you, son."

"I love you too, Mom."

Suzy chuckled. "Good luck telling your dad. I wish I could see his reaction. The great white hunter and sportsman might be a bit of a challenge."

"Oh, he knows," Jon said. "In fact, we stayed at his house last night. It was late and I didn't want to bother you."

She had just taken a drink and spewed coffee down the front of her shirt.

"What? He knows and he's okay with this? Your macho, macho dad?"

John shrugged and grinned.

"I know. Weird, isn't it? I wanted to get it over with and tell him first. I figured he'd go nuts. His reaction definitely wasn't what I expected."

Suzy looked at her son wide-eyed.

"Go on. I can't wait to hear this."

"Dad was amazing. He told me one of his hunting buddies recently told him he's gay. Dad says the guy still likes sports and is a great hunter."

Jon shoved his hands in his pockets, smiling.

"Dad said they're still good friends—he just doesn't want to sleep in the same tent with the guy."

Suzy threw her head back and laughed.

"Now, *that* sounds like your dad."

Chapter 48

For once, Alex got to the bank early to crunch numbers. Marketing budget time rolled around too soon. She always put it off until the last minute, cursing herself. Every year Alex reported to the board with marketing budget highlights and a year in review.

She much preferred the creative process. Alex walked to her credenza and pulled files for television, billboards, radio, print, yellow pages ads, and trade shows. She plunked the invoices on her desk. She was prepared to chain herself to her chair until the budget was finalized.

Needing to make copies, she tramped across the back of the lobby. The whirring fax machine caught her attention. Alex hovered over the machine, waiting for the fax. As the machine spit it out, she noticed there wasn't a cover page. She lifted the page and her eyes widened.

In large, bold letters with a scary Transylvania-like font, the fax read:

I'M WATCHING YOU.

Alex shivered. She glanced at the back door. It was locked. Suddenly the small copy room looked dark and ominous. She noted the message was about the same as the index card that had appeared in her mailbox. Hair rose on her neck.

She scanned the fax looking for an indication of the sender. Normally, an individual or corporate name would be printed at the top but that portion was blank. It only indicated the date and time.

How did the sender know how to block that information?

Shakily, she padded toward her office, holding the fax. As employees filtered in, she showed the fax to them, hoping it was some kind of dumb, practical joke. No one claimed ownership.

"It's not mine. Do you think it's for you, Alex?" a teller asked.

When Stu, the security officer, arrived, Alex showed him the fax. "It's probably nothing. Just some techy smartass who wants to play a joke on a bank. I wouldn't worry about it."

She nodded and sat down at her desk, trying to concentrate on her budget. She wished she could talk to Tony.

Driving home after work, Alex was still jumpy. A black cat crossed in front of her car.

Just what I need. Bad luck.

As she pulled into her driveway, her bald-headed neighbor, George, approached her car. Alex rolled down her window.

"Hi, Alex. What's going on? I got up last night to take cough syrup and couldn't help but notice a cop car outside your house. Everything okay?"

"Yes and no. I thought I heard someone trying to break in. There was a loud pounding on my back door. It sounded like someone was trying to break in. I was scared to death."

She broke out in a sweat recalling the incident.

"What did the cops say?"

"They assured me there would have been footprints on my deck since it was dewy outside. I guess I'm going nuts."

George shook his head. "You're not crazy. My Lab was maced last night. Some kind of high-powered mace, too. My dog's still not the same. He crawled under our deck and stayed there for hours, rubbing his eyes. He acted skittish. Still does."

A chill ran down Alex's spine.

Whoever was in her backyard didn't want the dog to bark. They were prepared with mace. God. What if they had planned on using the mace on her—or worse?

Alex gaped at George with fear in her eyes. He pulled a piece of paper out of his wallet and took out a pen. George scribbled something and handed it to Alex.

"Here's my number. Keep it by your bed and call me if you hear anything. You might want to keep a light on. Maybe it'll make you feel better."

Alex took the paper and nodded, near tears.

"Thanks, George. I will."

She pulled into her garage, double checked the locks, and settled in for the evening with the television blaring and lights blazing. Sleep was the last thing on her mind so she got on her computer and found an email from Dr. Holmes, the principal of Hilltop High School.

Chapter 49

Alex called Suzy.

"We've got to go to Hilltop in the morning. Apparently, they have several letters for Hope."

They agreed to meet and Alex, glad to get out of her house, arrived first. Her eyes bulged when she saw the boxes of letters. When Suzy appeared at the front door of the teacher's lounge, she ran toward her.

"Wait until you see this. You won't believe how many letters there are. I think everyone from the entire school wrote a letter and then some. They've put them inside three large boxes. They also made a big banner using red and black school colors.

"That's wonderful. I can't wait to see Hope's face," Suzy said, wishing she could tell Alex and Hope about Jon and Fernando. But this was Hope's moment.

After they put the boxes in Alex's trunk, Suzy picked up pizza and wine.

Alex sat in the driveway and checked her email waiting for Suzy to arrive.

As they walked toward Hope's front door, Alex beamed.

"This is a celebration. A big one." She decided not to spoil the festive mood by talking about the scary fax and possible attempted break-in. Hope had given her friends a key since she didn't want to get out of bed most days. Balancing two boxes on her left hip, Alex opened the door. Suzy carried another box, the pizza and wine.

"Hellllloooo," Alex said. No one answered.

"Hope, are you here?" Suzy asked. "We have a surprise."

"We're coming into your room." Alex sat the box on the floor as they walked toward Hope's bedroom. She wasn't in bed. The bathroom door was closed. Alex knocked on the door but no one answered. Exchanging worried glances, Suzy jiggled the locked door handle.

"Hope, are you in there?"

"Hoooooooope!" Alex yelled. "Open up. We have good news for you."

The women exchanged glances. The quiet house wasn't a good sign.

"I knew we shouldn't have left her alone so soon after the funeral with all those pills," Alex said.

She looked around for something to smash the doorknob and found a tall, heavy, silver candlestick. Alex banged on the doorknob.

"What in the world are you doing?" came a voice from behind. "I'm right here."

The women threw their arms around Hope.

"Why is the bathroom door locked?" Suzy asked.

"I'm not sure how I managed it, but just like everything else, I somehow locked it." Hope gave them a quirky smile.

"I was in the backyard putting food in my hummingbird feeder. I've called a locksmith. By the way, what are those boxes in my living room?"

"You have a way of scaring me." Alex grabbed Hope's hand and led her to the living room. "We have something to show you."

"Now, sit down," Suzy said. "Alex had a great idea the other day and she's going to tell you all about it."

Alex blushed. Hope looked puzzled. She sat on her sofa while Alex and Suzy flanked her.

"Hope, we've been worried about you and tried to think of something to make you feel better. It seems a *lot* of people are worried about you. They also miss you and love you. Here's proof."

Alex opened one of the boxes and spilled hundreds of letters onto the floor. Some were written in pencil, others in ink, while some envelopes had lipstick kisses, hearts or pink glitter on them. A few smelled perfume-y, had drawings of flowers and animals and others were adorned with red and black HHS block letters.

Hope stared at the mound of envelopes, taking it all in. Suzy and Alex unrolled the banner.

We Love You and Miss You, Miss Truman

They hung it above her patio doors near the kitchen. Hope stared at the banner for several minutes. She blinked away tears and grabbed a handful of letters. As she read quietly, Alex and Suzy opened the other two boxes which also overflowed with creative envelopes and letters. They dumped them all onto the floor into a heaping, colorful pile.

Alex broke the silence. "Now that you know that everyone loves you and misses you, can we please eat? My blood sugar is low and the pizza's getting cold. Do you mind?"

Hope said, "Do whatever you want. I have the best friends, the best students, and the best co-workers in the world. I can't believe you orchestrated this. I can't believe how many heartfelt letters there are. I'm overwhelmed."

She wiped away a happy tear and blew her nose. "I guess someone does need me and want me. This is amazing. *You* are amazing. Thank you. I know that's not much but I mean it from the bottom of my heart."

They group hugged and Alex said, "Honey, you're back."

"Welcome back," Suzy added.

Hope smiled, looking like she meant it for the first time in weeks.

"Go ahead and start eating. I have to do something. I'll be right back." Suzy and Alex exchanged glances as Hope disappeared into her bedroom.

When she returned, Suzy let out a wolf whistle. "You

look great, Hope. I've never seen that shirt. Teal suits you, and I love your hair up like that. Wait. Is that makeup I see?"

"Thanks," Hope said sheepishly. "Know anywhere I can donate my smelly gray sweats?" she laughed as she dangled them in the air. "I'm tired of moping around. This is the jolt I needed. I'll never be able to thank you enough. Now, let me get my wine opener."

Ding dong.

"That must be the locksmith." Hope opened the door and showed him to the locked bathroom. Meanwhile, between bites of pizza, Alex set out Hope's best china while Suzy lit candles and poured wine into crystal glasses.

"Just because we have pizza in a box, doesn't mean we have to eat it out of a box," Alex said.

Before the locksmith left, they offered him a slice but he declined. He gave Hope a double-take and nearly careened into the front door.

"He's cute." Suzy looked at Hope with raised eyebrows.

"Don't start," Hope warned. "One thing at a time. Getting dressed is a big step right now."

The friends giggled, ate pizza, drank two bottles of red wine and sat on the floor reading Hope's letters. As they walked to their cars, Hope kissed each one goodnight on the cheek.

"You're like sisters to me. I never could have gotten through this without you."

"We love you, too," Suzy said.

"Ditto and kisses from me," Alex added.

Hope went inside, read several more letters and touched the banner lovingly. She blew out the candles and knew she was ready to go back to work—and to life.

Chapter 50

Suzy arrived home to find Jon and Fernando watching a musical. Jon never liked musicals before. *Did he? Do I even know my son?*

Suzy loved Jon more than life itself but needed time to adjust to this bombshell. She still couldn't believe how well her ex, Bill, had taken the news. Suzy poked her head in the living room, exchanged greetings, and headed to bed. As she put on her pajamas, she recalled Hope's reaction to the letters and fell asleep smiling.

At one in the morning, the phone trilled.

"Hello."

"I was just thinking it will be a logistical nightmare for the groomsmen to ride in on horses. What if the horses, you know, did their business?" Mrs. B clucked her tongue. "How disgusting. Who would clean it up? I guess *you* would as the wedding planner, but still I—"

"Mrs. Biltmore, don't you ever sleep? I've had a very long, very rough day. Can we talk about this tomorrow?"

"Just a bit more. I, we, want lots of flowers. Hundreds and hundreds."

Suzy scrambled for a pen and paper on the nightstand.

"What kind of flowers?"

"Magnolias, white roses and lilacs." She paused. "And we need a signature drink."

"Do you have one in mind?"

"Mint juleps, of course. You do know what those are, I hope. Don't you know anything about southerners, Suzy?"

"Yes, I know what Mint Juleps are. I can't say I've ever had one but I'll check into it."

Undeterred, Mrs. Biltmore plowed on. "We'll need a large tent in case of rain. Better yet, make certain it won't rain and you'll get a bonus check."

Suzy wondered if she could make a deal with the local meteorologist or a higher power. "I'll do the best I can, but for now, I've got to go to sleep. I'm exhausted."

"Just one more th—th—th—"

Suzy heard a loud clatter and moaning. She sat upright, pressing the phone against her ear. "Mrs. Biltmore, are you okay? What was that noise?" She paused. "Mrs. Biltmore? Are you there? Your voice sounded strange—sort of slurry."

There was no answer. Suzy started to panic. "Mrs. Biltmore? Can you hear me?"

In a weak, slurred voice she replied, "I can't m-m-move my left arm."

"Where are you? I'm calling 9-1-1."

"At the coun—try—"

"The Biltmore Country Club?"

"Ye—es."

"Is anyone around?" *Who would be there at one in the morning?* "Hold on. I'm calling an ambulance. I'll be there in fifteen minutes."

Suzy dialed the emergency number and explained Mrs. B's symptoms.

"We'll send an ambulance right away, ma'am." Suzy cradled the phone as she put jeans on and gave the address for the Biltmore Country Club.

After the dispatcher confirmed the details, Suzy ran to Jon's room and told him where she was going. While driving to the country club, she called Emma, thankful Mrs. B's daughter had gotten in touch with her and she had her number.

They both arrived at the same time, rushing toward the front entrance. Suzy introduced herself to Emma as the ambulance sirens got closer. Lights swirled and two paramedics scrambled out the back. Suzy and Emma held the massive wooden doors open and watched with dread as they assessed Mrs. B and placed her on a gurney. After they wheeled her into the ambulance, Emma climbed in with her mother.

"I'll follow you to the hospital." Suzy was surprised by how tiny and frail Mrs. B looked on that gurney.

Clustered in the tiny emergency room with doctors, nurses and techs on either side of Mrs. Biltmore, Suzy watched beeping monitors as Emma held her mother's hand. Mrs. B was strangely quiet and pale while lab techs drew blood and a doctor listened to her heartbeat. When a nurse rolled her away, Suzy and Emma moved to a small waiting room and drank stale hospital coffee while hospital employees further tested Mrs. B. After an hour, a kind-looking, middle-aged man wandered in wearing regular clothes and a hospital badge around his neck. He introduced himself as the stroke coordinator and explained Mrs. B had had a stroke. He told the women it was lucky they got to her so soon.

"We have a three-hour window or less before possible permanent damage, paralysis, or worse, sets in. Whoever called the ambulance did the right thing." The coordinator looked from face to face and Emma smiled gratefully at Suzy. "She called 9-1-1."

The stroke coordinator continued. "She may need physical and speech therapy for a few weeks or months. In time, hopefully, she'll be herself again."

Emma grabbed Suzy's hand. "Thank you. I don't know how we'll ever repay you for saving Mom's life—definitely her quality of life."

Suzy patted Emma's hand. "You're welcome. For once, I'm glad she called during the wee hours. Your mother's a tough woman. If anyone can pull through, she can."

Chapter 51

Alex settled onto her couch and flipped through a magazine, thrilled Hope was finally on the mend.

Ring. Ring. Ring.

She walked to the kitchen and picked up her phone. The Caller ID was blocked.

Shakily, she answered, "Hello."

"Hey, Alex. I've just got a minute but wanted to tell you I won't have this stupid job much longer. I'll be able to talk to you soon. I'm dying to see you," Tony said.

Her stomach lurched. "I've missed you. You won't believe what's been going on around here. I've been so afraid."

"What? Tell me."

Alex told Tony about calling the officers to her house, the strange fax, and about the neighbor's dog getting maced. She mentioned she had been sleeping with the hall light on every night.

Tony paused.

"I'll have to check the emergency dispatch records. Keep that fax and I'll take a look at it after I'm unchained from this damn desk. I can see why you're scared but it's not a good idea to leave the lights on when you're asleep."

"Why?"

"You're giving a criminal the advantage. You know the layout of your house in the dark and a criminal won't. I know you're scared but try to sleep with the lights off."

Alex glanced at her brightly lit kitchen and hallway. "Okay, I'll turn them out. When can I see you? I'll feel much safer when you're around."

"A few days. I can't wait."

Alex went to bed giddy about seeing Tony again. She turned out all the lights and pulled the covers tightly under her chin. In the darkness, she tossed and turned, jumping with every house creak.

The next morning she had bags under her eyes. When she arrived at work, two loan officers chatted in the break room as her boss read the paper. She poured a cup of coffee and walked downstairs to work on her marketing budget. She sorted through several advertising invoices and walked to the copy room. The fax machine whirred. She stared at it as if it were a cobra.

Trembling, she pulled the paper out of the tray and tensed when she saw the same large Transylvania-like font. Again, the sender's name and location were blocked. Her hands trembled as she read the fax.

GLAD YOU FINALLY TURNED OUT THE LIGHTS. SWEET DREAMS.

Alex shivered and took the fax straight to her boss. He knitted his brows, studied the paper, and then placed it in the center of his desk.

"Do you think this was meant for you?"

"Unfortunately, yes. Let me fill you in." She told Jim about the recent occurrences at her house as well as the other fax. The president's frown deepened.

"This concerns me. I take the protection of our employees seriously." He paused. "I want you to tell me immediately if anything else occurs. And be careful, Alex."

She bobbed her head. "I will." Alex went upstairs to the employee lounge and poured another cup of much-needed coffee. When she returned, the message light blinked on her phone. *Probably another sales person wanting to sell ad space.* Half listening, she pushed her voicemail button.

Holding the phone between her ear and shoulder, she checked her appointment calendar.

Hey baby, baby,
I want to make love to you,
I want to have sex with you,
And go down on you-"

Sitting ram-rod straight, Alex pressed the phone harder against her ear to listen.

Baby, baby,
You know you want it too,
And if ya don't, I'll just give it to you.
Baby, baby,
I'm comin' for you.
Put the lights down low,
Baby, baby,
You know you want me, too.

Oh. My. God. Whoever this is wants to have sex with me. Mouth dry and heart pounding, Alex gingerly pressed the button to save the message. She had a feeling she was going to have to play this embarrassing song for her boss, the security officer or both.

She felt nauseous and called Suzy. She relayed what had happened with the creepy song and fax. "What should I do? Who could this be?"

Suzy sounded shaky but firm. "Tell your boss. This guy is obviously trying to get to you. First at home and now at work. This scares me. Maybe he thinks you know how to get into the bank vault. Maybe he thinks you'll wire him money? Listen to me. You need to tell your boss right now. This person is obviously watching you."

Alex broke out in a cold sweat.

"I hadn't thought about the money aspect. I thought it was all personal. I'll go tell Jim right now."

She knocked on Jim's door. He waved to usher her inside.

"You look pale. Everything okay?"

"No, actually it's not. I just got a sexual voicemail on my phone in my office. And that's not all." She told Jim about the strange incidents at her house and about the dog's being maced. Jim's jaw clenched.

"Did you save the message on your phone?"

Alex nodded.

"I want to hear it."

Jim followed Alex to her office. His mouth was set in a grim, straight line as he listened to the voice mail. When the song ended, he closed her door.

"Don't delete that. I'm calling our bank attorney, Leonard Jarrett. Mr. Jarrett also happens to be the city mayor, as you know, so that makes him the chief of police's boss. Do you get my drift?"

He narrowed his eyes. "I'm not going to have one of my employees threatened—"

"But," Alex interrupted, "I don't want our attorney to know my personal business."

"It's no longer your personal business. This person contacted you using bank property. First our fax machine and now your voicemail on a bank line. Sorry, Alex, but this has to go up the ladder. I'm going to give Leonard a quick call. I'll let you know what he says."

With Jell-o legs, Alex trudged up the stairs to the coffee machine hoping it would suddenly pour a whiskey sour. *Why me? What did I do to deserve this?*

When she returned, she spilled coffee on her desk calendar. "Shit." Her nerves were shot as she blotted the coffee with a tissue.

She glanced at her boss through her glass walls. He was still on the phone. He talked animatedly, waved his hands in the air, and stared in Alex's direction the entire time.

Alex jumped as her phone rang. "Alexandra Mitchell. Marketing."

"Hey, Alex. I'm joining you back on Earth sooner than expected," Tony said easily.

Alex was quiet.

"Are you there?"

"Listen, it's crazy around here. I got another scary fax and then, something even worse."

"What?"

Her voice caught. "Someone played a sex song on my voicemail. It shook me to the core so I told my boss. He's talking to our bank attorney right now."

Tony was unusually quiet. After several seconds, he said, "Who is your bank attorney?"

"Leonard Jarrett, the city mayor."

"Shit."

"What does that matter? Who cares who our attorney is? Aren't you worried about *me*?"

"It might have been me."

"What are you talking about?"

"It might have been me," he repeated.

Tony's pseudo-admission hit Alex like a bat upside the head.

"What the hell do you mean it 'might' have been you? Either it was or it wasn't." Alex's voice hardened.

"Why would you scare me like that? Was it you or not?"

"It might have been me."

Alex's heart pounded. "Did you scare me at home, too? Did you send those faxes? If you did you're a bastard." She slammed the phone down. Her entire body shook. Somehow, she staggered across the lobby and appeared at her boss's door. Jim motioned her in.

"You look a little gray around the edges? Do you want to go home?"

She slumped in a chair. *Where do I begin? How am I going to tell my boss that the still legally married cop with whom I've been having an almost-affair all summer is the one who "might" have left that stupid sex song on my voicemail.*

Alex took a deep breath. "Have you already called our bank attorney?"

"Yes and he's very concerned about your safety, Alex. He's acting on this immediately."

"Well, uh, the thing is—" She swallowed. "I may have discovered who left the message. It was possibly just a prank and had nothing to do with anything else that's happened to me recently."

Jim raised his eyebrows and leaned forward on his elbows. "I'm all ears."

Alex told Jim about her relationship with Tony and about his recent phone call.

Jim listened, arms crossed. "Is he the one you've called each time something has happened to you?"

"Yes. When he was around anyway or when he happened to call. He hasn't been able to call me for weeks. I've been lucky to have an 'in' with the police department and—"

"Don't you get it?" Jim stood up. "He was most likely the one all along. He probably did everything."

"What? Why would he do that? I'm falling in love with him and he cares about me. He wouldn't do this to me."

"My guess is he scared you so he could be your hero. He loved being your knight in shining armor. He didn't want to lose contact with you, so he kept frightening you hoping you would continue to talk to him even though he was married. He got exactly what he wanted—you."

Tears filled Alex's eyes. She reached for a tissue. Her mind was a jumble of terror, anger, and confusion. After blowing her nose, she said, "I think you're wrong. I hope you're wrong. How will I ever know for sure?"

"For a start, I'm going to let our attorney know my suspicions about this officer. I'll let you know what he says." Jim picked up the receiver and glanced at Alex. "Why don't you leave for an early lunch? Get a breath of fresh air."

Alex walked to her office, still wobbly, grabbed her purse, and left. The bright sunshine hurt her eyes. She wanted to drive home, bury her head in a pillow and cry.

How could he do this to me? Too upset to eat lunch, Alex drove around and around thinking about what Jim had said.

He might be wrong. She glanced nervously in the rearview mirror. A little voice told her he could also be right. She had never once suspected Tony until he halfway admitted to leaving the voicemail. She slammed her fist on the steering wheel. *It makes sense that he wanted to continue to be in my life. To be my hero. How could I have been so stupid?*

Chapter 52

After driving for an hour, Alex returned to the bank in a daze. Her head was swimming. Jim was apparently at lunch since his office light was turned off.

She picked up the phone to call Suzy but set it firmly back in its cradle. She wasn't in the mood to talk about this. Not yet. Staring at her computer screen, she willed herself to write radio copy but her mind was on the cop. She couldn't create a 30-second spot if she had to.

Since she had driven the entire lunch hour, her stomach rumbled. Alex went upstairs and raided the vending machine. She bought peanut butter and crackers, chips, a Diet Coke and ate in the employee lounge. She was in a fog, completely unaware of conversations around her. Not wanting to chit-chat, she doodled and made notes on a legal pad.

When Jim returned to the bank, he made a beeline for her office. He shut the door which she took as a bad sign.

"I just had lunch with our attorney. He wants you to act on this now. He said you need to file a report with Internal Affairs at the police department."

"What?!" Alex shrieked. "I don't want to do that. I don't want to get Tony into trouble."

She collapsed into her chair. "I just want to be safe." As mad as she was that Tony might have done this, she couldn't bear to get him into trouble. What if she caused him to get demoted or worse—fired? She could never live with herself. And what if he did do the unthinkable and harassed her to garner attention? She didn't want to think about it.

Jim frowned. "I can tell you're not crazy about this but it's procedure. There's no stopping this now. Mr. Jarrett has alerted the police chief and someone from Internal Affairs will be calling you within the hour."

"Already?" Alex ran her fingers through her hair. "I guess I don't get a say in the matter?"

Jim's eyebrows shot up. "Why are you protecting this officer?"

"I don't want to report him. Don't ask me why. If he did this, he certainly scared me to death but I don't think he'd really hurt me—"

The ringing phone made her jump.

"That's probably Internal Affairs now. I'll leave you alone." Jim left and closed her door.

Her voice quivered when she answered.

"Ms. Mitchell," the baritone-voiced man said. "This is Detective Bradley from Internal Affairs. I understand you would like to file a report."

"Well, I don't think I have a choice in the matter."

"What do you mean, Ms. Mitchell?"

"Nothing. How do we do this? I don't want the officer to know about our conversation. Is that possible?"

"Absolutely. We protect our citizens. I'd like for you to come to the police department tomorrow morning at ten. Do you know where the station is located?"

"Yes." Alex barely recognized her subdued voice.

"Good. Use the unmarked, gray door on the side. I'll be there to greet you."

Alex's mouth was dry. She could barely answer. "Okay. Uh, goodbye."

Tony's fate was possibly in her hands. His entire life he wanted to be a police officer like his dad and grandfather. He had told her he'd be able to take early retirement in ten years.

What if I destroy that? Maybe he really will come after me. Maybe he is a bad cop. Oh, God. Why did this happen? What am I going to do?

Suzy decided to check on Mrs. B. She hadn't been to the hospital for two days since Jon and Fernando had kept her busy with eating out, movies, and the theater. She figured Mrs. B needed her rest anyway.

She stopped by Artistic Blooms and asked Marc to prepare a bouquet of magnolias. Marc air kissed both her cheeks and sashayed around the shop as he plucked flowers from containers.

"What kind of vase do you want, Miss Suzy?"

"Just clear."

Marc frowned. "Let's put a big colorful bow on it. He held up a long strand of red and white dotted ribbon."

"She isn't a polka-dot kind of person. What else do you have?"

Marc put his finger on his cheek. "I have a beautiful silky plum, hmmm?"

Suzy nodded her approval. "Perfect. Mrs. B loves your work, you know."

Marc put both index fingers on his cheeks and formed an "O" with his mouth. "She does?"

"Yes and she's also in my life because of you. Apparently, you recommended me to her. Do you realize how *hellish* my life has been since I met her?" Suzy teased. "I should throw this vase at you and never use you for my brides' weddings again."

He stiffened. "I'm sorry. I didn't mean to—"

"I'm half teasing. I was just learning how to handle her when she had this terrible stroke. I feel sorry for her now."

Marc clucked his tongue. "Yes, the poor dear. Please give her my love." Marc finished the floral arrangement and created a big bow with a flourish.

"Card?"

"No. I'll deliver these personally."

Suzy gathered the massive bouquet and drove to the hospital.

When she entered the quiet, plain, sanitary-smelling room, Emma and a man Suzy had never met were sitting in chairs beside the hospital bed. Mrs. B looked fragile attached to non-stop beeping monitors and IV cords draped around her small, liver-spotted arm.

Suzy held up the large bouquet Marc had created.

"Mag-nol-ias." Mrs. B's speech was still affected. "You reeemem . . . berrred." Mrs. B. pointed a bony finger toward the window ledge and Suzy placed the arrangement where she could easily view it. She was surprised Mrs. B's voice was still difficult to understand and wondered with despair if it would always be this way.

Emma hugged Suzy and gestured toward the man who was now standing and smiling. "Meet Bernie."

The shorter, olive-skinned man shook Suzy's hand and offered his chair. Suzy liked his big, warm smile and soft brown eyes—and the fact that he was a gentleman. As she shook his hand, she noticed he had long, thick lashes.

"So *you're* Bernie. I've heard a lot about you."

Suzy stiffened, afraid to look at Mrs. B's expression. She had nearly let the cat out of the bag about knowing Emma's true love.

Emma patted the gentle, slightly bald man's arm.

"My Bernie has been here every day. More than me some days. Hasn't he, Mom?"

Mrs. Biltmore nodded but her lips were pursed. Suzy assumed the jury was still out on Bernie. Mrs. B pointed toward an enormous arrangement of red gladiolus.

"From Lin-coln."

Suzy thought they looked more like funeral flowers but nodded favorably.

Emma glanced at Suzy and scrunched her nose. Suzy stifled a giggle and walked toward the bed. She placed her hand over Mrs. B's.

"I've been worried about you. You look good," she lied. "How are you feeling?"

"A-bout the same."

"I'm sure it'll just take time. You'll probably have speech therapy."

Emma interjected. "The therapists work with her every day. She has physical therapy in the morning and speech therapy in the afternoon. They said she should be fine in a few weeks since she got here so fast after her stroke." Emma's eyes filled with tears. "Thanks to you."

Suzy blushed. She didn't handle compliments well.

"I'm glad I could help. I can't stay long. Please keep me posted on her progress."

"She needs your num-ber," Mrs. B said.

Suzy winked at Emma. "She's got it." She patted Mrs. B's frail leg through the thin sheets and blankets. "I've got to go but I'll see you soon. You'll be better before you know it."

Emma walked Suzy out.

"Can you believe it? She's so proud of those stupid flowers from Lincoln. I'm sure he sent them via his assistant. I guarantee you he didn't order them himself." Emma rolled her eyes.

"He hasn't visited or called. I talked to his mother so he'd be aware that Mom had a stroke. This from the man she wants to be her son-in-law." Emma crossed her arms defiantly.

"Bernie on the other hand has been here every single day. I wish she could respect and accept him."

Suzy saw the annoyance and sadness in Emma's face. "Just give her time. Maybe she'll come around. Bernie seems very nice—he's sweet and cute. I've got to run. My son is home after being away all summer. He's keeping me busy."

Emma nodded. "Thanks for everything. I'll keep you posted."

From across the hall, Suzy glanced once more at Mrs. B. She thought about how quickly life can change and realized she had to embrace her son and his life decisions. She was pretty sure she already had.

Chapter 53

Being back at Hilltop High felt like home. Hope craved the familiar routine, and most of all, she couldn't wait to see her students.

When she walked inside the familiar halls, she was greeted with hugs, an office full of balloons, and a "welcome back" banner across her desk. Hope brought several of her students' letters and taped them to her office walls. The letters made her feel secure and needed. She realized she needed her students as much as they needed her. Probably more.

Hope jumped right into her work after thanking Dr. Holmes and her fellow colleagues for their support. She met with honor student Billy first, and after several phone calls to HHS alumni, she helped him secure an after-school internship with a local public relations firm. Billy hugged Hope. "I'm glad you're back, Miss Truman. We missed you." He glanced at his shoes. "I missed you."

Tears sprang to her eyes. She loved these kids. After Billy left, she glanced at her watch. It was already lunchtime. Hope fished in her purse for money and came across the business card from the mystery man at the funeral. She stared at the tan and green card.

Paul Walker, Attorney at Law
Walker Hemphill Jones

Hope felt uneasy about his urgency that she call but picked up the phone and dialed before losing her nerve. She had to get back on track and decided to extract whatever problem this was like a sore splinter. After all, if it had to do with Larry and Montana, sadly, it must involve a problem.

On the fourth ring, she started to hang up, then heard a man's voice.

"Hello. Paul Walker speaking."

Hope cleared her throat unsure of what to say. "Hi. It's Hope. Hope Truman. You were at my parents—"

His gentle voice interrupted her. "Yes, I'm glad you called. I was afraid you—" his voice trembled "might not call me."

Hope was on high alert. "I can't imagine what this is about, Mr. Walker."

"Please call me Paul."

"Okay, Paul. I assume this has to do with my parents." Hope braced herself.

"Well, yes and no. I'd rather not talk about this over the phone. Can you meet for lunch?"

Hope stared at her watch. "We don't exactly get long lunch hours at school. I've already used up ten of my thirty minutes." She chuckled.

"How about after work? I'll buy you dinner."

Hope wasn't sure if she wanted to have dinner with a stranger but remembered his kind eyes and the fact that he was an attorney. Surely it would be safe. Hope weighed her options—she could go on with her life and never know what he had to say or meet him and get it over with.

"Are you still there?"

"Yes, I was thinking. Okay, I'll meet you. Do you like Mexican?"

"I love it. My favorite. How about Rosa's Mexican Restaurant?"

Hope smiled to herself. At least she'd get a good meal. "That's my favorite restaurant. I'll meet you at six."

"I'll look forward to it. Goodbye."

Hope walked to the lunchroom wondering what he wanted to tell her.

Did her parents have a life insurance policy she didn't know about? Do they owe someone money? Are there back taxes or a lien? She shuddered thinking about the likely scenarios and possible legal fallout. She was almost certain it would not be good news.

As Hope entered the large cafeteria sporting winning sports banners and the smell of non-award-winning food, the excited students broke her worrisome mood. Students and staff who spotted Hope rushed toward her, throwing their arms around her.

Others paid their condolences and young Britney linked her arm through Hope's. "I've missed you, Miss Truman. How are ya holdin' up?"

"Better each day. Thanks for your sweet, pink sparkly letter. It meant the world to me. I hung it above my desk."

Britney beamed. "Really. Glad you liked it." She squeezed Hope's arm. She seemed a different person from the sullen student who had run away from home.

They walked toward the cafeteria line and each grabbed a tray. Both asked the cook for a burger and fries.

"I'll start my diet tomorrow," Hope said.

"You don't need to diet. You're beautiful, Miss Truman."

As they walked toward the drink dispenser, Britney peered at Hope. "Mom and I have been getting along much better. I'm back at home. She even took me shopping the other day. We're going to a movie tonight and then out for pizza." Britney radiated. Her excitement was palpable.

Hope tried to hide her surprise. "That's great, Brit. What turned the situation around?"

"You."

Hope raised her eyebrows. "Me?"

"After you took me home that day and talked to my mom. She was really mad at first and said you had no business butting in. Then, I guess she started thinking 'bout what you said."

Britney looked at Hope with admiration. "She broke up with that awful man and we've been gettin' along great ever since."

"I'm so glad." Hope put her arm around Britney's shoulders.

"Me too."

They walked through the cafeteria line in satisfied silence. Hope ate quickly and returned to her office. She spent the afternoon fielding calls and catching up on mounds of paperwork. Every hour, she glanced at her watch, anxious about her dinner meeting with the attorney.

When Hope entered Rosa's, she saw the lawyer from the funeral home was seated in a booth. Chips and salsa were on the table but he appeared to be waiting for her before he ate a bite. When she neared the booth, he stood, gave her a genuine smile, and extended his hand.

"Thanks for coming. I hope you're hungry because I'm starving."

Hope was famished but her stomach was doing back flips. She wasn't sure if she could eat and wondered if Mexican food was such a great idea.

"I am hungry. And a little nervous to be honest."

The man smiled. "There's nothing to be anxious about. No bad news. Let's enjoy dinner then we'll talk."

Hope stared into his large chocolate brown eyes. He looked around sixty, was well groomed, and wore an expensive-looking brown suit and yellow tie. Studying the menu, Hope tried to focus on the food.

"What do you like to eat?"

"I could eat guacamole like mashed potatoes." She giggled. "And I love their spinach enchiladas."

He closed his menu. "Sounds like we have the same taste. Those are my favorites, too." His eyes twinkled.

They ate mostly in silence with occasional chatter about weather and traffic. Hope was hungrier than she expected, finally relaxed, and polished off her food.

"Would you like dessert and coffee?" Paul asked as he pushed his empty plate away.

"Coffee would be nice. No dessert, though. I'm trying to lose weight."

He patted his belly. "You look great. I, on the other hand, could stand to lose thirty pounds."

He shrugged. "Must be in the genes. I have the same body type as my par—" He stopped and fidgeted with his napkin. "I'm going to the restroom. Would you mind ordering two coffees?"

Hope nodded as he rose from the booth.

When Paul returned, two cups of hot coffee were on the table. Hope observed him. Paul's forehead glistened. He sipped his coffee while Hope added sweetener to hers.

She didn't know how much longer she could wait before she screamed *Tell me already.* Her stomach was in a knot and she wasn't in the mood for bad news.

Paul inhaled, blew out his breath, and stared into her eyes.

"I'm beginning to wonder if we should have met outside in a park or something."

Hope looked startled. "Please just tell me."

He stared at the table. "I don't know how else to break the news other than to blurt it out."

Hope felt a sudden chill as she waited with dread. The attorney set his cup down. "You were adopted by Claire and Larry when you were five months old."

He watched Hope's reaction before continuing.

She gasped, her eyes filled with tears.

"How do you know? Did you handle the adoption? Why didn't anyone tell me?"

"I was hoping Larry and Claire would tell you when you got older. It was their place to tell you. Not mine."

He looked into Hope's expectant eyes.

"I didn't handle the adoption but I know your biological mother died two months after giving birth to you."

Hope felt faint. "How did she die?"

His face was grim. "She contracted a staph infection in the hospital. While giving birth, she had an emergency C-section because the baby—you—were in distress. The infection spread and they couldn't save her. She was allergic to penicillin and the other antibiotics didn't work."

His eyes became glassy. He turned toward the window before continuing. "Your father tried to raise you by himself but couldn't handle an infant alone." His chin trembled.

Hope wondered how the kind attorney knew all of this. He must have handled the man's affairs.

"Larry did handyman jobs and cut your father's lawn for over a year. Claire cleaned his house and took care of the flower beds. They watched your father try to raise you. He gave it a valiant effort but had a demanding job. After observing his feeble attempts, Larry and Claire asked if they could adopt you. Apparently, they weren't able to conceive."

"I never knew they couldn't conceive. Of course, that subject wouldn't have come up with me." Her mind raced, wondering who her biological father was.

"The legal documents contained a privacy clause. Only they could tell you about the adoption. When I saw the obituary in the paper for Larry and Claire, I knew I had to attend the funeral and let you know. At first, the name Montana threw me but as I read the obituary I noticed she had changed her name."

Hope scanned Paul's face for answers. Then, it hit her like a semi-truck.

"*You're* my biological father aren't you?"

Paul hesitated, nodded, and then smiled. "Yes, I am. It's important that you know I always wanted to tell you, to call you, to watch you grow up, to be involved even if at arm's length. I contacted Larry and Claire a few times over the years and asked if I could see you on whatever terms they chose but they denied any interaction between you and me. They wanted the adoption kept a secret. I guess they had their reasons and I had to abide by their legal adoption."

He shifted in the booth. "Early on, I knew I made a mistake. Within a month, I tried to contact them to tell them I wanted you back. I was miserable. I lost Nancy and then I lost you."

A tear slid down his cheek. He pulled out his handkerchief and blew his nose.

"What happened?"

"They had already moved away. They moved often. I couldn't find them. When Claire changed her name it was even more difficult. I hired a private detective and made contact once. They wouldn't let me see you and moved again. After I heard about the horrible train wreck on the news, I was sorry for them but happy I could finally find you, my daughter."

Hope sat in stunned shock.

"I know this is a lot to grasp." He folded and refolded his napkin.

Hope stared into Paul's gentle eyes. She felt anger, betrayal—and excitement. *If this is true, it explains why my parents and I didn't mesh. Why we didn't act or look alike. And my biological father actually has a job. A good job. Plus, we look alike.*

Hope couldn't speak. Tears pricked her eyes. She sat as still as a Sphinx. She swallowed, trying to take in the news and her life as she knew it.

She gawked at Paul. Even though their similar features already told the story, she wasn't convinced.

"I want proof."

He reached into his jacket pocket.

"I thought you might. Here are the adoption papers." Hope noted Claire's loopy signature and the heart shape above the letter "i." She read the birth date and name of her biological mother, Nancy. She scanned the documents and returned them to Paul.

"You can have the documents if you want," he offered. "I have a copy."

Hope placed the paperwork carefully in her purse.

"I need time to digest this. I'm shocked to be honest. This is a lot to process, especially after Mom and Dad's, er, Larry and Montana's, horrible death."

"I imagine your head is swimming. I'm sorry to tell you so soon after the funeral but wanted you to know the truth. I couldn't risk losing you again."

Paul cleared his throat. "I'd love to get to know you, Hope, in whatever capacity you'll have me—as a friend or as your biological father. You set the pace. I hope you'll let me be a part of your life. Nothing would give me greater joy-" A sob caught in his throat. "than to be a good father to you."

Hope studied Paul. She smiled. "I'm glad you told me. Thank you but I'm overwhelmed and need to sort this out. I'll be in touch soon. I'm going home now. It's been an exhausting day to say the least."

Paul stood as Hope left. They shook hands, then awkwardly hugged. As she neared the front door, she turned to behold her newfound father. He was still standing. She saw a sweet tenderness in his eyes and a ready smile. She drove home in a confused but hopeful state.

Chapter 54

Alex awakened with a headache after a sleepless night. The last thing she wanted to do was get Tony in trouble—even if he were the one behind the creepy messages and faxes. She still cared about him. She couldn't help it. Of course, she also knew her boss was right. She had to get to the bottom of this. She had to know the truth.

She pulled a silky black robe around her and padded to the kitchen. A strong pot of coffee was in order. She wanted to be fully alert while being interviewed by Internal Affairs. The thought of meeting with another officer to talk about Tony made her stomach churn.

While the coffee brewed, she walked back to her closet.

What should I wear to rat out my sort-of cop boyfriend who might be a freakin' stalker?

A little voice told her she had no choice, and if he purposely tried to scare her, he deserved to be punished. But she didn't *want* to punish Tony. She was falling in love with him, like it or not.

Alex chose a charcoal gray blazer, black pencil skirt, and a silky turquoise blouse. She wanted to look professional. Between showering and dressing, she drank four cups of coffee. She was wired and jittery as she drove to the police station.

What will Internal Affairs ask me? Will Tony find out I was there? What will happen to him? What will happen to me if I don't go through with this? What will happen if I do report him?

She pulled into the parking lot and spotted an unassuming gray side door at the Crystal City Police

Department. She got out of her Mustang with dread. Her sluggish feet moved as though she were dragging giant logs. Her stomach did back flips. She wiped her sweaty palms on her skirt and took a deep breath. Facing the door, she knocked tentatively. Much too soon, a very tall, blond uniformed officer swung the door open wide.

"Good morning. You must be Alexandra Mitchell," he boomed.

Why do all of these cops have such loud, authoritative, scary voices?

Alex nodded, unable to speak. Her mouth felt like it was full of cotton. She forced a smile and extended her clammy hand.

"Come in. I'm Detective Bradley." Alex recognized his baritone voice from their phone conversation.

He motioned toward a chair opposite his desk and Alex plunked herself down. She placed her hands in her lap as she scanned the stark room. It was a dull, filing-cabinet-color gray with a cheap-looking metal desk and hard metal-framed chairs. There were no paintings or certificates on the wall. No family pictures. No signs of sports memorabilia or anything warm and fuzzy. It was a no-frills room that looked like it could be used to question criminals. Alex shivered.

"Are you cold? I can turn up the heat."

"I'm fine."

Detective Bradley splayed his large hands across his desk. "Let's get started." He placed a small recorder in the center of the desk.

"Do you mind if I tape this?"

Alex wondered if she had a choice. She felt perspiration appear on her top lip. Sweat dripped under her arms.

"Is that necessary?"

"It's procedure." He patted the small device, then stared directly at Alex.

"We always record formal complaints against our officers."

Alex shifted in her chair, wondering how much to say.

"Before you turn that on, I'd like to say something—off the record if that's permissible."

The office eyed her wearily, leaned back in his metal chair and crossed his arms.

"I'm listening."

"The thing is Tony—Sgt. Montgomery—and I have been sort of involved these past few months."

Detective Bradley's eyebrows shot up and he leaned forward.

"What do you mean sort of involved?"

"We've had a relationship. Probably beyond friendship. We haven't had sex because I know he's married." She scolded herself for already divulging too much.

"Anyway, the last thing I want to do is get him into trouble."

The detective leaned forward, eyeing her warily.

"So, exactly why are you here making a formal complaint?"

A loud sigh escaped her mouth.

"I received alarming faxes at work and the sexual voicemail on my office line. I was afraid and told my boss, who is the bank president. Since these occurrences happened on bank property, he got our attorney involved." She paused and took a deep breath before continuing.

"Our bank attorney happens to be the city mayor. After that, it was out of my control. Do you see my dilemma?"

The officer nodded. "I believe I get the picture."

He tapped his fingertips together. "This is *also* off the record. I know about Tony's troubled marriage. Have for years. Not sure why he puts up with that but it's his business. Tony and I are good friends. He's a good guy—a really good guy."

Detective Bradley leaned back in his chair.

"So, you see, I have a dilemma as well. I must report what you tell me, Miss—" He looked at his notes "Mitchell. After that, my report will be reviewed by Internal Affairs.

This could go either way, depending on what you tell me." His eyes challenged hers.

"Tony could lose everything—his pension, future promotions, and possibly his job. I'd like for you to think long and hard before I turn this recorder on. I'm not trying to influence you whatsoever. It's just a fact. Do you understand?"

Alex squirmed in her chair. She sat on her hands, staring at the gray door, wishing she could bolt.

"Detective, if I don't report *something*, I could lose *my* job. My boss will expect some kind of action. Besides, what if Tony really did this? I've been scared to death." Her eyes glistened.

"Do you really think Tony is behind this?" the detective asked.

"Not really but I honestly don't know. It's hard to believe he would purposely scare me. Actually, I'd be shocked if it were him. See how confused I am?"

The officer touched the recording device and was all business again. "Let's start with your telling me what you do know—what you know for sure."

He turned the recorder on and noted the date and time.

"This is Detective Bradley and I'm interviewing Ms. Alexandra Mitchell. Ms. Mitchell, I understand you have a complaint against one of our officers. For the record, this conversation is being recorded and I'd like for you to state your name and acknowledge such. Please go ahead."

Alex's heart thrashed. She straightened her skirt, stalling. Finally, she began.

"This is Alexandra Mitchell and I'm aware I'm being taped. Um. I don't know where to start. Several odd and scary things have happened to me lately. I'm not at all sure if they're related or if any of the things were caused by the same person." She started to ramble, gave the detective a deer-in-headlights look, and shrugged.

"Simply tell me the facts in the order in which they occurred, please."

Alex tried to get everything straight in her whirling brain. She reported the first fax, the possible attempted break-in at her house, the neighbor's dog being maced, the second fax at the bank which noted her lights being out, and finally, the sexual song on her office voicemail. She decided to forego the frog in the mailbox and white van that nearly hit her, chalking both up to coincidence.

Even though the information was being recorded, Detective Bradley also made a few notes.

"And do you think one of our officers is behind this, Ms. Mitchell?"

Alex wiped sweat from her top lip.

"Possibly."

"Can you name that officer?"

She took a deep breath. "Sgt. Tony Montgomery."

"What makes you suspect Sgt. Montgomery?"

Alex leaned forward and spoke softly.

"Actually, I never suspected him until the song played on my voicemail. I wouldn't have suspected him then except he called afterward and when I told him about the sexual lyrics he said 'it might have been me.'"

The detective's thick brown eyebrows formed in the shape of one long woolly worm.

"What do you mean?"

"He was vague but kept repeating 'it might have been me.' What else could that mean? He never would come out and say he played the song. I guess it was just a stupid way of telling me he wanted—" She stopped.

"On top of everything else that had happened, I flipped out, told my boss, and he got our attorney involved. So here I am. That's my report." She sat back in her chair wishing she were at Coconuts—or anywhere but here.

"Do you have anything to add?"

Alex thought for a minute and leaned forward, gaping at the tape recorder.

"Yes. I do. I think Sgt. Montgomery is a fine police officer and a good person. I hope he didn't do this and I hope this doesn't get him into trouble." Tears rolled down her cheeks as she scooted her chair back.

"That's all I have to say, officer."

"Thank you, Ms. Mitchell. I'll file your report with Internal Affairs."

Alex watched gratefully as the detective turned off the damn recorder. She stared at him wide-eyed.

"Do you think Tony will get into trouble over this?"

The detective had a poker face. Alex couldn't read his expression and he was obviously finished with their personal chit-chat about Tony.

"Thank you for coming in, Ms. Mitchell. I'll file your report and we'll investigate this matter. Call me if you have any questions or want to add to your statement."

He plucked a business card out of a holder. "Here's my number if you think of anything else related to this case."

Alex took it, shook his hand and walked through the door. Like a zombie, she stepped into the bright sunshine and squinted. She fumbled in her leopard print purse for her car key and sunglasses. As she peered into her purse, she jumped as a uniformed cop popped out from behind a patrol car.

"Hi," he said. "I was in the hallway getting a drink of water and couldn't help overhearing your conversation about Sgt. Montgomery. I can give you some information but it has to be on the QT."

Alex stared at the cop who looked and sounded hauntingly familiar. She couldn't place him and decided she was just on edge.

"You have information about Sgt. Montgomery? Like what?"

"Not here." He looked over his shoulder. "Meet me at The Pancake House at six o'clock." The cop disappeared as quickly as he had appeared.

Alex drove to work wondering what he wanted to tell her. Then something struck her.

How could he have overheard the conversation with Internal Affairs? Both doors were closed and Detective Bradley and I were the only two people in the room. Weren't we?

At five minutes after six, Alex arrived at The Pancake House. She saw the officer and approached his table.

"You're late," he growled while tapping his watch.

Alex glanced at the clock on the wall. "Sorry. I'm just five minutes late."

The officer glared. "Do you know what kind of trouble people can get into in five minutes? Do you know what can happen if we're late on the scene by five minutes?"

Alex stiffened. *What a hard ass.*

"Okay, okay. I get your point. Let's start over." She extended her hand. "Hi, I'm Alexandra Mitchell."

The officer shook her hand. "I'm Sgt. Sean Montgomery."

"Montgomery? Are you related to Tony Montgomery?"

"Good. You're quick. As a matter of fact, he's my little brother."

Alex stared at the man with new intensity. Now she knew why he looked and sounded familiar. Both men were tall with broad shoulders and chiseled faces. Each had those amazing aquamarine blue eyes, short tousled brown hair and slight sideburns. Sean was slightly smaller than Tony.

Sean eyed Alex, recognition now obvious in *his* eyes.

"Wait a minute. You're that broad. That reporter, aren't you? The one who was at the scene in Tony's car during the car chase."

Alex's heart pounded. She had been so lucky. No one had discovered her secret until now.

"Yes. I was there. I remember you, too. You yelled at me and stuck your head in the window. Then, you said something to Tony."

Sean threw his head back and laughed far too long and loud.

"Tony caught so much shit for having you in the car that night." He smiled a wicked smile. "Served him right."

Sean motioned impatiently for a server. When she appeared, he ordered two coffees—not bothering to ask Alex if she wanted anything different.

Alex decided immediately she didn't like Tony's abrasive brother. If she closed her eyes, and heard him talk, she'd swear it was Tony except with a harder edge. The server brought their coffee and wiped her calloused hands on her dirty apron. She took out a small pad and pulled a pen from over her ear.

"Can I get you folks anything to eat?"

They both shook their heads and she shoved the pad back in her apron pocket.

There was an uncomfortable silence at the table. Luckily, the server reappeared with rolled up paper napkins and broke the discomfort. "In case you change your mind. Would either of you like creamer?"

"Yes, please." Alex stared at the server's nametag. "Thelma."

While she waited for the creamer, she examined her silverware for spots and placed the utensils on her lap, rather than on the germ-laden table.

Alex felt her stomach growl and called the server back. "I've changed my mind. I'd like a small house salad. I'm starving."

Thelma glanced at Sean. "Would you like anything?" He shook his head and she walked away.

Stirring her coffee, Alex wondered how much Sean knew and how much she should tell him.

Why hadn't Tony ever mentioned him?

She was wary of telling Sean too much. Very wary.

"So, in the parking lot you said you overheard me talking."

Sean gazed at Alex. "Yeah. I could tell you were ratting out Tony."

She shifted nervously, crossed her legs, and fidgeted with her cup. Alex tried willing the server back to break the silence.

"Don't worry. He deserves it."

"Deserves what?"

"Oh, come on. You're the one who was at Internal Affairs. Why else would you be there unless it was to get my little brother into trouble?"

Alex opened her mouth but words wouldn't flow. The server appeared with her salad and stood beside the table.

"You can leave now," Sean huffed.

Thelma glanced sideways at Alex and walked away. Then, she reappeared.

"I forgot to bring your salad dressing. What would you like?"

Alex was glad for the diversion. "What do you have?"

Thelma rattled off several possibilities and Alex chose balsamic vinegar. After Thelma left, Alex studied Sean.

"I want to be clear. I wasn't trying to get Tony into trouble. I care about him. A lot. But—"

Sean snorted. "You care so much about Tony you went to I.A. to rat on him?" Sean did a great squinty-eyed Clint Eastwood impression that made Alex's heart thrash. She took a long sip of coffee, stalling.

The waitress appeared with the dressing. "Anything else?"

Sean glared at her.

"Can we have some fucking privacy? Got any of that on your damn menu? Just get us another refill and go away."

She refilled their coffee and left with stooped shoulders. Alex felt sorry for the server but decided now wasn't the time to speak up.

"Why were you talking to I.A.?"

Alex explained the weird occurrences at her house, the bank and the disturbing phone call.

Sean listened while stroking his chin as though he had a beard.

"Go on."

Alex noticed his nails were short and decided he must bite them, which disgusted her. She wasn't sure how much to say to Tony's irritating brother.

"As an officer, I'm sure you can understand it is bank policy for all employees to report any hostile or strange behavior to the bank president. After I told my boss, who happens to be the president, he reported it to our attorney. The news rose quickly to the top."

She sipped her coffee and inspected the cop's reaction as he, in turn, studied her.

"Is that everything?"

"Not exactly. After I told my boss about the voicemail, Tony happened to call."

"Always did have great timing." Sean chuckled.

Pushing her hair out of her eyes, Alex continued. "I told Tony about it and he said it might have been him. He never admitted to playing the song—just alluded that it was him."

Sean blew out a long whistle.

"What a dick. I can't believe he was so stupid. What did you do after you found out it was him?"

"I told my boss I'd handle the matter on my own."

"And?"

"He wouldn't allow that. Said it was out of my hands and a bank matter. That's why I was at Internal Affairs."

Alex took a bite of salad.

"You said you have something to tell me."

"I'll be blunt. I usually am."

No kidding.

The server approached their table with a handful of crackers.

"I forgot these earlier. Thought you'd like them with your salad." She placed them on the table and lingered at a nearby booth.

"Dumb broad," Sean muttered.

"As I was saying, Tony is no longer a police officer. He was fired after the chase when you were in the car. What a dumb shit." Sean looked almost gleeful.

Alex gasped. "What? He was fired? He told me he had a desk job. Oh, my God. It's all my fault. I've ruined his life. Do you think he was trying to get revenge by scaring me?" Her mind raced.

"Tony's my little brother. Growing up, he never wanted to be a cop. He actually wanted to coach football. He felt he *had* to be a cop because it runs in the family. It's what we do. Protect and serve. Tony resented the family legacy and the unspoken expectation of being a cop. That's why he became so damn jaded and started making mistakes."

Alex didn't feign her surprise. Tony had never talked about any profession other than a police officer. In fact, he seemed proud to carry on the family legacy.

"Do you think your father would have minded if Tony had become a coach?"

"I don't know. They did enjoy having three generations of officers in the family. Since I was a cop, I think Tony felt pressured to follow in my footsteps. He hates me for it to this day. We're not close."

"He made mistakes? What mistakes?"

"This is off the record. Way off record." His voice was stern.

"Of course." Alex leaned forward.

The waitress reappeared to refill their coffee while Sean talked.

"For one thing, he got involved with his snitches. Had affairs with a couple of them."

Alex felt her cheeks burn.

"What do you mean he had affairs? I thought his horrible wife was the one having multiple affairs."

"She probably did it in self-defense."

Alex wasn't sure she wanted to hear more but curiosity got the best of her.

"What else did he do?" She stirred her coffee so fast some sloshed over the side.

"He strong-armed people to get what he wanted. He was harder than necessary on most of the criminals we picked up. I think he took out his frustrations on the bad guys." Sean laughed.

"Believe me this isn't his first I.A. investigation."

Alex could imagine this hard-nosed Sean doing bad things but not sweet Tony. She hardly recognized her voice. "I always held him in such high regard. I felt *sorry* for him because of his wife. I can't believe he told me he was working a desk job. He lied."

Sean shrugged. "Whatever floats his boat. He's gone from the force, Alex."

"I'm scared. What if he's unstable? I thought I was in love with him."

"You're not alone. All the women fall for him—snitches, emergency room nurses, female cops—he has the touch, man." Sean leaned back and folded his arms.

"Even his wife adores him. She could do a lot better."

Alex stared at Sean in disbelief. "His wife? The adulterer who—"

Sean's face hardened. "She's a good woman. Listen, I don't think Tony will harm you but he may be desperate right now. He's lost his job and he's embarrassed. Now, he'll be facing an interrogation from Internal Affairs. Whatever you do, don't let on that you know he's no longer with the CCPD. And definitely don't let him know that you met me. That could send him over the edge. Just go along with his game, whatever that is."

Sean drained his coffee and glared at the server who swept the floor nearby.

"We're trying to have a discussion here. Do you have to do that while people eat?"

Thelma gave Sean a disgusted look and walked away.

Sean's pager beeped. He laid down a ten dollar bill and handed Alex his card.

"Here's my number in case you need anything. Stay alert and act normal if you see him."

Hands trembling, she reached across the table, took his card, and watched in disbelief as the other Sgt. Montgomery disappeared out the restaurant door.

Chapter 55

Suzy sat at her kitchen table while Fernando sashayed around the room cooking dinner and swaying to Latin music. He took Suzy's hand.

"Let me teach you the Salsa."

Suzy laughed and took Fernando's hands.

"Only if you want bruised toes. I have two left feet."

Fernando ignored her and showed Suzy a couple of dance moves. Suzy clumsily tried to mimic him and soon threw her hands in the air.

"Thanks but no thanks on the dance lesson. Maybe another time. I'm famished. That garlic smells wonderful. What are you making?"

Fernando smiled. "Angel hair pasta, roasted garlic, fresh parsley, pine nuts and parmesan cheese."

"It smells delicious." She rubbed her belly.

"I made the salad," Jon added.

Suzy and Fernando both laughed.

"He's better with laundry than in the kitchen." Fernando winked at Jon. "But he didn't inherit his mother's dance genes, thank goodness."

Suzy playfully punched Fernando in the arm as he opened the refrigerator door. She peeked inside, expecting it to be nearly empty. He had obviously stocked the fridge and pulled out a large tray.

"For dessert, I made tiramisu. I hope you like it."

"Do ducks quack? Who doesn't like tiramisu? Thanks for buying all this food." Suzy smiled at Fernando.

"No problemo. Jon, will you pour the wine?"

Jon filled three crystal wine glasses with red wine. Suzy could see Jon was happy. Very happy. In fact, he beamed like her brides. It was hard to refute. Her shock had subsided. She wanted her son to be content, even if it meant no grandchildren or a glorious wedding.

Suzy set the table and lit candles as her mind wandered to Mrs. Biltmore. She decided to call Emma after dinner.

After the scrumptious pasta and two glasses of wine, Suzy insisted on cleaning up. She shooed the guys out of the house and they left to catch a movie. After she loaded the dishwasher, washed and dried the pans, she called Emma.

"Hi. How's your mom?"

"Oh, hi. I was going to call you. She's better, I guess. Her mouth is still slightly crooked." Emma whispered. "We hide the mirrors. She's so vain. It would really bother her."

"Poor thing. Has her speech improved?"

"She sounds a little better. She still slurs her words. Bernie can understand her better than anyone. He's been amazing. He's such a great caretaker. He even brought one of those small wipe-off boards so she can write her marching orders."

Suzy laughed.

"That was thoughtful of Bernie. I'm glad he's good with her. Maybe she'll change her mind about him."

"I think she already has."

"If there's a silver lining to her stroke, it's going to be how she now views Bernie. He has a special touch and a heart of pure gold. Turns out, his grandmother had a stroke years ago and he cared for her, so he knows exactly what to do."

Suzy smiled even though no one could see her.

"He sounds like a wonderful, caring man. Does she still talk about Lincoln?"

Emma huffed. "Lincoln's a jerk. He finally paid a visit since he was here on business anyway. I happened to be in Mom's room. It was awful."

"What do you mean?"

"When he saw Mom, he was visibly horrified by her face and speech and didn't try to hide it. He was in her room maybe five minutes and left. She didn't say much but I could tell she was hurt." Emma sighed. "I just hope she improves soon. I never thought I'd say it, but I miss her cranky self."

Suzy chuckled. "I know what you mean. I *almost* miss her cantankerous barking but I don't miss the middle-of-the-night phone calls. I'm finally rested." She laughed. "Keep me posted. I'll visit soon."

Chapter 56

After meeting with Sean Montgomery, Alex called Suzy and Hope and asked them to meet her at Coconuts. They had all been too busy and stressed out lately to meet at their Thursday haunt. Alex couldn't wait to catch up with her friends.

She rubbed her tense shoulders while driving and arrived in record time, quickly ordering a glass of much-needed chardonnay. Suzy walked in next and plopped down on a bar stool beside Alex.

"Let's go sit in that corner. I don't want anyone to hear us."

"Why?"

"Trust me. Just order a drink while I grab that booth." Alex pointed. I'll be over there."

"Okay, mystery lady."

Suzy walked to the bar and ordered a cabernet. She carried it to Alex's table. "What's up?"

"Let's wait for Hope." At that moment, Hope bounded in the front door. She slid into the booth all smiles. "You won't *believe* what I have to tell you."

"I bet I can top it," Suzy added.

"I doubt if either of you can trump my story," Alex said.

The friends laughed and waited for Hope's margarita to arrive.

"Should we flip a coin to see who goes first?" Suzy asked.

"Suzy, go ahead. Did Jon make it home?" Alex asked.

Suzy twirled her wine glass in her hand.

"Oh, he's home alright. And so is his friend."

"That's right." Alex leaned forward. "Do you like her? What's her name?"

A smile crept across Suzy's lips.

"Fasten your seatbelts, girls. *His* name is Fernando." She leaned back and watched her friends' reactions.

"I'm confused," Hope said. "Where's the girl he was bringing home?"

Alex's mouth flew open, then a look of amusement filled her eyes.

Suzy splayed her fingers.

"There's no girl. Apparently, my only child is gay and I didn't even know it."

She rested her head on her hand. "I'm okay with it but don't know how I, an almost helicopter mom, could have missed the signs."

"Lots of people are gay. It's sort of vogue right now," Hope offered.

"Don't get me wrong. I don't have anything against homosexuality. I'm just mad at myself for not realizing sooner. I feel like a bad, unobservant mother."

Alex cocked her head. "Don't be ridiculous. You're a great mom. So, what's this Fernando like anyway?"

"Actually, he's great. He's nice, smart, and handsome. I can tell Jon's happy."

"That's what matters," Hope said.

"That is quite a bombshell, Suzy. Not sure if I can top that but let me tell you what's been going on."

Alex talked about her scary happenings and lowered her voice when she discussed going to Internal Affairs.

The women sat riveted. Alex mentioned meeting Tony's older brother and Sean's bombshell about Tony's being fired. She raised her glass to get the attention of a new female server.

"I need another glass of chardonnay, please. And fast."

Suzy blew out her breath. "I'm worried about you. You

should have called before today. I've had an uneasy feeling about this cop all along. You need to stay far, far away from him."

Suzy placed her hand on Alex's arm.

"None of these crazy things ever happened to you before you met him. If he got fired, he deserves it."

"But I have feelings for him," Alex protested. "I'm falling for him. In fact, I think I'm in love with him." She stared at the table afraid of her friends' expressions.

Hope put her hand on Alex's shoulder.

"You may *think* you have feelings for him but those feelings are for someone you obviously don't know. Besides, he's still married, right? Maybe he has become a criminal now. Gone rogue, full circle and all that. You did the right thing by reporting him. Suzy's right. You need to give this guy a wide berth."

A cute ponytailed redhead appeared with Alex's wine. She took a long sip before answering.

"I haven't heard a word from Tony since the phone call at work. Once he finds out I reported him, I probably never will."

She stared into her drink and looked around Coconuts nervously. She wondered if one of the newcomers was actually a spy for Tony. Paranoia was setting in.

"I don't want to talk about this anymore. I appreciate your concern but I'm drained. I'll handle this on my own. Hope, what's your news?"

Hope scanned her friends' faces and broke into a huge smile.

"You wouldn't believe me if I told you. I can't quite believe it myself."

Suzy gladly accepted another drink from the server and studied Hope.

"Surely your news can't top ours?"

"Actually, I think mine tops everyone's. You be the judge." Hope took a deep breath, studying her two loyal friends. Alex and Suzy's eyes were locked on hers.

"Remember that mysterious man in the back of the chapel at the funeral home? The one I talked to after the service?"

Alex nodded. "Yeah, I think so. I remember a guy motioning you over."

"I remember him too," Suzy said.

"Did you notice his looks?" Hope asked.

"Nothing outstanding. I believe he was in a suit like most of us that day," Suzy added.

"Seems like he was kind of short for a man," Alex added.

Hope smiled. "I've had a few days to digest this news so it's going to shock you. Brace yourselves."

The women leaned forward. "You've got our attention," Alex said.

"Do you want a drum roll?" Suzy teased.

"He's my real dad," Hope blurted.

"What do you mean?" Suzy asked with a bewildered look on her face.

Alex's mouth flew open but words failed her.

Hope took another drink of her margarita and chuckled.

"I warned you this was big news. His name is Paul Walker. He told me my real mother died shortly after childbirth and he tried to raise me himself. He worked long hours and couldn't handle a baby—me—on his own."

Hope paused, looking into her drink as if for answers.

"Paul said Larry and Montana worked for him around the house. Montana—Claire helped babysit me some when I was a baby. Paul said Montana was really good with me." Hope's eyes filled with tears and she looked away. Suzy placed her hand on Hope's arm. "Go on, hon."

Hope sniffed.

"Larry and Montana asked if they could adopt me. They saw how he struggled as a single parent. Apparently, they couldn't conceive." Hope paused. "They worked out an agreement and officially adopted me. Paul's an attorney so that made it fast and easy, I suppose." She reached into her purse for a tissue, dabbed her eyes and blew her nose.

Suzy and Alex didn't speak at first.

Finally, Suzy found words.

"This explains so much—why you didn't look like Larry and Montana and why your values and work ethics were vastly different."

Hope nodded. "I know. It's unbelievable. I'm still trying to get my head around it. Paul said he wanted to tell me for years that he was my biological dad but the legal documentation didn't allow him to approach me."

Tears trickled down her cheeks.

"Paul saw the obituary in the paper and knew I'd be at the funeral. That was his opportunity to tell me the truth. We've had lunch a few times and have talked on the phone almost daily. Actually, I feel like I'm dreaming."

"You're not dreaming. This is amazing news. What a turnaround from the tragedy. You still have a Dad, Hope." Alex jumped up and hugged her friend.

Suzy nodded. "I'm glad he told you. You'll have many years to get to know one another. I'm sure you're still sad about Larry and Montana but this gives you a fresh, new start." She joined the group hug.

Hope bobbed her head while tears flowed. "This doesn't take away from Larry and Montana whatsoever. I almost feel guilty because I'm excited about my new dad. I did love them and know they loved me in their own crazy way but this explains a lot." She blew her nose again and thrust the wadded tissue in her purse.

Alex drained her wineglass. "We've got to get back on schedule every Thursday. I can't take this much drama every time we meet."

The women laughed and nodded in obvious agreement. Suzy turned to Hope. "I'm thrilled you're getting to know your biological dad. You deserve happiness more than anyone I know."

Chapter 57

Alex drove home from Coconuts flabbergasted by Suzy's new revelation about Jon and Hope's new dad.

Then, her thoughts shifted to Sean and Tony. Her body tensed with fear. After arriving home, she rattled around her empty house and straightened glasses in the cabinet. She cursed herself for not allowing them to touch.

Why am I like this? She sat on the sofa and stared at a stack of magazines but wasn't in the mood to read. She did the next best thing and alphabetized them according to date with the oldest on the bottom and most current issue on top. Then, she rearranged her spice drawer, again in alphabetical order. Feeling a bit more relaxed, she looked at the black screen on her television but wasn't in the mood for a reality show featuring happy couples and their extreme adventures.

Restless, she walked to the kitchen and rooted around in the fridge. She chose a Diet Coke, block of cheddar cheese and grapes for dinner, too nervous to eat more but knowing she needed food on her stomach after two glasses of wine.

The brisk soda was refreshing and Alex munched on cheese and grapes as her mind raced. Pacing while she alternately popped grapes and cheese in her mouth, she decided fresh air might help. She threw the front door open to breathe in the outdoor air. The cool breeze assured fall was around the corner. A bright moon glowed and she started to relax.

Alex decided to water her dried-up flowers on the front porch. She turned to get the hose when she heard a car motor. She peered toward the road as Tony parked the car. She froze and steadied herself in the doorway. Tony sauntered toward her. His hair was longer, disheveled and he had a stubbly, short beard. He looked sexy, gorgeous, rugged, and suddenly scary.

"Hi." He smiled wide. "You're a sight for sore eyes." Tony reached for Alex and buried his head in her hair. "Mmm. You smell good. I've missed you."

Alex stiffened and pulled back.

"Didn't you miss me? I missed you."

He nuzzled her neck and moved toward her mouth.

She turned her head and his kiss landed in her hair. She saw the bewilderment in his eyes and remembered Sean said to act naturally. She leaned over and gave him a peck on the check.

He cocked his head.

"That's not much of a welcome back."

Alex tried to sound convincing. "Welcome back. I missed you." She forced a smile. "I'm tired. I was with the girls tonight and have an early meeting tomorrow." She stayed in the doorway. "I really need to go to bed soon."

"That sounds good to me." Tony's eyes twinkled.

Alex felt herself weaken against his boyish, sexy grin but remained firm. "No really. I need to sleep—alone."

Tony looked confused. "If I didn't know better, I'd say you were trying to get rid of me. I've been unavailable for a month, yet you don't seem happy to see me. What's up?" He looked hurt as he touched her hair and twirled it between his fingers.

"Have you met someone else?" Concern filled his voice.

Alex shook her head. "No, no. Absolutely not. There's no one else. I'm—I'm very happy to see you." Alex shifted and stared at her feet.

She decided to test him. "How's work?"

"The chief is still pissed so I'll be on desk duty for a couple more weeks reviewing cold cases while dad is on vacation. He knows I hate working inside. I'm still being punished." Tony blew out his breath.

"Shouldn't be much longer, though. He'll get mad at someone else soon and the focus will be off me." Again, there was that boyish grin.

Tony planted himself on the porch.

"Do you want to grab a bite at Rosa's? I'm starving and Mexican sounds good." He draped his arm around her shoulders. "Not as good as you, though." He paused, stroking her cheek.

She pulled away.

Tony's brow furrowed. "I've missed you. I thought a lot about you—about us—and our previous conversations. Alex, I—"

Alex put her finger to his mouth to stop him from finishing. How she would have loved to eat out with him a few short weeks ago. She was surprised he wanted to be seen with her in public. Surprised he'd take the risk.

"I can't. I have a meeting tomorrow, as I said. Besides, I just ate. I'm going to hit the sack. Rain check, okay?"

"How about this weekend? Let's go out. Maybe dinner and a movie. I have something I want to say to you." He stared at her hungrily.

Alex avoided his gaze.

"I'm really busy this weekend. The girls and I may go to a thing. An event."

Tony cocked his head and frowned.

"You'll have to find time for me one of these days." He stepped closer. She could smell his spearmint gum.

"Just one big juicy kiss, and I'll be on my way."

Alex did her best to return the kiss because she didn't want to raise his suspicions. Her knees nearly buckled as his tongue probed her mouth. All the while she wondered if she was kissing a bad cop. A cop that still pushed all her buttons. Every. Single. One. Tony looked like he had lost his favorite toy as he hugged her goodbye. Alex locked the door handle and slid the deadbolt into the door jamb.

Chapter 58

The antiseptic smell hit Suzy in the face as she pressed the elevator. She wondered how anyone could work in a hospital but then they probably wondered how she could plan weddings.

When she entered Mrs. B's room, she found her attempting to eat lunch while seated in a wheelchair. A tray of food was balanced unsteadily on her lap.

Suzy wrinkled her nose at the sight of thickened beef broth, cherry gelatin and nectar-like coffee.

Just two weeks ago Mrs. B was eating blackened salmon and lamb as she ordered everyone around the Biltmore Country Club.

Mrs. B shakily brought the spoon of gelatin up to her crooked mouth. Taking just one bite took forever. Suzy wondered if she should feed Mrs. B but didn't want to embarrass her. Luckily, a hospital employee entered the room.

"How's my favorite patient today?" asked a tall, pretty brunette as she bent over and checked Mrs. B's I.D. on her wrist band.

The employee patted Mrs. B on the arm and glanced toward Suzy.

"I'm Marsha, Mrs. Biltmore's speech therapist."

Suzy introduced herself as she shook Marsha's hand. She sat quietly and watched Marsha assist Mrs. B with her food. After she finished, the therapist set the food tray aside and asked Mrs. B simple questions—starting with the days of the week. When she answered those correctly, the therapist followed up by asking her to repeat family members' names. It was agonizing how long it took, but eventually, Mrs. B answered each question correctly.

Next, the therapist held up everyday objects and instructed Mrs. B to identify them.

"C-C-comb."

"What do we do with the comb?"

Mrs. B pointed to her hair.

"Good."

Suzy marveled at the interaction as Marsha pointed to other objects such as a toothbrush and salt and pepper shakers. Mrs. B answered correctly every item, although she was difficult to understand and spoke slowly. Suzy wanted to clap with glee after each correct answer like a proud parent at a ballet recital.

After they completed the exercises, Marsha turned toward Suzy.

"Are you family?"

Suzy shook her head. "A friend." She smiled. "I'm her daughter's wedding planner."

The therapist beamed. "Bernie is a wonderful man. Her daughter is lucky."

Suzy froze, afraid to look at Mrs. Biltmore but she heard a faint voice say, "Ber-nie. Good man."

Marsha patted Mrs. B's bony hand.

"That's right. He certainly is. Now, let's do some exercises for your beautiful face."

The therapist donned fresh gloves, pulled a long string out of a package, and opened a packet of colorful Life Savers. She placed the string through the hole in the candy and asked Mrs. B to place her lips around the Life Saver while the therapist held both ends of the string.

"Mrs. Biltmore, hold on to that cherry candy as hard as you can. Don't let me pull it out of your mouth. We're going to have a little tug of war."

Suzy watched with amazement.

"What does that do?"

Still holding the string, Marsha pulled on it but Mrs. B kept the candy securely in her mouth with her lips clamped.

"Great job."

Mrs. B smiled another crooked smile as Marsha turned to Suzy.

"This is a resistance exercise to help strengthen her lip muscles."

Suzy watched as they did the exercise a few more times. Marsha squatted down until she was eye level with Mrs. B.

"Tomorrow, I'll bring the vibrating massager again. We want to stimulate those weak muscles in your face, okay?"

Mrs. B nodded with her eyes half closed.

"You're tired, aren't you, sweetie? Let's get you into bed."

She helped Mrs. B into bed, lifted the railings, and patted her arm.

"Tomorrow, we'll go over some breathing techniques and do these exercises again. You're doing very well."

Marsha turned to Suzy.

"She's making good progress. It always seems slow to family and friends but she'll come around as long as she keeps working hard. She has physical therapy, too. That will give her strength and get her out of the wheelchair eventually. She may need a walker for a while but she'll be up and around in no time."

The therapist walked toward the door, then turned to say, "I understand you called the ambulance."

"Yes. We were on the phone about a wedding matter and I could tell something was terribly wrong."

"You did the right thing. With stroke victims, time is of the essence. Your call made all the difference. I know she's grateful to you."

Marsha glanced at Mrs. Biltmore. "I'll see you tomorrow."

"O-kay."

The therapist left and Mrs. B pointed to her wipe-off board on the tray near her bed.

"I thought you were sleepy. I don't want you to overdo it."

Mrs. B ignored her and kept pointing with her bony finger. Suzy handed her the board and marker. After what seemed like an hour, Mrs. B scrawled out two words:

No Lincoln

Suzy knitted her brows.

"Lincoln isn't here."

Mrs. B shook her head and wrote a big "X" through Lincoln's name.

Suzy's mouth flew open as reality set in.

"Are you saying Lincoln is out of the picture as far as Emma is concerned?"

Mrs. B slowly erased the board and scribbled:

Marry Bernie

Tears pricked Suzy's eyes. She felt a rush of joy.

"Are you telling me you want Emma to marry Bernie rather than Lincoln?"

"Y-es." She punctuated her answer with another crooked smile.

Suzy carefully embraced her small body and kissed her cheek.

"That's wonderful news and a great decision. I'm thrilled and Emma will be too. You're a smart woman, Mrs. Biltmore."

Later that day, Emma called Suzy, breathless.

"You'll never believe this. Mom wants me to marry Bernie. I'm going to get the wedding of my dreams after all."

Suzy could hear pure joy in Emma's voice.

"I know. She told me—or wrote it out, rather. I'm thrilled. Let me know the date and I'll review my notes with you."

"Oh, it'll be months from now. Maybe a year. I want Mom to be in good health so she can enjoy the ceremony. Bernie and I can wait for as long as it takes. We have each other and now we have her blessing. We're beyond ecstatic."

Suzy wished Emma could see her broad smile.

"I'm very happy for you and Bernie. I truly am. Thanks for call—"

"Wait. I have a couple more things to tell you. They're discharging Mom tomorrow."

Really?" Suzy asked with surprise.

"She wants to go home so they're arranging for home health therapists to go by her house every day. She'll have physical, occupational, and speech therapy. The best money can buy. You know."

Suzy chuckled.

"Also," Emma paused. "Mom asked me to bring her bank statements to the hospital yesterday. She noticed you still haven't cashed her fifty thousand dollar check. She told me to tell you to cash it by tomorrow. Her orders."

Suzy squeezed the phone.

"That's very generous of her."

"The way she looks at it you saved her life. And that's worth much more than fifty thousand dollars, plus you'll be planning my real wedding now. Please cash it. It'll make her feel better."

"Okay, I will." Suzy could hardly contain her excitement.

"Good. And there's one more thing. It's very exciting."

"What?" Suzy couldn't imagine how this phone call could get any better.

"Mom has decided she—rather the Biltmore Foundation—will make a one million dollar donation to the hospital. Her entire donation will be earmarked to benefit the hospital's stroke department. It's going to be a naming gift. Guess what it'll be called?"

Suzy chuckled. "Let me guess. Something with the word 'Biltmore?'"

Emma giggled. "Naturally. It'll be called the Biltmore Stroke Center. Mom's idea."

"I think that's a perfect name. Please tell Mrs. Biltmore I said so. Thanks for all the great news. And congratulations to you and Bernie. Talk to you soon." Suzy hung up and twirled across the floor trying to remember the salsa steps Fernando had tried to teach her.

Chapter 59

Suzy bubbled over with excitement. She walked to her office and removed the check from her desk drawer. She ogled it and placed it in her purse. She made a mental note to go to the bank later that day. Not that she'd forget.

She walked to the living room and peered out the window. The warm sun on her face was inviting. She walked outside and extended her arms like an airplane, twirling like a child. After Mrs. Biltmore's stroke and watching her rehabilitation, Suzy had made an oath to enjoy every day.

She breathed in the fresh air and observed the neighborhood children playing across the street. A redheaded little girl did cartwheels while two boys rode bikes. She rubbed the neighbor's Lab behind his ears and bent down to smell the fragrant red roses in her yard.

She wondered why she hadn't always snipped roses to enjoy fresh centerpieces at home and immediately plucked several roses and walked inside. She left the door open so she could hear the children's laughter.

As she searched for a vase, Suzy knocked a pile of catalogs onto the floor. A red and black envelope fell beside the dishwasher. Suzy picked it up, recognizing her high school logo. She opened the envelope. In bold red and black letters an invitation read:

Central High School
20th Reunion
Go Bulldogs!
Save The Date: August 30
Crystal City Hotel ~ 2222 W. Oak Street

We need volunteers for our reunion committee. That means you!

To volunteer or RSVP, email Bob Jackson at bjackson@chsreunion.com.

Suzy gasped when she reread the date. *It's this weekend.*

She suddenly felt old. A has-been at thirty-eight. She knew she'd probably get the prize for the oldest child since she got pregnant the first semester of college.

Another thought occurred to Suzy.

I wonder if Ken will be there. I wonder if he's still married.

When she checked Facebook years ago, he was married. She checked it once after that but he wasn't anywhere to be found on the social networking site. She had breathed a sigh of relief at not being tortured by his happy family pictures. Butterflies filled her stomach as she clutched the invitation.

Half scared, half excited, she called Hope to see if she had received her invitation.

Hope groaned.

"You must be joking. I threw my invitation away two months ago. You just read yours?"

"Yep. It was in a pile of magazines. Are you going?"

"Why would I want to show everyone what twenty years has done to my body?"

"Oh, please." Suzy paced the kitchen floor. "Why didn't you mention the reunion invitation when we were together?"

Hope sighed. "Let's see. We've all been a tad busy this summer. Guess it slipped my mind."

Suzy held the phone between her ear and shoulder while pouring a glass of water.

"Let's go. It'll be fun. I'm going to call Alex."

Hope sighed into the phone.

"Do you know of a forty-eight hour diet? You two are going to make me look bad. I'm not standing near you." She laughed.

"Stop. Let's go together for moral support. We'll make it a girls' night. What do you say?"

Hope paused. "All right. If you insist. But I'm not going to have fun."

"I do insist and yes you will. I'm calling Alex now. Bye."

Suzy hung up and called Alex who also sighed into the phone at the mention of the reunion.

"I hate those things. I completely forgot it was this month. I've been so worried about Tony I don't even know what year it is. I think I'll pass."

"Please, Alex. We have to go together. Hope's going. Maybe it'll be a good distraction for all of us. Plus," Suzy hesitated.

"What?"

"Ken might be there."

"Your high school sweetheart? The one you never should have let go? You're not playing fair. Okay, okay. Just for you. But I'm not going to have fun," Alex said.

"Yes you will. Thanks. Gotta run."

Suzy hung up and walked to her office to email Bob Jackson to see if she could help with any last-minute details. If she went to at least one committee meeting before the main event, maybe she could find out who would be attending—specifically, Ken. She sat down at her computer and emailed the class president.

Bob, I just found my reunion invitation! I can't believe it's been twenty years. Time sure flies. I know it's late notice but I'll be happy to help out if there's anything left to be done. Just let me know.

Go, Bulldogs! Suzy Jacobs

She hit "send" and stared at the screen, reminiscing about high school. She and Ken Dixon had been soul mates. They never should have drifted apart nor married other people. They belonged together. Of course, the little fact that she had gotten pregnant by Bill after a freshman romance didn't bode well for her relationship with Ken. It no longer mattered. He was probably happily married.

Wistfully, she remembered their trips to The Crescent Hotel, supposedly haunted, in Eureka Springs. Ken had held her all night because she was frightened. She smiled as she pictured them huddled under a blanket while cheering on the Kansas City Chiefs during a cool fall day or attending a tailgate party at a St. Louis Cardinals baseball game. She flashed back to the day they went inside the tip of the St. Louis arch and saw Cher in concert after eating at an Italian restaurant on the Hill. She'd give anything to relive that day now.

Her favorite times were simple ones—a picnic at the park, watching a movie, camping and eating roasted marshmallows or simply sharing a pizza. Suzy grinned thinking how cute Ken was in his catcher uniform. She cheered at all of his games even if she was sick. One special memory was the time he baked an apple pie for her birthday. She never asked why he didn't bake a cake instead and certainly didn't tell him she didn't care for apple pie. She and Ken ate every bite—right out of the pie plate, nearly making themselves sick.

Suzy pictured Ken as he looked in his high school baseball uniform with his brown, wavy hair, broad smile and dimple. Ken, always the gentleman, was sweet, handsome and smart. She hoped he'd come to the reunion. Alone. Suzy stretched and jumped as her computer beeped indicating an incoming email.

Chapter 60

Suzy peered at the screen. The email was from the class president, Bob, who explained there was a committee meeting in two hours at Coconuts. He invited Suzy to join them.

"I'll be there. Can't wait to see everyone." Suzy hit send and undressed on the way to the shower.

With a towel wrapped around her still-damp body, she painstakingly chose a cute-but-not-desperate outfit. She wore an above-the-knee khaki skirt, a yellow v-neck ruffled shirt, and brown wedge sandals. She added a floral purse, dangly gold earrings and dug in her jewelry box to find the perfect necklace. *I have to find it.* After rooting around for several minutes, she pulled out a small gold heart-shaped necklace.

I wonder if Ken will remember giving me this?

She applied glossy nude lipstick, brown eye shadow and curled her long, red hair. She drove around town to kill time before the meeting and scanned seemingly every radio station on the dial before she had the nerve to walk inside. Her stomach was in knots wondering if Ken would be there.

After the meeting, Suzy called Alex in tears.

"I hate men. I give up. I'm never going to date a—"

"What's wrong? Slow down." Alex took the phone outside and sat on her deck. She settled into a bright blue lawn chair and watched fireflies circle in the night as she listened to the strain in her friend's voice.

"You know how some people have the Midas touch where everything turns to gold?"

"Yes."

"Well, I have the Suzy touch where everything turns to rust." She sobbed.

"No, you don't. Will you please tell me what happened?"

"I went to a reunion committee meeting tonight." Suzy sniffed.

"What's so bad about that?"

"Ken was there. My Ken." Another sob escaped.

"He acted so happy to see me and came on strong. We stared at each other like lustful school kids throughout the meeting. I don't even remember what I volunteered to do. I couldn't tell you anything about the meeting. I was completely mesmerized by Ken. Afterward, he walked me to my car. We chatted until the other classmates left. Then, we hugged and kissed. I mean *really* kissed. I melted in his arms. I haven't felt that way since, well, since high school. Alex, I was about ready to jump into bed with him. It felt just like the old days. Like we hadn't missed a beat."

"I must be missing something. What's wrong with this picture?"

"I didn't realize how much I've missed him all these years. How much I still love him." Suzy blew her nose loudly.

"Ken said he had to leave. He had something important to do. When I got home, I had an email from Bob, our class president. He thanked me for helping with the reunion and added it was too bad that Ken is newly engaged since we made such a great couple in high school. He mentioned he still detected a 'spark' between us."

"Oh, no." Alex groaned.

Suzy sobbed louder.

"Oh, no is right. He didn't even have the nerve to tell me. Ken even said he has carried a torch for me all these years. How could he lie like that? How could he kiss me if he's engaged? I'm not going to the reunion now. I don't want to see her. I can't handle seeing *them*."

"Sorry. I'm overriding your decision."

"What? You didn't want to go in the first place."

"Changed my mind. We're going. And you're going to be in a drop-dead gorgeous dress and make him regret his decision."

Alex added, "And I can throw a—a pie in Ken's face. A messy meringue one that tastes really crappy and sour. I'll ask the kitchen for some cayenne pepper, distract Ken, and sprinkle it all over his food, or better yet, you could just spit on his plate when he isn't looking."

Suzy chuckled.

"What would I do without you? I almost feel better."

"Good. Why don't you come over? We can have a glass of wine and toast all the bad men we've dated."

"Can I have a rain check? I'm a mess. I just want some hot tea and to curl up with a good book about revenge or murder. Alex, thanks for listening."

"He doesn't deserve you. See you tomorrow."

Chapter 61

The women decided to have an impromptu meeting at Coconuts. Without their having to order, Gus brought their usual drinks over and greeted Alex, Suzy and Hope. Gus never talked much and had a way of knowing when the discussion was serious. He rarely hovered.

Grateful, Alex touched his bicep. "Someone's been working out."

He blushed, then puffed out his chest. "A little. You ladies enjoy."

When he was out of earshot, Alex mentioned she had been dodging calls from Tony.

Suzy's eyebrows shot up.

"Funny you should say that because Ken has called nonstop since last night. He probably left ten messages before I came here this morning. I didn't pick up."

"What did he say?" asked Alex.

Hope looked confused. "Ken? What are you two talking about?"

Alex brought Hope up to speed on the reunion committee meeting and the news that Ken is newly engaged.

Hope glanced at Suzy's rounded shoulders. "Oh, no. What are his phone messages about?" Hope asked.

"I only listened to one message. He said I *have* to attend the reunion. That he wanted to talk." I deleted the other messages without listening. "Guess he wants to flaunt his fiancée." Suzy sat back in her chair.

"I've got to find an ultra-sexy dress to wear."

"You'll be the most gorgeous woman there. Well, next to me," Alex teased.

Hope grunted. "You don't have to do anything to look better than me. Just show up."

Alex gave Hope a sideways glance.

"That's not true. We're all going to be gorgeous. You just wait and see."

On Reunion Day, Alex, Suzy, and Hope met for breakfast and went on a whirlwind shopping marathon for drop-dead dresses. Alex was intent on finding a gorgeous dress for herself but wanted to be sure Suzy's dress left Ken's mouth hanging open.

After finding three amazing dresses in two short hours, they decided to get a relaxing manicure and pedicure. Leaning back in the comfy salon chairs, they sank their feet into warm, soothing, lavender suds.

"You two know how to live. I've never done this before." Hope glowed at her friends.

"You must be joking. You've got to treat yourself once in awhile," Alex said as she noticed Suzy's clenched jaw and right eye twitching.

She patted her arm. "Relax. It'll be okay."

"That's right. It's his loss," Hope chimed in.

Suzy loved her girlfriends but kept quiet. Their supportive words didn't help the fact that she was miserable.

Alex swished her feet in the sudsy water.

"After our pedicures, come to my house. Let's get dressed together. It'll be fun. Just like high school. Okay? Done." Alex rarely took no for an answer.

She leaned forward and squinted at her French manicure. She loved how fresh and clean it looked. A nail technician applied bright red polish to her toes while another employee painted a light plum on Hope's toes. Suzy chose a deep pink.

"Turn your chair massager on, Hope." Alex pointed to the buttons on the chair arm. Hope obliged and leaned forward each time the massager rolled up and down her back. She smiled. "Nice touch."

Suzy's eyes were closed so Alex left her to her thoughts.

The three women were surrounded by the Perfect Nails staff—six to be exact. One woman was seated at each set of toes while another applied a top coat to their nails. The salon staff laughed and chatted in Vietnamese. Alex stared blankly at the television wondering if they were talking about them. She didn't care if they were. She was too worried about Suzy's reaction when she saw Ken with his fiancée.

Later that afternoon Hope and Suzy appeared on Alex's doorstep with dresses, shoes, makeup and jewelry draped over their arms. Hope rang the doorbell with her elbow. Alex threw the door open while balancing a tray supporting three glasses of wine.

"It's about time. Come in, girls. Let's get this party started."

Suzy and Hope draped their dresses over a chair and eagerly accepted the drinks. Suzy downed hers in record time.

"Whoa. Slow down. You don't want to get drunk before you see who your competition is, do you?" Alex teased.

Suzy rolled her eyes.

"Let's just get this over with."

"Amen," Hope added.

Alex topped off their wine and the women followed her into the bedroom where she had neatly laid their dresses on the bed. As they dressed Alex played a soothing Nora Jones song, followed by Beyonce's "Single Ladies." She laughed.

"Now, *that's* the attitude we need for tonight, girls."

Suzy stepped into a sexy, low-cut, form-fitting black halter dress with a slit up to there. She added large silver chandelier earrings, a black and silver statement necklace, a silver charm bracelet, and black stilettos. Somehow, she'd found time to get a spray tan.

Alex whistled.

"You look fantastic. If I were a guy, I'd ask you out."

Suzy smiled gratefully and blushed.

"Thanks. Put yours on."

Alex decided to go the romantic—but-sexy route and wore a strapless ivory dress with a bustier dotted with silver and gold sequins. The silky bottom half hugged her curves and the flowing high-low hemline was long in the back and above her knees in the front. She added gold ankle-strap stilettos, large gold hoops, and a chunky gold bracelet.

Suzy and Hope nodded approvingly.

"My turn."

Hope put on a long, slimming black skirt and a satin red blouse. "School colors." Hope laughed. She added pearl drop earrings and a glistening pearl necklace.

"What a gorgeous pearl necklace," Alex said.

Hope's cheeks pinkened.

"My new dad gave this to me. He said the necklace belonged to my biological mother. Apparently, this was her favorite necklace."

Her eyes moistened. "He told me the pearls would be my good luck charm from now on."

Suzy and Alex rushed toward Hope and enveloped her in a hug.

"That's right, honey. From now on, your luck will change," Suzy said adding, "Hopefully, mine will too."

"And mine," Alex said. "Maybe we should take turns wearing those pearls. We could form The Traveling Girlfriend Pearls."

Chapter 62

Bolstered with confidence from the wine and the fashion show at Alex's house, the three women walked into the Crystal City Hotel arm in arm. Alex could see their reflection in the ivory tiled floors underneath a massive chandelier with what looked like a thousand sparkling lights. An enormous waterfall trickled down a large wall and long, leafy greenery hung from the balconies. A calming string quartet played as several classmates gathered around the registration table. Alex noticed others mingled near the bar and wondered if Ken was there. She squeezed Suzy's hand. Suzy was silent.

Alex whispered, "Relax. It'll be fine."

Hope pointed toward the red and black color scheme on the tables.

"See, I'm color coordinated."

The women laughed as Alex stared at clusters of balloons anchored by a miniature stuffed bulldog, the school mascot, on every table.

"Someone sprinkled red and black confetti "20's" on the tables," Hope said.

"Nice reminder that we're getting old," Alex said as she fished for her cell phone.

"Squeeze together. Selfie time." Alex held her phone at arm's length. "Say 'monkey breath.'"

Hope burst out laughing as Alex clicked the photo.

"I bet my mouth was wide open." Hope laughed.

Alex noticed Suzy was still zombie-like. She held Suzy's hand as the women walked around the room. The DJ tested the microphone while servers put spinach salads on the tables.

Suzy suddenly smacked herself on the forehead. "I just remembered I'm supposed to help with registration. I'm such a mess."

Alex and Hope looked at one another, then watched Suzy amble downtrodden toward the registration table.

Suzy took a seat at the long registration table, forced a smile, and handed out nametags to former students who arrived in droves. The tags were in alphabetical order. She could see Ken had not yet arrived. She relaxed slightly.

Nearly two hundred classmates and their guests were expected but Suzy only had eyes for one. She couldn't stop staring at Ken's nametag and jumped every time a male walked up to the table. After several minutes, she decided he wasn't coming and caught Alex's eye from across the room. Suzy shrugged while Alex did a thumbs down.

Guess he didn't have the nerve to show up after all.

When all but ten nametags were picked up, Suzy laid the rest neatly on the table and decided to get another glass of wine. God knows she'd need one if Ken decided to make an appearance with his new fiancée.

Chapter 63

Alex observed her classmates. Everyone seemed to be mingling comfortably with a little help from their cocktails. She was glad one of the organizers had the bright idea to put the students' ugly high school picture on their nametags, otherwise, she never would have recognized most of them.

She approached her classmates with ease and found it interesting how some of the ugly ducklings were now attractive and vice versa. She wondered what everyone thought of her and suddenly wished she had a date—at least someone to dance with—other than Suzy and Hope.

Alex's thoughts turned to how everything had turned sour with Tony, the great white cop. She rarely let herself think about him. She was crushed by his betrayal but still yearned to see him. Her emotions ran the gamut. Occasionally, she cried herself to sleep but she'd never admit that to anyone. She liked being the strong one and hated herself for being weak. When she did allow herself to think about Tony, she admitted—if only to herself—that she was still in love with the guy. Bad cop or not. She couldn't help herself.

Bob, the class president, jolted her back to reality as he spoke into a cordless microphone.

"Please find a seat, everyone. Dinner will be served soon."

Alex sat next to Suzy and noticed Hope chatting with friends at another table. Alex glanced at Suzy. "Maybe she's reconnecting with someone. That'll be good for her. Let's try to have fun. We deserve it."

Suzy leaned over. "Ken isn't here. Looks like he chickened out."

As the lights dimmed and the food arrived, Suzy noticed a latecomer walk in and go straight to the bar. She couldn't make out his face until he turned around. It was Ken. Her stomach lurched.

She poked Alex in the ribs. "There he is. I wish I could fall through a trap door." Her eyes widened. "Why did I let you drag me here?"

"It looks like he's alone," Alex observed.

"She's probably in the ladies' room," Suzy said.

Hope appeared at the table and sat down. She looked in the same direction as her friends.

"Oh. I see Ken is here—cute as ever. Still has lots of that great hair," Hope said.

Ken walked deliberately toward their table, never taking his eyes off Suzy. Naturally, there was an empty chair. Suzy turned her chair to face the speaker. She couldn't look at Ken. She couldn't bear to be at the same table. She was too embarrassed, hurt, and still in love with the guy.

How could he do this to me? I can't believe he had the nerve to kiss me while he was engaged. I fell for him all over again. And where the hell is she?

Suzy stared intently at the class president, not hearing much of what he had to say. She heard Bob welcome the classmates to their twentieth reunion and thank everyone for coming. He discussed the evening's upcoming events. Suzy zoned out and picked lint off her lap.

When she heard the president ask for a moment of silence for their deceased classmates, Suzy instantly hated herself for being self-absorbed. She scanned the program and noted ten names. Already, ten classmates had died. Seven guys and three girls.

Seeing the daunting list of the deceased, Suzy felt

ridiculous for her own predicament and said a silent prayer for her former classmates and their families.

A student walked to the front and lit a candle to remember each person as Bob called their name. Suzy, Hope and Alex held hands. Several people wiped their eyes and cleared their throats as Teresa sang the school song. Thank goodness the song was printed in the program. Suzy never knew the words in school, much less now.

When Teresa finished singing, servers brought out entrees. Out of the corner of her eye, Suzy detected movement and could tell Ken shifted in his seat. She sat as still as a statue and hoped Bob would talk all night so she wouldn't have to make conversation.

Suddenly, Suzy heard a whisper in her ear. Ken was behind her. She jumped and glared at him.

"What are you doing here and where is your fiancée? You know, the one you failed to tell me about." She didn't give him a chance to answer.

"I guess you thought I wouldn't find out but Bob informed me." Suzy flipped her hair behind her shoulder. "I can't believe you kissed me knowing you were engaged. I thought more highly of you, Ken. Do you have to sit at this table? I'm sure there are plenty of empty seats." She looked around the room, avoiding his gaze.

"Yes, I do have to sit here. We've got to talk." Ken's eyes bored into her.

"I don't want to talk. Everyone is watching."

"Let me buy you a drink while everyone is eating their salad. I need to talk to you. It's important. Please."

Reluctantly, Suzy let Ken pull out her chair and walked with him toward the bar.

"Make it fast. I can't think of anything you could say that would make it up to me." Her heart beat double time.

Alex and Hope watched the interaction. Both picked at their salads while casting nervous glances in Suzy's direction.

Chapter 64

"Please let me explain. I *was* engaged when we worked on the committee, but after we talked and kissed, I knew I had to end it with Melissa. I broke it off with her that very night. She stayed at another hotel and I bought her a plane ticket back to Ohio the next morning."

Ken ran his fingers through his brown, wavy hair.

"I have two women who are furious with me right now but I had to end it with Melissa and take a chance on you. I couldn't risk losing you again, Suzy. Will you give me another chance?"

Suzy opened her mouth to speak but Ken placed his finger on her lips.

"Let me finish. Please. I want to explain."

Suzy took a gulp of wine as butterflies danced in her stomach. Ken locked eyes with her.

"I want you to know something. I've always loved you—even in high school when we were kids. In fact, I never stopped loving you. I always regretted that we never married. When I found out you had a son and got married, I kicked myself every morning for letting you get away."

Blinking back tears, Suzy said, "I still love you too. I've wondered about you all these years. When I'd allow myself anyway. I knew you were my soulmate and always regretted we slipped apart."

She pinched her arm. "I must be dreaming. Things like this don't happen to me. What about Melissa? I almost feel sorry for her."

"She's as mad as hell but she'll be okay. She's a strong woman. Besides, we were never right as a couple. I know now that I was settling. I think she was, too. We were both lonely and wanted to be married. I never loved her the way I love you." Ken touched Suzy's cheek.

Suzy felt herself melt.

"Go on."

"You feel like 'home' to me. Always have. It wouldn't be fair to marry someone else when I'm still in love with you. I knew that the minute I saw you at the meeting."

"Why didn't you reach out to me?"

"I knew you had a son. After my divorce, I didn't want to mess up your family life. I figured you'd find me if you wanted to."

Suzy shook her head. "I can't believe this."

Ken stared into Suzy's eyes, as if trying to read her mind. He wiped tears off her cheeks with his thumb.

Feeling lightheaded from the wine and no food on her stomach, Suzy steadied herself against the wall. She was elated yet wary. After all, she was known as the wedding planner who couldn't find wedded bliss.

"Why didn't you tell me this before tonight? I almost didn't come. I didn't want to see you with her."

"I called you a million times the past two days. You never picked up nor returned my calls. I didn't want to leave the message on a machine. I wanted to tell you in person. That's why I said it was important for you to come tonight."

Suzy took a deep breath.

"I've got to let this soak in. Do you mind if we sit down and eat? I'm feeling woozy from the wine. From everything."

Ken looked relieved.

"Sure, sure. Let's eat. As they walked back, Suzy's mind swirled with what Ken had just said. When they reached the table, he pulled out her chair. Suzy managed a shaky smile and glanced at Alex and Hope.

Alex raised her eyebrows. Hope looked grim.

Hungrily, Suzy stabbed her lettuce, and poured too much dressing over the top of her salad. With each bite, she considered their discussion. She wanted to believe him more than anything. Maybe her luck *had* changed. Maybe her touch was no longer rust-or maybe it was Hope's good luck pearls.

She noticed Bob, the class president, inspecting her.

Great. He probably assumes Ken is still engaged and we're cheating.

Suzy's brain worked overtime. Her stomach butterflies were tap dancing. She was afraid to get her hopes up.

"Suzy, for the third time, will you pass me the pepper?" Alex asked. She leaned forward and whispered in Suzy's ear.

"Everything okay?"

When Suzy stared ahead, Alex waved her hand in front of Suzy's face.

"Earth to Suzy."

Suzy jerked her head and passed the pepper.

"Here's the salt, too. Sorry."

She leaned over and whispered. "Everything's great. I think."

Bob clinked a spoon against his glass.

"It's time for awards. Suzy, since you were class secretary, will you come forward and present the awards?"

Full of newfound energy, Suzy bounded to the front of the room. Her red hair glistened and her jewelry sparkled almost as much as her eyes.

Alex noticed an immediate transformation from the previous hour and wondered what in the world Ken had said to her best friend.

Bob handed Suzy the microphone and the list of questions they had discussed at the reunion committee meeting. She scanned the list and looked at the crowd.

"Hi, everyone. Great to see you tonight. It doesn't seem

like twenty years, does it? Let's find out what you've been up to. First we have an award for the classmate who traveled the furthest. So where do you all live?"

After lively shouts from New Yorkers and residents of Los Angeles and Mexico, Rick Kern stood at the back of the room. "Athens, Greece."

"Can anyone top that?" asked Suzy. The room fell silent.

"I didn't think so. Rick come forward for your prize."

"Now, who has the most kids?" Suzy stole a quick glance at a smiling Ken.

Alex and Hope exchanged glances and made faces. Neither of them had even thought about having kids at this point. Well, maybe they had given it a little thought but it wasn't a topic of conversation, even though their biological clocks were ticking loudly.

Suzy started by asking if anyone had ten kids and worked her way down. Evonne Fisher was the winner with eight children, including two sets of twins.

"What are they, rabbits?" Alex whispered to a giggling Hope.

The award for the oldest child was awarded to Lori Evans who has a bouncing twenty-one-year old.

"Oops," Suzy said as she presented a plaque to a laughing Lori.

Suzy stared at her notes.

"Folks, we have two more awards and you get to vote on these. First up is the classmate who has changed the most. Please nominate whomever you wish."

There were giggles, murmurs and whispers among the crowd. The guys boisterously nominated their friends.

"Mike, get on that stage. You're as bald as a cue ball," said the former basketball star, Jim.

"George, with that beer gut, no one would recognize you. I nominate George Lucas."

There was raucous laughter as Suzy stifled a giggle. No

one had the nerve to nominate a female for most changed, so the two men stood at the front.

"We'll decide this by applause," Suzy said. She walked in front of Mike and waited for everyone to clap. Then, she walked over to George. The applause was deafening.

"Guess we have our winner. Sorry, George."

Suzy was eager to sit near Ken again.

"Okay, one last prize. This is for the student who has changed the least. Any nominations?"

Hope nominated Alex and Alex nominated Suzy. Dale, seated at the back, nominated the class president.

"Anyone else?" Suzy looked around the room.

"Let's determine this by applause again." Suzy and Alex both received whistles and wolf calls but Bob won.

When Alex sat back at the table, Hope leaned over.

"You and Suzy look even better than you did in school. Bob looks exactly the same."

Bob took the mic as Suzy switched places with Hope to sit beside Ken. A video of class highlights appeared on a large screen.

Alex mouthed to Suzy, "Meet me in the ladies' room" and jerked her head in that direction.

When the women got inside, Alex looked under the stall doors to make sure they were alone.

"What gives? What did Ken say to you? You were so depressed and angry. Now, you look like you just received a huge lottery payout."

Hope followed them in and waited for Suzy to answer.

Suzy explained how Ken broke up with his fiancée after they saw one another at the committee meeting." Suzy's eyes filled with tears. "I can't believe this. Ken said he's loved me all these years and wasn't going to let me get away again." She dabbed at her eyes while Hope handed her a tissue.

"Can you believe it? We may actually have a chance after twenty years."

Alex hugged her friend. Hope threw her arms around both of them.

"I'm glad someone has a happy ending. You deserve a break in the relationship department. I'm glad Ken realized what he had in you. Well, don't just stand there."

Alex gave Suzy a gentle shove. "Go back out there to your man!"

Suzy removed the mascara from under her eyes and practically bounced out the door like a kangaroo.

Alex reapplied her lipstick and turned to Hope.

"I'm happy for Suzy but what a miserable night this is going to be. What are you and I going to do? Slow dance with each other?" Alex powdered her nose without waiting for a reply.

Hope fluffed her brown curls, straightened her necklace, and watched Alex in the mirror.

"It's not that bad. Come on. We'll have fun even if we do have to dance together. Let's go back out. I promise I won't step on your feet when we slow dance."

Alex laughed. "You're right. Let's go."

She placed the powder in her small purse while edging toward the table. Alex noticed the video was still playing and whispered to Hope, "Do we really have to be reminded of the jocks and drama students in the same footage?"

Hope shrugged.

"Oh, look. The finale is one more photo of the homecoming queen. Perfect."

Hope patted Alex's arm. "I know you lost by two votes. You've only told me that, what, a thousand times?"

Alex stuck out her tongue.

When the video ended and the main lights were turned on, Alex squinted. She observed servers dressed in black scurrying to every table. They expertly balanced the entrees—either roasted chicken or pork medallions.

As a server set down her plate, Danny, the class-clown-turned-psych worker, leaned over.

"I thought *you* were the homecoming queen."

Alex rolled her eyes.

"If you must know, I was told by a student senate member that I lost by two votes." Alex sniffed and took a drink.

Chapter 65

Hope reappeared from the bar with a cocktail for each of them. Alex gulped half her wine, knowing she had already had too much but she didn't care. She was miserable.

Her thoughts wandered to Tony. She got mad at herself for even thinking about him. Alex glanced at Suzy who appeared to be in her own fairytale. Suzy and Ken had moved to a smaller table by the wall. Alex was happy for Suzy. She really was. She just wished she could conjure up a happy ending for herself. She knew that wasn't going to happen. Not with a married cop and definitely not with a bad cop.

As the servers cleared the plates, Bob walked back toward the microphone.

"After dessert and coffee, put on your dancing shoes—or kick them off, whichever you prefer. Let's show everyone what our class is made of!"

"Yeah," yelled a basketball star.

"Let's do it," shouted a football player, not to be outdone.

"Bring it ooonnn," Danny bellowed, trying to be cool.

Everyone laughed.

Let's get this party started and over with, Alex thought.

After inspecting her fork, she plunged it into a slice of chocolate cheesecake and took a huge bite.

Who cares about calories now? She swiveled around and tapped a server on the back.

"Excuse me, sir. May I have some coffee?"

As the server turned to face Alex, she gasped. It was Tony. He was dressed in all black like the other servers. Alex composed herself and narrowed her eyes.

"Undercover assignment?" she asked sarcastically.

"I've got to talk to you," Tony said as he balanced a coffee pot and pitcher of water on a tray.

Alex searched for Hope who was on the other side of the room chatting with a group of women. She surveyed the room for Suzy who was still in a corner cocoon with Ken.

Hair bristled on her neck as she swiveled around to face Tony.

"We don't have anything to talk about. My friends told me to stay away from you. My boss told me to stay away from you. Everyone was right and I was wrong. They said I would get hurt and I did." Tears threatened her eyes. Alex hissed, "Go away. Go back to your wife." She turned back around so Tony wouldn't see tears streaming down her cheeks.

Then, just as quickly, rage rose and her face hardened. She swung back around to challenge him.

"You scared me half to death. Do you know how many sleepless nights I've had because of you? Do you know how frightened I was for weeks? Just go away. Go back to sleep on that couch of yours."

Danny leaned in, no doubt hanging on every word.

Tony touched Alex's arm but she jerked it away.

"Alex, please. Listen to me."

Tony set the coffee pot and water down. He squatted beside her. "Give me fifteen minutes. Please. Sean, my asshole brother, lied to you. I didn't do the things he told you. I can prove it."

Alex stared at Tony. "You know about my meeting with Sean?" She softened somewhat, wanting to believe him. "How can you prove he lied?"

"Sean planted evidence to make me look bad. He's a dirty cop and an even lousier brother. That's why we're not close."

Alex's mouth gaped open.

"You never even told me you *had* a brother. He said something to you after the car chase. I remember. Why didn't you tell me he was your brother?"

Tony rubbed his stubbly cheek, eyes hard.

"I should have told you about Sean. We've always had a sibling rivalry and competed professionally. Give me fifteen minutes to explain. In private. Then, if you want me to leave, I will. I promise."

Tony had turned her world upside down more than once. She was afraid of being hurt yet again and was now slightly afraid of him.

"I don't think so. You've caused enough trouble for me. I don't care what you have to say. Besides, how can I believe you? Why don't you just leave?"

Alex's eyes darted around the room. Everyone was laughing and most likely exchanging stories and photos, completely unaware of her plight, except for her eavesdropping neighbor.

"Do you want me to handle him, Alex?" Danny asked.

Alex stifled a giggle. The five foot five skinny classmate wouldn't stand a chance against the six foot four cop.

"No. Thanks anyway, Danny."

Tony touched her shoulder.

"Fifteen minutes. If you feel the same way after you hear me out, I'll never bother you again."

Alex studied Tony. She saw considerable strain in his face. He looked tired and haggard, had bags under his eyes, and stubble on his face. She felt herself starting to yield, stood, and flipped her blond hair behind her shoulders.

"You have *ten* minutes."

Chapter 66

Alex pointed toward a quiet corner away from her classmates.

"We can talk there."

Alex strode ahead of Tony with wobbly legs. She cursed herself for giving him another chance—and for looking so damn handsome, albeit haggard. Her heart pounded with excitement— and fear. She couldn't imagine what he could say to gain her trust.

She stole one more glance toward Hope and Suzy. Hope was laughing with friends and Suzy appeared to be in a love nest. So much for their buddy system.

Tony pulled out her chair, then sat down.

Without saying a word, he took a piece of paper out of his shirt pocket and slid it toward Alex. She glanced at the folded document.

"What's this?"

"While we were apart the past month, I knew Sean would feed you a pack of lies after he spotted you in my car. He's always been jealous of me. He couldn't stand the fact that I was about to become a lieutenant before him, especially since he's older. He did everything he could in the department to make me look bad, both personally and professionally."

Alex sat very still trying to absorb everything as her mind raced. She scolded herself for thinking about how good Tony looked.

He leaned forward.

"Plus, he's always had a thing for my wife. She dated Sean first. He tried to win her back over the years. They probably had an affair while we were married. I could have followed them or wired the house but I guess I didn't want to see my big brother in bed with my wife. Besides, he knows how to hide his tracks."

Alex frowned. "I could care less if your brother had sex with your wife. It sounds like they deserve each other. Is that what you came to tell me because I'm not interested."

Alex scooted her chair back so hard it screeched on the bare floor. Several classmates turned in their direction except for Hope or Suzy, naturally.

Alex shifted in her seat trying to decide whether to leave.

"People are watching. You're embarrassing me. Are you trying to completely ruin my life with everyone I know past, present, and future? God, Tony. I'm going back to my table now."

He reached across the table for her hand but she kept it on her lap.

"Wait. There's more. Much more. I know you don't care whether or not Sean had sex with my wife but after the lies he fed you, I started wondering about my son."

Alex was half standing when something occurred to her. She sat back down.

"Wait a minute. How do you know Sean fed me a pack of lies as you put it?"

Tony smiled, looking pleased with himself.

"My snitch. She works at The Pancake House where you and Sean met."

Tony's eyes danced. "She must have been as annoying as hell because she sure had a lot of information."

Alex thought back to that night. She remembered Thelma who made several trips to their table and smiled remembering how irritated Sean was with her.

"That waitress drove Sean nuts. Guess Big Brother—or Big Sister in this case—is everywhere, huh? Go on. I'm listening."

"My wife was pregnant when I married her, and like I said, she dated Sean before she dated me. So, a few weeks ago, I started wondering if Joey's really mine. I guess deep down I've always been curious but I never wanted to consider that possibility. Until now."

Tony studied Alex's face.

Alex softened and stared at the folded paper. Her mind raced with possibilities.

Tony patted the document and blinked back tears.

"This is a paternity test. First, let me say I never knew I could love another human being as much as I love Joey."

Tony's voice wobbled. "Until I met you, that is. I care more about you than you know. I think I'm in love with you. In fact, I know I'm in love with you." He stared into her eyes, searching for a reaction.

"Do you want to ask me anything?"

Alex braced herself.

"What did the test say?"

Tony unfolded the document and pushed it toward her.

"Joey is not my biological son. He's Sean's son. I took some DNA off Sean's coffee cup at work."

He tapped the paper. "Here's the proof."

Alex cupped her hand over her mouth.

Tony's voice caught. "My little boy isn't my little boy. He's my nephew."

Alex watched a tear slide down his chiseled cheek. She longed to hold him, cradle him.

"I'm sorry, Tony." Alex rubbed his muscular, hard forearm.

"I can't imagine how hard this must be for you. Are you going to tell Joey?"

"I haven't worked that out." Tony sighed.

"I just got the results yesterday. He's so young. I'll always love him whether or not I'm his biological dad. Of course, he'll need to know some day. I'm just not sure when."

Alex nodded and took Tony's hand in hers. She felt terrible. She had cursed him every day not knowing he was going through his own personal hell. He wasn't trying to make her life miserable—or scare her—that was his dirty brother, Sean. Alex's thoughts swirled as she tried to take in what Tony had said. She felt horrible that she had found Tony guilty before the trial.

Alex rubbed her forehead trying to recall all the scary events. She wanted answers.

"What about that sexual phone call at the bank? The one that got me sent to Internal Affairs?"

"Sean did that. Our voices sound similar. After he saw you at the chase scene, he asked some questions and found out where you worked. That asshole did that to scare you and to frame me. He probably heard I was getting a promotion and did his best to get me demoted or fired."

"Why did you say it might have been you?"

"Cops don't rat out other cops. Good ones don't anyway. I had no idea it would go that far up the ladder. I'm sure he was the one who sent the faxes and probably the one who tried to scare you at home. It certainly wasn't me."

"Why would Sean try to scare me?"

Tony gritted his teeth.

"He's a bastard. Since you were associated with me, he wanted to get to you. See why I never mentioned him?"

He glanced at his watch. "Since I only have ten minutes, let's move to another subject."

Alex smiled. "Take all the time you need."

Tony reached into his other pocket. "Knowing the paternity results made it easy for me to go ahead with something else." He pushed another letter toward Alex.

"I filed for divorce. I'm not living with a woman who betrayed me. I'm not staying married to a woman I no longer love. I moved out. I'm living at this hotel. That's how I landed the server uniform."

Alex shook her head. “I can’t believe all of this.”

“You were right about my marriage all along. The paternity test made everything clear. Sorry it took me this long to figure it out.” He studied her face.

Alex leaned back, wishing she were anywhere but at a class reunion.

“This is a lot to comprehend in one fell swoop. I feel like I’m dreaming—or watching a soap opera.”

Tony grinned. “You’re not dreaming. And I hope you and I can start dating—in public. No more hiding around. I want to be a part of your life. A big part if you’ll have me.”

Alex wished she hadn’t had so much wine. She wanted to remember every single word Tony said. She didn’t want to forget one syllable of this conversation. She leaned in and smiled.

“You know I’ll have you. I’ve been in love with you for a while now. But we have to take this slowly. I’ve been frightened and confused. I need time to heal. *We* need time to heal. Together.”

She reached across the table for his hand. “I’m sorry about your son but we’ll always include Joey in our lives.”

Tony looked genuinely touched.

“I’m glad to hear you say that. Joey will always be my son even if he doesn’t have my blood running through his veins. As for Sean, I wish I never had to set eyes on him again. I could get him fired if I went to the chief but I don’t think I will. It’ll catch up with him. Karma, you know?”

“You’re a good man, Sgt. Tony Montgomery.” Alex’s shoulders felt relaxed for the first time all summer.

“That’s *Lt.* Tony Montgomery.” He beamed.

“Got a promotion huh? Looks like we’ve got a lot to celebrate. Why don’t we go back to the table? Hope and Suzy are here. I want you to meet Suzy’s new beau. Actually, he’s her old beau.”

Tony looked puzzled.

"Long story. I'll fill you in."

Alex took Tony's hand and walked toward the table. Danny ogled them as they sat down. Alex ignored him and caught Hope's attention. She motioned her over as Ken led Suzy onto the dance floor.

Hope walked up, looking bewildered. She whispered to Alex. "Did you pick up a server?"

"Ha ha. I guess it does look like that. No, this is Tony. He was in disguise as a server."

"Tony?" Hope's eyebrows shot up.

"Don't worry. It's okay. More than okay, actually. He wasn't the one scaring me and he's getting a divorce." Alex beamed. "I'll tell you everything later."

"Are you sure?" Hope asked.

"Very sure."

They were interrupted by the DJ asking classmates to clear the dance floor as he focused a large spotlight on Ken and Suzy.

Chapter 67

The song, "At Last," by Etta James blared as Ken and Suzy danced.

"What's going on? Why are we dancing alone?" Suzy asked.

Ken grinned from ear to ear.

"Shhhh. Just enjoy the music."

Suzy snuggled close as Ken held her tight. She listened to the words and giggled.

"At last is right."

Suzy didn't care that everyone was watching. She felt like they were the only two people in the world. She put her head on Ken's shoulder, enjoying the moment. She never wanted it to end and never wanted to lose sight of Ken again.

When the song ended, Ken dropped to one knee and took Suzy's hand.

Her eyes widened as her mouth gaped open. Goosebumps pricked her arms. She forgot to breathe. Suzy heard gasps and shushes, then the room fell silent in anticipation.

Ken stared lovingly at Suzy. His eyes glistened.

"I can't believe it took me twenty years to realize we were meant to be together. Suzy, you were my first love and I want you to be my last love."

He pulled a black velvet box out of his pocket and opened it.

Suzy stared agog at the huge, glittering diamond solitaire.

"Will you marry me and spend the rest of your life with me?"

Suzy was speechless. She gazed into Ken's gentle, moist eyes and knew he was the one. He had always been the one.

"Yes, yes, yes!" She bent down and threw her arms around his neck.

Everyone was silent as they watched Ken place the diamond on Suzy's finger. Then, the room erupted with loud whoops and whistles. The entire class clapped and cheered as the DJ played the song, "Celebrate." The classmates rushed toward the blissful couple.

Guys slapped Ken on the back and gave him high fives. Hope and Alex embraced a tearful Suzy and kissed her on both cheeks.

As everyone danced, Alex whispered to Suzy.

"Why don't you get married now?"

"Now? As in right now? Right here?" Suzy gaped.

"Yes, right here. Right now," urged Alex. "Why not?"

Suzy looked incredulous.

"Let's see. I don't have a dress, flowers, cake nor a photographer. Nothing is planned, and you know, I'm a wedding planner. I like to do that sort of thing."

"Exactly. Let us plan a wedding for you for a change. We can pull this off. Just watch."

Hope bobbed her head. "I agree. Do it. Why wait any longer?"

The women looked from Suzy to Ken. He grinned.

"Why not? We've already lost twenty years. Let's get married."

Alex took charge, scanning the room.

"We have a DJ for music and can use the flowers on the table for your bouquet. Everyone is here who loves you. I'll call Jon and Fernando and get them here right away."

"I'll call my dad," Hope said. "He used to be an ordained minister. Hopefully, his license is still up to date."

Suzy's head spun. As long as her son was there, along with her best friends, she didn't care where she got married as long as she was with Ken. She looked down at her black halter dress and frowned.

"I can't get married in black."

"We're the same size," Alex said.

"I'm wearing ivory. Wear my dress. Let's go change in the restroom."

Suzy laughed. "I guess you have thought of everything except the marriage license. We'll have to go to the courthouse tomorrow to fill out paperwork."

"Details, details," Alex scoffed.

While Suzy and Alex switched dresses, Hope and several other female classmates plucked flowers out of the table centerpieces and made a bridal bouquet. They tied it with ribbons they cut off the balloons. Disposable cameras were on every table, plus most had cell phones, so the photographs were handled. Luckily, the DJ had a wedding scheduled the following day so several wedding songs were preprogrammed and loaded.

Hope's dad arrived wearing a brown suit and light blue tie. Paul held a Bible and Hope ran to his side, hugging him.

Then, she and her classmates pieced together two lacy table runners from the dessert buffet to create a makeshift veil.

Alex and Suzy reappeared wearing each other's dresses. Suzy walked toward Ken while Alex noticed females working on the veil. It needed something.

She looked around and spotted Diana who always wore her homecoming crown to every reunion. Alex didn't bother to ask permission. She walked over and plucked the tiara off Diana's head. She placed it on top of Suzy's veil and smiled. Taking the homecoming crown was one of her favorite parts of the last-minute wedding ensemble.

A sweaty Jon and Fernando rushed in wearing tailored suits and artful ties. Jon carried a large layered white cake with a bride and groom on top. Suzy recognized the cake from the local grocery store but didn't care.

Fernando placed the wedding cake on a small table while Jon rushed to his mom's side. She hugged her son and introduced him to Ken. They started to shake hands, then hugged instead.

"Make my mom happy," Jon said.

"I will," Ken promised as he tucked Suzy's red hair behind her ear and gazed into her eyes. "I love her and always have."

Suzy kissed him then plucked a compact out of her purse to reapply lipstick. When she looked up, the entire class had formed into two lines, making an aisle for them to walk down. Alex handed Suzy the bouquet tied with red and black ribbons. Hope took off her pearls and placed them around Suzy's neck.

"Here's your something old and borrowed."

"And lucky," Suzy added as she winked at Hope.

Alex pulled her blue topaz ring off her finger and gave it to Suzy.

"This takes care of the blue requirement and the dress is new. Whew. All the bases are covered."

She kissed her best friend on the cheek.

"I love you. Be happy."

All three women embraced then stepped aside as Ken took Suzy's hand. Tony stood beside Alex. Jon and Fernando giggled as they watched Ken and Suzy start down the aisle. Hope's Dad stood at the end of the aisle, his Bible open.

The DJ played the bridal march. Alex noticed several women dabbing their eyes as tears pricked hers. Jon and Fernando cried, too.

The ceremony went by too quickly. As Hope's father read the vows, Suzy and Ken beamed. It was as though they were the only people in the crowded room.

When Paul told Ken to kiss the bride, he gave Suzy a long, tender kiss then dipped her backward.

After Ken steadied Suzy, Paul said, "May I be the first to introduce Mr. and Mrs. Dixon."

Cameras clicked like paparazzi. Classmates clapped wildly and cheered as Suzy and Ken walked down the man-made walkway.

Several threw handfuls of red and black confetti "20's" at the happy couple who walked hand in hand. Hope wiped her eyes and slipped her arm through her father's, happy he had served such an important role.

Alex shouted, "Where are you going on your honeymoon?"

Suzy and Ken looked at one other.

"Haven't had much time to think about that." Suzy winked at her new husband.

Ken looked at his bride. "Any place is a honeymoon as long as I'm with you."

Ken turned to the crowd. "Looks like our first stop will be the Crystal City Hotel." He picked up his beaming bride and carried Suzy out the door.

CPSIA information can be obtained
at www.ICGtesting.com
Printed in the USA
BVOW11s0436230917
495684BV00010B/69/P